Henry R. Montgomery

Memoirs of the Life and Writings of Sir Richard Steele

Vol. II

Henry R. Montgomery

Memoirs of the Life and Writings of Sir Richard Steele
Vol. II

ISBN/EAN: 9783337055585

Printed in Europe, USA, Canada, Australia, Japan

Cover: Foto ©Raphael Reischuk / pixelio.de

More available books at **www.hansebooks.com**

MEMOIRS

OF THE

LIFE AND WRITINGS

OF

SIR RICHARD STEELE,

SOLDIER, DRAMATIST, ESSAYIST, AND PATRIOT,

WITH

HIS CORRESPONDENCE, AND NOTICES OF HIS CONTEMPORARIES
THE WITS AND STATESMEN OF QUEEN ANNE'S TIME.

BY

HENRY R. MONTGOMERY,

AUTHOR OF "THOMAS MOORE: HIS LIFE, WRITINGS, AND CONTEMPORARIES,"
"ISAAC BICKERSTAFF," ETC.

TWO VOLUMES.

VOL. II.

EDINBURGH:
WILLIAM P. NIMMO.
1865.

EDINBURGH:
PRINTED BY BALLANTYNE, ROBERTS, AND COMPANY,
PAUL'S WORK.

CONTENTS.

VOL. II.

CHAPTER XIX.

CHAPTER XX.

CHAPTER XXI.

THE RETIRED VETERAN.

Errata.—Vol. ii. p. 32, middle of page, for " organ of the opposition," read " opposite party." Vol. ii. p. 227, line 15 from bottom, after "golden visions were conjured," read " up." Vol. ii. p. 284, 9th line from top, after the word " final," insert comma instead of period. Vol. ii. p. 254, for "was only remained in office," read "retained." A letter has been misplaced in vol. ii. p. 107, owing to the author's distance from the press, for which the reader's indulgence is requested.

SIR RICHARD STEELE,

AND

HIS CONTEMPORARIES.

CHAPTER XI.

THE POLITICIAN AND PATRIOT.

Steele makes a dash into politics—He starts the *Englishman*, with a political bearing, in place of the *Guardian*—His friend Hughes proposes to occupy the deserted ground of literature—His letter to Addison announcing the discontinuance of the *Guardian*, and proposing a literary successor—Political retrospect with reference to Steele—Drawn into an unfortunate controversy with the *Examiner* relative to the Dunkirk article of the *Guardian*—Steele publishes a pamphlet in reply, and in defence of his paper in the *Guardian* on the importance of Dunkirk—Publication of "The Crisis"—Close of the *Englishman* newspaper—Is elected member for Stockbridge.

THE *Guardian*, having been summarily relinquished, was in a few days succeeded by the *Englishman*, which was political in its character, and published thrice a week. Mr Hughes, in a letter dated October 6, 1713, written to Addison, then at his country seat, Bilton, near Rugby, says: "I do not doubt but you know by this time that Mr Steele has abruptly dropped the *Guardian*. He has this day published a paper called the *Englishman*, which begins with an answer to the *Examiner*, written with great bold-ness and spirit, and shews that his thoughts are at present entirely on politics. Some of his friends are in pain about him, and are concerned that a paper should be discontinued which might have been generally entertaining without engaging in party matters." The writer then proceeds to make a proposition to occupy the literary field to which Steele, for the present at least, seemed hopelessly lost. He lays before Addison his plan of a literary paper for his approval and co-operation. It was to consist of the con-versations of an imaginary literary society on all sorts of subjects, reported by their secretary, and to be called the *Register*. "By this means," he says, "I think the town might be sometimes entertained with dialogue, which will be a new way of writing, either related or set down in form under the names of different speakers; and some-times with essays, or with discourses in the person of the writer of the paper." Addison, after expressing his ap-proval of the outline, adds, "To tell you truly, I have been so taken up with thoughts of that nature for two or three years last past, that I must now take some time *pour me delasser*, and lay in fuel for a future work. In the mean-time, I should be glad if you would set such a project on foot, for I know nobody else capable of succeeding in it and turning it to the good of mankind, since my friend has laid it down. I am in a thousand troubles for poor Dick, and wish that his zeal for the public may not be ruinous to himself; but he has sent me word that he is determined to go on, and that any advice I can give him, in this par-ticular, will have no weight with him."* Without any

---

* Correspondence and Memoir of Hughes, by Duncombe, vol. i. p. 67.

disrespect to the talents of Hughes, we may well believe that Addison felt Steele to be his true partner in such matters, and was satisfied to wait. In order not to have to refer to it again, it may be mentioned, with reference to the suggestion of Hughes, that a paper somewhat similar in design to that proposed by him, and to which he became a contributor, was started not long after by another Sir Richard,—Blackmore, the poetical physician, who appears to have been ambitious to emulate the labours of Steele; but the paper does not seem to have been much of a success at the time, and is now more unknown, perhaps, even by name than his voluminous epics, which were a dose posterity has not been inclined to swallow. Its title was the *Lay-Monk*, and it was continued from the middle of November 1713 till the 7th of the following February.

But, to resume our immediate subject, the political fever with which Steele was now seized, and which displayed itself in the publication of the *Englishman*, had been latent in the constitution for some considerable time. It has been supposed that it was to the articles in which the *Tatler* shewed a strong tendency that way that the existence of the *Examiner* was owing, though this is scarcely probable, as the importance of having such an organ could not have failed to suggest itself to the opposite party. One thing at least is certain, that their publication and the recriminations to which they led, aggravated materially that tendency to descend from the dignity and serenity of his literary character to mingle in the strife of party. Some of these were drawn from him by his high sense of the claims of friendship as well as of loyalty to his party.

When the Whig ministry was tottering to its fall, Steele

rushed to the rescue by several publications under the title of *Pasquin.* But his zeal was in vain, for the party had committed a sort of political suicide by the very foolish and rash step they took in elevating a weak and contemptible bigot, Dr Henry Sacheverell, who had desecrated the pulpit by indulging in violent declamations of a political tendency, into the dignity of a martyr. In a sermon which he preached in St Paul's on the 5th of November 1709, he not only denounced resistance to kings as unlawful, which was construed into a censure on the Revolution, but was supposed to allude to the Whig Lord Treasurer, Godolphin, under the name of *Volpone.* The result was his impeachment in March 1710, when he was sentenced to a suspension from preaching for three years, and his sermon, which had been published, was ordered to be burned by the common hangman. The Tory party, who had long raised the cry of the Church in danger, seized on the opportunity of identifying him with the cause, and creating a popular ferment on that ground, which enabled Sacheverell to make a sort of triumphal progress through various parts of the kingdom.* In a subsequent publication, under a feigned name, a letter to Sir Miles Wharton, dated March 5, 1712,† Steele says, " When the minds of

---

* " The charge against Sacheverell was not for impugning what was done at the Revolution, which he affected to vindicate, but for maintaining that it was not a case of resistance to the supreme power, and consequently no exception to his tenet of an unlimited passive obedience. The managers of the impeachment had therefore not only to prove that there was resistance in the Revolution, which could not, of course, be seriously disputed, but to assert the lawfulness in great emergencies, or what is called in politics, necessity, of taking arms against the law—a delicate matter at any time, and not least so by ministers of state and law officers of the crown, in the very presence, as they knew, of their sovereign."—*Constitutional History,* vol. iii. p. 202.

† This letter was written on the occasion of the royal prerogative being un-

men are prejudiced, wonderful effects may be wrought against common-sense. One weak step in trying a fool for what he said in a pulpit, with all the pomp that could be used to take down a more dangerous and powerful man than England yet has seen, cost the most able ministry, that ever any prince was honoured with, its being. The judgment of the House of Lords was by this means insulted, and the anarchical fury ran so high, that Harry Sacheverell swelling, and Jack Higgins laughing, marched through England in a triumph more than military." The popular reaction in favour of the Tory party exactly accorded with the views of Queen Anne, who had long only tolerated the Whigs, from the ascendency exercised over her by the more commanding mind of Sarah, Duchess of Marlborough. That influence had long been declining, and the long-tried favourite, notwithstanding the kindness she had shewn the Princess Anne in her days of disfavour and her long services, was now completely supplanted by a poor relation of her own, Mrs Masham, for whom she had procured a subordinate and almost menial situation in the royal household. The Queen, thus freed from the sway of the imperious duchess, and seeing that she would be justified by popular feeling in being so from that of the Whigs also, made an unwonted effort of vigour to throw off the hated yoke. On the 10th of August 1710, the seals of the Treasury Office were transferred from Godolphin to Robert Harley, afterwards Earl of Oxford, whilst

scrupulously strained to insure a majority in the Upper House, and twelve new peers were created. Sir Miles had declined the honour, and Steele awards him high applause on the occasion. To prevent such unconstitutional influence, Steele proposes the introduction of a bill to prevent any newly-created peer from voting until three years had elapsed from the date of his patent.

the more brilliant and intriguing Henry St John, afterwards Lord Bolingbroke, was raised to the post of Secretary of State.

Harley was a man who, both from policy and more disinterested motives, took pride and pleasure in rewarding merit, and he sought by every means of flattery and more substantial considerations to win over Steele, as he had done Swift, who was now the presiding genius (though unattached) of the administration, to the interests of his party. He had raised the salary of one of his offices, that of Gazetteer, from a comparatively nominal sum to L.300 a year, and offered, if he would name any other more in accordance with his wishes to give it to him. Steele, however, firmly withstood all these allurements and blandishments, but they of course imposed upon him a certain degree of political neutrality—a tax which we may believe was paid with some reluctance. When, however, he saw the attempt made to degrade and ruin the great captain of his age, who had covered England with glory, and effectually humbled the overweening ambition of her rival, and that on a charge trumped up after he had resisted every solicitation to renounce his principles; when he saw him stripped of all his accumulated and well-earned honours and emoluments, the same system of degradation carried out with his wife and family at Court, his patience could hold out no longer, and on 1st January 1712 he addressed to their victim a letter, "An Englishman's thanks to the Duke of Marlborough," in which he gave expression to the indignation and sympathy with which he thought such treatment should inspire the minds of all.

In the 41st No. of the *Guardian*, under date of April

28, 1713, Steele was drawn into an unfortunate personal altercation with the *Examiner*, the violent organ of the Tory party, which was for a time conducted by Swift, in consequence of what he deemed a gross and unwarrantable attack upon a young lady of rank, merely because she was the daughter of an obnoxious nobleman. The article in question referred to Lady Charlotte Finch, daughter of the Earl of Nottingham, and afterwards Duchess of Somerset, as "knotting in Saint James's Chapel during divine service, in the immediate presence both of God and her Majesty, who were affronted together, that the family might appear to be entirely come over." This appeared such an outrage upon the sanctity of private life, that Steele indignantly protested against it. "If life be," he says in the conclusion of the article, "(as it ought to be with people of their character whom the *Examiner* attacks,) less valuable and dear than honour and reputation, in that proportion is the *Examiner* worse than an assassin. We have stood by and tamely heard him aggravate the disgraces of the brave and the unfortunate. We have seen him double the anguish of the unhappy man,—we have seen him trample on the ashes of the dead; but as all this has concerned greater life, and could touch only public characters, it did but remotely affect our private and domestic interests." He returns to the subject, in a letter to the *Guardian*, his own organ, in No. 53, in reply to the *Examiner*, defending himself by the example of the *Tatler*, and shews, what indeed required little ingenuity to do, the wide difference between the imaginary characters of the *Tatler*, which were representative men and "knights of the shire," and "the license of printing letters of people's real names," with "things

affixed to men's characters which are in the utmost degree
remote from them." "I have not," he says, "like him,
fixed odious images on persons, but on vices." Though he
says he will give himself no manner of liberty of making
guesses at the writer, he evidently referred to Swift when
he concluded by saying: "I have carried my point, and
rescued innocence from calumny; and it is nothing to me
whether the *Examiner* writes against me in the character
of an estranged friend." This inference, aggravated by some
of the epithets used, led to the unfortunate correspondence
between them previously given. In the same letter he
returns to the subject of the Duke of Marlborough, who
had fallen under the animadversions of the *Examiner*.
"He is welcome from henceforth," he says, "to treat me
as he pleases; but . . . never let innocence or merit be
traduced by him. In particular, I beg of you never let the
glory of our nation, who made France tremble, and yet has
that gentleness to be unable to bear opposition from the
meanest of his own countrymen, be calumniated in so impudent a manner." Though he alluded to others as equally
with the "estranged friend" open to suspicion as the
writer, Steele had grounds, in addition to the known fact
that Swift *had* been at least intimately connected with the
paper, known only to himself, for believing him not inca-
pable of writing this article ; for among the few papers he
had contributed to the *Tatler*, two were most unwarrantable satires upon most accomplished and amiable ladies,
because they were blues, so wholly was his temper unfitted .
for that species of writing.

But these were mere squibs compared to the blaze in
which he was enveloped by the famous political *Guardian*,

No. 128, when his opponent did not fail to make use of the
liberty he had given him to treat him as he pleased. That
memorable paper, of August 7, 1713, contained a letter by
Steele, with the signature of "English Tory," in which he
directs attention to a paper hawked about the streets,
printed in French and English, being a Memorial to the
Queen from the magistrates of Dunkirk, that she would
remit that part of the treaty of Utrecht which stipulated
for the demolition of the harbour and works at Dunkirk,
on the ground of the ruin it would entail upon those connected with the trade of the place, and that such a course
would even be beneficial to the interests of British trade.
After quoting one of the sentences of the memorial relative
to the "dreadful sentence pronounced by her Majesty
against the town," and requesting that the *Guardian*
would set the memorialists right, and acquaint them that
her Majesty had pronounced no sentence against the town,
he proceeds to put a number of statements in the briefest
and most forcible form, in detached sentences, completely
upsetting the sophistry of the memorial, and having this
sentence at the beginning, middle, and ending—*That the
British nation expect the immediate demolition of Dunkirk.*
As it was believed that this affair was connived at by the
ministry, though her Majesty had officially announced her
intention of not complying with the prayer of the memorial, the *Examiner*, with rabid malignity, endeavoured to
fasten upon him a charge of disloyalty, as if the sentence
had been addressed to her Majesty, and not to disabuse
the minds of the memorialists. If something like a popular
appeal was not intended, with what view was the paper
handed about?

This *Guardian* appeared on the 7th of August, the day preceding that of the dissolution of the Parliament, and was replied to by the *Examiner* of the 21st of the same month, and in a pamphlet entitled, "The Honour and Prerogative of the Queen's Majesty vindicated and defended against the unexampled insolence of the author of the *Guardian* : in a Letter from a country Whig to Mr Steele." The paternity of the letter might be traced to Swift, if there were no other clue than that furnished by the writer retorting on Steele his remark in the private correspondence between them, when Swift claimed the merit of having, by his influence, retained him in his public employments, namely, that they laughed at him if they persuaded him so. A passage from each may be given as a specimen of the literary ruffianism of that polite age. In the ninth and tenth pages of the pamphlet the writer says :—

"See how the villain treats the best of sovereigns, the best mistress to him, whose bread he has eaten, and who has kept him from a gaol. Read it again, say they. Put it into English, said a neighbour of mine to me ; come make the best of it. Then he reads the abominable language as follows :—

" 'The British nation expect,' &c., and again, 'the British nation expect the immediate demolition of Dunkirk.' And a third time, with a tone of threatening, 'the British nation expect it.'—See *Guardian*, Aug. 7, 1713.

" I would have pleaded for you that this was not to be understood to be spoken to or pointed at the Queen, but to the people of Dunkirk, and I searched the whole paper for something to have brought you off with that way.

" But it would not do, they laughed at me. How could it be spoken to him, say they ? His memorial is to the Queen, and if it should be directed to Monsieur Tugghe [the deputy] it would be still worse ; for that would be to talk thus to him, viz—What do ye petition the Queen for ? We tell you, the British nation will not suffer it, the Queen dares not do it, for the British nation expect it to be immediately demolished. This stopped my mouth indeed with respect to that part of the excuse, and then they went on with me. Come, says my neighbour, if you cannot put it into words, I'll do it for you.

" 'The British nation expect the immediate demolition of Dunkirk.'

" We all know her Majesty has possession of Dunkirk, and though the work is to be done by the French, her Majesty may appoint the day. Now, says he, read the words.

" What is it but thus ?

" 'Look you, madam, your Majesty had best take care that Dunkirk be demolished, or else,' &c.

" And again—

" 'Madam, we expect; and we would have you take notice, that we expect that Dunkirk be demolished, and that immediately.'

" Just thus an imperious planter at Barbadoes speaks to a negro slave, ' Look you, sirrah, I expect this sugar to be ground, and look to it that it be done forthwith. 'Tis enough to tell you I expect it, or else,' &c., and he holds up his stick at him, take what follows."

It is amusing to find the writer professing to be the would-be apologist of " the villain," and pretending to look through the whole paper for anything to bear the construction that it was addressed to the deputy of the memorialists, though it will not bear any other construction. The words of the letter to the *Guardian*, after saying that he gave him an opportunity not only of manifesting his loyalty to his Queen, but affection to his country, by treating an insolence done them both with the disdain it deserves, are : " Mr Ironside, I think, you would do an act worthy your general humanity if you would put the Sieur Tugghe [the deputy] right in this matter, and *let him* know that her Majesty has pronounced no sentence against the town, but his most Christian majesty [of France] has agreed that the town and harbour shall be demolished.

" That the British nation expect the immediate demolition of it."

But this pretended apologist, after vainly seeking for any evidence that it was meant for the deputy, discovers that, even so, it only made the matter worse, inasmuch as it was attempting to shew the uselessness of an appeal to her Majesty, and that she dare not comply with the demand. But the application is stated in the document of the deputy to have *been* made, and to have been unsuccessful, so that the paper publicly handed about bore the construction of an appeal from the Queen to the people. It was thus an insult offered to the authority of the Queen, and by sophistical arguments, to the understanding of the people. The pure malignity of the pamphleteer is therefore obvious.

The article in the *Examiner* of the 21st of August is in similar style :—

"I believe," says the writer, "I may challenge all the nations of the world, and all the histories of this nation for a thousand years past, to shew us an instance so flagrant as what we have now before us,—viz., whenever a *subject*, nay a *servant* under a *salary*, and favoured in spite of ill behaviour past, with a considerable employment in the government, treated his sovereign in such a manner as the *Guardian* has done the person of the Queen, and went unpunished.

"If the clemency of the Queen prevails to save such a man ; if her Majesty thinks it below her to resent an injury from so contemptible a wretch, by so much the rather should every subject resent it, and shew their duty and respect to their sovereign by trampling under their feet the very name and memory of the man that can have boldness enough to insult his prince in a printed, and for that reason scandalous libel, and can have ingratitude enough to do it while he is eating her bread.

"How can any man shew himself a faithful subject to her Majesty, and not resent such a piece of conduct ! to see a subject hold up a rod at his prince ! and openly threaten the Queen if she does not cause Dunkirk to be demolished ! to threaten her Majesty with the nation's resentment if it be not forthwith entered upon, and command her to do it immediately ; it ought to fill every faithful subject with abhorrence, and cause them either to shun the man, or to let him know they detest his behaviour.

"And yet this man was never so dear to the Whigs as since he let them know he durst assault his Queen. This has made him their favourite ; and one of their authors has made his dull panegyric upon him already for it ; while another set of them are endeavouring to get him chosen for the next parliament that he may carry on his insult there, and obtain the

honour, as another of their haughty leaders has already done, of being
expelled the House."

All this insolence and slavish reference to prerogatives
and princes only shewed that there was something rotten
in the matter, or the party would not have felt the blow so
sensitively. As the sovereign can do no wrong, a ministry
that is conscious of doing wrong is sure to shelter itself, at
least through its tools, under the shield of the sovereign
and of prerogative. When Burke on one occasion was
treated with this sort of insolence, he said, "He had every
wish to speak respectfully of the sovereign, but was not
disposed to accord the same privilege to his man-servant
and his maid-servant, his ox and his ass." This ministry
had concluded a premature peace, which neutralised the
effect of the advantages which had been so gloriously
achieved at so much cost to the treasure of the nation,
and they were suspected of conniving at the infraction of
one of the leading articles of the treaty they had concluded,
by suffering the port of Dunkirk to remain undestroyed.
Certain it is that the period stipulated for its demolition
had then elapsed several months. No wonder, then, that
they should have set up such a howl of disloyalty, ingratitude, and every foul name at any one who brought in a
light where they wanted darkness.

These attacks, in which the unscrupulous nature of
party warfare was aggravated and embittered by personal
animosity, induced Steele to draw up a reply in his own
vindication, which he entitled, "The Importance of Dunkirk considered : in defence of the *Guardian* of August
the 7th, in a Letter to the Bailiff of Stockbridge." In this
pamphlet he included a copy of the memorial circulated

by the deputy of the Dunkirk magistrates, together with the obnoxious letter in the *Guardian*, and extracts from the replies of his opponents, containing the most offensive passages, accompanied with a map of the coast adjacent to Dunkirk. Besides his personal vindication, he enlarged his former statements on the subject in dispute, and illustrated them with more ample details, in which the extent of his information on such a subject seemed wonderful. After quoting his own communication in the *Guardian*, he merely says, in reference to his opponents, " This letter happened to disoblige some people," but in reference to the charge of being under salary when he commenced this discussion, he states—

"Mr Bailiff, it is so far otherwise, that to avoid the least appearance of it, I did not attempt doing what proceeded from a true, grateful, and loyal heart,—viz., the laying before her Majesty's ministry that the nation had a strict eye upon their behaviour with relation to Dunkirk, before I had resigned all which their interposition with her most gracious Majesty could take from me. I am so far from eating her bread with a disinclination to her service, that I had resigned a plentiful income I had from her favour, in a considerable office and pension, which incapacitate a man for sitting in Parliament, to render myself more useful to her and my country in the station with which your borough has since honoured me."

He then proceeds to say—

" The author of the Letter from the Country Whig personates that character so awkwardly, and the *Examiner*, without entering into the point, treats me so outrageously, that I know not how to offer against such adversaries reason and argument, without appearing void of both. However, since it has for some time been the fashion to run down men of much greater consequence than I am, . . . these writers shall treat me as they think fit, as I am their brother scribbler ; but I shall not be so unconcerned when they attack me as an honest man. I shall therefore inform them that it is not in the power of a private and an indifferent man to hurt the honour and prerogative of the Crown without being punished, if the ministry think fit, as he deserves, by the laws of our country ; but true and real danger to the Queen's honour may arise if persons in authority tolerate men (who have no compunction of conscience) in abusing such instruments of glory and nonour to our country as the illustrious Duke of Marlborough, such wise and faithful managers as the late Earl of Godolphin, &c.

"There is no man will deny but that it is in the power of the ministry to call the *Examiner* to an account, as well as the *Flying Post.* It is not for me to enter into the reasons why they do not do themselves that justice ; but where is honour, where is government, where is prerogative, while neither age nor sex, virtue nor innocence, can have any redress from the assaults made upon their reputation, which is dearer than life ? But such injuries the *Examiner* repeats every week with impunity."

With reference to the prerogative, after a variety of arguments to shew the absurdity of its introduction into the discussion, he remarks—

"I say again and again, if once men are so intimidated as not to dare to offer their thoughts upon public affairs, without incurring the imputation of offending against the prerogative ; that prince, whatever advantage his ministers might make of his prerogative, would himself soon have no prerogative but that of being deceived. . . . What ! are majesty and ministry so consolidated, and must the people of Great Britain make no distinction between the one and the other ? We very well know the difference, sir, and humbly conceive that if a whole ministry were impeached and condemned by the people of Great Britain in Parliament for any notorious neglect of duty or breach of trust, the prince could not suffer by it."

He then gives in a few words the gist of the question—

"My adversaries," he goes on to say, "are so unjust, they will not take the least notice of what led me into the necessity of writing my letter to the *Guardian.* They know, if they stated it honestly, they must acknowledge that instead of what they call me I was a faithful servant to the Queen, and an honest fellow-subject to the ministry. My Lord Bolingbroke tells the Sieur Tugghe, [French deputy,] as a Secretary of State from the Queen, that his request cannot be complied with : the Sieur prints a memorial, which is no other than an appeal to all the weak people in England against her severity. Nay, if the translator has done him justice, he has used the very word *severe.* This I take for the utmost insult against the Queen and her ministry. . . . But I deserve well of them in this question about *Tugghe, or else they are not so angry as I am at what Tugghe has done against their Queen.*

"We know not," he says, "what is the equivalent for Dunkirk, but, according to the circumstances of France before the suspension of the

English arms under the gallant Duke of Ormond, (who would certainly have done his duty,) the French have owned that the equivalent might have been Paris.

"When," he adds with withering sarcasm, "such was our case, and such is our case, some men lately preferred, and grown too delicate, would have men of liberal education, that know the world as well as themselves, afraid, for fear of offending them *in their new clothes*, to speak when they think their Queen and country ill-treated."

Then alluding to the prevalent impression, "That a man of so small a fortune must have secret views or supports, which could move him to leave his employments and lose a crowd of well-wishers, to subject himself, as he must know he has, not only to the disesteem, but to the scorn and hatred of very many who, before he meddled with the public, had a partiality towards him," he goes on to express the nature of those enlarged principles and sentiments of public spirit which were powerful enough to make him "lay aside" the common views by which the mistaken world are actuated."

"Great qualifications," he says, "are not praises to the possessor, but from the application of them, and all that is justly commendable among men is to love and serve them as much as it is in your power, with a contempt of all advantages to yourself (above the conveniences of life) but as they tend to the service of the public. He who has warmed his heart with impressions of this kind, will find glowings of good-will which will support him in the service of his country against all the calumny, reproach, and invective that can be thrown upon him. He is but a poor creature who cannot bear being odious in the service of virtue. Riches and honours can administer to the heart no pleasure like what an honest man feels when he is contending for the interests of his country, and the civil rights of his fellow-subjects."

Referring to "the prostituted pens which are employed in a quite contrary service," he says :—

"It is the disgrace of literature that there are such instruments, and to good government that they are suffered. But this mischief is gone so far in our age, that the pamphleteers do not only attack those whom they believe in general to be disaffected to their own principles, but even such as they believe their friends, provided they do not act with as sincere a prejudice as themselves. Upon the least deviation from an implicit hatred of the opposite party, though in a case which in the nearest concern affects their country, all their good qualities are turned to ridicule; and everything which before was valued in them is become contemptible.

"It is as frivolous as unjust to hope to stop our mouths, when we are concerned for so great a point as the business of Dunkirk, by mention of the prerogative, and urging our safety in our good and gracious Queen. . . . But I persist in it, that it is no manner of diminution of the wisdom of a prince that he is obliged to act by the information of others.

"If I might make an abrupt digression," he pointedly concludes, "from great things to small, I should on this occasion mention a little circumstance which happened to the late King William. He had a Frenchman who took care of the gun-dogs, whose business it was also to charge and deliver the piece to the king. This minister forgot to bring out shot into the field, but did not think fit to let so passionate a man and eager a sportsman as the king know his offence, but gave his majesty the gun loaded only with powder. When the king missed his aim, this impudent cur stood chattering, admiring, commending the king's skill in shooting, and holding up his hands, he had never seen *sa majesté* miss before in his whole life. This circumstance was no manner of argument (to those who afterwards found out the fellow's iniquity) against the king's reputation for a quick eye and shooting very finely."

With this anecdote he concludes his letter of vindication to the civic representative of his constituents, of whom Gay subsequently says,—

> "Of all our race of mayors shall Snow alone
> Be by Sir Richard's dedication known." *

But whatever may have been the importance of Dunkirk, fears and misgivings were entertained by the Whigs, in reference to the ministry in power, of a graver character than any it could inspire. They feared lest the hasty treaty which had been concluded on the 5th of May 1713, should be accompanied by secret articles subversive of the great principles in Church and State for which they had contended with their lives and fortunes at the recent

* Journey to Exeter, 1716.

Revolution, and lest that struggle would have to be repeated on the death of the Queen, by an attempt, which there was too much reason to dread, on the part of France, in concert with the ministry, to introduce the Pretender and set aside the Act of Settlement, which vested the succession to the crown in the house of Hanover.

It was these signs of the times, by indications which appeared too truly like coming events casting their shadows before, that induced Steele, regardless of all personal consequences, to put himself forward, as he thought became a true patriot, a good citizen, and an honest man, who prized too dearly those principles which he now saw in danger, to permit them to be sacrificed without raising a warning voice. With this view he had started the *Englishman;* and relinquishing those literary pursuits in which he delighted, and by which he had acquired so high a reputation, as well as domestic leisure, he acceded to the offer of the Duke of Newcastle to put him in nomination for the borough of Stockbridge, in Dorset, where accordingly he was duly elected.

With the view of still further enforcing the constitutional doctrines which he believed to be in the most imminent peril by the intrigues of France and the Jacobite party, he prepared early in the following year (1714) a pamphlet, entitled " The Crisis," setting forth the just causes and results of the late Revolution, on the authority of the most important state documents. These included the Declaration of Rights and Settlement to the Succession of the Crown ; the Resolutions of the Convention of the Lords and Commons of Scotland in 1689, reciting the grounds for abjuring the authority of James—viz., his assumption of the royal authority without having taken the required oath, his invasion of the fundamental constitution of the kingdom, his assumption of arbitrary power, his violation of the laws and liberties of the state, illustrated by a variety of details ; two acts *for the further limitation of the crown* in the Protestant line, by fixing the entail on the Princess Sophia and the house of Hanover, in consequence of the death of Queen Mary without issue, and the Duke of Gloucester, son of the Princess Anne ; an act of the first year of Queen Anne for enlarging the time for taking the oath of abjuration ; an act of the fourth year of the same reign for the better security of her majesty's person, and the succession to the crown in the Protestant line ; an *act for the union of the two kingdoms,* of the fifth year of Queen Anne, reciting some of the leading articles.   The first hint of this publication, he tells us afterwards in the preface to "The Apology," was given by Mr Moore of the Inner Temple, a gentleman thoroughly skilled in the history, laws, and constitution of the kingdom, and who undertook the supervision of the legal and technical part.   " When I thought it my duty," he says in the same place, " I thank God I had no further consideration for myself than to do it in a lawful and proper way, so as to give no disparagement to a glorious cause from my indiscretion or want of judgment." Before finally making it public, he submitted copies for the opinion of several friends for whose judgment he had the greatest respect.   " When ' The Crisis,' " he adds, " was written hand in hand with this gentleman, I, who was to answer for it with my all, would not venture upon our single judgment ; therefore I caused it to be printed, and left one copy with Mr Addison, another with Mr Lech-

mere, another with Mr Minshall, and another with Mr
Hoadley. From these corrected copies (no one of these
gentlemen knowing till this day that the other had seen
it) 'The Crisis' became the piece it is."*

With reference to the supposed spurious birth of the
pretended Prince of Wales, he refers to the fact, though
considering it "not material to mention," "that at the time
of the pretended birth, the Princess Anne, now our most
gracious queen, was at Bath; that the bishops were
clapt up in the Tower; that the women about the queen
were Papists; that the presumptive heir was not present;
. . . that our own history informs us that the first Queen
Mary was prevailed on to feign herself with child, to exclude her Protestant sister, the Lady Elizabeth; that the
imposture had been carried on, and a birth been imposed
upon the nation, had not King Philip, her husband, wisely
considered that the impostor would not only succeed to the
crown of England, but also to that of Spain, and so prevented it."

In reference to the settlement of the crown, he says,—

"I cannot forbear to express my wonder that there can be found any
Briton weak enough to contend against a power in their own nation which
is practised to a much greater degree in other states. . . . How hard is
it that Britain should be debarred the privilege of establishing its own
security, even by relinquishing only those branches of the royal line which
threaten it with destruction, whilst other nations never scruple, upon less
occasions, to go much greater lengths. There have been, even in France,
three different races of their kings: the first began with Pharamond, the
second with Charles Martel, the third with Hugh Capet; and I doubt
whether, if the direct line of the blood-royal of France were to be followed,
it would make for the title of his present most Christian majesty. But,
to come to fresh instances, in which Great Britain itself hath not been
unconcerned, what right, by the contrary rule, could the Duke of Savoy

* "Apology," &c., Preface, pp. 14-15.

have to the kingdom of Sicily, or the Elector of Bavaria to that of Sardinia? Can Great Britain help to advance men to other thrones, and have no power in limiting its own? Has not Louis XIV. given us fresh instances of such innovations in his own family? Or can men think he is not in earnest in excluding his grandson the King of Spain and his descendants from the crown of France, and the Dauphin and the Duke of Berry and their descendants from the crown of Spain? And if sacred things as kingdoms themselves may be thus disposed of out of the right line, not by any resignation that can, in any equitable sense, be called voluntary, but apparently for mere reasons of state and ambition, certainly the English and Scotch, for the preservation of religion, liberty, and property, the essential benefits of life, might with more justice settle their crown in the Protestant line in the manner they have done."

All these cogent arguments, strengthened with the " barrier of laws and oaths, of policy and religion, of penalties without and conscience within," were apparently enough to banish all fear ; but on considering certain indications both at home and abroad, his misgivings revive. He then takes a vivid retrospect of the state of Europe for some years past, before the conclusion of the war, contrasting it in a melancholy manner with the existing condition of affairs. " I shall not presume," he says, " to enter into an examination of the articles of peace between us and France ; but there can be no crime in affirming (if it be a truth) that the house of Bourbon is at this juncture become more formidable, and bids fairer for a universal monarchy, and to engross the whole trade of Europe, than it did before the war."

The obligations of the house of Stuart to the crown of France were notorious. The last two kings of that race had been pensioners upon it ; and if it possessed the power to serve them, the will could not be doubted.

" We cannot help it," he concludes, " if so many thousands of our brave brethren who laid down their lives against the power of France have died in vain; but we may value our own lives dearly, like honest men.

Whatever may befall the glory and wealth of Great Britain, let us struggle to the last drop of our blood for its religion and liberty. The banners under which we are to enter this conflict, whenever we are called to it, are the laws mentioned in this discourse. . . . Her Majesty's parliamentary title, and the succession in the illustrious house of Hanover, is the ark of God to Great Britain, and, like that of old, carries death to the profane hand that shall dare to touch it."

About the same time Steele published also, as a distinct pamphlet, " The Englishman : being the close of the paper so called, with an Epistle concerning the Whigs, Tories, and New Converts." This was No. 72 of the political successor of the *Guardian*, and dated Feb. 15, 1714. The writer says,—

" I was once so happy in the kind thoughts of the generality of people of all conditions in this town that I cannot, without regret, look back upon them ; and indeed I should be still more concerned had I not forfeited it for such considerations as only are to be preferred to their good opinion, . . . the testimony of a good conscience.

" That which moved in me," he adds, " an indignation not to be suppressed was the licentious abuse of great and good men who had served their country with honour and success. I thought what favour I had obtained by being the author of an instructive way of representing the manners of men, and describing vices and virtues in a style that might fall in with their ordinary entertainments, could not be more worthily employed, improved, or lost, than in defence of such men, and of the constitution itself, which they had supported.

" When the subjects of peace or war were all the conversation in town, I took upon me to be as concerned as I thought I had a right to be, and speak my sentiments with the freedom of an English gentleman.

" This behaviour brought upon me the invectives of many unknown authors, each of whom has writ against me with as much violence as if I had been personally his most inveterate enemy ; for they have been succinct enough in what concerned the argument, but have largely dwelt upon the author they writ against, in the articles of birth, education, and fortune.

" If empty words are all that are required to make up the virtue we express by the word loyalty, I must own that he (the *Examiner*) and his friends are the best subjects that either king or queen were blessed with ; . . but I will suppose loyalty to be only, what it should be very much, a love and zeal to the queen's person, honour, interest, and safety ; and even on these heads it is visible that their zeal hath been shamefully to their own interests and places, and that her honour, and interest, and love of her people, hath been sacrificed to a scandal.

" To pass by the blackening and ridiculing all the noblest parts of her reign, the inhuman usage of her old servants, and the last insolent jest the *Examiner* made on the report of her death, and his sudden triumph and joy, even while the life of the queen was yet doubtful,—to pass all these, and many a real injury besides, I will only ask whether it be for the queen's honour and interest to have one-half of her people's affections alienated from her by studied provocations ? . . . If her Majesty, in great complaisance to them, will throw off one-half of the people as enemies that have no right to any favour that is worth having, and lend them her name and purse and power to keep those hated people under, or else ruin them, then they in requital will stand by her in distributing all places and preferments among themselves ; and so will the worst sect we have amongst us, and the worse they are, the higher they will strain their un-limited loyalty in sacrifices of the nation's rights. . . . Though flattery carries witchcraft, yet when she shall see that these men . . . cannot carry their elections but by representing all others as under her displeasure ; when she shall see that they overbear the rights of corporations by the impertinent interposition of her power and name ; . . . when she shall see that those noisy men who embarrass the nation in every question by calling out the Church, are but like the weathercocks and clappers of the steeple ; and that the sober and laborious and peaceable churchmen are its real supports and pillars ; when a little more time shall bring out things that begin to appear pretty plain already ; then the queen will shew selfish men who would engross her favour, that she will be mother of all her people ; and as, in spite of these men's studied provocations, she hath their hearts and affections, so she will rule with equal justice towards all. . . . And for those who shall dare to insult and exasperate the other as enemies, they are sycophants instead of friends, and rob her of her best treasure, which is the love of all her people."

Referring to all the designs of the opposite party being carried on under the watchword of the Church, he com-pares the Church and State to the union of soul and body, so that one cannot suffer without injury to the other. " I have enlarged the more upon this head, because, since the *Examiner* and oracles of policy have opened themselves, many of the clergy are for giving unreasonable preferences of the Church to the State, and advance such notions fo the securing of the former as, if put in practice, will infallibly destroy the whole."

After alluding to one of the scurrilous publications of his opponents as " a very notable piece," though we believe the writer was one of the understrappers of the party, named Wagstaff, Steele says, " I think I know the author of this," (evidently referring to Swift,) "and to shew him I know no revenge but in the method of heaping coals on his head by benefits, I forbear giving him what he deserves; for no other reason but that I know his sensibility of reproach is such, as that he would be unable to bear life itself under half the ill language he has given me." This doubtless alluded to some confession in the intimacy of their early friendship. But what an example of magnanimity! He would neither employ licentious ridicule, of which he was no contemptible master, out of consideration for him who had been his friend, nor would he on his own account stoop to retort the low arts of his opponent by flinging dirt from the gutter.

Among other matters in this pamphlet, it rectifies the misstatements of the *Examiner* in endeavouring to throw the odium of some rumours originating in the illness of the queen upon the Whigs, and in treating with contempt some reported affidavits respecting enlisting recruits for the Pretender in Ireland, and in reference to the latter quotes a resolution of the Grand Jury of Waterford, and a proclamation of the Lord-Lieutenant in confirmation of the fact.

This pamphlet has been dwelt upon the more, as it was the last of those political writings which the ardour of his patriotism led him to publish, to denounce a violent, reckless, and infatuated faction, who were madly drifting the ship of the state upon the rocks and quicksands, and hazarding the wreck of the constitution in their blind fury. These publications drew upon their author, as we shall see, the unbounded rage of his opponents; and he was made to expiate the offence against them by being expelled the House, and elevated to the honour of a political martyr and patriot.

It may be proper here to refer to a statement by Dr Somerville, the historian,[*] who, after remarking · that " perhaps there never was in the annals of political literature a book more universally read, or so much the subject of conversation as 'The Crisis,'" proceeds to quote a letter written by Mr Moore, in the year 1716, bringing his claims before Lord Chancellor Macclesfield as the writer of "The Crisis," from which he infers that Steele only lent his name to it. But the internal evidence, as well as the positive statement of Steele, is opposed to this inference. In his " Apology," published two years previous to the date of this letter, Steele, as previously noticed, had acknowledged Mr Moore as the proposer and joint-executor of the work, and had paid him many compliments on his legal and constitutional knowledge, but stated at the same time that "'The Crisis' was *written hand in hand with this gentleman*," so that there can be no doubt of the general literary portion being his.

* " History of Great Britain," &c., Appendix, No. xxxvi.

CHAPTER XII.

Meeting of the new parliament—Steele takes his seat as member for Stockbridge—Petition against his return on the ground of bribery—Display of factious opposition to him on the occasion of his first remarks in the House—Arraigned by the Ministry as guilty of libel and sedition in his political writings—His defence—Is supported by Walpole, General Stanhope, Lord Lumley, Lord Finch, and others —Memorable incident on the occasion—His expulsion voted by a large majority—Hallam on the right of expulsion, and its unscrupulous exercise—Publishes his "Apology" for himself and his writings—Reflections of Pope, and ribaldry of Dennis—Correspondence to the time of his expulsion.

THE new parliament met in the beginning of March 1714, and Steele took his seat for Stockbridge in Dorsetshire, where he had been elected the previous August. His election was followed up by a petition against his return, on the ground of bribery, which was probably merely a piece of party vindictiveness; but as he was exposed soon after to other proceedings, which had no doubt been fully concerted in the interim, the validity of the petition was never tested. He had an early intimation of the treatment in store for him. After two or three gentlemen had proposed Sir Thomas Hanmer as Speaker of the House of Commons, Steele took on him to say he had the same honourable sentiments of that gentleman in the following words to the Clerk of the House :—

"Mr Jodrell,—At the close of the last parliament her majesty was graciously pleased to declare from the throne that the late rejected bill of commerce between Great Britain and France should be offered to this House. That declaration was certainly made that every gentleman who should have the honour to be returned hither might make himself master of that important question. It is demonstration that was a most pernicious bill, and no man can have a greater merit to this House than his by whose weight and authority that pernicious bill was thrown out. I rise up to do him honour, and distinguish myself by giving him my vote for that his inestimable service to his country."

We have his own account of the reception of this his first parliamentary effort. It will be impossible, he says, for the reader to conceive how this speech was received, except he has happened to have been at a cock-match, and has seen the triumph and exultation which is raised when a volatile, whose fall was some way gainful to part of the company, has been necked. At the mention of the bill of commerce the cry began; at calling it pernicious, it increased; at the words "doing him honour," it grew insupportably loud. Having no reason, however, he adds, for being confounded for other people's folly or absurdity, he bore the insolence well enough to speak out what he intended. At the same time he did not attribute this particular outrage to the House, he said, any further than that they ought to have suppressed, and severely observed upon it, by turning out the offenders, who, it is supposed, were a parcel of rustics who crowded in with the members before the election of the Speaker, from a received error that there is no authority in the House till he is chosen. Whether this was meant as a satiric touch, he tells us, he could hear those loud critics as he came out remarking to one another, " Oh, 'tis not so easy a thing to speak in the House;"—"He fancies because he can scribble——," and the like deep animadversions.

On March 12 complaint was made to the House against certain paragraphs in three printed pamphlets,—one entitled "The Englishman," from Saturday, Jan. 16, to Tuesday, Jan. 19, 1713-14, wherein is a printed letter to the *Englishman*, to which is subscribed the name of Richard Steele ; another, entitled "The Crisis," in the title-page whereof it is said, "By Richard Steele, Esq.;" and the other, entitled "The Englishman," being the close of the paper so called, in the title-page whereof it is also said, "By Richard Steele, Esq.,"—as containing several paragraphs tending to sedition, highly reflecting on her Majesty, and arraigning her administration and government. Upon which the accused member was ordered to attend in his place the next morning. He attended accordingly on Saturday the 13th, and heard the several paragraphs in the pamphlets complained of read. He afterwards stood up and read from a paper the following statement :—

"Mr Speaker,—I have written and caused to be printed several books and papers, with a sincere zeal and good intent to serve my queen and country, the present happy establishment in Church and State, and particularly the Protestant succession in the house of Hanover. . . .

"Though I was ordered to attend in my place before any particular passages, if I am rightly informed, were read or objected to in the House, yet now that I have heard what they are, I trust to the justice of this House that I shall have a reasonable time to peruse and compare them, and if I find them, upon perusal, to be really the same which I wrote and published, I shall ingenuously own them, and hope to make such a defence of them as will be satisfactory to this House ; for which I doubt not but you will allow me sufficient time."

Mr Auditor Harley moved that the following Monday be the day appointed for hearing his defence. Steele, however, after reminding the House that the only intervening day was Sunday, and that, besides collating the papers, much more must be supposed as material to his defence, said he did not think he abused the indulgence of the House by desiring till Saturday following.   After some further discussion, Thursday was named by him, in which he was seconded by Mr Pitt of Worcestershire, and it was finally agreed to.

Believing that a great part of the ill-will against him was owing to what he had written respecting Dunkirk, and that it would make for his defence that the affairs relative to the collusive demolition should be brought before the House previous to the day appointed for his defence, Steele, on the following Monday, determined to act on that impression.   He accordingly moved, " That a humble address be presented to Her Majesty, that she will be pleased to give directions that the several representations of her Majesty's engineers and officers who have had the care and inspection of the demolition of Dunkirk, and all orders and instructions given thereupon, be laid before this House." The motion passed in the negative, and this, he tells us, tended to heighten the depressing impression he had of the issue of his cause.   He fortified himself, however, as he best might, for the worst, considering all that was to follow, he says, as a farce wherein heedless men were to indulge their curiosity, mirth, or cruelty, without any regard to justice, or how far what they were doing would affect him or themselves.

The important day, Thursday the 18th,

" Big with the fate of Cato and of Rome,"

arrived in due course.   The order of the day for taking into consideration the printed pamphlets complained of to the House being read, Mr Foley, the accuser, demanded that the matter appointed for the day might be entered upon. The other leading opponents were, Sir William Wyndham, Sir Edward Northey, the Attorney-General, and other friends of the administration. Steele had chosen to make his appearance near the bar of the House, and had on either side of him Mr Stanhope and Mr Walpole, the afterwards celebrated minister, who, he tells us, condescended to take upon them the parts of his advocates—a circumstance of the scene, he says, which very much sweetened his affliction. He was also assisted by his friend Mr Addison, member for Malmsbury, who sat near him, to prompt him when occasion required. The first question proposed was, whether the member accused acknowledged the writings or not ; upon which Steele stood up and said,—

"Mr Speaker,—When I was called upon the other day, upon the same occasion, I suspended the utter acknowledgment of the papers laid on your table against me. I was advised to do so. What has hitherto been insisted upon by me was mere formality in favour of other innocent men who may hereafter fall into my circumstances. I now frankly and ingenuously own all these papers laid to my charge to be parts of my writings. I wrote them in behalf of the house of Hanover, and I own them with the same unreservedness with which I abjured the Pretender. I humbly submit myself to this honourable assembly, and depend upon your justice."

Though he had too much at stake, he tells us, to be in humour enough to enjoy the scene, there was, with all the cruelty of it, something particularly comic in the affair. All the men of sense in the majority of the House, though they did not deny a friend a vote, stood off and left the whole management to the family and the office.

The onset, he says, was made in the poorest manner, and the accusation laid with an insipid action and cold expression. The accuser arraigned a man for sedition with the same indolence and indifference as another man pares his nails. What was spoken appeared only a rheum from the mouth, and Mr Foley, as well as do what he did, might have blown his nose and put the question. But though the choler of his accusers, he says, was corrected by their phlegm, yet had they perseverance to go on, insensible of the raillery of the contrary party, and the contempt of their own. The most lamentable thing of all to consider, he adds, was that, though there was not one man of honour who spoke on the side of the ministry but did it upon general terms, wherein he apparently discovered his disapprobation of the work he was about, so many honest gentlemen should join in a vote of expulsion.*

A person of much less knowledge of the world and of human nature need hardly have been surprised at such a result in the then state of parties, and the passions by which they were actuated. He might have been surprised that a minister should convert the legislative assembly into a judicial body to take cognisance of what had not passed within the walls of the House, and of acts and writings by one not at the time a member of it, and with which the courts of justice were competent to deal; but having done so, it was no matter of surprise that he should accomplish his purpose, under the existing state of things. The circumstances of the legislative body at that time were directly the reverse of what they are now. The majority of the House of Commons was Tory, and the Whig strength lay in the Lords.

After some considerable discussion as to the mode of proceeding, the call became general, "Mr Steele," "Mr Steele;" but his friends induced him to sit still, until it was intimated that, if he omitted taking advantage of the present

---

* Preface to Apology for himself and his writings.

occasion to make his defence, he would have no further opportunity to do so, when he rose and addressed the House.

He commenced by bespeaking the indulgence of those whom he addressed, in consideration of the disadvantages under which he laboured, the shortness of the time allowed him for preparation, the natural excitement of his feelings, the want of rest, and the confused state of the mass of papers to which he had to refer. He showed that if he had committed any errors or displayed undue warmth in contending for the rights of his country in reference to Dunkirk, or the succession of the house of Hanover, of which he was not sensible, that he had been betrayed into it by the statements of the organ of the Opposition, as well as by its personal outrages and abuse; that if statements originating in a paper warfare were to be taken cognisance of in that place, they were constituting the *Examiner* one of the ministry, and must have a mean opinion of the dignity of a British House of Commons, if they made themselves parties on either side in such a case.

"I say, Sir," he argued, "there are many who have written with as great zeal in a cause which is condemned as treasonable by our acts of Parliament, and yet have had the good luck to escape the notice of those who have either the making of laws or the putting them in execution. . . . Those writers who declared themselves the professed advocates of the ministry, and gave themselves the air of being in the secrets of the administration, were the first aggressors. . . . Those papers I am now speaking of prejudged my election, denounced to me the displeasure of men in great places, and foretold that storm which is now falling upon me, unless it be averted by the justice and honour of gentlemen, who are the only persons that can interpose in this case between an innocent man and an offended minister. Such has been the cruel and ungenerous usage which I have met with from an author who has professed himself a champion for the ministry, that no longer since than last Friday, he has fallen upon me with that rage and malice which are unbecoming a scholar, a gentleman, or a Christian, at the time that so great a misfortune befel me, as to be accused before this House. As if he did not think that weight heavy enough upon me, he makes his court to his superiors by determining the cause which lay before this honourable assembly, and represents me in such a character as, I hope, is due to no man living. I cannot but take notice of his last paper, which if any gentleman will be at the pains of perusing, he will find (by what strange accident, or concerted measures, I know not) that it is a brief of the charges against me before this House. It was in answer to this writer that I first employed my pen, and, as I thought, for the service of my country. This man has represented half of her Majesty's subjects as a different people, who have forfeited the common protection allowed them by the constitution; but has never been called to account for it, *as a writer of matters tending to sedition.* He has treated the fathers of our Church like the basest among the people, torn in pieces the reputation of the most eminent names in Great Britain, marked out several members in both Houses of Parliament, and endeavoured to render them odious to the nation when they have disagreed with him in opinion, or rejected any Bill which the Ministry had seemed to promote. He has vilified those in friendship and alliance with her Majesty, and condemned treaties which are still in force. He has trifled upon so melancholy a subject as that of her Majesty's late indisposition, and represented her as actually dead, for the sake of a poor conceit which the greatest part of his readers were not able to take, and those who did, could not but regard with horror. All this, Sir, the author I am now mentioning has done, without being called to account for any reflection *tending to sedition, highly reflecting on her Majesty, and arraigning her administration and government.* In the opinion of the world he has not only done all this with impunity, but with encouragement. It is chiefly in answer to this author, that those papers were written which are now upon your table. I could not see without indignation an endeavour set on foot to confound truth with falsehood, and to turn the whole history of the present times into a lie."

He then refers to and quotes the paragraph objected against him in No. 46 of the *Englishman,* which has these words :—

"I speak all this because I am much afraid of the Pretender, and my fears are increased because many others laugh at the danger. I presume to say, those who do laugh at either do not think at all, or think it will be no day of danger to themselves. But I thus early let go my fire against the Pretender's friends, because I think myself a very good judge of men's

mien and air, and see what they intend at a distance. I own I have
nothing to say . . . . when nobody else talks in the same style, but what
the sailor did when he fired out of the stage-coach upon highway-men
before they cried, ' stand '—*Would you have me stay till they have boarded
us ?* "

The interest of the defence, as a whole, was injured by
the necessity he was under of applying himself to the
particular passages marked against him in the different
publications referred to, and the consequent introduction
of a variety of minute and unconnected details and explanations.

Referring to the first passage marked in " The Crisis,"—
from which he supposed, he said, those who marked it would
fetch an inuendo out of it that he spoke disrespectfully of
the Universities,—after quoting some passages to shew that
the general tenor of his writings was directly opposed to
such an insinuation, he adds, " It appears by these, and
many other passages in my writings, that I have retained
the greatest honour and esteem for those learned bodies,
in one of which I received my education, and where I can
still boast of much personal friendship and acquaintance."

Alluding to the next passage marked in the same work,
the imputed inference from which was supposed to reflect
upon the clergy (to whom the pamphlet was dedicated)
in reference to the Hanover succession, he said, " Sir, I
am afraid that those who stir up this accusation against
me, only make use of the name of the clergy to give it a
more popular turn, and to take off the odium from themselves, by the use of such venerable names." He then
alluded to the notorious fact, that his writings had been
noted for their advocacy of virtue and religion, as well as
the defence of their teachers ; and after having cited

various passages in confirmation of this, he added, "I can't tell, Sir, what they would have me do to prove me a Churchman, but I think I have appeared one in so trifling a thing as a comedy; and considering me as a comic poet, I have been a martyr and confessor for the Church; for this play ('The Lying Lover') was damned for its piety." Among other passages, he quotes from the *Tatler* the favourable notice he had given of an anonymous pamphlet by Swift, entitled "A Project for the Advancement of Religion," and adds these pointed words:—"The gentleman I here intended was Dr Swift; this kind of man I thought him at that time. We have not met of late, but I hope he deserves this character still."

After explanations in reference to various passages marked against him, he protests against forcing a meaning from his words to bear a censurable construction contrary to their natural and literal sense, and insists "that if an author's words, in the obvious and natural interpretation of them, have a meaning which is innocent, they cannot, without great injustice, be condemned of another meaning which is criminal."

In defence of what he had said in reference to Dunkirk, he remarked:—

"I have regulated my thoughts on that subject by the treaty of peace, which has been published for the perusal of her Majesty's subjects. It was thereby stipulated that the mole and harbour should be first demolished; but, instead of this, the French (for it is there I lay the blame) have only demolished the fortifications towards the land; and thus, as I have said in another place, the Queen's garrison is exposed, by levelling the works, to the mercy of the French; and the mole and harbour, which were first to be demolished, stand as they did. Will any one say that this proceeding of the French, so contrary to what was stipulated by the articles of peace, is not begun contemptuously and arbitrarily their own way?

The time stipulated by the same treaty for the demolition of the mole and harbour, is long since elapsed, and no longer since than a week ago, as I can prove by incontestible evidence, they were actually repairing that very mole, which should have been long before this a heap of ruins."

In reference to some further passages, he says :—

" But here the gentleman finds another inuendo, and has marked out a seditious blank: that is, in reality he is very angry with me, not for anything I have said, but for something I have not said ; or rather, because I have not written what he would have had me write. But if he finds both my silence and my words criminal, I must confess I don't know how to please him."

In conclusion, he says :—

"I must declare, sir, that upon the perusal of those paragraphs which have been marked against me, I have been more puzzled to know why I ought to defend them, than how they ought to be defended !   And I dare appeal to any gentleman who is used to read pamphlets, whether he has seen any of either side for some years past, that have been written with more caution, or more thoroughly guarded against giving any occasion of just offence.

"Upon the whole matter, I do humbly conceive that no words which I have made use of can be censured as criminal, in the candid and natural interpretation of them, and can only be construed as such by distant implications and far-fetched inuendoes."

He then quotes the words of the then Lord Chancellor of England, on the trial of Dr Sacheverell, shewing that in such cases, if a man's words admitted of an innocent interpretation in their plain and natural sense, the mercy of the law gave him the benefit of it, and did not sanction the departing from the words, by resorting to an imputed criminal meaning, and that though there were formerly too many instances of this nature, the late happy revolution put an end to such arbitrary constructions.   After this felicitous reference to such a high authority, and a case the result of which might serve as a warning to his accusers, he wound up in the following admirable manner :—

"I have heard it said in this place, that no private man ought to take the liberty of expressing his thoughts as I have done, in matters relating to the administration. I do own that no private man ought to take a liberty which is against the law of the land. But, Sir, I presume that the liberty I have taken is a legal liberty, and obnoxious to no penalty in any court of justice. If it had, I cannot believe that this extraordinary method would have been made use of to distress me upon that account. And why should I here suffer for having done that which perhaps in a future trial would not be judged criminal by the laws of the land ? Why should I see persons whose particular province it is to prosecute seditious writers in the courts, employing their eloquence against me in this place ? I think that I have not offended against any law in being ; I think that I have taken no more liberty than what is consistent with the laws of the land ; if I have, let me be tried by those laws. Is not the executive power sufficiently armed to inflict a proper punishment on all kinds of criminals ? Why then should one part of the legislative power take this executive power into its own hands ? But, sir, I throw myself upon the honour of this House, who are-able, as well as obliged, to screen any commoner of England from the wrath of the most powerful man in it, and who will never sacrifice a member of their own body to the resentment of any single minister."

With these words he concluded a most able and temperate address, which had occupied about three hours, and with a courteous obeisance to the Speaker, withdrew. When he was withdrawn, Mr Foley rose and said, without amusing the House with long speeches, it was plain the writings they complained of were scandalous and seditious, injurious to her Majesty's Government, the Church, and the Universities, and called for the question. A very warm debate then arose, which lasted till eleven at night. The first who spoke on behalf of Steele was Robert Walpole, Esq., who had himself been the victim of a similar factious expulsion, with the addition of incarceration in the Tower. He had only recently resumed his seat, and now distinguished himself, and added to his popularity with his party, by his able advocacy of the liberty of the subject to freedom of speech, and the privileges of the Commons of England. He was followed by his brother Horace, and Lord Lumley, Lord Hinchinbroke, and Lord Finch. A memorable incident occurred when the latter rose to address the House. He was the eldest son of the Earl of Nottingham, and brother of the young lady in whose defence Steele had broken the bounds of neutrality to which he had restricted himself in the *Guardian*, in reply to the *Examiner*. It was the young lord's maiden effort, and, in addition to any other motives by which he may have been actuated, he had a debt of gratitude to pay; but, after rising to address the House, overcome with ingenuous diffidence, he was about to resume his seat, muttering audibly, however, at the same time, "It is strange how I can't speak for this man, though I could readily fight for him." The first appearance of a young member naturally created an interest, and his muttered words spreading through the House like wildfire, he was greeted with the cry of "Hear him, hear him," from all quarters, when again stepping forward, he made a first speech of which it is recorded that every word told. In a dedication which Steele afterwards addressed to him, he alluded to "the noble motive which first produced your natural eloquence, as what should be the great purpose of that charming force in all who are blessed with it, the protection of the oppressed."

Eloquence and argument, however, were alike impotent against the force of numbers, and it was "resolved," by a majority of 245 against 152—

" That a printed pamphlet, entitled " The Englishman," being the close of the paper so called, and one other pamphlet, entitled " The Crisis," written by Richard Steele, Esq., a member of this House, are scandalous and seditious libels, containing many expressions highly reflecting upon her Majesty, and upon the nobility, gentry, clergy, and universities of this kingdom, maliciously insinuating that the Protestant succession in the house of Hanover is in danger under her Majesty's administration, and tending to alienate the affections of her Majesty's good subjects, and to create jealousies and divisions among them—

" Resolved—That Richard Steele, Esq., for his offence in writing and publishing the said scandalous and seditious libels, be expelled this House "

Thus prematurely terminated for the present Steele's Parliamentary career. It may not be uninteresting or inappropriate here to refer to the strictures on this right of expulsion exercised by the Commons, by the highest authority on constitutional history :—

" It was carried to a great excess," remarks Mr Hallam, " by the Long Parliament, and again in the year 1680. These, however, were times of extreme violence, and the prevailing faction had an apology, in the designs of the court, which required an energy beyond the law to counteract them. The offences, too, which the Whigs thus punished in 1680 were, in their effect, against the power, and even the existence of Parliament. The privilege was far more unwarrantably exerted by the opposite party in 1714 against Sir Richard Steele, expelled the House for writing 'The Crisis,' a pamphlet reflecting on the Ministry. This was perhaps the first instance wherein the House of Commons so identified itself with the executive administration, independently of the sovereign's person, as to consider itself libelled by those who impugned its measures." *

Steele had so little of the courtier or politician about him, that he seemed to think the way to success was to speak the honest truth, and he tells us that the kindness and discretion of his friends at his defence prevented his adding many statements of that nature which would only have exasperated the feeling against him. Truth is said proverbially to lie at the bottom of a well, and it is often

* Hallam's Constitutional History, vol. iii., p. 265.

the only reward of those who are sedulously bent on drawing it up to tumble in headforemost themselves.   The
mere fact of resuscitating the most solemn acts and resolutions of the legislature at and subsequent to the Revolution, with some strictures upon them, (in "The Crisis,") was
an unpardonable offence.   But now that he had suffered
the worst that an unscrupulous and vindictive Ministry
could inflict upon him, he felt himself as much concerned,
he says, to shew why this sentence should not be a reproach
to him, now it was passed, as he was before to speak against
its being pronounced.   With this view he prepared for the
press the substance of his defence, with some additions,
and published it, with an elaborate dedication, by way of
preface, to Mr (afterwards the famous Sir Robert) Walpole,
in which he indulges in some very severe strictures on the
minister by whose influence he was sacrificed, and de-
nounces " the arbitrary use of numbers in the most odious
colours, that gentlemen may have a just detestation of
practising a thing in itself unwarrantable, from the support only of the insolent and unmanly sanction of a majority."   He entitled the work an " Apology for Himself
and his Writings," occasioned by his expulsion from the
House of Commons; and it may be regarded as not the
least masterly of his productions.   It has been quoted to a
considerable extent in the preceding notice of his defence
in the House.   Speaking of the minister, as he does in
very severe terms in the dedication, among other statements he expresses the opinion he had always entertained
of him, that "whatever became of his country, which I
believe had little share in his lordship's cares, he would,
with the wand in his hand, raise powers which he would

want skill to command, and which, consequently, would
tear himself in pieces."

In the supplementary statements he says :—

"It may be objected that I am sure to come off when I, who am the
criminal, am also to be the judge.   I may make the same objection against
the determination of the House ; they who were the judges were also the
accusers.   .   .   .   But my fate is so extraordinary, that I am punished by
the House of Commons, (where freedom of speech is an essential privilege),
for saying what was criminal nowhere else.   Had what I have written been
spoken in the House of Commons, no man will pretend to say it had been
criminal.   How, then, when it was innocent in another place, came it to
be criminal when produced there ?   I was safe, when in circumstances
that rendered me more accountable, and run into danger by being privi-
leged.   .   .   .

"There was not one argument used to support this heavy accusation ;
but I suppose, upon consideration that his reflecting upon the Queen so
directly . . . was just the quite contrary to what he had done, the ill-
behaviour towards her Majesty is in the resolution scattered among her
subjects.   .   .   .   Let this resolve be taken out of its formality, and it is
just as if they had said, he has been guilty of treason and also of ill
manners.

"There are many instances of punishment in the House for being too
obsequious to the Court against the people, but Mr Steele is the first that
fell there for being audacious towards ministers in behalf of his country.

"But let those who were for an oppressed gentleman, their fellow-
citizen, . . . be had in everlasting remembrance, . . . who have nobler
prospects in view than to follow mercenaries with their vote against a poor
and impotent patriot, who attempted to rouse his country out of a lethargy
from which she has awakened only to behold her danger ; and upon seeing
it too great, has only sighed, folded her arms, and returned to her trance."

Among the various publications of Steele at this period,
was a volume of "Poetic Miscellanies," consisting of a collection of pieces contributed by himself and his poetical
friends, with a dedication to Congreve.   He also published
another collection in three volumes, of an instructive
character, entitled, "The Ladies' Library," dedicated to
three accomplished ladies—the first to the Countess of Bur-
lington, daughter of Henry Noel, second son of Viscount

Campden ; the second to Mrs Boevey ; and the third to Mrs Steele. The last will be referred to on another occasion. The second is the only one on which it is necessary to dwell at present, and that from the circumstance of there being a tradition of Steele having had an early attachment to this lady, and of her having been the original of the perverse widow of Sir Roger de Coverley. This surmise was communicated first by the Rev. Duke Yonge of Plympton, in Devonshire, through Archdeacon Nares to Mr Chalmers, the editor of the "Essayists."

"My attention," says the reverend gentleman, "was first drawn to this subject by a very vague tradition in the family of Sir Thomas Crawley Boevey, of Flaxley Abbey in Gloucestershire, that Mrs Catherine Boevey, widow of Wm. Boevey, Esq., and who died January 21, 1726, was the original from whence the picture of the perverse widow in the *Spectator* was drawn. She was left a widow at the early age of twenty-two, and her portrait (now at Flaxley Abbey, and drawn at a more advanced period of her life) appears to have been a woman of a handsome, dignified figure, as she is described to have been in the 113th No. of the *Spectator*. She was a personage well known, and much distinguished in her day, and is described very respectably in the *New Atlantis*, under the name of Portia.
. . . "No. 113 of the *Spectator*, as far as it relates to the widow, is almost a parody on the character of Mrs Boevey, as shewn in the dedication. Sir Roger tells his friend that she is a reading lady, and that her discourse was as learned as the best philosopher could possibly make. She reads upon the nature of plants, and understands everything. In the dedication Steele says, 'instead of assemblies and conversations, books and solitude have been your choice: you have charms of your own sex, and knowledge not inferior to the most learned of ours.' In No. 118, 'her superior merit is such,' says Sir Roger, 'that I cannot approach her without awe ; my heart is checked by too much esteem.' Dedication,—'Your person and fortune equally raise the admiration and awe of our whole sex.'
"She is described as having a confidant, as the knight calls her, to whom he expresses a peculiar aversion, No. 118 being chiefly on that subject. 'Of all persons,' says the good old knight, ' be sure to set a mark on confidants.' . . . Mrs Boevey certainly had a female friend of this description, of the name of Pope ; who lived with her more than forty years,

whom she left her executrix ; and who, it is believed in the family, did
not execute her office in the most liberal manner." *

This coincidence is certainly curious, and the inference
not improbable. It may be added that though Mrs Boevey
at her decease in 1726 was interred in the family vault
at Flaxley, there is also a splendid monument to her
memory in Westminster Abbey, under that of Lord Howe,
with a bust on a small medallion, and with a suitable
inscription. This was erected by Mrs Pope, the executrix
and confidant above-mentioned.

Before proceeding to notice the engagements of Steele
after his expulsion, a few letters may here be introduced,
bringing his correspondence up to that event:—

LETTER CCXXII.   *To Mrs Steele.*
                      Bloomsbury Square, Dec. 24, 1713.
  DEAR PRUE,—I dine with Lord Halifax, and shall be at home half hour
after six. For thee I die, for thee I languish.   RICH. STEELE.

LETTER CCXXIII.   *To Mrs Steele.*
                      Jan. 20, 1713-14.
  DEAR PRUE,—I am gone to Buckley's,† and from thence am to go and

---

  * Chalmers' edit. "Essayists"—*Spectator*, introduction to vol. i. pp. 76–78.
  † " *Sam. Buckley* at the Dolphin, in Little Britain, for whom seven volumes of
the original *Spectator* in folio had been printed. The *Spectator* being discontinued at the close of the seventh volume, was succeeded by the *Guardian ;* and
Pope informs us that Steele was engaged in articles of penalty to Jacob Tonson,
for all the papers he published under this last name. The same author says,
' The true reason why Steele laid down the *Guardian* was a quarrel between him
and the bookseller above-mentioned ;' he adds, ' that Steele, by desisting two days,
and altering the title of his paper to that of the *Englishman*, got quit of his
obligation.' At the date of this letter, the periodical paper to which Steele gave
the title of the *Englishman* was in course of publication ; it was printed by S.
Buckley in Amen Corner, and announced as the sequel of the *Guardian.* The
title of *Spectator* was resumed some months after. Number first of the eighth
volume, printed by S. Buckley, in Amen Corner, *folio*, is dated on the 18th of the
June following, in 1714."

dine at a place where I am to be with the Elector's Envoy. From thence I shall again return to Buckley's. I trust I shall bring home good news. I want clean linen, being very dirty with running about. I have left Mr Cragg's subscription* books at his house.—I am, dear Prue, yours faithfully,   RICH. STEELE.

LETTER CCXXIV.   *To Mrs Steele.*
                                                      March 11, 1713-14.

DEAR PRUE,—I send you this to let you know that Lord Halifax would not let me go to the House, but thought it would be better to have the first attack made in my absence. Mr Foley† was the gentleman who did me that honour ; but they could not bring it to bear so far as to obtain an order for my attending in my place,‡ or anything else to my disadvantage, than that all pamphlets are to come on on Saturday. Lord Halifax, in the House of Lords, told the Ministry that he believed, if they would recommend "The Crisis" to her Majesty's perusal, she would think quite otherwise of the book than they do.

I think they have begun very unhappily and ungracefully against me, and doubt not but God will turn their malice to the advantage of the innocent.—Your faithful husband and humble servant,
                                                                RICH. STEELE.

LETTER CCXXV.   *To Mrs Steele.*
                                              Bow Street, March 12, 1713-14.
DEAR PRUE,—I am going to Mr Walpole's, to meet some friends. There

---

* Of Steele's celebrated political pamphlet, "The Crisis," which was printed and published by Buckley. On the subject of this subscription, see some severe remarks in Swift's "Public Spirit of the Whigs." A few days before the date of this letter, Swift published a paraphrase of an ode of Horace, beginning—

> "Dick, thou 'rt resolved, as I am told,
> Some strange *arcana* to unfold;
> And, with the help of Buckley's pen,
> To vamp the good old cause again.
> Which thou (such Burnet's shrewd advice is,)
> Must furbish up, and nickname 'Crisis,' " &c.
>   *Supplement to Swift.*

† "The motion which Mr Auditor Foley particularly levelled at Steele, in a debate on the bill for limiting the number of officers in the House of Commons, was ' to take into consideration that part of the Queen's speech which related to the suppressing seditious libels and factious rumours.' "

‡ "They obtained it, however, on the next day."

is nothing can arise to me * which ought to afflict you, therefore, pray be a Roman lady, and assume a courage equal to your goodness. The Queen is very ill.—Your faithful, very cheerful husband,

RICH. STEELE.

Do not mention, if you see Harris, the business of the Queen.

LETTER CCXXVI.   *To Mrs Steele.*

March 13, 1713–14.

DEAR PRUE,—They have given me till Thursday. The House is in very good inclination to me. I will come home to dinner if Lord Halifax does not detain me. Your merit is what saves yours,

RICH. STEELE.

LETTER CCXXVII.   *To Mrs Steele.*

March 18, † 1713–14.
Temple, seven o'clock.

DEAR PRUE,—I have made my defence,‡ and am ordered to withdraw. Addison was sent out after me, by my friends, to bid me not be seen till I heard what will be the censure. If you please to go to Mrs Keck's I will send to you thither by a porter an hour or two hence. Nothing can happen to make my condition in private the worse, and I have busied myself enough for the public. The next is for you and yours,

RICH. STEELE.

---

* "On this day a regular complaint was made to the House by Mr Foley, of three pamphlets by Steele, ("The Crisis" and two single numbers of the *Englishman*,) as containing 'several paragraphs tending to sedition, highly reflecting upon her Majesty, and arraigning her administration and government.' Mr Steele was ordered to attend in his place on the 13th, which he did accordingly, and was then allowed four days for making his defence."

† "The original is misdated, March 17."

‡ "He owned, in his place, 'that he wrote and published the pamphlets complained of;' and read the paragraphs to the House 'with the same cheerfulness and satisfaction with which he abjured the Pretender.' Steele spoke on this occasion with such a temper, modesty, unconcern, easy and manly eloquence, as gave entire satisfaction to all who were not inveterately prepossessed against him. He was strongly supported by Mr Walpole, General Stanhope, the Lord Finch, the Lord Hinchinbroke, and the Lord Lumley. His principal opponents were Mr Foley, Sir W. Wyndham, Sir Edward Northey, (the Attorney-General,) and other courtiers. After a long and interesting debate, Steele was expelled the House by 254 voices against 152. He took ample revenge, however, three days after, on the Harleys and the Foleys, under the name of the *Crabtrees* and the *Brickdusts*, in the eleventh number of the *Lover*."

It is certainly edifying (whatever our opinion of the prudence of Steele may be) to find sentimental Mr Pope delivering himself of a homily on this occasion against violence, in a letter to Congreve, dated the 19th of March. After stating the result of Steele's affair, and his opinion that he had not only been punished by the others, but suffered much even from his own party, in the point of character, without receiving any amends in that of interest, he proceeds to say, " I wish all violence may succeed as ill; but am really amazed that so much of that sour and pernicious quality should be joined with so much natural good humour, as I think Mr Steele is possessed of." Of course, the mild, sweet author of the "Dunciad," good, easy man, had none of this "sour, pernicious quality," nor had ever displayed any violence. He only libelled and stabbed *individuals* on all hands, with initial letters attached to his verses, including all who had ever given him any offence, real or imaginary ; but not excluding some of whom he professed to think favourably, and to number among his friends, and when taxed with it, prevaricated and shuffled in the most paltry manner. In the case of his friend Aaron Hill, he referred him to an edition he had altered, to shew that his name would not have suited the measure.* Nay, among the victims of his atrocious virulence was Lady Montagu, for whom he had formerly professed the most romantic devotion, and to whom the fact of her being a married woman did not

---

* Hill repaid him with a character similar to his own satire on Addison, as one who

"———— sneakingly approv'd,
And wanted soul to spread the worth he lov'd."

prevent him making the most extravagant declarations. In other cases, where personal chastisement had been threatened, some of his biographers have given him very equivocal credit for courage in carrying pistols. If ever Dennis was justified in the exercise of his "sour and pernicious quality," it was surely when he reminded him of what the initial letters of his own two names and the final one would make.

We hear nothing of the violence of his reverend frien.1, Dr Jonathan Swift, who was employing anonymously all the roughest weapons of party warfare,—scurrility, satire, and libel, with a violence and unscrupulousness almost without example, at least in any writer of reputation, and which, if it had been exerted against the Government instead of for it, might had a very different result. But it was only one who wrote in a manly, straightforward way, who signed his name, or if he satired anonymously, did it under a fictitious name, and within the bounds of decency, and who could say, as he did to Swift, that his controversy was with principles, not men—that incurred the censure of the author of the "Dunciad." Verily

> " One fool thinks himself more wise than t' other,
> And shakes his empty noddle at his brother."

Nor was Pope the only Job's comforter that Steele found. Another mild individual, John Dennis, the critic, indulged himself in a characteristic piece of ribald humour on the subject. Steele one time gave the title of hangman of the gospel to a furious preacher. He might have called John Dennis the hangman of literature. Indeed he was worse than the hangman, who merely executes a painful but necessary duty. Dennis, on the contrary, indulged in

wanton cruelty; and if he had been the functionary referred to, would have treated his victim to a preliminary
rehearsal of his office before executing it.   He now took
the opportunity, when Steele was suffering both in mind
and in fortune, to aggravate his adversity by publishing, in
the *Post-Boy* of the 27th April, the advertisement of an
insulting poetical epistle, in imitation of Horace.*

* "John Dennis, the sheltering poet's invitation to R. Steele, the excluded
party writer and member, to come and live with him in the Mint.   In imitation
of Horace, Ep. v., lib. i.   Price 3d.   Fit to be bound up with 'The Crisis.'"

CHAPTER XIII.

FROM HIS EXPULSION TILL THE DEATH OF QUEEN ANNE.

Steele not unduly depressed by his political martyrdom—Displays great industry on literary and political subjects—Publication of the periodical papers entitled the *Lover* and the *Reader*—Satirises his political opponents under the titles of the *Crabtrees* and *Brickdusts*—Proposes a " History of the Duke of Marlborough "—Publishes various political pamphlets, besides literary works, including " Poetic Miscellanies" and ".The Ladies' Library"—Short-lived triumph of his enemies—The tables turned by the death of the Queen—Correspondence up to that event.

NOTWITHSTANDING what Steele has said in deprecation of the censure of the House, there were not wanting some who professed to think that, so far from being surprised at his expulsion, he even courted that honour, and was not ill pleased that he did not attain to political martyrdom, like some of his predecessors, through the Tower. Without stopping to discuss this point, there is no reason to believe that, after the first excitement was over, he was unduly cast down by the event. Though his circumstances were no doubt in a critical position, he immediately applied himself to a variety of work with an industry in which, with all his excitability, he appears never to have been wanting. The *Englishman* * had terminated on the 15th

---

* It may be worthy of mention that it was in this paper that the history of Alexander Selkirk first appeared, which formed the groundwork of that romance by De Foe which has been the delight of boyhood since—" Robinson Crusoe."

of February, at the end of fifty-seven numbers. Previous to
the event, he had started, on February 14th, a fresh literary
periodical paper, after the manner of the eminent ones he
had brought to a close. It was entitled the *Lover*, and
was published three times a week, under the fictitious
name of Marmaduke Myrtle, Esq. In the eleventh number
he took his revenge on the Harleys and the Foleys, under
the titles of the Crabtrees and Brickdusts. The paper
generally bears a resemblance to a sequel of his series of
sketches in the *Tatler* under the character of Cynthio. It
was perhaps on too narrow a foundation, but from whatever cause,—in which the fact of his mind running on
more exciting topics no doubt had a considerable share,—it
only reached to forty numbers, and came to a close on the
27th of May. Indeed, so much was he preoccupied with
political matters that, better than a month previous to
the close of the former paper, he had started a second,
the *Reader*, in opposition to the *Examiner*, the brazen
mouthpiece of the administration. It only reached to nine
numbers, however, beginning on the 22d of April and
closing on the 10th of May. In both papers he had Addison as an occasional contributor.

The *Lover* was dedicated by Steele to Sir Samuel Garth,
the benevolent and poetical physician, whom he celebrates
as " the best-natured man."   Dr Garth was a leading
fellow-member of the Kit-Cat. This eminent man was
descended of a good Yorkshire family, pursued his studies
at Cambridge, and took his degree of M.D. in 1691. He
then became a member of the College of Physicians in
London. A plan for the appropriation of an apartment
in the college for giving advice gratis, and medicine at a

trifling cost to the sick poor, proposed in the year 1696, was warmly espoused by Dr Garth ; but being stoutly opposed by some members of the profession and the apothecaries, he called his muse to the aid of the cause, and in a mock-heroic poem, "The Dispensary," exposed the selfishness of its opponents with the happiest effect, and covered it and them with deserved ridicule. The poem was published in six cantos, with a dedication to Anthony Henley, and was much read and admired, running through several editions. Among numerous complimentary verses to the author on the occasion were those of Codrington, containing the lines,—

> " I read thee over with a lover's eye ;
> Thou hast no faults, or I no faults can spy ;
> Thou art all beauty, or all blindness I."

In the year 1697 he gave evidence of his eminent professional, as well as classical attainments, by a Latin oration delivered before the Faculty. On the death of Dryden in 1701, Dr Garth took upon him the chief care of the last offices ; and, after pronouncing a suitable discourse on the occasion, had the remains interred in Westminster Abbey, in the same grave with Chaucer. In 1702 he was chosen one of the Censors of the College of Physicians, and shortly after, on the formation of the famous Kit-Cat Club, became a member. The eminent professional skill of Dr Garth, his literary reputation, his unaffected good-nature and agreeable conversation, gained him an immense practice among the higher classes, and a private esteem equally extensive.

On the resignation of the Whig Ministry in 1710, Dr Garth addressed some complimentary verses to Lord Godolphin, in which occur the following lines :—

" So much the public to your prudence owes,
    You think no labours long for our repose.
    Such conduct, such integrity are shown,
    There are no coffers empty but your own."

They were, however, so hastily penned as to lay them
open in some degree to the severe cavilling animadversions
they received in the *Examiner.* These were written by
Prior, one of the Tory converts, who had been dismissed
from the Kit-Cat in consequence. They were, however,
vindicated by Addison in a *Whig Examiner* of Sept. 14.
In 1711, Dr Garth wrote a dedication for an intended
edition of Lucretius, addressed to the Elector of Hanover,
which was much admired as one of the purest specimens
of Latinity. The Elector, on his accession to the throne
as George I., conferred on Dr Garth the honour of knighthood with the sword of Marlborough, and made him his
own Physician-in-Ordinary and Physician-General to the
army.

He died, after a short illness, Jan. 18, 1718-19, and was
interred in the church of Harrow-on-the-Hill, in a vault he
had prepared. His only daughter was married to Colonel
the Hon. William Boyle.

Spence, on the authority of Tonson and others, speaks
very highly of his social character, and mentions a rumour
of his having died a Catholic, which is the more remarkable, as his enemies accused him of wanting any fixed
notions on religion. Pope, in one of his letters, says, " The
best-natured of men, Sir Samuel Garth, has left me in the
truest concern for his loss. His death was very heroical,
and yet unaffected enough to have made a saint or a philosopher famous. But ill tongues and worse hearts have
branded his last moments, as wrongfully as they did his

life, with irreligion. You must have heard many tales on this subject ; but, if ever there was a good Christian without knowing himself to be so, it was Dr Garth." *

Almost immediately after his expulsion, Steele issued proposals for a "History of the Duke of Marlborough," who was still living, to date from his commission of Captain-General and Plenipotentiary to the expiration of those commissions. That the history, if it had been destined ever to have been written, whatever it might have been otherwise, would have been drawn in partial colours, we cannot doubt, from the admiration he had for his extraordinary abilities, and the great regard in which he was held personally by the illustrious subject of his intended history. Singularly enough, that feeling had its beginning in a pleasantry of Steele's on his grace's taking good care of his own relations, which, being reported to him, to the credit of his good-nature was taken in good part. What Steele's history of the duke might have been we cannot of

* Several amusing anecdotes are recorded of Dr Garth. It is said, at the Kit-Cat, on one occasion, after mentioning his having a number of patients to visit, he sat for a considerable time enjoying himself. At length Steele, who was of the company, partly perhaps out of consideration for the sufferers, and possibly as much in banter, said, " Really, Garth, you ought to have no more wine, but be off to see those poor devils." " It's no great matter," replied Garth, " whether I see them to-night or not ; for nine of them have such bad constitutions that all the physicians in the world can't save them, and the other six such good ones that all the physicians in the world can't kill them." On another occasion, at a coffeehouse, writing a letter, he found himself overlooked by an Irishman, whose curiosity seemed to be in proportion to his stature. Bringing his epistle to a conclusion without appearing to notice the impertinence, he added, in his most legible hand, " I would write you more by this post, but there's a d——d tall, impudent Irishman looking over my shoulder all the time ! " " What do you mean, sir ? " cried the other in a fury ; " do you think I looked over your letter ? " " Sir," replied Garth, " I never opened my lips to you." " Ay, but you 've put it down for all that." " 'Tis impossible, sir, you should know that, as you never looked over my letter."

course tell, but, in the absence of it, it may not be uninteresting to quote a succinct sketch he has given in " The
Crisis" of his career during the war :—

" The first thing that meets my imagination is, the French army
broken, routed, flying over the plains of Blenheim, and choosing rather to
throw themselves headlong into the Danube than face about upon their
conqueror.   I see the just honours done him by the emperor and the whole
empire ; I hear him, with loud acclamations, acknowledged the deliverer
of Europe.   He is introduced into the college of princes, and takes possession of the principality of Mindelheim.   Triumphant columns are
erected in the plains of Blenheim, recording the seasonable assistance of
the British arms, and the glories of that immortal day.

" The British leader returns from the Danube to the Rhine ; he and
his brave companions are the delight of the nations through whom they
march, and are styled their good, their guardian angels.   After passing so
many different nations in a triumphant manner, he lands in his own
country a humble, unattended subject, honouring and adorning his nation
by privacy and modesty at home, much more than by the highest triumphs
and ostentations abroad.

" The Queen and Senate pass in religious pomp to thank the Almighty
for victory over their common oppressor.   But the prospect does not
end here ; the plains of Ramillies are a new scene of glory to the confede-
rate arms, and a second happy day ends the bondage of many cities.

" His most Christian Majesty [Louis XIV.] conceives new hopes from
changing his generals, and from the conduct of Vendosme promises himself to repair the diminution of his glory by Villeroy.   The branches of his
royal family, the Dukes of Burgundy and Berry, are to animate the
soldiery by their presence ; but Vendosme, Burgundy, and Berry are not
strong enough for the genius of the Duke of Marlborough at Oudenarde.

" The French still change their general, and Villars is in command.
He soon shares the same fate with his predecessors, by being beaten out
of his camp by an inferior number of troops ; a camp so strong by nature
and art, that as none but the Duke of Marlborough would have attempted,
so none but that captain, at the head of his brave countrymen, would
have succeeded in it.   In short, methinks I see Ostend, Menin, Lisle,
Tournay, Mons, Aire, Doway, and innumerable other towns held im-
pregnable, all besieged, taken, and restored to their lawful prince and
ancient liberties.

" The English general, during the course of ten campaigns, besieged no
town but what he took, attacked no army but what he routed, and returned each year with the humility of a private man.

" If beating the enemy in the field, and being too vigilant for their councils in foreign courts, were effectual means towards ending the war, and reducing them to a condition too low for giving fresh disturbance to Europe, the Duke of Marlborough took just measures; but however unaccountable it may appear to posterity, that general was not permitted to enjoy the fruits of his glorious labours; but, as France changed her generals for want of success in their conduct, so Britain changed hers after an uninterrupted series of conquests. The minds of the people, against all common sense, are debauched with impressions of the Duke's affectation of prolonging the war for his own glory; and his adversaries attack a reputation which could not well be impaired without sullying the glory of Great Britain itself; his enemies were not to be softened by that consideration; he is dismissed, and soon after a suspension of arms between Great Britain and France is proclaimed at the head of the armies. The British, in the midst of the enemy's garrisons, withdraw themselves from their confederates. The French, now no longer having the Britons, or their great leader, to fear, affect no more strong garrisons and fortified camps; but attack and rout the Earl of Albemarle at Denain, and necessitate the brave Prince Eugene to abandon Landrecy, a place of such importance that it gave entrance into the heart of France, of which the French king was so sensible that, before he recovered from his fright, he acknowledged he in a manner owed his crown to the suspension of arms between him and Great Britain. The suspension is followed by a treaty of peace at Utrecht. The peace is concluded between Great Britain and France, and between France and the States-General. The emperor and the empire continue the war! I shall not presume to enter into an examination of the articles of peace between us and France; but there can be no crime in affirming (if it be a truth) that the house of Bourbon is at this juncture become more formidable, and bids fairer for a universal monarchy, and to engross the whole trade of Europe, than it did before the war." *

Still pursuing a subject of which he professed to have grown sick, Steele drew up a pamphlet, after laying down the *Lover* and *Reader*, entitled " French Faith in the Present State of Dunkirk ; a Letter to the *Examiner* in Defence of Mr Steele." It was written shortly after the

* " The Crisis," pp. 30, 31. The task of biographer to Marlborough, after his death, was committed to Mallet, who received a thousand pounds, but never did the work, which was reserved for Archdeacon Coxe.

delivery of the place to the French. The harbour had
indeed been destroyed, in which result, it is not improbable, the agitation in which he had taken so prominent a
part may have been instrumental; but the French were
evading the spirit of the treaty by making a new and
equally commodious one at Mardyke, a piece of material
casuistry which Steele regarded as giving just ground of
alarm and reprehension. At the same time he entered
the field as the champion of toleration in defence of the
civil and religious liberties of his fellow-subjects and fellow-
Christians, the Dissenters, occasioned by a narrow and
bigoted measure introduced into Parliament for preventing the growth of schism, in which, despite the measures
for their relief passed in the previous reign, it was proposed not merely to enact penalties against the free exercise of their religion by Dissenters, but against secular
teachers who had not conformed. Against this measure,
Steele, though himself bred up in the Established Church,
entered his protest in very spirited terms, in " A Letter to
a Member of Parliament:"—" The first thing that occurs
to me is that, by the Act of Union, the Churches of England and Scotland are equally exempted from any innovation. The schism seems to be too geographical; for as
the whole United Kingdom is equally under the care of
the Parliament, it seems a great omission that Dissenters
in the north part of Britain should not be as much dis-
couraged as they are in the south. According to justice,
Episcopal clergy should be under the same disadvantages
in Scotland, as Dissenting teachers are in England." After
a great variety of the most cogent arguments,—among
others, that they were setting an example of greater in-

tolerance than the Turks, and interfering with the in-
alienable rights of the Dissenters as fellow - men and
fellow-subjects, as well as doing a real injury to the
Establishment itself,—he thus throws derision upon the
measure :—" Prodigious! that a church adorned with so
many excellent and learned members, supplied by two
famous universities, both endowed with ample revenues,
immunities, and jurisdictions, should be affronted with
the offer of being reinforced with penal laws against the
combination of women and children! You might with
the same propriety provide against schismatic nurses!"
The bill ultimately fell to the ground in consequence of
the death of the Queen.

But though he was prepared to do battle for the rights
of all as men and citizens, he claimed for himself the
privilege which he accorded to others, of meeting those
with whom he differed with the weapons of reason and
argument. Another treatise which he published at this
time, entitled " The Romish Ecclesiastical History of late
Years," he no doubt deemed a seasonable sequel to the
various warnings he had already given against the Pretender. It had an appendix containing a variety of
curious information on the subject-matter. It was accompanied by a dedication to his generous and spirited
defender, Lord Finch, in which, after referring to the subject-matter, he compliments him on his eloquence, and
gratefully alludes to the occasion, previously noticed, of
its first exercise in his own favour.

It was followed up by a volume on " The State of Roman
Catholic Religion throughout the World." This was a
translation from the Italian, written for the use of Pope

Innocent XI. The dedication to the Pope, which was a fine piece of grave irony, was understood to be by Dr Hoadley, then Bishop of Winchester; and Steele, by fathering it, laid himself open to the sarcasm of Swift :—

> " Steele, who own'd what others writ,
> And flourish'd by imputed wit," &c.

Dr John Hoadley, son of the bishop, seemed to think that Swift considered himself so much the undisputed monarch of this sort of irony, and so ill brooked any rival near his throne, as thus arrogantly and characteristically to resent this invasion of the territory of his wit.

In the midst of these engagements in defence of civil and religious liberty, and of what he deemed needful reminders, in the exisiting state of his country, for the maintenance of the precious and dear-bought privileges she possessed, an event not unlooked for occurred, the effect of which was to compensate him for the short-lived triumph of his enemies at his expulsion, to scatter to the winds that insolent majority, and to produce a recoil that covered them with confusion, whilst it elevated him to a degree of moderate prosperity, such as he had never previously enjoyed. This event was the decease of Queen Anne, after a lengthened illness, on the 1st of August 1714.

Previous to narrating the result, it is necessary to bring up his correspondence to that event, or rather, for convenience, a little beyond it.

LETTER CCXXVIII.   *To Mrs Steele.*

March 19, 1713–14.

MY DEAR LIFE,—I will take immediate care of what you send about.

Pray, let nothing disquiet you, for God will protect and prosper your innocence and virtue, and for your sake, dear Prue, your faithful husband and humble servant,   RICH. STEELE.

LETTER CCXXIX.   *To Mrs Steele.*

March 19, 1713–14.

DEAR PRUE,—I am in very good humour, and in no concern but fear of your being uneasy. I will go to the club to-night; for, as you say, I must press things well now or never.—Your faithful   DICK STEELE.

LETTER CCXXX.   *To Mrs Steele.*

Bloomsbury Square, March 20, 1713–14.

DEAR PRUE,—I will do all you desire; and, after I have been with Lord Wharton and the rest in the morning, I will come to Bloomsbury, where the Mayor of Stockbridge dines with your most faithful husband,   RICH. STEELE.

LETTER CCXXXI.   *To Mrs Steele.*

March 24,* 1713–14.

DEAR PRUE,—All I know further is that, when I was a-bed last night, Ashurst called here, and left word he had been about the business, and all would go beyond expectation.—Your reprehended spouse and humble servant,   RICH. STEELE.

LETTER CCXXXII.   *To Mrs Steele.*

Tonson's, March 25, 1714.

DEAR PRUE,—All I hear now is this morning from Ashurst, that L.3000 is to be paid in to Mr Warner for my use; but when, and by what hand, I am still in the dark. I suppose Ashurst will in the afternoon be here, and I am to be in the evening with young Minshull.

I am very impatient to have this matter ended some way or other, that I might be with you and the brats. God will preserve us, and let us meet with joy.—Your most obedient husband,   RICH. STEELE.

---

* "The Case of Richard Steele, Esq., with an Impartial Account of the Proceedings against Him, in a Letter to a Friend," was published on this day.

LETTER CCXXXIII.   *To Mrs Steele.*
                        Easter Sunday, March 28, 1714.

DEAR PRUE,—I write this to acquaint you that I am going to Dr West's chapel.

I cannot learn anything of our great business more than it is a-doing, and my chief creditor seems easy in expectation of his money that way.

I am going this morning to a very solemn work,* and invoke Almighty God to bless you and your little ones, beseeching Him to spare me a little life to acquit myself to you and them, whom of all the world I have hitherto least endeavoured to serve. But you, and Betty, and Dick,† and Eugene, and Molly, shall be henceforth my principal cares next to the keeping a good conscience.—Yours, good Prue,   RICH. STEELE.
Service to Mrs Keck.

LETTER CCXXXIV.   *To Mrs Steele.*
                        March 30, 1714.

DEAR PRUE,—I sit down to give you some account of our affairs. The affair with Ashurst, he says, is in great forwardness; but I cannot dive into the secret by what hands I am to be obliged. I had the good fortune to be with Mr Cadogan‡ alone yesterday after I dined with him. His discourse was much to my satisfaction, but I cannot write it; therefore, if you please to come hither in the evening, between seven and eight, we will talk all over. After I had been with Cadogan till six in the evening, he carried me to a ball, where were his mother, sister, and several relations, among whom was Lady Blundell. I did not come home till three in the morning, which is the reason that you hear from me so late as now, at twelve o'clock. It is a mighty silly thing for you and I to be melancholy; but let us cheer one another, and be a comfort to each other. According to the situation of affairs, nothing but Divine Providence can

---

* A short prayer of Steele's on a similar occasion has been preserved, and is here quoted in proof of his devotional feeling:—

"O Almighty Lord God and Saviour, look down with compassion on me, and give me grace to approach the mysterious ordinance of salvation with fear and reverence.

"O Lord, I love, I adore, I believe in Thee. Give me, O Lord, a life suitable to my faith; and let me not [be] cast away, with a soul conscious of, and adoring, Thy unspeakable goodness. But wash out my offences; and give me the benefit of this cup, in order to a good mortal, and a glorious immortal, life; through the merits and mediation of Jesus Christ our Lord and Saviour!"

† His eldest son, who died soon after.
‡ The famous General, afterwards Earl Cadogan.

prevent a civil war within a few years; and against such disasters there can be no remedy but preparing our minds for the incidents we are to meet with, with cheerfulness.—Dear wife, I honour, I love, I dote on you,

RICH. STEELE.

LETTER CCXXXV.   *To Mrs Steele.*

April 1, 1714.

DEAR PRUE,—I want the lease and all receipts about the house in York Buildings, to which Mr Reason is landlord. Pray, send them by Harris. I have heard no news to-day, but expect some by and by, of which you shall have an account—Your faithful husband and humble servant,

RICH. STEELE.

LETTER CCXXXVI.   *To Mrs Steele.*

Devereux Court, April 3, 1714.

DEAR PRUE,—I cannot come home, having the Under-Sheriff to speak with first at five o'clock; from thence I shall go to the play, which I make a place of business, for I am in hopes of seeing two or three people in the boxes whom I cannot see elsewhere. I desire Will may carry the three bottles of wine of mine, at Tonson's, to Bloomsbury. I will be at home as soon as the play is done.—Yours, yours, ever, ever,

RICH. STEELE.

LETTER CCXXXVII.   *To Mrs Steele.*

May 21, 1714.

DEAR PRUE,—I will come for you at six o'clock, to go by land or water to Chelsea. I think things go pretty well. I am gone to Fox Hall. I must come to London again before I go to Chelsea.—Yours ever,

RICH. STEELE.

LETTER CCXXXVIII.   *To Mrs Steele, fifth door, Bloomsbury Square.*

May 21, 1714.

DEAR PRUE,—I send this to let you know that we do not go out of town to-night.—I am your affectionate, faithful husband,

RICH. STEELE.

Pray pardon impatiences, which have their foundation in care and solicitude for you, and vexation that I have not been so just as to prefer my family to all the world.

LETTER CCXXXIX.   *To Mrs Steele.*

Bloomsbury Square, May 28, 1714.

DEAR PRUE,—I will come to you as soon as possibly I can. I hope you will like the lampreys which I left at home. I am going to the Hanover Club, but must be back at the press before half-hour after seven.—Your most obedient husband,   RICH. STEELE.

LETTER CCXL.   *To Mrs Steele.*

Tonson's, Bow Street, June 2, 1714.

DEAR PRUE,—I stay here to attend this thing* close, or it will not be ready, for I am forced to make alterations according to new intelligence about the bill. When I have done I will come to you.—Yours over,

RICH. STEELE.

LETTER CCXLI.   *To Mrs Steele.*

Bloomsbury Square, June 24, 1714.

DEAR PRUE,—Lord Wharton, whom I met at the House, engaged me at the Kit-Cat at three o'clock; so that, had I come home, I should have had time but just to come back again. I will wait on you after six.—Yours most obediently,   RICH. STEELE.

LETTER CCXLII.   *To Mrs Steele.*

July 8, 1714.

DEAR PRUE,—After having settled with Tryon to pay Tishmaker, I am attending other business, and wait Mr Walpole's motions. I will be at home at seven o'clock.—Yours,   RICH. STEELE.

LETTER CCXLIII.   *To Mrs Steele.*

Charing Cross, July 15, 1714.

DEAR PRUE,—Mr Walpole going out of town to-morrow, I am obliged to dine where he does, to get an opportunity of speaking to him.—I am, dear Prue, your most affectionate, obedient husband,

RICH. STEELE.

---

* "The second edition of 'A Letter to a Member of Parliament, concerning the Bill for Preventing the Growth of Schism, by Richard Steele, Esq.,' was published June 5, 1714. His 'Romish Ecclesiastical History of late Years,' appeared on the 25th of the preceding month."

LETTER CCXLIV.   *To Mrs Steele.*

St James's Coffeehouse, July 31, 1714.

DEAR PRUE,—The news is come hither that the Queen is dead.*—I am, dear Prue, your most affectionate and most obedient husband,

RICH. STEELE.

LETTER CCXLV.   *To Mrs Steele.*

Thatched House, St James's Street, Aug. 4, 1714.

DEAR PRUE,—I have been loaded with compliments from the Regents, and assured of something immediately, but have not heard what answer Philips brings from Scott. I desire you to send me a guinea. I shall have cash in the morning. I wait here to speak with Cadogan, with whom I would explain the posture of my affairs more earnestly.—Faithfully yours,

RICH. STEELE.

LETTER CCXLVI.   *To Mrs Steele.*

Aug. 6, 1714.

DEAR PRUE,—I was obliged to borrow of Mr Minshull † money to pay Scott £50.

He obliged me to dine with him, after which I must go to Mr Moore,† and after that to Mr Ashurst, and after that, to the delight of my eyes, your dear self.

RICH. STEELE.

LETTER CCXLVII.   *To Mrs Steele.*

Aug. 8, 1714.

DEAR PRUE,—I send Wilmot ; but stay at St James's, because they talk of great news, which I will bring you ; and am, your most obedient husband,

RICH. STEELE.

LETTER CCXLVIII.   *To Mrs Steele.*

St James's, Aug. 15, 1714.

DEAR PRUE,—I have been with Cadogan, who gives me great hopes of

---

* "She actually died next morning, a little after seven o'clock, Aug. 1, 1714, in the fiftieth year of her age, and thirteenth year of her reign."

† "Mr Minshull, Mr Moore, Mr Lechmere, Bishop Hoadley, and Addison, were all said to have been concerned with Steele in the composition, revisal, and correction of 'The Crisis,' which was published in Steele's name, Jan. 19, 1714."

success in the patent for farthings.* Baron Bothmar dines with him, and he will have me be there.

If I do not deserve good fortune, I hope being joined to you and yours will be, in the sight of Heaven, a motive for blessing me, who, with God's grace, shall grow better.—Your obedient husband, RICH. STEELE.

LETTER CCXLIX. *To Mrs Steele.*
             St James's, Aug. 23, 1714.

DEAR PRUE,—I have ordered Wilmot to carry home the things you speak of in Covent Garden. I shall be with the Brodericks † and others till after eleven o'clock this night, for which I hope you will pardon me ; but I will not drink.—Your obedient husband, RICH. STEELE.
Wilmot will tell you about the house in this street.

LETTER CCL. *To Mrs Steele.*
                Sept. 8, 1714.

DEAR PRUE,—I shall dine at Cleland's,‡ in order to see Lady Marlborough§ as soon as she is at leisure after dinner. I have spoken to two or three of the justices, and I think all will do well.—Your most obedient husband, RICH. STEELE.

---

* "This seems to have been an abortive project."

† "Thomas Broderick, Esq., was elected at the same time with Steele a representative for Stockbridge."

‡ "The friend and correspondent of Pope, and supposed to be the Will Honeycomb of the *Spectator*. Of his son, . . . see 'Anecdotes of Mr Bowyer,' p. 366."

§ "On the subject, possibly, of the history of her lord. In the sixth number of the *Reader*, May 3, 1714, Steele gives an account of his design to write the history of the Duke of Marlborough from the date of his commission of Captain-general and Plenipotentiary to the expiration of those commissions. The materials were then in his custody, but the work afterwards devolved to Glover and Mallet, to whom the Duchess gave by her will £1000 for that purpose, with as little result."

CHAPTER XIV.

Character of Queen Anne—Return of the Whigs to power on the accession of George I.—Steele appointed surveyor of the royal stables
at Hampton Court, and governor of the royal company of comedians—Is placed in the commission of the peace for Middlesex, and
appointed a deputy-lieutenant of the county—Elected member of
Parliament for Boroughbridge—Is knighted by the King on the
occasion of receiving an address from the lieutenancy of Middlesex
—Gives a grand entertainment in honour of the event and of the
King's birthday—Lines spoken on the occasion—Republishes his
political writings—New literary papers, the *Town-Talk*, *Tea-Table*,
and *Chit-chat*—Correspondence to close of 1715.

QUEEN ANNE, destined to be the last of the Stuart race
to sit on the throne of these kingdoms, whose recent decease produced so important a revolution in the affairs of
Steele, was a well-intentioned but weak and commonplace
princess. She was of a dignified presence, though latterly
too much inclined to stoutness, but was by no means intellectual, nor distinguished by any accomplishments or social
qualities. She was very strict in attention to her devotional duties, but her religion consisted too much in a
scrupulous observance of forms, to which indeed, in all
the concerns of life, she appears to have been a slave, and
savoured strongly of the dogged bigotry of her father.
She seemed to feel the necessity of some one to lean upon,
and was addicted to favourites, on whom she lavished all

her regards, but degraded at pleasure. She professed to have been a believer in the supposititious birth of the Prince of Wales; but latterly her own son, the Duke of Gloucester, of whom great hopes had been entertained, having died young, she became strongly desirous of promoting the interest of the Pretender; and as Harley, probably, was not deemed sufficiently pliant on that subject, she dismissed him a few days before her death, leaving his rival, Bolingbroke, in power, and the treasurer's staff in the hands of Shrewsbury.

Immediately on the death of the Queen, a regency was appointed. Steele's friends, the Whigs, as the supporters of the house of Hanover, were once more in the ascendant, and Bolingbroke, who had been left in power, was at once dismissed, and fled to avoid the result of rumoured measures affecting his personal safety.

On the arrival of George I. in England, Steele was of course recommended to his notice as a zealous friend of his house, and an able writer in its interests; and, as a reward of his services, was at once appointed surveyor of the royal stables at Hampton Court, put into the commission of the peace for Middlesex and the liberties of Westminster, and nominated one of the deputy-lieutenants of the county.

At the same time, the licence of the royal company of comedians of Drury Lane having expired at the death of the Queen, they immediately applied to Steele for his interest in procuring its renewal, expressing, at the same time, their desire that he would do them the honour of having his own name inserted with theirs in the commission. A full account of this transaction is given by Colley

Cibber, who was one of the managers in conjunction with Wilks, Doggett, and Booth, which, not only from its being written in his usual lively style, but from the honour it reflects on Steele, it would be injustice to give in any other than his own words :—

" Their licence, however, being of course to be renewed, and since they knew the pension of L.700 a year which had been levied upon them for Collier* must still be paid to somebody, they imagined the merit of a Whig might now have as good a chance of getting into it as that of a Tory had of being continued in it. Having no obligations therefore to Collier, who had made the last penny of them, they applied themselves to Sir Richard Steele, who had distinguished himself by his zeal for the house of Hanover, and had been expelled the House of Commons for carrying it (as was judged at a certain crisis) into a reproach of the government. This we knew was his pretension to that favour in which he now stood at court. We knew, too, the obligations the stage had to his writings, there being scarce a comedian of merit in our whole company whom his *Tatlers* had not made better by his public recommendation of them, and many days had our house been particularly filled by the influence and credit of his pen. Obligations of this kind, from a gentleman with whom they all had the pleasure of a personal intimacy, the managers thought could not be more justly returned than by shewing him some warm instance of their desire to have him at the head of them. We therefore begged him to use his interest for the renewal of our licence, and that he would do us the honour of getting our names to stand with his in the same commission. This, we told him, would put it still further in his power of supporting the stage, in that reputation to which his lucubrations had already so much contributed, and that therefore we thought no man had better pretensions to partake of its success. He was highly pleased with the offer, and his spirits took such a lively turn upon it, that, had we been all his own sons, no unexpected act of filial duty could have more endeared us to him. The licence being obtained, the managers agreed to give Sir Richard L.700 per annum, as they had done before to Mr Collier. Soon after this, the house in Lincoln's-Inn-Fields being finished by the old patentee, who had been silenced, he procured, by the interest of Mr Craggs the younger, his suspension to be taken off; upon which, that playhouse being opened, proved at first a great drawback upon the profits of the old house. On this occasion the managers remonstrated to Sir Richard that, as he now

* Wm. Collier, M.P. for Truro.

stood in Collier's place, his pension of L.700 per annum was liable to the same conditions, which were, that it was only payable during their continuance to be the only company permitted to act; but in case another was set up against them, this pension was to be liquidated into an equal share with them, and which they now hoped he would be contented with. While they were offering to proceed, Sir Richard stopped them short by assuring them that, as he came among them by their own invitation, he should always think himself obliged to come into any measure for their use and service; that to be a burden to their industry would be more disagreeable to him than it could be to them; and as he had always taken a delight in his endeavours for their prosperity, he should be still ready on their own terms to continue them. Every one who knew Sir Richard in his prosperity (before the effects of his good-nature had brought him to distress) knows that this was his manner of dealing with his friends in business. Another instance of the same nature will immediately fall in my way.

" When we proposed to put this agreement into writing, he desired us not to hurry ourselves; for that he was advised, upon the late desertion of our actors, to get our licence (which only subsisted during pleasure) enlarged into a more ample and durable authority, and which he said he had reason to think would be more easily obtained if we were willing that a patent for the same purpose might be granted to him only, for his life and three years after, which he would then assign over to us. This was a prospect beyond our hopes, and what we had long wished for; for, though I cannot say we had ever reason to grieve at the personal severities or behaviour of any one lord chamberlain in my time, yet the several officers under them, who had not the hearts of noblemen, often treated us (to use Shakespeare's expression) with all the insolence of office that narrow minds are apt to be elated with. But a patent, we know, would free us from so abject a state of dependency. Accordingly we desired Sir Richard to lose no time. . . . In a few days after, Sir Richard told us that his Majesty, being apprised that others had a joint power with him in the licence, it was expected we should, under our hands, signify that his petition for a patent was preferred by the consent of us all. Such an acknowledgment was immediately signed, and the patent thereupon passed the great seal; for which I remember the Lord Chancellor Cowper, in compliment to Sir Richard, would receive no fee." *

The patent was received on the 19th of the ensuing January 1715,† and the patentee being obliged to start the

---

* Cibber's Apology, c. xv., 1740.

† An example occurs in this matter of the facility with which literary errors

next morning for Boroughbridge, in Yorkshire, where his
return to Parliament was pending, the managers were
obliged to draw up hastily his assignment to them of equal
shares in the patent, till their counsel might more ad-
visedly perfect it, with further conditions of partnership.
The result of this haste may be stated in the words of the
same writer. " But here," says Cibber, " I ought to take
shame to myself, and at the same time to give this second
instance of the equity and honour of Sir Richard ; for this
assignment (which I had myself the hasty penning of) was
so worded, that it gave Sir Richard an equal title to our
property, as it had given us to his authority in the patent ;
but Sir Richard notwithstanding, when he returned to
town, took no advantage of the mistake, and consented,
in our second agreement, to pay us L.1200, to be equally
entitled to our property, which at his death we were
obliged to repay (as we afterwards did) to his executors."
The writer adds that Steele's equity and moderation had
their reward, for his income from the theatre averaged
L.1000 a year, while the former patentee, by his stiffness
in insisting on his pension, lost annually to the extent of
the difference.

A few days after Steele's arrival at Boroughbridge, he
was elected one of the representatives for that place. Mrs
Steele accompanied him as far as York, where she awaited

are perpetuated. The date of the patent had been erroneously given in the life
of Cibber as 1718, probably by a typographical mistake, which has been repeated
in a late edition, (Hunt and Clarke, 1826.) This erroneous statement was followed in the sketch of Steele by Dr Drake ; and the " Biographia," though it does
not adopt this error, gives in a marginal note a retrospective one, still more unaccountable—namely, 1714, making the patent date before the death of the Queen,
and adds that Cowper was made Chancellor the same day (19th Jan.) that the
patent was signed, though he entered upon office in the previous September

his return, and the following letters passed between them in the interim, the first of which may perhaps require a reference to the circumstances in which it is stated to have been written, in the reading, and gives reason to fear that he had not then, as he states in the next one, followed her directions " exactly : "—

LETTER CCLI.   *To Mrs Steele.*

Jan. 27, 1714-15.

DEAR, DEAREST PRUE,—I hope this will find you well, as I am at this present writing. I send Wilmot to know how you do only, and to bring the books concerning the law of elections ; or, what is better, let him bring the green covers with him. If you have a letter with a note of Warner's, send it hither, and I will have it of his neighbour, Mr Jessop. I write now among dancing, singing, hooping, hallooing, and drinking. I think I shall succeed. My dear, I love you to death.

If the bill is not come, and you have a guinea or two, send them ; for I would not borrow till my bill comes, which will certainly be next arrival of the post to York.   RICH. STEELE.

LETTER CCLII.   *To Mrs Steele, at Mr Harrison's, over against the Black Man, in Coney Street, York.*

Boroughbridge, Twelve at Night, Jan. 28, 1714-15.

DEAR PRUE,—I obey your directions exactly, and avoid drinking, and everything else that might give you any trouble. The precept for electing members for this place came hither to-day, and the election is to be on Wednesday. It looks with a good face on my side. I take the opportunity of writing by the gentleman who keeps the Black Man. He has very much pleased me with an account that you had a river at the end of your garden. There will be there, I doubt not, a thousand prayers offered up to grant me discretion, and the ease of this world. You and yours, I fear, will make me covetous ; I am sure you have made me value wealth much more than I ever thought I should ; but indeed I have a reason which makes it worth the pursuit : it will make me more agreeable to you.*

I hope Nanny does not misbehave, so as to disturb your tranquillity.

---

* " See Letter 257 and note, *ad finem*."

If the post should not this night bring me money, I find I can have money in the country, and draw a bill on Mr Castleman at London.

LETTER CCLIII.   *To Mrs Steele.*

Boroughbridge, Feb. 1, 1714–15.

DEAR PRUE,—I am astonished Warner has not sent me a bill before now. Mr Jessop * is at the neighbouring borough, where he is to be chosen this morning.

I will take twenty pounds of him, and send you money by an express, which I will send to you to-morrow, with advice of our success here. The election is to be between eight and eleven in the morning.—I am, dear Prue, ever thine,   RICH. STEELE.

LETTER CCLIV.   *To Mrs Steele, at Mr Harrison's, at York, Coney Street.*

Feb. 4, 1714–15.

DEAR PRUE,—This is to acquaint you that I will be with you on Saturday, and then settle your journey home, which I propose shall be in the coach this day se'nnight.

I have got money, and you shall hear of me again to-morrow morning.

Mr Jessop has been very zealous in my election, and stood by with his skill and knowledge on the spot.—Yours ever,   RICH. STEELE.

On his return to town, Steele took his seat in the first Parliament of the first George, and on the 7th of April following joined with the other deputy-lieutenants of Middlesex in giving a splendid entertainment to the Earl of Clare, their Lord-Lieutenant, when an address to the King was agreed upon, which was drawn up by Steele, and on the following day presented by Lord Clare at the head of his deputy-lieutenants.   On this occasion, his Majesty, as a mark of his gratification and favour, conferred on Steele and two other of the deputies, Thornhill and Cooke, the honour of knighthood.   To celebrate this

* "William Jessop, Esq., elected in this and several succeeding Parliaments for Aldborough, in Yorkshire."

event, as well as the fifty-sixth birthday of the King, Sir Richard, on the 28th of May following, invited a distinguished company of upwards of two hundred persons of both sexes to partake of an elegant and sumptuous banquet, where, amid every variety of delicacies, "the feast of reason and the flow of soul" were not omitted. A prologue, written by Mr Tickell, and spoken by Mrs Younger, was succeeded by an abundant supply of burgundy, champagne, and other wines of the choicest kind, while pyramids of various sweets towered on the board. The company afterwards adjourned to the concert-room, where in the mazy dance they "chased the glowing hours with flying feet." An ode of Horace, and several songs composed for the occasion and set to music, were performed, and the entertainment was wound up with an epilogue, written by Addison, and spoken by Mr Wilks. These verses have been attributed, though erroneously, to Steele himself, and he was supposed to have amused the company with pleasant allusions to a variety of circumstances relative to himself ; but the humour of the raillery lost nothing by being by his illustrious friend.*

"The sage whose guests you are to-night, is known
To watch the public weal, *though not his own;*
Still have his thoughts uncommon schemes pursu'd,
And teem'd with projects for his country's good.
Early in youth, his enemies have shewn
How narrowly he miss'd the chemic stone : †

---

* See Nichol's Select Collection of Poems.

† It has been stated that one of the earliest projects of Steele was with reference to the discovery of the philosopher's stone, and that the laboratory at Poplar, where his experiments were conducted, was afterwards converted into a

Not Friar Bacon promised England more ;
Our artist, lavish of his fancied ore,
Could he have brought his great design to pass,
Had wall'd us round with gold instead of brass.
That project sunk, you saw him entertain
A notion more chimerical and vain :
To give chaste morals to ungovern'd youth,
To gamesters honesty, to statesmen truth ;
To make you virtuous all ; a thought more bold,
Than that of changing dross and lead to gold.
But now to greater actions he aspir'd,
For still his country's good our champion fir'd ;
In treaties versed, in politics grown wise,
He look'd on Dunkirk with suspicious eyes ;
In a few months he is not without hope,—
But 'tis a secret,—to convert the Pope :
Of this, however, he'll inform you better,
Soon as his holiness receives his letter."

If we could imagine a man of so much good-nature and
so humane a spirit as Steele, indulging in vindictive and
revengeful feeling, he might now have done so to his heart's
content, in seeing the men who had persecuted and pursued
him with the utmost malignity fallen from their high
estate—Bolingbroke a fugitive in a foreign land, Harley a
captive in the Tower, with impeachment for treason hang-
ing over him. Still he had no ground for a very exalted
opinion of the gratitude of princes or of parties. He saw
his friend Addison, to the highest and best part of whose
literary reputation he had been materially instrumental,
elevated to the important posts of Secretary for Ireland,
and afterwards one of the Secretaries of State in England,

garden-house. Whether this was true, or founded on some experiments of a
more practical character, is of course impossible now to ascertain.

The moral experiment alludes to his *Tatlers*, *Spectators*, and *Guardians*, and
the other allusions are to his political pamphlets.

on the sole ground of his literary merit, whilst he who had
accomplished such literary services to the country, both in
his own person and by drawing out the resources of others,
who had distinguished himself, moreover, by his courage
and ability in defence of the existing dynasty, now in
power, at a time when its interests were in peril, and had
suffered by his exertions in the cause, was rewarded with
the surveyorship of the royal stables.   What the remuner-
ation of that appointment may have been has not been
stated, and it is a secondary consideration ; but it could not
have required the abilities of Steele ; and as to the gover-
norship of the theatre, that he might perhaps have had as
good a chance of obtaining if he had never made any sacrifices to his political zeal.   He might naturally, therefore,
feel that his reward was none of the most liberal.   When,
therefore, he collected his various pamphlets, and repub-
lished them this year, under the title of his "Political
Writings," with a dedication to the Earl of Clare, we may
believe that it was with no view of trampling on his
fallen enemies, but of drawing attention to his legitimate
claims.   In his dedication to the Earl of Clare, formerly
Lord Pelham, and afterwards Duke of Newcastle, then
one of the existing government, he says, in reference to
the origin of these writings, "The painful struggle under
so great a difficulty as explaining with a ministry in open
contradiction to their proceedings, is what can be supported by nothing less than the testimony of a good conscience, and a heart pure from avaricious ambition.   And
these are such supports as will keep a man from languishing in discontent, should he, among the prosperities of a
cause he has endeavoured to serve, live to find zeal for the

public, of all human virtues, the most exposed to the cool comfort of being its own reward; and that which was undertaken against the inclinations to mirth and pleasure, out of a sense of duty and honour, to have little other effect than to become a man's characteristic, and by that means to give a turbulent air to all his other pretensions, and even to sink the agreeableness of the friend and companion in the appearance of somewhat supposed to be demanding in the patriot." These remarks leave little doubt as to the feelings he justly entertained of the princely reward of his services in the cause of princes. In August, however, of this year he received L.500 from Sir Robert Walpole for special services, which was entered in the name of Mr Leonard Welsted, a gentleman holding a situation in one of the secretaries' offices, who, on account of his literary talents, was highly esteemed by Steele, and from whom he received the amount. It was intended, doubtless, to remunerate him for his actual loss by relinquishing the places he formerly held.

Among the other publications of Steele this year, besides " The State of the Roman Catholic Religion," previously noticed in anticipation, in connexion with another kindred publication, were the second volume of " The Englishman," and " A Letter from the Earl of Mar to the King, before his Majesty's arrival in England, with some Remarks on my Lord's subsequent conduct."

Though much allowance may be made for one who had had all the weight of power, as well as its meanest tools, exerted against him to crush him in the cruellest manner, both by injury and insult, for some tenacity in self-vindication, yet it would have been more gratifying to our idea

of his general character, and more in keeping with that
forbearance and lenity which he invariably displayed in
other cases, and for which he even incurred blame,—in
reference, for instance, to the rebels of 1715, and those
concerned in the disastrous South Sea scheme,—if, now
that his enemies were fallen and powerless, he had avoided
anything having even the appearance of vindictiveness ;
but the sea will labour after the storm has passed, and it
is not always that philosophy has power to still the passions
that have been lashed into disorder by the malignity and
baseness of others.

It is gratifying to find him turning from his unhappy
politics to his old, best mistress, Literature, though with
but a divided heart.   On the 17th of December he started
a new weekly paper on something of the old model, entitled
the *Town-Talk*, in a series of letters to a lady in the
country.   It has been supposed to have formed the substance of genuine letters written to his lady, then in the
country, giving an account of the principal events of the
week in the busy and fashionable world.   In the following
letter to his friend Hughes, the poet, he refers to it :—

LETTER CCLV.   *To Mr Hughes.*
                                    St James's Street, Jan. 8, 1715-16.
  DEAR SIR,—A paper, called the *Town-Talk*, is particularly designed to be
helpful to the stage.   If you have not sent " The Mask,"* which is to come
out on Thursday, to press, if you please to send me the copy, it shall be
recommended to the town, and published on Thursday night with that
paper.—Your affectionate friend, and most humble servant,
                                          RICHARD STEELE.

It appears to have only reached nine numbers, termin-

---

* " Apollo and Daphne," a masque by Mr Hughes, set to music by Dr Pepusch.

ating February 13; but a week previously he brought out
another under the title of the *Tea-Table*, which was of still
shorter date, and, ending on the 2d of March, was succeeded by *Chit-chat*, which, like the *Town-Talk*, was in the
form of letters to a lady in the country, and was equally
brief in its existence with its immediate predecessor,
coming to a close on the 16th of March. These changes of
arrangements, including even the very days of publication,
which were altered from one number to another, indicate
either that his mind was not fully given to the work, or
probably that these spasmodic efforts were mere tem-
porary expedients to tide over some pressing emergency,
a state of things in every point of view to be regretted.

The following letters, with those previously given, bring
up his correspondence to the close of the year 1715 :—

LETTER CCLVI.   *To Mrs* Steele, at her house, over against Park Place,*
                                   St James's.
                                   Claremont, April 10, 1715.
DEAR PRUE,—My Lord Clare † (who you will own to have some pretence
to command me) will not let me come away from hence this night. Pray,
forgive your most obedient, humble servant,   RICH. STEELE.

LETTER CCLVII.   *To Lady Steele.*
                                   Speaker's Chambers, Aug. 14, 1715.
DEAR PRUE,—I write this before I go to Lord Marlborough's, to let you

---

* " This *might* have been addressed to *Lady* Steele."
† " Afterwards the patriotic Duke of Newcastle. Steele had just before dedicated to him the collection of his ' Political Writings.' This nobleman, who was
then Lord-Lieutenant of the county of Middlesex, had, not long before, placed
Steele in the commission of the peace for that county, and appointed him one of
his deputy-lieutenants. It was in this capacity that, two days only before the
date of this letter, he was knighted on presenting to the King an address from
the lieutenancy of Middlesex and Westminster, which Steele had the honour of
drawing up."

know that there was no one at the Treasury but Kelsey, with whom Welsted* left the order, and he is to be at the Treasury again to-morrow, between two and three, when, without doubt, the money will be paid.†
I have no hopes from that, or anything else, but, by dint of riches,‡ to get the government of your ladyship.—Yours,   RICH. STEELE.

---

* " Leonard Welsted, an ingenious young clerk in the office of one of the Secretaries of State, whom Steele very highly esteemed. Welsted had, not long before this, addressed to him two several pieces, an imitation of an ode of Horace, under the title of ' A Prophecy,' and ' An Epistle on the King's Accession.' "

† " In the notes on the ' Dunciad,' (among much equally wanton abuse,) Mr Welsted is reproached with having ' received at one time L.500 for secret services, among the other excellent authors hired to write anonymously for the ministry.' This idle calumny (which arose from that sum appearing in the report of the Secret Committee, 1742, as issued ' to Leonard Welsted, gent., for special services, August 27, 1715') was refuted on the authority of Welsted's own declaration to Walthoe, an alderman of St Albans, ' that he received the money for Sir R. Steele and paid it to him.' If any further proof of this assertion were wanting, we have here the express testimony of Steele himself that the money was issued for his use. And we are so far indebted to the author of the ' Dunciad,' that he has unwittingly contributed to illustrate this letter, which would otherwise have wanted a clue."

‡ " It appears from this, and other passages in these letters, that Lady Steele had an undue love of money, which was a source of much vexation to herself, and of some uneasiness to her husband. There is presumptive proof of this in the following quotation, which is happily illustrated in this publication. Steele, in his *Englishman*, celebrates the greatness and equanimity of a poor man with a *tar neckcloth*, who, with perfect *sang-froid*, was first informed at a coffeehouse of his having got a prize of L.10,000 in the lottery. After strictly and coolly examining into the truth of the information, he turned out of his pocket half-a-crown and sixpence. Presenting the half-crown to the waiter, ' It is all I have got now,' said he ; ' but I will call another time, and give you more for your good news.' Having related the incident with his usual spirit and high approbation, Steele adds, ' I speak it sincerely, I had much rather have his temper than his fortune ; for had it happened to me, alas ! I should have given it, like a slave as I am, to a *woman who despises me without it.* Hang her, however, I wish I had it for her sake.'—*Englishman*, No. 47, Jan. 21, 1714."

CHAPTER XV.

DURING the greater part of the two ensuing years, there is
little incident to diversify the record in Steele's life. His
time was occupied in great part by his parliamentary
duties ; and the few events that ruffled the even current of
his daily course are to be gleaned from his correspondence,
which during this period was more than ordinarily ample,
from the circumstance of Lady Steele, owing to failing
health, having retired into Wales for the benefit of her
native air.

It is a proof of the political sagacity of Steele that he
foretold, as we have seen in one of his letters to his wife,
the certainty, unless Providence interfered to prevent it,
of a civil war. Yet, perhaps, some of the appearances on
which his heated imagination had formed its conclusions
were more apparent than substantial. Neither can it be
doubted that the Whigs themselves, in their intemperate
exultation on coming into power, and their apparent design
to drive their opponents to desperation, were the immediate
occasion of precipitating the event. If any measures had
been kept with the chiefs of the party, they would undoubt-

edly have waited at least for a more convenient season, and the crisis might have been tided over. If no subordinate agent had been found to take the initiative, Prince James, the young Chevalier as he was called, was not likely to have taken any active steps himself, and he had just lost the most powerful of his friends by the death of Louis XIV. He was then about his twenty-sixth year, a person of most sweet and amiable disposition; but, though displaying a highly intellectual countenance, not at all gifted with intellectual vigour, and indeed considered rather weak and deficient. This was in the next generation rectified by the infusion of the heroic blood of the Polish royal family of Sobieski. It has been made a subject of speculation whether the subsequent civil dissensions might not have been avoided if, at the time when, according to a picturesque tradition, the Queen his mother stood with him, then an infant, in her arms under Lambeth Church, waiting for an hour for a hackney coach to convey her in her flight, the young prince had been seized and educated so as to remove the obstacles to making the succession hereditary. The neglect of this step at one time or other is said to have been the grand error of the chiefs of the Revolution.* But, not to speak of the questionable right of interference with the liberty of the prince, even for his good, another great doubt arises of any certainty of its success, judging from the history of his family, or whether other evils might not have arisen from a race so fickle, and so extravagant, that the two last kings of the family had been pensioners upon the crown of France. In fact, they had been tried in the balance too often and found wanting to give

* Chambers's History of the Scottish Rebellions, vol. iv. p. 158.

much hope of the favourable result of another experiment.
The nation did wisely in again repudiating practically that
astounding figment, which royalty had the influence to get
inculcated in all countries, of nations being made for kings,
and not kings for nations,—yet with as little violence as
possible.

George Louis, who now ascended the throne as George
I., owed his elevation mainly to the ambition of his mother,
rather than any strong inclination of his own, which it is
understood led him to prefer the quiet of his little Hanoverian court. Not so, however, the Electress Sophia, his
mother, a woman of vigorous mind and unbounded ambition, who, when the failure of issue by William or Anne
became apparent, set up her claim through her mother
Elizabeth of Bohemia, who was the daughter of James I.
By her indefatigable exertion she got it recognised ; for,
though there were about forty nearer, yet they had the
same disqualification as the Chevalier himself ; and had
any of them even made profession of Protestantism, which
to their credit none of them did, it may be doubtful whether
a suspicious conversion would have availed them. At the
suggestion, probably, of his ambitious mother, he had come
over to England in the year 1680, and made a proposal to
the Princess Anne, hoping thereby probably to facilitate
the splendid prospect which had dazzled the imagination
of the Electress. He was not successful, however. She
afterwards married Prince George of Denmark, and had
several children, but by the death of them all, the former
pretender to her hand was destined to be her successor.

Scarcely had he ascended the throne when the standard
of insurrection was raised in the north. This result must

be attributed, at least at that time, to the reception which
he gave to the heads of the Tory party, when, on his land-
ing at Greenwich, Sept. 18th, they greeted his arrival with
an appearance of cordiality that the most loyal could not
have exceeded.   But he had been taught by the Whigs,
who seemed bent upon crushing their opponents beyond
redemption, to consider them his secret enemies ; and
though perhaps a wiser policy would have led him to con-
ciliation, his mind had been so poisoned against them, that
he did not affect to conceal his feelings.   He scarcely received them with civility.   To the Earl of Mar, who had
been one of the Secretaries of State, he is said to have
turned his back.   At the close of the previous month that
nobleman had addressed a letter of congratulation to the
king, expressing the utmost duty to his house, with the
hope for the nation of his prolonged sway over them, and
for himself deprecating any insinuations of his loyalty that
might be made to his disadvantage.   He further reminded
the king that his family had been hereditary custodians of
the persons of his Majesty's Scottish ancestors when minors.
He is even said to have endeavoured to procure from the
leading Highland families a written document congratulat-
ing him on his accession.   Either his duplicity or his selfishness must have been unbounded.   But he and his party
soon learned that they had nothing to hope for; and despair
is a bad counsellor.   Bolingbroke was displaced, and, to
avoid rumoured steps against him, fled to the Continent.
Ormond was forbidden the royal presence, and soon followed ; and Oxford was shortly after sent to the Tower.
The two former, as if to justify the suspicions of their
enemies, soon took office under the Chevalier.

With regard to Mar, he became fixed in his hostility, but carried out his duplicity to the end, by paying his respects to the king the very day previous to proceeding to the north to organise a hostile movement. He had already changed with every change of government since entering public life. He had been one of the leading agents in bringing about the legislative union, which had drawn on him much odium in his own country; and he was now about to make open confession of penitence (as he did) for that act, and to make reparation by restoring to Scotland not merely its legislature, but its ancient crown under James VIII. It may be added, as some palliation for his versatility, that his family had been impoverished by their attachment to the cause of Charles I. Such was John Erskine, eleventh Earl of Mar, a man of the most insinuating address, who had succeeded so often in making his pliability available, but who, finding that he could do so no longer, did not scruple to plunge his country in all the horrors of a civil war. It was certainly damaging to a great cause to be intrusted to such hands.

While Mar was proceeding to arouse the north against the new settlement of the Crown, the popular feeling, fostered most likely by the gentry, the bulk of whom in both parts of the kingdom were in favour of the exiled family, displayed itself in serious riots, which assumed the safe watchword of "The Church." In the south the Jacobite faction was less ardent and more cautious of consequences. In England, the greater part of the nobility and the mass of the middle classes, except in Lancashire and the more northerly counties, where Catholicism prevailed, were in favour of the Protestant succession; and the same may be

said of the lowland or southern part of Scotland. The High-
lands of Scotland, and the north and west of England,
were the great strongholds of the Jacobite interest.

There was a great deficiency of concerted plan in reference to the movement. A memorial of Mar had stated the
necessity of twenty thousand foreign troops, to insure a successful issue, without which the English Jacobites would
not make any move ; yet the Chevalier, though conscious
that he could command no force at all approaching that
amount, and professing to his more prudent advisers that
he yielded to the necessity of delay, at the same time gave
Mar secret encouragement to proceed. Whether this step
was the result of an over sanguine temperament, or a necessity he felt compelled to in consideration of the large funds
that had been raised by the Catholic potentates and
wealthy individuals of that persuasion, which has been
stated at upwards of twelve millions, it was unquestionably
rash and ill-advised. However, Mar, having received his
instructions, proceeded on the 2d of August to Scotland by
way of Newcastle in a coasting vessel, (having the previous
day paid his compliments to the king,) and as the first step
of concerting measures, got up a hunting-match, to be followed by a festive entertainment, to which all the leading
Jacobites were invited. An occurrence of such an ordinary
kind appeared the best cover for such a purpose.

At Aboyne, which was the appointed place of rendez-
vous, the Earl of Mar made an elaborate harangue to the
noblemen and gentlemen assembled, which he began by
professing the deepest contrition for the prominent part
he had taken in the matter of the union, and his resolution to use his best endeavours to undo the mischief. He

denounced the Hanoverian usurpation, and the measures consequent upon it. He then entered into particulars respecting the proposed movement, of which he had been appointed generalissimo by his exiled sovereign, who had furnished him with funds for the defraying of all expenses. He spoke of large foreign supplies already obtained, and promises of more, which should be shipped as soon as convenient, and concluded by expressing his confident hope that all present would zealously join in a cause involving their best and dearest interests. He then displayed to them his powers and instructions to organise the movement. Before the assembly broke up, it was resolved that they should return to their respective homes and raise their retainers to co-operate in such ways as should be determined on at a future occasion.

In the meantime the Government having received intimation from the Earl of Stair, the English minister at the court of France, of the designs of the party, by means of the imprudent openness of discourse of its friends and agents in Paris, had taken such steps in anticipation as seemed most suited to the emergency. Besides an addition of seven thousand to the army, a force of six thousand men, which the Dutch had promised to furnish, was obtained, and the fleet reinforced to an equal extent. The Habeas Corpus Act was suspended. The half-pay officers were sent throughout the country to organise bodies of local militia, and an act was passed for the prevention of riots. A reward of a hundred thousand pounds was offered for the apprehension of the Pretender if taken within the British dominions. The stringent laws existing against Catholics were put in force. Persons of that

persuasion were prohibited coming within ten miles of the
metropolis ; and on the 30th of August, an act was passed
for the purpose of summoning all suspected persons in
Scotland to Edinburgh to give security for their loyalty.
This was an unfortunate step, and very injurious in its
operation. Summonses to this effect were sent to all
suspected persons, requiring their appearance within seven
or fifteen days, according as they resided north or south
of the river Tay; and probably many who might have
taken no active part, finding they were compromised, and
ashamed, from a point of honour, openly to give in their ad-
hesion against their sympathies, were, as they might think,
left no honourable alternative but in turning out. It was
following out the course they had adopted with the heads
of the Tory party, and, as it were, forcing them over the
edge of the precipice.

Urgent entreaties were now forwarded to the Chevalier
that he would no longer delay appearing in person among
them. But without waiting for that event, Mar, on the
6th of September, erected his standard at Kirkmichael, in
Braemar, with only a small retinue, not amounting to one
hundred men. A trifling accident, in the falling of the
gilt ball from the top of the pole on the occasion of its
being fixed in the ground, was construed into an ill omen
by a superstitious people.

A letter written in the after part of this eventful day by
the Earl to the bailie of his barony of Kildrummy, (and
which Steele published in his *Town-Talk*, it having probably got into the hands of the Government,) in addition
to the ludicrous and familiar tone, gives a curious view of
the man who was lately haranguing the nobles and gentry

on the recovery of their lost liberties, now threatening his tenantry with fire and sword if they did not turn out, which, it appears, they were in no hurry to do. On the following day he published an elaborate manifesto, explaining at large the objects and policy of the Jacobite party.

A very well-contrived plan for a very important object, the capture of Edinburgh Castle, was at the same time defeated by the most culpable negligence and mismanagement in the execution. In addition to the prestige of such an exploit, they would have gained possession of the bulk of the military stores in Scotland, and a sum of a hundred thousand pounds which had been deposited there after the Union in compensation of certain inequalities which affected Scotland. They had bribed four of the garrison to their interest, had contrived scaling ladders admitting of four at a time, which were to be placed against the least precipitous side of the rock on which the castle stands, and had fixed on nine o'clock on the night of September the 9th for the attempt. Yet, though the authorities had got notice on the same night, though not till after the appointed hour, the conspirators delayed their task two hours, drinking their courage up to the mark at a tavern ; and when they made the attempt, the guard was just being changed, and the plan failed. Its success would have been of paramount importance to the Jacobite interest, and would, in fact, have been tantamount to giving it the supremacy in Scotland.

This incident, which a little better management might have made disastrous to the Government, led to more energetic measures for the repression of insurrection. In addition to the seizure of a number of suspected persons of note, the commander of the forces in Scotland was directed to form a camp at Stirling, so as to command the passage of the Forth. This command was now assumed by the Duke of Argyle. Still the force he had was quite inadequate, amounting only to about a thousand foot and five hundred horse; the Government imagining that the movement in Scotland was only intended as a diversion to lure the troops from the protection of the richer prize in the south; and had the Jacobite levies been under more skilful and energetic command, notwithstanding the failure of the hopeful scheme in the metropolis, they might have swept any force in Scotland from the field.

By the middle of September, Mar's force had become considerable, and the seizure of Perth by his orders, in anticipation of a movement for that purpose by the loyalist party, had been attended with credit and advantage, it being the key of the country north of the Forth. On the 28th, at which date his force amounted to about five thousand, though it ultimately increased to about double that number, he himself entered the town, and the same day received letters from the Chevalier by the Hon. Mr Murray, who, strange to say, had landed at Dover, and made his way in safety from thence. Twelve ships, laden with munitions of war and officers, were announced as about to start, and the Chevalier himself shortly to follow.

The Fabian policy pursued by Mar was perhaps natural to a prudent man whose experience was not in military affairs, but it was probably injurious to the cause. He seemed bent upon not risking an action till the risk of failure was out of the question, and he had succeeded in surrounding the enemy on all sides, in what he termed a "hose-net." Yet it was almost a necessity, in his position, that some decisive blow should be struck, both as regards those who had already joined, and those who were inclined to join, as the fiery spirit of the Highlanders made them impatient for action. One dashing and brilliant achievement he did accomplish with promptitude, in intercepting a vessel laden with 400 stand of arms for the use of the loyalists beyond Inverness, where the Earl of Sutherland had gone to raise volunteers. This vessel had started from Leith, but had put in in a gale on the Fife coast, where she was captured by a detachment ordered by Mar on that service.

A detachment of 2000 men was now sent by Mar, under the command of Brigadier Macintosh, an experienced veteran officer, across the Forth, to co-operate with the insurgents in the Border country. The crossing was effected by taking the most unobserved route, and by a feint made openly in the face of the enemy to act as a diversion in favour of the crossing party. After being diverted from their main design by a tempting chance of capturing Edinburgh, which was relinquished, and paralysed by distracting counsels as to the plan of operations, arising from the decided objections of the Highlanders to cross the English border, which were at last overcome after much valuable time had been spent and opportunities lost, they ultimately joined with the Jacobite forces in the north of England. In the south the system of repression adopted in the disaffected districts by a judicious distribution of the Government forces had been

perfectly successful. In Northumberland alone had there
been any demonstration. The command of this force had
been given to Mr Forster, a member of Parliament, not
because he was the most influential among the party, or
the most suited to the command, but from a consideration of policy, he being a Protestant. Among the other
leaders was the Earl of Derwentwater, son of one of the
natural daughters of Charles II. They had been forestalled by General Carpenter, the commander of the
Government force, in their design of getting possession of
Newcastle, then a fortified place. The two bodies formed
a junction at Kelso. The reluctance of the Highlanders
having been ultimately removed, they marched through
Warkworth, Alnwick, and Morpeth, gathering strength as
they proceeded, and proclaiming James III., to join their
friends in Lancashire, and took up their position in Preston, which they fortified in the best manner they could.

Meantime Mar had made a movement towards an action
with Argyle, and on the 13th of November the two forces
met on the rising ground of Sheriffmuir, which resulted in
the defeat of one wing of each army. Though a drawn
battle, Argyle seemed to have borne off the trophies and
honours ; and such was the characteristic timidity and
want of decision of Mar, that when the exhausted party of
Argyle's army returned from the pursuit of his defeated
wing, seeming to fear an ambuscade, he allowed them to
wheel quietly round the rising ground on which he was
posted, and from which he had only to descend to anni-
hilate them. He then fell back once more upon Perth,
which he prepared to defend.

Almost at the same time the party in the south had

taken up their position at Preston, which they prepared to fortify as well as it would admit of. This was Mr Forster's policy; but it appears to have been a fatal mistake to allow themselves to be cooped up behind walls, and even those such as could not be defended for any time, instead of contesting the approaches to it and the passage of the Ribble, where, if they did not even cut off the enemy, they might with certainty have maintained their position and kept the communication open with their friends. They succeeded in maintaining their position, and inflicted considerable loss upon the besiegers by lining the houses with their troops and by barricades. But despairing of doing so long, especially as the besieging forces had been reinforced by General Carpenter from Newcastle, (on the very day on which the battle of Sheriffmuir was fought,) they proposed terms of capitulation. The bearer of them was astonished and confounded to find that they were not eagerly received, the general in command expressing doubts whether he ought to treat with rebels who had sacrificed the lives of the king's troops. Even after every remonstrance as to not accepting the proposal of men willing to submit, the utmost that he would accede to was an unconditional surrender till the pleasure of the Government was known. This they ultimately accepted, giving hostages for their compliance. When, however, the Highlanders heard of it, they were furious, and would, it is believed, have sacrificed Mr Forster, through whom they considered themselves to have been betrayed, had he not kept out of the way. Indeed, an attempt was made to shoot him, and these fiery mountaineers were inclined, even after they were, as they considered, sold, to cut their way through the enemy and return to their own country.

While these events, so fatal to the cause of the Chevalier, were occurring, he himself was delayed, by one cause or another, long beyond the period at which he had proposed to embark, and at length arrived at Peterhead, a small seaport in Aberdeenshire, only on the 22d of December, when all hope of the cause had almost gone. On the 4th of February following he secretly re-embarked, leaving instructions for his followers to disband, and taking Mar with him, on the ground that those left behind would make better terms in his absence. Thus ended the unfortunate and ill-advised insurrection of 1715.

By the unconditional surrender at Preston, six noblemen, who were among the insurgent leaders, were tried by their Peers at Westminster Hall, early in the following February, and condemned to death. They were the Earl of Derwentwater, Lord Widdrington, the Earl of Nithsdale, the Earl of Carnwath, Viscount Kenmure, and Lord Nairne. Some of them succeeded in effecting their escape. Steele has given some account of the proceedings in the 9th number of the *Town-Talk.*

After alluding to " the transactions of that High Court of Parliament, wherein the exercise of royalty itself was, in a kind, vested in the Lord High Steward,* who indeed performed it with a certain air and meekness of majesty which . . . could be exceeded only by what appeared in the countenance of that very prince then present,"† he

---

* Lord Chancellor Cowper.

† The King and Prince of Wales were both present in the box prepared for the royal family.

proceeds to give a brief notice of the imposing and solemn scene :—

" You are to suppose Westminster Hall, in a kind, amphitheatrically disposed. The Lord High Steward, placed under a canopy of state, surrounded by the *regalia*, carried by proper officers ; Garter-king-at-arms at his right, and the Black-Rod at his left ; the peers of Great Britain in their robes, facing towards him in the area of the hall ; on his right hand, by a rail dividing them from that court, were seated the Commons of Great Britain, in ascending rows behind each other ; over against them, on the left, divided also from the House of Lords, were disposed, on like ascents, people of the first quality of both sexes, which filled and completed the solemnity of the appearance. When silence was thrice proclaimed, the Lieutenant of the Tower was commanded to bring forth his prisoners. The gentleman gaoler, accordingly, bearing the point of his axe from the offenders, marched before them, so as to place himself on the left hand of him of first quality, when they stood at the bar,—to wit, the Earl of Derwentwater on his right ; next to him the Lord Widdrington ; to him the Earl of Nithsdale ; to him the Earl Carnwath ; to him the Viscount Kenmure ; to him the Lord Nairne ; and this unhappy rank was closed on the right by the Deputy-Lieutenant of the Tower. . . . There was a structure particularly appointed on the left of the prisoners for the accommodation of the managers of the House of Commons. . . . Their [the prisoners'] quality, change of condition, the vigour of their days, and the present inability to offend further, pleaded very strongly to a good-natured and generous people, who are quick to anger, but slow to revenge. The youth of one, the equanimity of another, the plain honesty in the countenance of a third, the pathetic simplicity and sorrow of a fourth, and nothing but what was to be pitied in a fifth, the sixth expressing only despair, jointly and severally moved the heart in behalf of each and all of them. But when they had all said what they could to excite pity, and frankly, after being asked in direct words, acknowledged they had nothing to say in arrest of judgment, the Lord High Steward, . . . in conclusion, with a voice and air of as deep and undissembled sorrow as they were in upon whom he pronounced it, uttered the fatal sentence." *

When called upon to plead, after some introductory remarks, Lord Derwentwater said :—

" But the terrors of your Lordships' just sentence, which at once deprive

---

* *Town-Talk*, No. 9.

me of my life and estate, and complete the misfortunes of my wife and innocent children, are so heavy on my mind, together with my inexperience, that I am scarce able to allege what may extenuate my offence, if anything can do it. I have confessed myself guilty ; but, my Lords, that guilt was rashly incurred, without any premeditation. . . . I was wholly unprovided with men, horses, arms, and other necessaries. . . . As my offence was sudden, so my submission was early. When his Majesty's generals thought fit to demand hostages for securing the terms of the cessation, I voluntarily offered myself. . . . And whilst I continued hostage, the great character of his Majesty's clemency, and the repeated encouragement I had to hope for mercy, by surrendering to it, soon determined me, and I accordingly . . . from that time submitted myself to his goodness, on which I still entirely depend."

He concluded by an appeal to the intercession of his brother peers, protesting that his future life should be found not unworthy of such an act of grace. But notwithstanding the strong public interest in his favour, the intercession of several peers and leading commoners, as well as the personal application of his Countess, accompanied by other ladies of distinction, to the Sovereign and both Houses of Parliament, all proved of no avail. His sentence was carried out, and he was executed on Tower Hill, February 24, 1716. Having concluded his devotions, he proceeded to read an address in favour of the Pretender, asking pardon of those whom he had scandalised by his breach of loyalty to his lawful and rightful sovereign, James III., by his plea of guilty. Notwithstanding, he added, if his life had been spared, he should have felt himself bound in honour not to take up arms again against the reigning sovereign.

James Ratcliffe, Earl of Derwentwater, was the son of a natural daughter of Charles II. His mother, Mary Tudor, was the daughter of an actress, Mrs Mary Davies, whom Charles had taken off the stage. Having married Francis,

Lord Ratcliffe, eldest son of the first Earl of Derwentwater, she became the mother of this last unhappy peer of the name. He was only in his 24th year, was distinguished by his private virtues, being equally noted for his munificent hospitality and constant acts of benevolence, in the practice of which he spent his time and estate, without reference to religious persuasion, though himself a Catholic. It appears that before he had given any ground of offence to the Government, he received information of a Secretary of State's warrant having been issued for his apprehension, on suspicion of his having secretly joined the Jacobites, who were going about the country at the time. Having presented himself to a justice of the peace, and failed to obtain information respecting the charges against him, he unfortunately secreted himself; and on the appearance of Forster's party in the neighbourhood, was induced to join them. The extending of mercy in such a case would surely have been a graceful exercise of the prerogative on the inauguration of the new dynasty, and have tended to make their throne

> " The centre
> Round which love a circle drew,
> That treason durst not enter."

Lord Somers was among those who shed tears for his fate.

Of the other condemned peers Lord Widdrington had the good fortune to effect his escape, but was attainted. The Earl of Nithsdale was equally fortunate, joined the Pretender at Avignon, and died at Rome in 1744. The Earl of Carnwath had both his life and estates remitted to him, and died in 1737, at the age of eighty-four. Lord Kenmure was executed; but his estate, though not the title, was restored to his son. Lord Nairne, brother to the Duke of Athol, received several respites, and in 1717 was included in the act of grace, and had his estate, but not his title, restored.

Of other prisoners taken at Preston, Forster, the leader of the northern insurgents, succeeded in making his escape ; as did Charles Ratcliffe, brother of Lord Derwentwater, who had been offered a pardon, but rejected it. He was one of the most active and courageous of the insurgent leaders. He subsequently obtained a naval commission in the French service, and being captured carrying stores for the use of the insurgents at the following rising in Scotland, was executed on Tower Hill, December 8, 1746.

Whilst the fate of the condemned peers was still in suspense, and their ladies and friends were making the utmost exertions on their behalf, Steele was one of the minority inclined to mercy, and was accused of inconsistency by the bigoted and narrow-minded, who thought they could not be too profuse in their zeal for the triumphant cause, by vindictiveness to the fallen ; who could not understand reprobation of the offence with mercy to the offenders, but who would infallibly have been the foremost and loudest in their homage to those they now persecuted, if the fortune of war had been reversed. Steele not only presented one of the petitions on their behalf, accompanied by a speech of some length, but advocated their cause through the press as well. He was seconded in Parliament by Mr Fuller, one of the members for Petersfield, (who had been a contributor to the *Tatler*), and by Mr Shippen. In reference to the misrepresentation he suffered on this subject, he published a "Letter to a Member" concerning the condemned lords, in which he said he advocated " mercy and clemency for the sake of his king and country, in whose behalf he dared to say that . . . all noble geniuses in the art of government have less owed their safety to punishment and terror, than grace and magnanimity."

This unfortunate rebellion having resulted in a large confiscation of property, a commission was appointed on the subject, of which Steele was made a member.

The following letters comprise the correspondence in 1716 and part of 1717 :—

LETTER CCLVIII. *To Lady Steele, humbly present.*

Jan. 10, 1715-16.

DEAR PRUE,—I have that in my pocket which, within a few days, will be a great sum of money, besides what is growing at the play-house. I prefer your ease to all things. I beg of you to send for coals and all things necessary for this week, and keep us only to the end of it out of your abundance ; and I shall ever add to it hereafter, instead of attempting to diminish it. I cannot indeed get money immediately without appearing most scandalously indigent, which I would avoid for the future.—Ever yours, RICH. STEELE.

LETTER CCLIX. *To Lady Steele, over against Park Place, St James's St.*

Baldwin's, East Street, near Red Lion Square,

Jan. 11, 1715-16.

DEAR PRUE,—I am here very busy, and shall be all night. Pray send me a book which is upon the 'scritoire in the dining-room. It is a History of Ireland, and many leaves of it turned down, and papers in it. It is a sad thing I must take such pains, but you are to be the better for it, which is the main comfort to yours ever, RICH. STEELE.

LETTER CCLX. *To Lady Steele.*

Chelsea, Monday, Feb. 14, 1715-16.

DEAR PRUE,—Mr Fuller* and I came hither to dine in the air, but the

---

* One of Steele's assistants as a writer in the *Tatler.*

maid has been so slow that we are benighted, and choose to lie here, rather than go this road in the dark. I lie at *our own house*, and my friend at a relation's in the town. I desire Willmot may come in the morning with my linen.—Your obedient husband,   RICH. STEELE.

LETTER CCLXI.   *To Lady Steele.*

March 26, 1716.

DEAR PRUE,—I did not come to town to-day, because I find my hand in, and, by the help of Dymock,* shall be able this evening to finish what I have deferred from day to day for two months last past. Lest you should be uneasy, I send Willmot to let you know that I shall not come home till to-morrow about eleven in the morning ; and am, dear creature, absolutely thine,   RICH. STEELE.

LETTER CCLXII.   *To Lady Steele, with a Case.*

St James's Street, Aug. 9, 1716.

DEAR PRUE,—You may observe in those excellent books which your polite cousin † reads to you that necessaries are often wanting to the heroes and heroines, for want of stowing their portmanteaus with proper materials.

The bearer brings you, with this, a case of instruments for eating and drinking, that may be upon the road both of ornament and use to, madam, your obedient husband,   RICH. STEELE.

LETTER CCLXIII.   *To Lady Steele, at Carmarthen, South Wales.*

Saturday, Nov. 17, 1716.

DEAR PRUE,—Molly's distemper proves the small-pox, which she has very favourably, and a good kind. Mrs Evans is very good ; nurse Jervase very diligent. Sarah has every good quality, and the whole family are in health beside the dear infant. I am very close at my papers, not having been two hours out of the house since I parted with you. I love you to distraction ; for I cannot be angry at anything you do, let it be ever so odd and unexpected, to the tenderest of husbands,   RICH. STEELE.

We had not, when you left us, an inch of candle, a pound of coal, or a bit of meat in the house ; but we do not want now.

---

* Steele's " amanuensis."
† Alexander Scurlock, son of a brother of Lady Steele's father.

LETTER CCLXIV.   *To Lady Steele.*

Nov. 20, 1716.

DEAR PRUE,—I am here under the double severity of your absence and Molly's sickness ; but I hope you are well, as the child is, in her condition. She has the small-pox, with very favourable symptoms, and is very well attended by Evans and her husband, Sarah, and nurse Jervase.—I am, with the utmost affection, your obedient husband, and most humble servant,

RICH. STEELE.

I hope to begin my journey* the day after Willmot's return. I opened this after [being] sealed, to let you know Willmot is come.

LETTER CCLXV.   *To Lady Steele.*

Nov. 26, 1716.

DEAR PRUE,—I hope this will find you safe at Carmarthen, and that you find all things easy there. There is nothing extraordinary has occurred here. Your daughter Betty was very well yesterday : I made her be out as I rode by.

I have been much upon horseback to prepare me for my journey, for which I expect orders on Monday next out of Scotland. This is the ninth day with my dear Molly in the small-pox; she has many in the body and face : they are, they say, very kindly. Nurse Jervase, with her duty, recommends herself to you for her extraordinary care and diligence about your child. Mrs Evans and her husband deserve very well of us.—I am, with the tenderest love, your most obedient husband and most humble servant,   RICH. STEELE.

My most humble service to the widow and all the family.

LETTER CCLXVI.   *To Lady Steele.*

Nov. 27, 1716.

DEAR PRUE,—I writ to my cousin Alexander this post, and desired him to excuse my not writing to you ; but, on second thoughts, fearing you might be displeased, I send this, though it has only to say that I am, with entire love and duty, your most obedient husband and humble servant,   RICH. STEELE.

LETTER CCLXVII.   *To Lady Steele.*

Nov. 29, 1716.

DEAR PRUE,—I am extremely obliged to you for your letter on the re-

---

* To Scotland, whither he was going as a commissioner of the forfeited estates.

verse of my cousin's. Your indisposition is a very great grief to me. I desire you to use brandy to bathe your head, till you hear Dr Garth's advice by next post. Betty is very well, and Molly up, and has this day taken physic, which shall be continued as much as proper, and at proper distances. I have a great packet to answer from Scotland, of which you shall have a further account in my next.—I am, devotedly yours,

RICH. STEELE.

LETTER CCLXVIII.   *To Lady Steele, at Carmarthen, South Wales.— Frank, Richard Steele.*

Dec. 6, 1716.

DEAR PRUE,—This is only to say we are all well. Among other little matters, I wait an answer from you before I set out for Scotland—I am, dear Prue, faithfully thine,   RICH. STEELE.

Garth advises your washing your head with water and salt.

LETTER CCLXIX.   *To Lady Steele.*

St James's Street, Dec. 11, 1716.

DEAR PRUE,—I have received yours with the enclosed bill for fifty pounds. I earnestly entreat you not to excruciate your spirit with what you ought to overlook and despise. I will write to you at large on Thursday about all matters, especially the method of my journey.—I am, dear woman, entirely yours,   RICH. STEELE.

LETTER CCLXX.   *To Lady Steele.**

[*undated.*]

DEAREST PRUE,—This is only to ask how you do.—I am your, Betty, Dick, Eugene, Molly's humble servant,   RICH. STEELE.

LETTER CCLXXI.   *To Lady Steele.*

Dec. 13, 1716.

MY DEAR PRUE,—Mrs Secretary Bevans† has acquainted me, by the

---

* " This scrap is placed here, most probably out of its proper order; a circumstance of no more consequence than the letter itself, which is only preserved as enumerating all his family in a way that no man but himself would ever have thought of."

† "Sister to Lady Steele's mother. . . . She was at this time a widow."— See letter of November 26.

7th instant, that you are well, and very much my friend and servant. Mrs Evans went to see Betty yesterday, who, she says, is grown a very fine lady. Moll sat by me a little as I was writing yesterday; she will not be at all marked, but is a dear child. Eugene is grown a very lively gentleman. After all this news, which takes in all the compass of whatever you care for,* you will not much regard politics, if I should write any. But it seems my Lord Townshend is out, and Stanhope and Methven the two secretaries for England, and Duke Roxborough † made a third secretary for Scotland ; for which place I intend to set out this day, with an opportunity of a gentleman's coach going down.—I am, dear Prue, your most affectionate, obedient, languishing relict,   RICH. STEELE.

The machine is almost ready.

LETTER CCLXXII.   *To Lady Steele.*

Dec. 18, 1716.

DEAR PRUE,—Whether I love you because you are the mother of the children, or them because you are their mother, I know not ; but I am sure I am growing a very covetous creature for the sake of both of you. I am making haste to Scotland ; have only a small affair, which I will acquaint you with in my next, and am entirely yours,   RICH. STEELE.

LETTER CCLXXIII.   *To Lady Steele.*

St James's Street, Dec. 20, 1716.

DEAR PRUE,—Mrs Secretary‡ writes me word you have a curiosity to know what bustle it was that you heard of at the play-house. It was occasioned by a gentleman's coming in very rough, in a riding habit, and the sentry inquiring of him where he was going, as he offered to pass into a box, he told him, if he opposed his passage, he would shoot him through the head. The soldier was the more alarmed at him, and persisted to deny him entrance ; at which the stranger pulled out a pistol, and shot the man

---

* "By this expression it appears their first boy, Dick, was now dead. Eugene died in November 1723."

† "John Ker, Duke of Roxborough, was appointed Secretary for North Britain December 16, 1716. He resigned that office August 25, 1725 ; and since that period, instead of a distinct Secretary for Scotland, there has been regularly a Keeper of the Signet under the other two secretaries."

‡ "Mrs Bevans." In playful allusion to her acting as secretary to Lady Steele.

in the neck. He was seized, and several pistols found about him, and proves one Mr Freeman, a madman. The house was in a very great uproar, crying out, " *The Prince !*" who only appeared indifferent and composed.*

I long to be gone from hence. The children are all well.—I am, dear Prue, ever thine,   RICH. STEELE.

Your man Sam owes me threepence, which must be deducted in the account between you and me ; therefore, pray take care to get it in, or stop it.†

LETTER CCLXXIV.   *To Lady Steele.*

St James's Street, Dec. 22, 1716.

DEAR PRUE,—This wishes you an agreeable Christmas. I have taken such care as to be as easy on the road‡ as travelling about this town.—I am, dear Prue, with the sincerest passion, ever yours,   RICH. STEELE.

LETTER CCLXXV.   *To Lady Steele.*

Christmas Day.

DEAR PRUE,—I went the other day to see Betty at Chelsea, who represented to me, in her pretty language, " that she seemed helpless and friendless, without anybody's taking notice of her at Christmas, when all the children but she and two more were with their relations." I have invited her to dinner to-day with one of the teachers, and they are here now in the room ; Betty and Molly very noisy and pleased together. Bess goes back again, as soon as she has dined, to Chelsea. I have stayed in to get a very advantageous affair despatched ; for, I assure you, I love money at present as well as your ladyship, and am entirely yours,

RICH. STEELE.

I told Betty I had writ to you ; and she made me open the letter again

---

* " The strange circumstance, here alluded to, happened at Drury Lane Theatre on the 6th of December 1716, when the Prince of Wales was present at the tragedy of 'Tamerlane.' A particular account of the whole transaction, of which Steele has here given his lady a good abstract, is in the 'Political State,' vol. xii. p. 547. Mr Freeman was a gentleman of Surrey, and had for several years been troubled with fits of lunacy. Though the soldier's wounds did not prove mortal, Mr Freeman was committed to Newgate on the additional charge of having killed a man in the country two days before."

† In playful allusion to Lady Steele's excessive attention to money.

‡ " In his journey to Scotland."

and give her humble duty to her mother, and desire to know when she shall have the honour to see her in town. She gives her love to Mrs Bevans and all her cousins.

LETTER CCLXXVI.   *To Lady Steele.*

St James's Street, Dec. 28, 1716.

DEAR PRUE,—It is matter of gain, not matter of gallantry, keeps me here thus long. I hope, within a post or two, to give an account of a thing that will bring us a great sum of money.*

All my endeavours and thoughts tend only to extricate my condition, and have no debt but that to a good wife and a few dear innocents.—I am, dear Prue, eternally thine,   RICH. STEELE.

The King leaves Hanover the 4th of January, our style.

LETTER CCLXXVII.   *To Lady Steele.*

St James's Street, Jan. 1, 1716–17.

DEAR, DEAR PRUE,—I wish you from my soul a happy new year, and many, very different from what we have hitherto had. In order thereunto, I have taken a resolution, which, by the blessing of God, I will steadfastly keep, to make my children partners with me in all my future gain, in the manner I have before described to you. That you may be convinced of this happy change, you shall be yourself the keeper of what I lay up for them by quarterly portions from this day.—I am, with the tenderest affection, your faithful husband and most humble servant,

R. STEELE.

Your children are all very well.

LETTER CCLXXVIII.   *To Lady Steele.*

St James's Street, Thursday, Jan. 3, 1716–17.

DEAR PRUE,—I have the pleasure to acquaint you that Gillmore's work † is just finished; and that there are some little matters besides, which will forthwith highly conduce to the good of you and your little ones. The courtiers are in a very great hurry, which cannot be composed till the king comes.‡ The order for the pay of our commission lies before the

---

* "A contrivance of a machine for bringing fish to London; of which a more particular account is given in the sequel."—See letter Jan. 3, 1716–17, &c.

† The project referred to in letter of December 28, 1716.

‡ "Who was then at Hanover."

Treasury ; when that is signed I shall leave the town, though but to go and come from Scotland—Ever yours,   RICH. STEELE.

You may be sure I mean to return by way of Carmarthen.

LETTER CCLXXIX.   *To Lady Steele.*

St James's Street, Jan. 4, 1716–17.

DEAR PRUE,—I have received your long letter, for which I thank you, and will punctually observe the directions. I have answered concerning my cousin Griffith to Mr Madocks, because you, being unacquainted with the methods of the university, would not have comprehended what I mean. You shall find Jonathan provided for in a short time. Every tittle shall be observed as you directed.—I am your most obedient and affectionate husband,   RICH. STEELE.

You are utterly mistaken in your suspicion of my having borrowed of my cousin ; there is indeed no such thing, directly or indirectly.

LETTER CCLXXX.   *To Lady Steele.*

Jan. 8, 1716–17.

DEAR PRUE,—Forgive me, that I can say no more now than just to tell you we are well, and am, with all truth, your faithful   DICK STEELE.

LETTER CCLXXXI.   *To Lady Steele.*

St James's Street, Jan. 10, 1716–17.

DEAR PRUE,—I have some matters of profit now on the anvil, which I cannot be able to explain till Tuesday's post, at which time you shall have a full account ; but, between that and this, little more than to tell you I am alive ; and, while so, inviolably thine,   RICH. STEELE.

LETTER CCLXXXII.   *To Lady Steele.*

Jan. 12, 1716–17.

DEAR PRUE,—I have yours of last post without a date, and shall, in every particular, govern myself as you direct. You know you are next week to have particulars concerning all the present views of, madam, your most affectionate husband, and most devoted humble servant,

RICH. STEELE.

Our little people are very lively and well.

LETTER CCLXXXIII.   *To Lady Steele.*

Jan. 17, 1716-17.

DEAR PRUE,—I have yours on a leaf of the widow's. If you knew how deeply it touches me, you would not write in so scornful and unkind style to, madam, your most affectionate, obedient husband,   RICH. STEELE.

LETTER CCLXXXIV.   *To Lady Steele.*

St James's, Jan. 19, 1716-17.

DEAR PRUE,—I have prepared the letter for Morgan Davies, &c., but they are at home, and I am at court, and cannot go to my own house till too late for the post. You shall have all your commands spoken to next post. The king came hither about five o'clock.—I am, dear Prue, eternally yours,   RICH. STEELE.

LETTER CCLXXXV.   *To Lady Steele.*

: [*Undated.*]

DEAR PRUE,—I have yours, and if I have ever offended you, I am heartily sorry for it, and beg your pardon. As to the next circumstance, the world is all alike everywhere, and I know no occasion for expecting great friendship and disinterested conduct, but maintain a discreet and distant correspondence, at the same time always ready to do what good one can to relations, without thinking of what return they will make. I do, as you advise, court and converse with men able and willing to serve me. But, after this, you grow very pleasant, and talk of L.800. Please to shew me in your next how you make out such a demand upon me, and you shall have my serious answer to it. Your words are, " the full L.800 you owe me." You advise me to take care of my soul; I do not know what you can think of yours, when you have and do withhold from me your body. I observe what you say of cousin Alexander, and shall be glad of his correspondence. I have not yet had any money as a commissioner, but shall next week, and then will pay Betty's schooling, &c.—Your most obedient humble husband and servant,   RICH. STEELE.

I enclose to you a letter from Morgan Davies, with my answer on the back. I believe you had better conceal that. I send you his letter ; you may be sure he shall have no consent of mine separate from yours, for you rule me entirely.

LETTER CCLXXXVI.   *To Lady Steele.*

Feb. 5, 1716-17

DEAR PRUE,—I write without having anything new to say. I am going to be very easy, God be thanked, in my affairs ; to throw off all hangers-on, put my debts in a regular way of payment, which I cannot immediately discharge ; and try to behave myself with the utmost circumspection and prudence in all the duties of life, especially of being, dear Prue, your most obliged husband, and obedient humble servant,   RICH. STEELE.

LETTER CCLXXXVII.   *To Lady Steele.*

Feb. 9, 1716-17.

DEAR PRUE,—I shall observe your directions concerning Dick Philips, but it gives me great indignation to observe that you are forced to go to law for the balance of your accompt. I hope you take care of your health, and let nothing discompose you, that, when we meet, we may have healthy bodies and easy minds, and enjoy the comforts of life with tranquillity.—I am ever yours,   RICH. STEELE.

LETTER CCLXXXVIII.   *To Mr M. Davies.*

Feb. 14, 1716-17.

SIR,—I have yours of the 9th inst., but am wholly unacquainted with the point on which you and my wife differ in your accounts. If I knew that, I should be more able to advise her. I daresay she is as averse to contests as you can be, but I can make no further answer till I hear from her. I am extremely concerned that there is any occasion of dispute ; for I was always very much disposed to continue, Sir, your most obedient humble servant,   RICH. STEELE.

I have writ to my wife, and believe you will hear from her.

LETTER CCLXXXIX.   *To Lady Steele.*

[1717.]

MADAM,—If I have a tender regard for every one that lives under my roof, so as to be uneasy if they want for any convenience, how much more am I concerned for my wife and children. I desire therefore, that, for the future, I may be well assured that there is enough with thankfulness, and my expense shall be hereafter much more confined within my own walls. I am coming home.   RICH. STEELE.

LETTER CCXC.   *To Lady Steele.*

[1718.]

DEAR PRUE,—I write this in very great haste, being just come out of the country, where I lay last night, with some friends, at a place called Carshalton, in Surrey.

I am very sorry for neglecting a post, and hastened now to town to prevent the like accident.—I am, dear creature, ever thine,

RICH. STEELE.

My Lord Cadogan * has sent hither this evening; he is labouring to do me good at court. I shall know more in the morning.

LETTER CCXCI.   *To Mr Alex. Scurlock.*

May 26, 1725.

COUSIN SANDY,—I have yours with the accompt, upon which you refer me to the last, which I have found among my papers. You will find the charge in the accompt ending Michaelmas, concerning collecting and returns, is for £313, 17s. 6d.

But I have not time to observe upon this matter carefully, so as to avoid errors, but my care is about the £100 to the king. Till that is over, I know not how to rest easy, but shall take a journey down to Wales to take it up rather than let it lie out, so much do I dread being accomptant to the crown.—I am, Sir, your most obedient humble servant,

RICH. STEELE.

LETTER CCXCII.   *To the Lady Steele, at Carmarthen, South Wales.—*
Frank, Richard Steele.

Feb. 16, 1716-17.

DEAR PRUE,—Sober or not, I am ever yours,

RICH. STEELE.

LETTER CCXCIII.   *To Lady Steele.*

Feb. 23, 1716-17.

DEAR PRUE,—I have not anything particular to say to-night, but that I am informed there will be, within a few days, further changes at court. Your children are all very well. I wait with great impatience for the receipt of my money. There is forfeited money in town, but it is not yet in the Exchequer.—I am, dear Prue, ever yours,   RICH. STEELE.

LETTER CCXCIV.   *To Lady Steele.*

Feb. 28, 1716-17.

DEAR PRUE,—I am very well pleased with the behaviour of David † at Oxford, who has rendered himself very agreeable to all the Whig world, on

---

* This nobleman (of whom see p. 304) was not created a Peer till May 18, 1718, so that this is one of the latest letters written by Sir Richard Steele to his wife.
† David Scurlock, probably a son of Lady Steele's uncle.

a very proper occasion, at Oxon.   He spoke contemptibly of the Pretender in a public speech, and the Proctor thought fit to reprove him thereupon. The Bishop of Bangor* takes occasion to espouse him in this juncture.

Your daughter Moll is noisy, Betty very grave, and Eugene very strong and lusty.   We are not yet paid a farthing ; when we are I shall send you down a receipt for Betty's schooling.—Ever yours,   RICH. STEELE.

LETTER CCXCV.   *To Lady Steele.*

March 2, 1716-17.

DEAR PRUE,—I usually write to you the first thing I do on a post-day, but to-day company came in and made me neglect it.   Afterwards I was called abroad, then came home, and Budgell,† Benson,‡ and Fuller,§ came in upon me to dinner.   The two last stayed till the evening, and Fuller carried me with him to the play, from whence I am now returned home.   Your friend Keck‖ was the finest, gayest figure there, and Captain Ferrers gallantly attending behind her.   All your family is well.   Good night.—I am, dear Prue, ever thine,   RICH. STEELE.

LETTER CCXCVI.   *To Lady Steele.*

[Undated.]

MY DEAREST PRUE AND BELOVED WIFE, &c.,—I have yours of the 7th instant, which turns wholly upon my taking care of my health, and advice to forbear embarking too deeply in public matters, which you enforce by reminding me of the ingratitude I have met with.   I have as quick sense of the ill-treatment I have received as is consistent with keeping up my own spirit and good humour.   Whenever I am a malcontent I will take care not to be a gloomy one, but hope to keep some stings of wit and humour in my own defence.   I am talking to my wife, and therefore may speak my heart, and the vanity of it.   I know, and you are my witness, that I have served the royal family with an unreservedness due only to Heaven, and I am now, (I thank my brother Whigs,) not possessed of twenty shillings from the favour of the court.   The playhouse it had been barbarity to deny at the player's request, and therefore I do not allow it a

* Bishop Hodley.
† Eustace Budgell, Addison's cousin.
‡ William Benson, Esq., Auditor of the Imprest.
§ See note to letter of Feb. 14, 1716.
‖ This lady afterwards proved herself an excellent friend to one of Steele's daughters, as appears from some subsequent letters.

favour. But I banish the very memory of things, nor will I expect anything but what I must strike out of myself. By Tuesday's post I think I shall be able to guess when I shall leave the town, and turn all my thoughts to finish my comedy.* You will find I have got so much constancy and fortitude as to live my own way (within the rules of good breeding and decency) wherever I am ; for I will not sacrifice your husband, and the father of the poor babes, to any one's humour in the world. But to provide for and do you good, is all my ambition.

I have a list of twenty-one leases for the setting out £199, 8s. *per annum.* I have not yet heard of Mr Philips.—I am, dear Prue, ever yours,

RICH. STEELE.

LETTER CCXCVII.   *To Lady Steele.*
Hampton Court, March 16, 1716–17.

DEAR PRUE,—If you have written anything to me which I should have received last night, I beg your pardon that I cannot answer till the next post. The House of Commons will be very busy the next week ; and I had many things, public and private, for which I wanted four and twenty hours' retirement, and therefore came to visit your son. I came out of town yesterday, being Friday, and shall return to-morrow. Your son, at the present writing, is mighty well employed in tumbling on the floor of the room, and sweeping the sand with a feather. He grows a most delightful child, and very full of play and spirit. He is also a very great scholar ; he can read his Primer, and I have brought down my Virgil. He makes most shrewd remarks upon the pictures. We are very intimate friends and play-fellows. He begins to be very ragged ; and I hope I shall be pardoned if I equip him with new clothes and frocks, or what Mrs Evans and I shall think for his service.—I am, dear Prue, ever yours,

RICH. STEELE.

LETTER CCXCVIII.   *To Lady Steele.*
March 19, 1716–17.

DEAR PRUE,—Mr Richard Philips was with me this morning, and I signed the leases to which I saw your hand. This day has been a great affair in the House of Commons. Mr Walpole, in very clear and excellent terms, laid before us the state of the debt of the nation, and proposed a way, by lowering the interest given to the creditors of the kingdom, and other methods, to ease our circumstances. I happened to be the only man in

---

* "If this was his 'Conscious Lovers,' it remained unfinished till 1721."

the House who spoke against it,* because I did not think the way of doing it just. I believe the scheme will take place ; and if it does, Walpole must be a very great man.

I am very well pleased with the project from Mr Gillmore's design ; and, from the integrity of my intentions in all my actions, in great tranquillity of mind. I contract my sails every day ; and when I receive my money, shall in such a way as will shew that you and my little ones are all my sincere delight.—1 am, dear Prue, ever yours,   RICH. STEELE.

LETTER CCXCIX.   *To Lady Steele.*

This goes to dear Prue, to comfort her in her absence from her husband. If she thinks the distance as painful as he does, hearing from him must be a great satisfaction. I am sure, as soon as I have made my affairs so easy as that we can be together without being interrupted with worldly care, I shall put an end to the distance between us. I every day do something towards this, and next week shall pay off Madam Dawson. You shall have, within a few days, a state of my circumstances, the prospect of bettering them, and the progress I have already made in this necessary work. The children do come on so well that it would make me even covetous to put them in a condition equal to the good genius, I bless God, they seem to be of. Moll is the noisiest little creature in the world, and as active as a boy. Madam Betty is the gravest of matrons in her airs and civilities : Eugene a most beautiful and lusty child. The Parliament goes on but coldly ; but I hope there is a warmer spirit will soon appear in the service of this nation, which, possessed of the most solid blessings, sacrifices itself to trifles.—Yours ever,   RICH. STEELE.

LETTER CCC.   *To Lady Steele.*

[*Undated.*]

DEAR PRUE,—Yours of the 18th lies before me ; and I am convinced that *generous* in my carriage should rather be what you call it, thoughtless. As for the company I am to meet with, I shall maintain a general complaisance, and think the sincerity of speaking all one thinks a great injury and insult towards the rest of the world. I assure you, we will have no quarrels on that score ; for, as I owe everybody civility, so I owe you to go on your own way ; nor will I debate with you on these subjects, but proceed in my own way. To shew you that I am grown a very hard-

---

* "This is confirmed by the account in the 'Political State' for March 1716–17."

hearted fellow, and fit for this world, Mrs Long* has been arrested, and I
have, upon her application, refused to concern myself in her affairs. It
was, I think, a little confident in her to ask it of me ; and, in such cases,
I think I may be as bold as to deny unreasonable things, as they are to
ask them.   The Lords of the Treasury have ordered us some money, and
I shall husband it to the best advantage, to keep above this ill-natured
world ; but it is a terrible circumstance to have one's money due to others
before it comes into one's own hands.

Dick Philips has been here to-day; and, after we had dined, I executed
the leases.   I am highly pleased and satisfied with your conduct, and think
you come up to the description in the Proverbs† of the good woman of whom
it is said that her husband shall be honoured from her character. I do
assure you, I am not ashamed to tell you, that I submit my conduct to the
imitation of yours, and shall take you with me in all matters of concern.
You are to know that I have been casting about how to turn a kind inclination towards me at present into what is solid.   There is an estate
forfeited to the king, of L.100 a year, by one who died for murder.   It is a
thing I have come to the knowledge of by the by ; and believe I shall
have a grant of it to help me out of the inconveniences my zeal brought
upon me, and I have not yet recovered.   One does not know what fate
any letter may meet with; therefore I can never find in my heart to
commit secrets to paper.   But take it for granted, I shall hereafter shew
very little romance in the temper and conduct of, dear Prue, your most
affectionate husband, and most obedient servant,   RICH. STEELE.

LETTER CCCI.   *To Lady Steele.*

[*Undated.*]

DEAR PRUE,—I have yours, wherein you mention Fuller, and the account
you have that he shewed an insolent joy at his wife's death.   I do not set
up to excuse his conduct towards his wife, but shall take care of mine
towards my own.

You tell me you want a little flattery from me.   I assure you, I know
no one who deserves so much commendation as yourself, and to whom
saying the best things would be so little like flattery.   The thing speaks
itself, considering you as a very handsome woman that loves retirement,

---

* "It might have been supposed that this was the celebrated beauty recorded
among the Kit-cat toasts, who retired from the world on account of pecuniary
distress; but it appears from the 'Supplement to Swift,' that she died at Lynn,
December 21, 1711."

† Chap. xxi. 23.

one who does not want wit, and yet is extremely sincere ; and so I could go through all the vices which attend the good qualities of other people, from which you are exempt. But, indeed, though you have every perfection, you have one extravagant fault, which almost frustrates the good in you to me ; and that is, that you do not love to dress, to appear, to shine out, even at my request, and to make me proud of you, or rather to indulge the pride I have that you are mine. This is all I wish changed in you, which I hope you will bring about, and condescend to be, what nature made you, the most beauteous and most agreeable of your sex, at the instance of, dear Prue, your most affectionate, obsequious husband,

RICH. STEELE.

A quarter of Molly's schooling is paid.
The children are perfectly well.

LETTER CCCII.   *To Lady Steele.*

March 23, 1716–17.

DEAR PRUE,—I write by your order though I have nothing new. My money is not yet come to hand, and I am very impatient for it, because I would show you, as soon as it is in my power, a reformation in the management of my expense.—I am, dear Prue, your most obedient, obliged husband,   RICH. STEELE.

LETTER CCCIII.   *To Lady Steele.*

March 26, 1717.

MY DEAREST PRUE,—I have received yours, wherein you give me the sensible affliction of letting me know of the continual pain in your head. I could not meet with necessary advice ; but, according to the description you give me, I am confident washing your head in cold water will cure you ; I mean, having water poured on your head, and rubbed with one hand, from the crown of your head to the nape of your neck. When I lay in your place, and on your pillow, I assure you, I fell into tears last night, to think that my charming little insolent might be then awake and in pain, and took it to be a sin to go to sleep.

For this tender passion towards you, I must be contented that your Prueship will condescend to call yourself my well-wisher. I am going abroad, and write before I go out, lest accidents should happen to prevent my writing at all. If I can meet with further advice for you, I will send it in a letter to Alexander.—I am, dear Prue, ever thine,

RICH. STEELE. ·

LETTER CCCIV.   *To Lady Steele.*

March 30, 1717.

DEAR PRUE,—The omission of last post was occasioned by my attend-ance on the Duke of Newcastle, who was in the chair at the Kit-Cat. Be so good as to forgive me. We have not yet one shilling from the com-mission, though L.750 is become due, nor indeed know we when to expect it. I hope, however, within a few days to take up as much money as will pay off all hangers-on, and to have no more for the future. I pant for leisure and tranquillity, which I hope to enjoy when we meet again—I am, dear Prue, your most obedient, affectionate, faithful husband,

RICH. STEELE.

LETTER CCCV.   *To Lady Steele.*

April 2, 1717.

DEAR PRUE,—I am just come from a parliamentary club, and can only say all your family is well, especially he who is ever yours,

R. STEELE.

LETTER CCCVI.   *To Lady Steele.*

April 9, 1717.

DEAR PRUE,—I write according to your advice, before I go out in the morning ; and indeed the House of Commons sit so late, that what with that, and being carried off to dinner, one is apt to run into the expense of the whole day, without having an hour to send to one's best friend. I gave Mrs Evans the part of your letter, but there is no occasion for that caution ; the child in her eyes, and everywhere else, is in perfect good health. God be thanked, the rest are in the same condition ; and we want nothing here but the receipt of money. I dined yesterday in Chancery Lane, and after dinner visited Mr Keck, who is very well, and much your ladyship's servant. Keep up your spirits, and let us live like a man and woman that love when we next meet.—I embrace you, and am your most affectionate, and most obliged, humble servant,

RICH. STEELE.

LETTER CCCVII.   *To Lady Steele, at Carmarthen, South Wales.*
Frank, Richard Steele.

[*Undated.*]

DEAR PRUE,—I am, as you observe, still in town, and have your rally-ing letter.* The claims of the fair sex are, you say, unaccountable. It is

* See letters of December 28, 1716, and May 30, 1717.

well for you they are ; for, I assure you, I think you both the fairest and the best of women.

I have been much at home and alone since we parted. I am come to a resolution of making my three children my partners, and will constantly lay up something out of all receipts of money for each of them, in a box bearing the name of the little one to whom it belongs. Betty grows tall, and has the best air I ever saw in any creature of her age. I am going to dine with the Speaker. Things at Court seem to be in a very uncertain way.—I am, dear Prue, eternally yours,   RICH. STEELE.

LETTER CCCVIIL   *To Lady Steele.*

April 10, 1717.

DEAR PRUE,—It is now Wednesday, and meeting with your letter, I write now, lest I should not have leisure to-morrow, when our Board are to meet very early. Now, as to your letter, you say I am reported a Tory. You know I have always an unfashionable thing called conscience, in all matters of judicature or justice. There happened, a little while ago, a petition to be brought into the House of Commons from the Roman Catholics, praying relief as to point of time, and the meaning of certain clauses which affected them. When there was a question just ready to be put upon this, as whether it should be rejected or not, I stood up and said to this purpose :—

"Mr Speaker, I cannot but be of opinion that to put severities upon men merely on account of religion is a most grievous and unwarrantable proceeding. But, indeed, the Roman Catholics hold tenets which are inconsistent with the being and safety of a Protestant people ; for this reason we are justified in laying upon them the penalties which the Parliament has from time to time thought fit to inflict ; but, sir, let us not pursue Roman Catholics with the spirit of Roman Catholics, but act towards them with the temper of our own religion. If we do so, we shall not expect them to do anything in less time than is necessary to do it, or to conduct themselves by rules which they do not understand," &c.

When I had adventured to say this, others followed ; and there is a bill directed for the relief of the petitioners. I suppose this gave a handle to the fame of my being a Tory ; but you may, perhaps, by this time have heard that I am turned Presbyterian ; for the same day, in a meeting of a hundred Parliament men, I laboured as much for the Protestant Dissenters. Now for the news. Mr Walpole, Mr Methuen, and Mr Pulteney have resigned their offices. Mr Stanhope is to go into the Treasury. Mr Addison and Lord Sunderland are to be Secretaries of State. Lord Townshend is removed from Lord-Lieutenant of Ireland ; he is to be succeeded by the Duke of Bolton, and the Duke of Newcastle to be Lord Chamberlain. We

have got no money. I recover very fast my gouty lameness ; and, now I
am in a better way, I own to you I have had a sad time—scarce ever well
of the gout since we parted. The children and all your family are well.
God bless you !   RICH. STEELE.

As soon as I have money, I will have Pall Mall searched for a house.

LETTER CCCIX.   *To Lady Steele.*
                                    St James's, April 13, 1717.
DEAR PRUE,—We are here all well. They tell me I shall be something
in the new changes ; but what, I know not, nor do I care, [but] as it may
make me, with more comfort and pleasure, your most obedient servant and
loving husband,   RICH. STEELE.

LETTER CCCX.   *To Lady Steele.*
                                            April 16, 1717.
DEAR PRUE,—I dined this day with Mr Secretary Addison, who received
the seals of office last night.

The employment of Commissioner, by the act which constitutes the
commission, forbids my having any other office. But I am not out of
humour, &c.—I am your most affectionate, obedient husband,
                                                         RICH. STEELE.

LETTER CCCXI.   *To Lady Steele.*
                                            [*Undated.*]
DEAR PRUE,—I had a letter from Mr Scurlock, coolly saying you ordered
him to let me know you were indisposed, and could not write.

I expect more fondness, and that you say, at least, some kind thing to
me under your own hand every post. The Lords of the Treasury, when
they went out of their post, ordered half-a-year's salary to our commission ; and when that comes out of the manager's hands, from the estates
forfeited, we shall be paid, and that, I believe, will be about a fortnight
hence. In the meantime I want it sorely, to pay off many things and
keep something by me, if ever I can bring myself to that economy. You
have the kindest of husbands.   RICH. STEELE.

I am very lame, but in good health otherwise.

LETTER CCCXII.   *To Lady Steele.*
                                            April 19, 1717.
DEAR PRUE,—Your family and children are in good health. We have

half-a-year's salary ordered to our commission, which will be paid as soon
as our country receivers can remit it out of Lancashire ; which is all that
at present occurs to, madam, your most obsequious, faithful husband,

RICH. STEELE.

LETTER CCCXIIL.   *To Lady Steele.*

April 22, 1717.

MY DEAR PRUE,—I have yours, which is full of good sense, and shews
in you a true greatness of mind.   But at the same time that, according to
your advice, I shun all engagements which may ensnare my integrity, I
am to seek all occasions of profit that are consistent with it.   Little Molly,
who is in the house with me, is a constant dun to get money ; for it gives
my imagination the severest wound when I consider that she, or any of
my dear innocents, with nothing but their mere innocence to plead for
them, should be exposed to that world which would not so much as repair
the losses and sufferings of their poor father, after all his zeal and super-
erogatory service.   You say well, "It will be well for them to have it to
say, their father kept his integrity ; but if they say, at the same time, he
left us competent estates, it will be so far from lessening, that it will advance his character."   But I shall not spend much time to convince you
that [I think] it is a good thing to get money, but solemnly promise I will
no more omit any fair opportunity of doing it.

You writ to me some time ago to order you a newspaper ; I have done
so, and the letter* from the secretary's office also will come every post to
you.

The scene of business will be very warm at the next session, but my
lesson is so short, (that of following my conscience,) that I shall go through
the storm without losing a wink of sleep.   I have told you, in a former
letter, that ever since you went, I have been almost as great a cripple as
your dear mother was,† and indeed I recover mighty slowly.   I take your
advice of temperance, and am, with my whole heart, yours for ever,

RICH. STEELE.

Mr Gillmore's affair is quite finished with great success, insomuch that
Sir Isaac Newton is desirous the machine may stand at his house, and be
carried from thence to the Parliament.   Benson, Gillmore, and I meet
to-morrow, to concert all matters relating to it against the House of Commons meet again, which is on the 6th of May.

LETTER CCCXIV.   *To Lady Steele.*

[*Undated.*]

DEAR PRUE,—I have yours, with your advice against temptation, &c.

---

* The *Gazette.*   † This intimates her decease.

All I can aver is, that I have learned a language, and written a book, to keep me out of vanities.* All shall be done as fast as I can. You have here enclosed what you directed I should send for Morgan Davies.

Thus far I writ on Saturday last; but went to Mrs Clayton's,† and with some people there, went to Court, and was detained, so as not to be able to get away to despatch my letter to you, for which I beg your pardon. If I do not do my business just now, I must be contented to go on in the beaten dull road, and aim no more at lively strokes.

O Prue, you are very unkind in writing in so cool a strain to the warmest, tenderest heart that ever woman commanded.—I am, dear Prue, your most obedient husband and most humble servant,

RICH. STEELE.

I have directed the cream of tartar to " Mr Alexander Scurlock."

LETTER CCCXV.   *To Lady Steele.*
                                     Wednesday, April 24, 1717.

DEAR PRUE,—I have a letter from your secretary,‡ intimating that you were going to see the entry of the judges, and could not write yourself. I would not use so harsh a phrase as *expect*, though I have formerly taken the liberty of that word, when it concerned a queen; § but I beseech you, when you have health, to employ your own fair hand to, madam, your most obliged and affectionate husband,   RICH. STEELE.

LETTER CCCXVI.   *To Lady Steele.*
                                     April 26, 1717.

DEAR PRUE,—I am much obliged to you for so long a letter in your own handwriting. I am glad you are in any way got out of Davies's clutches; there is no possibility of escaping out of such claws without some loss of blood. I am trying to get out of a huckster's hands here also.

It is not possible to describe to you the perplexities into which the business of this nation is plunged; and it is a melancholy reflection that one has no comfort in considering the affairs of this distressed people, but as ill-usage and a general corruption abate one's concern for the public— Yours ever,   RICH. STEELE.

---

* Steele assigns this among other reasons for the publication of his little book entitled " The Christian Hero."

† Afterwards Lady Sundon, bedchamber-woman and friend of Queen Caroline. In the life of Bishop Hoadly, prefixed to his work, are many letters from that worthy prelate to Mrs Clayton.

‡ Either Mrs Bevans or Mr Alexander Scurlock.

§ In his pamphlet on Dunkirk.

LETTER CCCXVII.   *To Lady Steele.*

April 30, 1717.

DEAR PRUE,—Yours, without date, lies before me. I am sorry you give yourself any inquietude about the frivolous little humours of others. There is a plain, affable way of acting, without engaging one's self with much concern, which you understand well enough if you please. I take Sir Thomas Stepney* to be a fair, worthy gentleman, and in the interest of his country.   That this may find you in ease and tranquillity is the hearty prayer of your affectionate husband,   .   RICH. STEELE.

LETTER CCCXVIII.   *To Lady Steele.*

[*May* 1, 1717.]

DEAR PRUE,—You never date your letters, which very much perplexes me.   To avoid the same fault, I tell you that I have received yours on Wednesday evening, May the 1st, and sit down to answer now I am alone and at leisure.   I am heartily concerned for your eyes.   I have often told you, I believe you have used enchantments to enslave me ; for an expression of yours, of *good Dick*, has put me in so much rapture, that I could forget my present most miserable lameness and walk down to you.   I have at this time interest enough to do what you ask for Sandy, but I do not ask Mr Secretary Addison anything.   Gillmore dined with me to-day, when Benson was expected but did not come, to our great uneasiness, for we were to have taken measures to bring the matter into Parliament, and concerted everything else relating to the machine, which is a most prodigious work.

My Lord Cadogan, who is now in the first degree of favour, sat with me here the other night above an hour.   I should, by his great frankness and generosity of mind, be rightly recommended and represented, but my decrepit condition spoils all.   The money is not yet come to hand, which makes me very uneasy and out of patience.   I think the affair which Sandy asks for is to be surveyor of glass windows for Carmarthen and an adjacent county.   I had not interest in the Treasury till this new commission† was constituted, but think there is not one in it that would not be ready to do me a little favour.   My dear little peevish, beautiful, wise governess, God bless you !   RICH. STEELE.

I do not write news to you, because I have ordered the letter from the secretary's office to be sent to you constantly.

---

* Sir Thomas Stepney, Bart., was then one of the members for the county of Carmarthen.

† The then Lords Commissioners were, Viscount Stanhope, Lord Torrington, with John Wallop, George Baillie, and Thomas Micklethwayte, Esqs.

LETTER CCCXIX. *To Lady Steele.*

Thursday, 3 in the afternoon, May 2, 1717.

I had a very painful night last night; but, after a little chocolate an hour or two ago, and a chicken for dinner, am much more at ease.—Your servant, R. STEELE.

LETTER CCCXX. *To Lady Steele.*

May 7, 1717.

DEAR PRUE,—I am glad to hear, by a letter from your cousin, that you are well: but have taken physic this morning, and cannot hold down my head to paper; therefore hope you will excuse your faithful, obliged husband, RICH. STEELE.

LETTER CCCXXI. *To Lady Steele.*

[Undated.]

DEAR PRUE,—I am under much mortification from not having a letter from you yesterday, but will hope that the distance from the post, now you are at Blancorse, is the occasion.

I love you with the most ardent affection, and very often run over little heats that have sometimes happened between us, with tears in my eyes. I think no man living has so good, so discreet a woman to his wife as myself; and I thank you for the perseverance in urging me incessantly to have done with the herd of indigent, unthankful people, who have made me neglect those who should have been my care from the first principle of charity.

I have been very importunate for justice to the endeavours I have used to serve the public; and hope I shall very soon have such reparation as will give me agreeable things to say to you at our meeting, which God grant to you and your most obsequious husband, RICH. STEELE.

LETTER CCCXXII. *To Lady Steele.*

[Undated.]

MY DEAR, HONOURED, LOVELY PRUE,—I yesterday received two letters from you by the same post, and am comforted from the fear of your want of health, which I thought occasioned the omission of a letter. The letter wherein you speak of the L.100 remitted to Mrs Clark has no date, which always creates puzzles. I highly admire and honour you for your good conduct in clearing your estate and paying your debts. Nothing on my part shall be omitted to render you cheerful in your endeavours for our common good; for I design to allow you to be the headpiece, and give as much into your power as I can, which is but justice to the good and skilful use you have made of the power already reposed in you.—The poor Spanish horse is dead ; the mule I shall make a present of to a young gentleman who is fond of him. I expect a horse fit for my own riding in return. I gave Mrs Evans your letter ; her brother-in-law is at present very ill, so that she cannot make any resolution. You ask about my chariot. Fuller made me a present of a very good one ; the old one, with ten pounds, will purchase a good chaise. Depend upon it, I abhor debt as much as treason.—Ever yours, RICH. STEELE.

You may be sure I have said nothing to Dick Philips which I should not have said, &c.

LETTER CCCXXIII. *To Lady Steele.*

May 9, 1717.

DEAR PRUE,—I have intelligence from Carmarthen that you are well at Blancorse. Upon serious reflection, your not giving me one line yourself is such a slight notice of me, that indeed I will not write you hereafter but in answer to your own hand. If Sandy tells me that " you are well," I will repartee, " I am well," to him, without further painstaking. I was forced to lie last night at a lodging next door to Mr Wilks, in Covent Garden.

The children and all your family are well.—Yours ever,

RICH. STEELE.

LETTER CCCXXIV. *To Lady Steele.*

May 11, 1717.

DEAR PRUE,—I have a letter from Blancorse of the 6th, from Mr Sandy. You might have made use of the same conveyance. I cannot, nor will I, bear such apparent neglect of me ; and therefore, if you do not write yourself, except you are not well, I will not write to you any more, than by telling your secretary " I am well," &c.—Yours,

RICH. STEELE.

LETTER CCCXXV. *To Lady Steele.*

May 14, 1717.·

DEAR PRUE,—I have your kind letter of May 7, which was a great pleasure to me. I begin to think I shall have my limbs very soon again, for I am in an unusual freedom in my faculties. If you have business to do in the country, do it, for things here are not yet in so good a way as I hope they will be soon. You must not put me off with excuses for want of paper, since I send you every post a sheet to answer with, enclosed with that I write to you.—I am, dear Prue, ever yours, RICH. STEELE.

LETTER CCCXXVI.   *To Lady Steele.*

May 18, 1717.

DEAR PRUE,—I was mightily pleased with a letter under your hand, for the length of which I thank you. I do not insist upon long epistles ; but to have a line is absolutely necessary to keep up our spirits to each other. I am obliged to you for your inclination towards the girls, and the thought of taking up the mortgage. You bid me write no cross stuff. I ask no unreasonable things to keep me in good humour. I cannot imagine what you and your cousin can have disagreed so much about ; but she is my relation, as she is yours. I am wonderfully recovered to what I was. Eugene, Betty, and Molly are in perfect health.—Ever yours,

RICH. STEELE.

Mrs Clark has just now been here. She pleads poverty ; and I have promised her, as soon as I get money, to pay her the interest which was due on the L.50 which you have paid off.

LETTER CCCXXVII.   *To Lady Steele.*

May 22, 1717.

DEAR PRUE,—Your son is now with me, very merry in rags, which condition I am going to better, for he shall have new things immediately. He is extremely pretty, and has his face sweetened with something of the Venus his mother, which is no small delight to the Vulcan [his father.]— Ever yours,   RICH. STEELE.

LETTER CCCXXVIII.   *To Lady Steele.*

May 22, 1717.

DEAR PRUE,—I have yours of the 18th, and am always pleased when I see anything under your fair hand ; but, by the way, I expect the sheet of paper I send to you to be sent up to me in the next letter, and not such scandalous half-sheets. The report of exempting me from pay is false ; for five hundred pounds, " for the time the commission was in Scotland," is already ordered me, which I daily expect to receive. As for your staying all the winter, I long to see you, and we will never part again till death separate us. Benson is so busy with great men that Gillmore's affair * is retarded by it. I will say nothing about my coming down till I see further about the duration of this session of Parliament.—I am ever yours,

RICH. STEELE.

Lest you should not read well the interlineation, I say the L.500 ordered me is for the time the commission was in Scotland.

---

* This alludes to his own Fish-pool invention, of which notice will be taken on a future occasion, and in the construction of which the person referred to was engaged.

LETTER CCCXXIX.   *To Lady Steele.*

[*Undated.*]

DEAR PRUE,—If you knew how glad I am to see a long letter from you, I daresay, as fantastically shy as you are of doing anything that should make your husband think you love him, you would oftener afford me that pleasure. When Jonathan answers my letters, I shall know what to do ; but if I thought quite so ill of him as the rest of his relations do, I should wholly decline the thought of serving him. I never had any thought of making an expense at Carmarthen but on a fairer prospect than I ever yet saw.

I have had abundance of reflection since we parted ; and in the future part of my life you will find me a very reserved man, and clear of all hangers-on. I find by all the care and industry which a man uses for others, if they are beholden to your pocket, they are only ashamed they were obliged to you, and leave your interest. I shall, therefore, hereafter make my expense upon my own way of living, and my own household and little family. Though my wife gives herself whimsical airs of saying, " If she is unworthy, yet the children,"—I say, though you talk of the children, if I will not mind you, I tell you they are dear to me, more that they are yours than that they are mine. For which I know no reason, but that I am, in spite of your ladyship's coyness and particularities, utterly yours,

RICH. STEELE.

LETTER CCCXXX.   *To Lady Steele.*

May 27, 1717.

DEAR PRUE,—To shew you how little I deserve, or understand what you mean by Mrs Bevans's insolence or Mr Philips's wrongs to you, I make no answer to such unreasonable intimations, as if they were supported by me. I assure you my head is too full at present to enter into what it is impossible for me, at this distance, to apprehend. I wish I could make you easy, I am sure I would do it ; for I have no tranquillity when I think you are under any discomposure.—I am ever yours,   RICH. STEELE.

LETTER CCCXXXI.   *To Lady Steele.*

May 30, 1717.

DEAR PRUE,—I have yours, wherein you rally about Venus and Vulcan.* I do not doubt but I shall see you as fine a lady as ever you were ;

---

* See Letter CCCXXVII., p. 121.

I am sure I shall think you so : but complacency and a little regard to a poor decrepit creature, ungratefully and barbarously used, I should think you owe me as a Whig, if not as a wife. This day there comes on in the House of Commons a debate,* whether the Earl of Oxford should be tried, and when.—I am, dear Prue, ever yours,   RICH. STEELE.

LETTER CCCXXXII.   *To Lady Steele.*
                                        June 11, 1717.

DEAR PRUE,—I have yours of the 5th instant, for which I heartily thank you. Your expedient of nurse Jervase is a very rough medicine ; but your own kind letters are a safe and pleasant cure against such evils as you, in raillery, seem to apprehend. I write this from Richmond, where I have been since yesterday morning at a lodging near Wilks, who, I believe, will bring matters to bear so as that there will be no playhouse but ours, allowing Rich, who is almost broke, a salary while there is but one house. I am in hopes, one way or other, let the courtiers do as unthankfully as they please, I shall pick up a comfortable fortune. When I said I would do towards you as to all mankind, you were to understand that if I am hard upon no part of mankind, I shall not be so towards the nearest relation in nature, a good wife. Do not talk of love taking leave of an object ; I tell you I love you to dotage. Gillmore is here with me ; I took him to talk over our affairs, which I doubt not will succeed.† I am going to London, whence you shall hear how the family does.

              June 11, *St James's Street, half hour after nine.*
I am just returned hither, where I find all things in good order, and your children in perfect health.—Your most obedient and obsequious husband,   RICH. STEELE.

LETTER CCCXXXIII.   *To Lady Steele.*
                                        June 15, 1717.

DEAR PRUE,—I am heartily glad my letter, which you received on Whitsuntide, was so agreeable to you. It is indeed in our power to make each other as happy as mortals are capable of being. I have, in pursuance of the resolution I told you of, parted with my new man, and have now only Willmot. If you think Sam would recover here, it is well to send

---

* " See an account of it in ' Political State,' vol. xiii. p. 724."
† " Mr Gillmore's place of abode was at Nettleton, in Wiltshire."

him ; but I cannot tell when I can leave the town, because the trial of my Lord Oxford will prolong the session : the managers for that purpose were named yesterday.   I have been a little intemperate and discomposed with it ; but I will be very sober for the future, especially for the sake of the most amiable and most deserving woman, who has made me her happy slave and most obedient husband,   RICH. STEELE.

LETTER CCCXXXIV.   *To Lady Steele.*

June 20, 1717.

DEAR PRUE,—I have yours of the 14th, and am infinitely obliged to you for the length of it.   I do not know another whom I could commend for that circumstance ; but where we entirely love, the continuance of anything they do to please us is a pleasure.   As for your relations, once for all, pray take it for granted, that my regard and conduct towards all and singular of them shall be as you direct.

I hope, by the grace of God, to continue what you wish me, every way, an honest man.   My wife and my children are the objects that have wholly taken up my heart ; and as I am not invited or encouraged in anything which regards the public, I am easy under that neglect or envy of my past actions, and cheerfully contract that diffusive spirit within the interests of my own family.   You are the head of us ; and I stoop to a female reign, as being naturally made the slave of beauty.   But to prepare for our manner of living when we are again together, give me leave to say, while I am here at leisure, and come to lie at Chelsea, what I think may contribute to our better way of living.   I very much approve Mrs Evans and her husband ; and if you take my advice, I would have them have a being in our house, and Mrs Clark the care and inspection of the nursery.   I would have you entirely at leisure, to pass your time with me in diversions, in books, in entertainments, and no manner of business intrude upon us but at stated times.   For, though your are made to be the delight of my eyes, and food of all my senses and faculties, yet a turn of care and house- wifery, and I know not what prepossession against conversation-pleasures, robs me of the witty and the handsome woman to a degree not to be expressed.   I will work my brains and fingers to procure us plenty of all things, and demand nothing of you but to take delight in agreeable dresses, cheerful discourses, and gay sights attended by me.   This may be done by putting the kitchen and the nursery in the hands I propose ; and I shall have nothing to do but to pass as much time at home as I possibly can, in the best company in the world.   We cannot tell here what to think of the trial of my Lord Oxford ; if the Ministry are in earnest in that, and I should see it will be extended to a length of time, I will leave them to themselves, and wait upon you. Miss Moll grows a mighty beauty, and she shall be very prettily dressed, as likewise shall Betty and Eugene ; and if I throw away a little money in adorning my brats, I hope you will forgive me : they are, I thank God, all very well ; and the charming form of their mother has tempered the likeness they bear to their rough sire, who is, with the greatest fondness, your most obliged and most obedient husband,   RICH. STEELE.

CHAPTER XVI

THESE letters of Steele, from which we gather all that is to be known of the daily life of the writer at this period, are certainly unique among the correspondence of literary men. They are of the most unpremeditated character, evidently written without the most remote thought to publication, most of them being in fact mere hastily-penned memoranda of the most familiar incidents of domestic life, of the most private thoughts, confessions, and hopes of the writer. Never man before, perhaps, was subjected to such a test, in having, as it were, his very breast laid bare ; yet those who cherish the memory of Steele with a love and tenderness accorded to few literary men, need feel little shrinking at the result of the unwonted and trying scrutiny. Most literary men have in their correspondence dressed out their thoughts with care, and frequently with scrupulous formality. The letters of Pope, in particular, are full of the most studied affectation of fine sentiment, and a straining after a philosophic turn of thought, and something of the same kind attaches even to the correspondence of Burns. In reading the present letters, the occasion on which they were written must ever be borne in mind. They are the mere familiar prattle of one who communi-

cated the most trivial incident to the partner of his life in
her absence, with a constancy that might have been expected in a lover ; and to the unexampled economy of the
receiver in preserving these documents we owe it that a
chasm is not left in this still period of the life of Steele.
But, though they are devoid of fine sentiments in a literary
sense, they are full of those the source of which is in the
heart, not the head, which are worth whole volumes of
Popish sentimentality.

We find him resenting with spirit, but without temper,
his wife's occasional negligence in not writing personally,
and expressing himself grateful for any communication of
unusual length. The whole correspondence abounds with
expressions of his ardent affection. A single word of kindness from her ; the epithet "good Dick" so transports him
that he says he feels as though he could forget his gout
and walk all the way down to Wales to her. He is never
tired of praising her amiability. He tells her at one time
that he sometimes recalls little trifling differences between
them with tears in his eyes. As Mr Thackeray has said
that he paid, in one of his *Tatlers*, the finest compliment
ever offered to a lady when he said that to love her was a
liberal education, so in one of these letters he pays perhaps
the finest compliment ever offered to a wife when, in reply
to what he calls one of her "whimsical airs," as if she
thought he had no regard for her, he says, in reference to
the children, to whom she had alluded, that they were
dearer to him in consideration that they were hers than of
their being his own. There is indeed something touching
in the tone of the last of the preceding letters, and to find
him laying his domestic plans for the future, in anticipation

of their reunion, in the way that he thought would contribute most to her ease and happiness, and putting, as it were, his house in order, little aware how soon it would be left to him desolate. An obscure remark which he makes in another about her urging him to have done with a "herd of indigent, unthankful people," whatever it means, is an addition to many other proofs that the extravagance which was so injurious to him was not all personal. Only in one single instance throughout this lengthened correspondence does anything occur bearing an unkind construction, and that was when accused of coldness, which he retorts certainly in very plain terms, but without bitterness, and simply as a matter of fact, but which must have been very mortifying, intensified as it was by an expression of thankfulness that his love had survived it. If he gave any ground for such a charge, it certainly has not been preserved with the rest of the correspondence, the whole tenor of which is as directly opposite as possible.

LETTER CCCXXXV.   *To Lady Steele.*

June 21, 1717.

DEAR PRUE,—I have yours of the 17th, and am beholden to you that you will be persuaded to dress when I am with you. As for my share about the brats, Gillmore's affair goes on so happily that I am in no manner of doubt but I shall be able to do amply for them. I like your expression about immortality, and know our happiness in next life will depend very much upon our behaviour to each other in this. We may promote or interrupt each other on the way thither by our conduct; and, as I do not now doubt your part to me, so I hope you will not mine to you. As for my vivacities, they are changed into, changed into, changed into cheerful endeavours for my family. I never can, I own at the same time, be what they call thoroughly frugal; but my expense shall be at home, in a plentiful supply of all things for you and the brats, with regard to pleasures as well as necessaries. Mr Hoadly, the Bishop of Bangor, has, in the sermon * for which he is so ill-treated, done like an apostle, and asserted the true dominion established by our blessed Saviour.—I am, dear Prue, your most affectionate, obliged, obedient husband, RICH. STEELE.

LETTER CCCXXXVI.   *To Lady Steele.*
                                        Chelsea, June 24, 1717.

DEAR PRUE,—I received a letter from you without date. Your first article is about Sam, for whom you have the enclosed advice. There was no danger of my being a manager against Lord Oxford, without I had sought for it, which I was far from doing; so far from that, that I had not the curiosity to be there to-day, which was the first day of his trial. I am at Chelsea with my books, and, by the help of God, will, for the future, avoid all odious offices, except where the safety of my country is immediately concerned. I wish the behaviour of selfish and unskilful people may not put us into the danger which we escaped only by the intervention of Providence. I have been at Chelsea ever since Saturday, and have enjoyed great satisfaction in my solitude. Betty and Molly were with me here yesternight—that is, on Sunday evening; they were very good company, and I treated them with strawberries and cream, and, according to my fond way, ate more than both of them. I do not design to be at the House of Commons during the trial, but pass my time, while it lasts, in what will, I hope, bring in a large sum of money in the winter. I am glad your opinion falls in with mine as to parting with Dymock, &c.—I am dear Prue, ever yours, RICH. STEELE.

LETTER CCCXXXVII.   *To Lady Steele.*
                                        June 27, 1717.

DEAR PRUE,—I am very uneasy upon not hearing from you last post. I have a great deal of merry and agreeable things to say, but the terror of

* "This was the famous sermon on ' the Nature of the Kingdom or Church of Christ,' preached before the King, March 31, 1717, which gave birth to the well-known Bangorian controversy. In the preface to a volume of sermons published in 1754, in which this discourse is preserved, Bishop Hoadly says, ' At whose request it was commanded to be published, I know not; but I know that it was not, either directly or indirectly, from any desire of mine.'—' An Account of all the considerable Pamphlets, &c., with Occasional Observations, by Philanagnostes Clericus,' was published in 1719."

my letters finding you out of order makes me forbear any such unseasonable gaiety. Pray write without fail next post, if you are able. You will best judge of the enclosed.—I am your most humble servant and obedient husband,   RICH. STEELE.

LETTER CCCXXXVIII.   *To Lady Steele.*

July 2, 1717.

DEAR PRUE,—Yours of the 25th of last month is inquisitive whether the affair of Gillmore passes the House this present session of Parliament. We have examined into the necessary method for such an invention. We must, in the first place, have a patent under the Great Seal for fourteen years, which is a thing cannot be denied. When we have this, we are to set forth to the Parliament by petition that we have such a patent ; and hope we shall appear to merit a longer term than the Crown is able to give us, and ask of the legislature power to add to the fourteen years twenty-one more ; so that, on the whole, the profits in the invention will be in our families thirty-five years. We are going to take the patent immediately, which secures at first, and shall bring our petition for the longer time next session. Benson is *at all the charge*—that is, the main expense ; but you need not doubt but I shall, one way or other, be out a hundred pounds before it is perfected. All this while you are to know that we are to have our charges placed in common when the thing comes to bear. It is demonstration that here is a very considerable estate ; but I am come to that, that, be it never so certain, I shall not act upon it in my expenses till I am actually in possession of the growing profits. Excellent reformation ! You shall be obeyed about Mrs Clark and Mrs Keck, and everything else in my power. The children are the most amiable things in the world, and I will keep them very gay and prettily dressed, for I grow a dull family creature. All my public spirit and gallantry is turned into the care of a wayward beauty called a wife, and a parcel of brats called children.

Last night my Lord Oxford was acquitted by the Lords without coming to a trial. The Commons exhibited articles of impeachment against him : when they came to place of trial, the Lords insisted that the articles of treason should be first tried. The Commons insisted on their own method, and would not come to the hall on those terms ; upon which the Lords acquitted their peer. But the Commons immediately went into a debate, to bring in a bill to punish him another way ; which debate is adjourned till to-morrow morning, and it is possible my Lord Oxford's triumph may be short.—Yours ever,   RICH. STEELE.

LETTER CCCXXXIX.   *To Lady Steele.*

July 4, 1717.

DEAR PRUE,—I have yours of the 30th of last month, full of concern and care for me, for which I am infinitely obliged to you. As to my journey, I cannot tell what to say as to the time of setting out; but can by no means think of the stage-coach. I must travel so as to have my hours my own, and halt when I please; for, you must know, I begin to take great care of your husband, as knowing he grows a very good one every way. As to money for our expenses, I assure you I will take care of that, and much approve your scheme as to the Bath, before and after Carmarthen visit.

I believe Madam Evans is not with child, so that you may have hopes of seeing her; but the House of Commons were at a Committee of Elections till twelve o'clock, at the end of which, instead of waiting in the cold for a coach, and other inconveniences in that wearied condition, I bid Willmot get me a bed in Palace Yard. He did get one next to St Margaret's Church, from whence I now write to you. And now, at ten o'clock, the House are coming together, the next morning, about an address to his Majesty.

The Lords have been so careful of that great patriot the Earl of Oxford, as to acquit him, upon a pretence of privilege, which they never exerted before. The Commons have much indignation at this usage; and address the King not to pardon him, that they, the next session, may prosecute him in a Parliamentary way.

But what are these things to us and brats? I am entirely devoted to you and yours.—Your most obedient husband,   RICH. STEELE.

LETTER CCCXL.   *To Lady Steele.*

July 11, 1717.

TEN THOUSAND TIMES MY DEAR, DEAR, PRETTY PRUE,—I have been in very great pain for having omitted writing last post. You know the unhappy gaiety of my temper when I get in, and indeed I went into, company, without having writ before I left my house in the morning, which I will not do any more. It is impossible to guess at all the views of courtiers; but, however, I am of opinion that the Earl of Oxford is not in so triumphant a way as his friends imagine. He is to be prosecuted by way of bill, or Act of Parliament, next session, in order to punish him as he shall appear to deserve; and in the meantime to be excepted out of the act of grace, which comes out next week.

Please to take the advice you give me on this subject, and keep your conversation out of the dispute. Your letter has extremely pleased me with the gaiety of it ; and, you may depend upon it, my ambition is now only turned towards keeping that up in you, and giving you reasons for it in all things about you. Two people who are entirely linked together in interest, in humour, and affection, may make this being very agreeable ; the main thing is to preserve always a disposition to please and be pleased. Now as to your ladyship, when you think fit, to look at you, to hear you, to touch you, gives delight in a greater degree than any other creature can bestow ; and indeed it is not virtue, but good sense and wise choice to be constant to you. You did well not to dwell upon one circumstance in your letter ; for when I am in good health, as I thank God I am at this present writing, it awakes wishes too warmly to be well borne when you are at so great a distance. I do not see any mention of your man Sam ; I hope the doctor's prescription has been useful to him.

Think, dream, and wish for nothing but me, who make you a return in the same affection to you for ever.—Your most obsequious, obedient husband,
RICH. STEELE.

Pray date your letters.

LETTER CCCXLI.   *To Lady Steele.*

St James's Street, July 16, 1717.

DEAR PRUE,—Yours of the 10th instant lies before me. You are very good in thanking me for, what is my duty, being in pain when anything disturbs you. You recommend care of health and money. God will, in His due time, restore me to the former by the use of my limbs, which is all I want of perfect health. As to money, I am grown very fond of it ; but, as you are a good keeper of it, I design your estate shall constantly be laid up after the mortgage is paid off ; and the allowance for you and children shall come from me, over and above what your estate brings. This will enable us to put our children into the world, if God shall please to continue us to see them disposed of. The contest of the Bishop * has ended in the confusion of his adversaries. Dr Edwards is, I suppose, of Bangor's side of the question in the main argument. I cannot tell what to answer you about the Bath ; but when I leave this town, my servants shall have board wages, and I will take a snap anyhow ; for I must keep myself to myself, and have my play † ready this ensuing winter, in order to be quite out of debt.

---

* " Dr Hoadly, Bishop of Bangor."
† "'The Conscious Lovers,' not acted till Nov. 7, 1722."

I approve your reflection, from what you see in others from want of education, to be careful of our brats in that point. They are all well. Moll is as great a charmer as her mother, and will prove as great a sharper. Dear thing, how I love you !   RICH. STEELE.

LETTER CCCXLII.   *To Lady Steele.*

July 24, 1717.

DEAR PRUE,—I have yours of the 20th. I lament the lamentable condition you are in, with relation to the place and other matters, there in described with great wit and spirit. But your letter is an argument against what you say—to wit, that it is impossible to write for a polite part of the world in that neighbourhood. The King is at Hampton Court, and I design next week to go thither, with a petition for a small grant, to make myself easy.

If I succeed, as I am encouraged to expect, our labour for ourselves will be very much shortened, and I have little more to care for than to enjoy the pleasure of being, dear Prue, your most affectionate husband and most obedient, humble servant,   RICH. STEELE.

As I was going to close this, I hear the voice of Mrs Keck talking to Molly ; but she is so great a Prue, that she comes and goes without seeing me, though I am in the house. But I have sent her word I am writing, and she gives her services.

LETTER CCCXLIII.   *To Lady Steele.*

July 26, 1717.

DEAR PRUE,—I have your kind letter, which expresses your fears that I do not take care of myself as to catching cold and the like. I am careful enough when I am awake, but in the night the clothes are kicked on the floor, and I am exposed to the damp till the coolness wakes me. This I feel at present in my arms and legs, but will be carefully tucked up hereafter. I wait with impatience for the receipt of money out of the Treasury to make further payments. I believe, when I have it, I shall wholly turn off my coach-horses ; for, since I am at my study whole days together, it is, I think, a senseless thing for me to pay as if I was padding all that while, and showing myself to the world. I have sent your enclosed to Mrs Keck. She came into the dining-room to me when I sent away my last letter, and we had some tea ; and, instead of such chat as should naturally arise between a great gallant and a fine lady, she took upon her to tell me that I did spend my money upon my children, but that they ought to be better accommodated as to their dress and the like. She is indeed a very good

Prue ; and though I divert myself with her gravity and admonition, I have a sincere respect for her.   I was last night so much enamoured with an author I was reading, and some thoughts which I put together on that occasion, that I was up till morning, which makes me a little restive to-day.   Your daughter Moll has stole away my very heart, but doubt not but her brother and sister will recover their share when we are all together, except their mother robs them all of him who is, dear Prue, entirely yours,

RICH. STEELE.

LETTER CCCXLIV.   *To Lady Steele.*

[*July* 27, 1717.]

MY DEAR WIFE,—I read your kind letter with a great deal of pleasure, and promise myself as much happiness as ever man knew when we meet again.   I hope it will please God to prosper our little affairs in such manner as that we may pass the remainder of our days in tranquillity ; that is a state I have never yet known, but it is very much in your power to contribute towards possessing it for the future.—You mistake when you say I wish to see Wales out of any suspicion ; I assure you I design that journey only out of curiosity to see what, by your favour, will one day be in my posterity, if it shall please God to continue our children to us.   They are now all three in good health, and I hope to tell you before this day se'nnight that I have paid Betty's schooling.   As to the persons you mention in your letter, I shall conduct myself towards them as you shall advise.   I cannot yet answer you as to the L.200 you speak of to be ready three months hence, but shall do all I can.   I place the utmost of the happiness of this life in you, and earnestly exhort you to meet me with the same disposition to be pleasing to me, as I have to manifest myself, in little as well as great occasions, your most affectionate and faithful husband and servant,   RICH. STEELE.

LETTER CCCXLV.   *To Lady Steele.*

July 29, 1717.

DEAR PRUE,—Yours of the 25th is before me.   I am always glad when you write a great deal ; but do not hurt your eyes to scribble longer than is easy to you.   Your kind expression is the most welcome and pleasing thing which could possibly arrive at me.—Mr Glanvill* of the Treasury asked me the

---

* "William Glanvill, Esq., one of the clerks of the Treasury, and receiver of the revenues of the First-fruits office.   He died in the January following, and was buried at Wooton in Surrey, where the following concise epitaph, dictated by himself, preserves his memory :—

other day " how my wonderful girl did ?" There is, it seems, a lady of his acquaintance who visits Betty at school, and cries her up for a greater wit than her father—that is not much—but than her mother either.—I am every day walking about the offices to get our salaries paid, that I might go into the country, particularly the Bath, whence you shall direct me further—that is, command my motions. But, if I find my limbs easy to me, I believe I shall vigorously pursue my journey to the dearest of women to the most affectionate of men.—Poor, dear, angry, pleased, pretty, witty, silly, everything Prue, yours ever,   RICH. STEELE.

LETTER CCCXLVI.   *To Lady Steele.*

[*July* 31, 1717.]

MY DEAR WIFE,—Yours of the 27th came to hand. I am very far from being insincere in my resolves about parting with insignificant people. I am ready to burst with indignation against my own folly, and melt with gratitude for your goodness in bearing so long as you have. I am in purgatory till it is otherwise, and am really in danger of falling into the contrary extreme of being too near and reserved. God Almighty grant we may meet together in such dispositions as to enjoy with our little ones the only true pleasures of religion and virtue.—Yours ever,

RICH. STEELE.

LETTER CCCXLVII.   *To Lady Steele.*

St James's Street, Aug. 3, 1717.

DEAR PRUE,—I have yours, wherein you dissuade me from Wales, and tell me you hear I am ordered for Scotland. Mine of Saturday is on that subject.—I come now from the most disagreeable place in the world, a great man's table, and am unfit for writing, &c., but will be very long on this affair on Thursday.—Your most obsequious husband and most humble servant,   RICH. STEELE.

'(Vicesimo secundo die Januarii,)
Anno salutis reparatæ,
(MDCCXVII.)
Hic sitæ fuerunt reliquiæ,
GULIELMI GLANVILL.
Requiescant donec veniat Redemptor.'

The substance of his charitable will may be seen in Aubrey's ' Survey,' vol. ii. p. 144."

LETTER CCCXLVIII.   *To Lady Steele.*

Aug. 3, 1717.

DEAR PRUE,—I am going to Hampton Court, where the King now is, to solicit some matters relating to our commission. I give a thousand thousand thanks for your very pretty and very kind letter of the 29th of last month. Forgive me that I am in haste, with a steadfast resolution in what you are so kind as to approve with so much affection.—I remain your most affectionate husband and most obedient, humble servant, RICH. STEELE.

LETTER CCCXLIX.   *To Lady Steele.*

Aug. 9, 1717.

MY DEAR WIFE,—Yours of the 4th is full of that natural terror you have upon you by the apprehensions of thunder. There is no talking away such fears. I earnestly recommend you to the protection of God, under that and all other amazement and failing of spirit. I take all the measures I am able to be a comfort to you, as you are a very great one to me; for I indeed, from reason and reflection, as well as tenderness and passion, take you for the best of women. How happy shall we be when we are out of debt, to have nothing to do but to please and exhilarate each other, and educate our children in the love of that God who made us their parents! The poor little things seem (as far as my partiality will let me judge) to have very good endowments. I hope we shall live to see these talents improved.

We have not had any thunder at all in these parts. God preserve you to your family, and, dear Moll, your most affectionate husband and most obedient servant,   RICH. STEELE.

LETTER CCCL.   *To Lady Steele.*

Aug. 17, 1717.

DEAR PRUE,—I am in the utmost concern to find you so very uneasy as you are in the country. I am confident if you had such a fellow as Dymock, whom you might command, it would be better with you, and you might be mistress of your estate as absolutely as you are of, dear Prue, your most obsequious husband and servant,   RICH. STEELE.

LETTER CCCLI.   *To Lady Steele.*

[*Aug.* 24, 1717.]

DEAR PRUE,—I have yours of the 19th. I have done about the mention of Dymock, and believe you are in the right. The other circumstance to

be considered in your letter is about removing. You say I did not tell
you I had resolved it when you left the town. I did not myself know it
then ; but your instructions to me were, Pall Mall, St James's Street, Ger-
ard Street, or a place near a church, which last you will have. I am confident, daily intelligence of what passes at the playhouse will be some
hundreds in my way ; and money is the main thing : get I always could,
but now I will get it and keep it. Your affair is to make and keep yourself cheerful; you shall have nothing to do but to enjoy—it shall be my
part to labour and get.

I have had much struggle by reason of ill payments, and unreasonable,
hasty, severe people ; among the rest that hog, Lady Vandeput. I have
paid her to the end of last quarter, and have given her warning, and can
remove any time between this and quarter-day without paying more than
this quarter.

I shall on Michaelmas-day have L.533 due to me. If I can find means
to have that advanced, I will pay off the coach-horses quite, and have no
charge of equipage of any kind till we are together again in London.

How can you let your spirits sink so as to mind what people say whom
you do not esteem ? Be yourself, and reserve your best self for, dear Prue,
yours ever,   RICH. STEELE.

I go to-morrow to Tunbridge, with Dr Garth, to visit Lady Marlborough
and the Duke ;* so perhaps you may not have a letter by Tuesday's post,
for I fear I shall not return till Wednesday.

LETTER CCCLII.   *To Lady Steele.*
                                            [*Aug.* 28, 1717.]
DEAR PRUE,—I returned last night from Tunbridge, whither my last
told you I was going on Sunday morning, to be back on Wednesday night,
which I did accordingly, and found yours of the 22d and that of the 24th.
Yours, 22d, speaks again of Dymock. I give that matter up, and believe
you in the right. Yours, 24th, concerning Mrs Philips ; I lament the poor
lady's fate, and share in the uneasiness the reflection upon it gives you.
Pray do not give way to fancies about your health, but bear up and expect
good days,—negligent of this world as to its duration, careful as to its un-
certainty. The enclosed letter I send you, to shew you a present difficulty
I labour under, and shall be determined.

---

* " Who had, in the December preceding, been seized with an apoplexy, which,
though by the skill of Dr Garth it was for some time palliated, impaired his
senses, and at length terminated in a total decay and his dissolution. His Grace,
however, had, after the year 1717, some lucid intervals."

When the Commissioners parted, they resolved to meet at Edinburgh on the 10th of the next month. But that I am not able to do, for many reasons. The gentleman who writes the enclosed, Sir Harry Houghton, will be ready to relieve me the middle of November, provided I hasten thither now; if not, I must stay till the latter end of January. The staying in Scotland till then would break all my measures. If I followed my own inclinations, I should go to Wales, though I stayed but two days, and cross the country into the Lancashire road. I got on horseback at Tunbridge, and am confident I can ride thirty miles a day with ease; however, I design to take the method you propose of a chaise. Suppose I should bring Madam Clark down with me, only to attend your journey; it would, I think, be right. Your opinion of these great points, next post, will be very welcome. Your daughter Betty, who is here two or three days for the holidays of Bartholomew-tide, desires to know whether I am writing to you or not; if I am, she desires her duty. Molly cannot endure any kindness I show this visitant, and I am not a little delighted to see a young lady jealous of my favour. If you and I were together, and all our children with us, I should never be a leisure moment out of my own house.

I am resolved, God willing, to have it so; and, for the future, even travel with my whole family. I will get the better of you in this matter; and you must submit to have me fond of you and yours, at what place and in what way I think fit. This is the harshest piece of arbitrary power I will ever be guilty of.—Yours ever,   RICH. STEELE.

LETTER CCCLIII.   *To Lady Steele.*

[*Undated.*]

DEAR PRUE,—I do not know how to give you an account of my present prospects; but can only say that the Commissioners of Scotland demand me there with so much impatience, that go I must. However, it is less painful to me, because Benson is now in town, and will take care, in my absence, of the greatest concern of all, which is now brought to perfection.* If I can value myself upon the half-year's pay already due to me, I shall leave the town without any murmur against me. God send us a happy meeting, and that the rest of our days may be free from debt.—I am, faithfully, affectionately yours,   RICH. STEELE.

LETTER CCCLIV.   *To Lady Steele.*

[*Undated.*]

DEAR PRUE,—The last I received from you, which was last night, had

---

* "The Fishpool."

no date. It is indeed, as you observe, a strange kind of life we lead, and the separation is painful to me for one reason more than it is to you.

If you think fit to go to the Bath, I cannot imagine but a woman of your estate will find friends enough to raise as much money as will carry you thither.

I alter the manner of taking my journey every time I think of it. My present disposition is, to borrow what they call a post-chaise of the Duke of Roxborough. It is drawn by one horse, runs on two wheels, and is led by a servant riding by. This rider and leader is to be Mr Willmot, formerly a carrier, who answers for managing on a road to perfection, by keeping tracks and the like. I think also at present to be off my new house, and let things be as they are till we meet, when you shall choose for yourself a house ; *which I will like because you like it.*

As to your desire of contriving plenty of money, I have made a bargain with our paymaster for so much, whether it is come out of the Treasury, to pay always within ten days of quarter-day from Christmas next, so that we will not want any more. I shall contrive also to have a quarter beforehand, and never let family tick more for victuals, clothes, or rent. I know this is better talk to you than if it were a paper of wit written by your beloved Cowley. But all shall, God willing, be punctually performed by, dear Prue, your most obsequious husband and most humble servant,

RICH. STEELE.

LETTER CCCLV.   *To Lady Steele.*

[Hampton Court, Saturday, Aug. 31, 1717.

DEAR PRUE,—A man of quality, going to town, waits to take this with him, so that I cannot say more till Tuesday.—Yours ever,

RICH. STEELE.

LETTER CCCLVI.   *To Lady Steele.*

Hampton Court, Aug. 31, 1717.

DEAR PRUE,—I wish you would once say you would like a thing because I like it. I know not whether what I have taken is to be called in a court. It is a fore-door, at which a coach can set down at the very threshold, in Hart Street, Covent Garden. I have taken no lease, and can part with it when I please to Mr Wilks,* who designs to buy it of the landlord. As to all other matters, I am contriving for the best. You talk of the cheapest way, &c., to get to town. I beg of you to be easy in such

---

* " Then one of the managers of Drury Lane Theatre."

points; you shall have everything your heart can wish, in the reach of a moderate fortune. Pray be contented with laying up all your estate, which I will enable you to do; for you shall be at no manner of charge on anything in nature, for yourself, children, or servants, and they shall be better provided than any other family in England, for I shall turn my expense and delight all that way. Therefore, in the name of God, have done with talk of money, and do not let me lose the right I have in a woman of wit and beauty, by eternally turning herself into a dun—forgive the comparison. When my heart is fixed to think of you as the object of love, esteem, and friendship, and all that is soft, it is in a moment turned into sorrow and anxiety, to find ways to make you contented about trash and dirt. Pray let it be otherwise; till you do, a thousand good qualities in you are (like a miser's wealth) mine without enjoyment. Your son grows a lusty boy, and is your servant, as is his father most heartily.   RICH. STEELE.

I writ to you a note to-day before, by one going to town, and write again, having occasion to send Willmot on other business.

LETTER CCCLVII.   *To Lady Steele.*

Hampton Court, Sept. 12, 1717.

DEAR PRUE,—Willmot brought me, yesterday, yours of the 2d and 5th instant. The first determines my Scotch journey before I see Wales. I shall take your advice in the manner of it, if I cannot yet do better; but I may possibly join with two or three gentlemen, and hire a coach for ourselves. You may depend upon it, I will take care of myself, now you say you value me.

I had altered my design of removing, for fear you should not like the house, and should have given a sum to be off; but Lady Vandeput has sent me word she has let the house, therefore I must go.

Yours of the 5th imports only that you are gone to Blancorse, bidding me take care of my health, and ending "yours entirely." This last phrase is easy to utter at this distance, but I fear, were we together, I should have you at the same coy tricks. But if I am, by the blessing of God, in as good health and as good plight as at present, when we meet I must banish all these for ever.—For ever yours,   RICH. STEELE.

Since I writ the above, I am to thank you for the receipt of a third letter, dated the 5th, from Blancorse. I have before said that I cannot help going to the house now, for Madam Vandeput has another tenant. But you shall do what you will, stay or leave it, when you have seen it.—Yours,   R. S.

LETTER CCCLVIII.   *To Lady Steele.*

Hampton Court, Sept. 14, 1717.

DEAR PRUE,—You hear from me so often from this place that I fear you think I am become, what you mortally hate, a courtier.   But, being obliged to defer my journey for some days, I have taken it into my head to spend that little wit and humour which they say I have, rather in the company of the greatest persons in the world, (who, if they do me no other good, are cheaper conversation,) than with such from whom I can neither reap experience nor any other valuable thing, and by whom I daily impoverish myself.   Madam Vandeput has thoroughly nettled me ; but, as she is of the fair sex, I shall not make answer to her usage in word or deed, but go to town on Monday, and move from her house that week, and towards Scotland the week after, so as to be at Edinburgh the beginning of October. Sir Harry Houghton has again writ me word he will relieve me when I let him know my business requires my return to London.—Yours ever,

RICH. STEELE.

LETTER CCCLIX.   *To Lady Steele.*

Sept. 18, 1717.

DEAR PRUE,—Yours of the 15th of September tells me you have got the amusement of the gout.   We must, in all cases, look upon everything in the most hopeful light, and not put the worst upon accidents.   If women are instigated . . . . as men when they are gouty, we shall have odd time of it ; and you will, in your heart at least, be tractable to me.   We shall be rich, and we must take the distemper peculiar to that circumstance in good part.   You see I obey your orders, and do not write peevishly; though I cannot but be out of humour at losing so delicious a morsel as your ladyship by frequent incapacities, as you will be in if this disease should frequently visit you.   Gillmore's project* is certain to succeed, and I bear the present, from the prospect of the future, with an equal mind.— I am, madam, your ladyship's most obliged husband and most obedient, humble servant,   RICH. STEELE.

LETTER CCCLX.   *To Lady Steele.*

Sept. 20, 1717.

MY DEAR PRUE,—I have yours of the 16th, and am heartily troubled that we share in a new calamity—to wit, having the same distemper.†   Pray take care of yourself, and you will find that we shall be in great plenty

---

* See letter of June 11th.   † " The gout "—see preceding letter.

before another year turns round. My dear wife, preserve yourself for him that sincerely loves you, and to be an example to your little ones of religion and virtue. If it please God to bless us together with life and health, we will live a life of piety and cheerful virtue. Your daughter Bess gives her duty to you, and says she will be your comfort, but she is very sorry you are afflicted with the gout. The brats, my girls, stand on each side the table, and Molly says that what I am writing now is about her new coat. Bess is with me till she has new clothes. Miss Moll has taken upon her to hold the sand-box, and is so impertinent in her office, that I cannot write more. But you are to take this letter as from your three best friends,

BESS, MOLL, AND THEIR FATHER.

Eugene was very well this morning.

Moll bids me tell you that she fell down just now, and did not hurt herself.

Betty and Moll give their service to Sam and Myrtle.

LETTER CCCLXI.   *To Lady Steele.*

Sept. 24, 1717.

DEAR PRUE,—I am still in the house at St James's Street, but shall leave it on Thursday, if I can despatch the business I expect to do to-morrow. I do hereby promise you never, directly or indirectly, to have anything to do with the Court ; for I am convinced there is nothing to be done with those poor creatures called great men, but by an idolatry towards them which it is below the spirit of an honest, free, or religious man to pay.

This, I hope, you will take for good news, for it brings my thoughts and cares into a narrower compass, and is what you have been ever persuading me to. My own studies at the theatre, Gillmore, &c., will amply do anything I can form to myself, without stooping to servilities. I have some reason to expect that the Royal Family itself would be glad to favour me, but there are many obstacles between poor me and them.

Now, if I have health, which, by the blessing of God, increases to a comfortable degree, this resolution of throwing away all pretensions from the Court may, perhaps, fortify me to be the more useful to my king and country in Parliament, and everywhere else. The children, God be thanked, are all well. Now let me answer to what you say, that I have not expressed anything about a desire of our meeting again. There is nothing upon earth I wish so much, provided always that you will be what you ought to be to me, . . . and that you will have the children in the house with us, for I am come to take great delight in them. When I return from Scotland, we will never part more.—I am, with the sincerest affection, your obsequious husband and obedient servant,   RICH. STEELE.

LETTER CCCLXII.   *To Lady Steele.*

[*Sept.* 28, 1717.]

DEAR PRUE,—I have your agreeable letter of the 23d instant ; the first time you ever so much as alluded to anything that way. My dear wife, let us strive to improve and recommend our persons to each other. As for the L.100 a quarter, I have secured it, during this commission, from Christmas next ; for I have agreed with a paymaster to let me have my salary ten days after the quarter shall become due ; and have provided that this will be having a quarter beforehand, for I shall be supported in Scotland by what is already due, and not what is growing due. When we once come to endeavour to please each other, we shall succeed, and be always in good humour. The brats are all well ; and I am ever truly thine,

RICH. STEELE.

LETTER CCCLXIII.   *To Lady Steele.*

Sept. 30, 1717.

DEAR PRUE,—I am sorry you have spent your time so as that you are at a loss for credit enough to bring you from a place you dislike. I have told you that I cannot pay a quarter beforehand till Christmas ; but from that instant, I think we shall be in as much plenty as any family in England. Gillmore* is an inestimable jewel ; he is now with his family at Nettleton, within eight miles of the Bath, but has this post sent me a letter, in which I find certain proof of the most useful work in the world.

The commission in Scotland stands still for want of me at Edinburgh. It is necessary there should be four there, and there are now but two ; three others halt on the road, and will not go forward till I have passed by York.

I have, therefore, taken places in the York coach for Monday next. I shall, I hope, be able to send you word, the post before I leave the town, that all things are left in a comfortable way.—I am, dear Prue, your most obsequious husband and most humble servant,   R. STEELE.

LETTER CCCLXIV.   *To Lady Steele.*

St James's Street, Oct. 3, 1717.

DEAR PRUE,—I have yours. As to the incivilities and the like, I wish I had known they were so great a degree sooner, I would have come and persuaded you to remove where you might have been mistress ; and it is a jest, for one who has of their own, to be uneasy for want of changing place.

---

* See p. 141 and note.

I fear I shall be detained here a day or two longer than I intended, for want of money; but in all things I will go as near as I can to your demands. I shall not have L.100 to lay down till Christmas.—Yours,

RICH. STEELE.

LETTER CCCLXV.   *To Lady Steele.*

[*Oct.* 5, 1717.]

DEAR PRUE,—Yours of the 30th of September now lies before me.   I have already told you that I cannot pay down L.100 beforehand, for your house and the like, till the 25th of December; from after which I have agreed to be paid punctually my salary as soon as due—that is, within ten days after it is due.   I take you at your word, to pocket none of it, but let it go to family uses; but you shall, if you please, leave the house-rent out of it, for I will spend on my children more than what is barely necessary. You are a coquette in the expression of " setting aside the agreeableness of my person,"—you well know no woman has a better.   I wish you would resolve to keep a discreet, orderly woman, to take care of your children ; and why may not Mrs Evans do for your business of providing the table and the like ?

I will not go in the chaise ; but will, according to your ladyship's advice, go in the stage-coach.   I observe that you are pleased that I do not move till you come to town : I am very glad it is agreeable to you.   I am very much troubled at your postscript ; but what has a woman of your spirit and fortune to do but to live in a house or lodgings where she is mistress ? But I cannot, at this distance, understand your reasons ; when we meet, I hope these kind of ails will be at an end for ever.

As to money, I have at this hour L.843 due to me, and find it a very hard matter at any rate to supply myself with cash to leave the town, paying the coach, the house bills, new clothing the children, and the like.   It is known by those to whom I apply that I want it, and I shall pay enough for it.   But nothing is dearer than asking a courtier anything.   There is no doubt of Gillmore's* affair being a considerable fortune, and the theatre seems to be in a very prosperous way.—I am, dear Prue, ever yours,

R. STEELE.

---

* " See note on Letter CCCXXVIII., p. 121, and Letter CCCXXXII., p. 123. The author of ' The Ode-maker,' a banter on Dean Smedley, printed in the ' Supplement to Swift,' thus glances contemptuously, though impotently, at Steele :—

" ' Or, lest thy chiming vein should cool,
What if thy friend Sir Richard's Pool
Thou didst describe, in lines and feet,
For that queer nick-nack, pat and meet;

LETTER CCCLXVI.   *To Lady Steele.*

Oct. 8, 1717.

DEAR PRUE,—I have been bustling about the town all day, and am come home when the post last rings.

Despise those who use you ill, and value those who love you, and you will make happy yourself and most humble servant, your fond husband,

RICH. STEELE.

LETTER CCCLXVII.   *To Lady Steele.*

[*Undated.*]

DEAR WIFE,—You cannot imagine the rage yours put me into. How can you believe I can bear the treatment you tell me you receive, as being affronted and called fool to your face by rude blockheads? I could not outlive such an injury done you, were I present at it; nor know I how to suffer it as it is, with all the excuses which I make to keep myself in countenance from their stupidity and brutality. If I had patience, I should debate with you on this subject, and ask how it is possible a woman of your sense could possibly fall into a dispute with such idiots and savages? But my heart is too much raised to chastise them, to enter into such cool expostulations with you.

Take it for granted, it is impossible to be easy but with mere correspondents and kind servants. You never will be with relations, who are often apt to think your being in the world an injury. For the remainder of our days, let us have an entire confidence in each other, with a mutual complacency and desire to please each other; and I shall be a protection to you, and you a comfort to me against all that can happen from without.

Mrs Evans is not to be expected down; and when I proposed to Mrs Clark what you bid me, she did not receive it as she ought, I thought; but made scruples, and seemed to be forming a merit in case she should comply, which shewed that she would have shynesses and airs that would have made you constantly uneasy. Pluck up a resolute calm spirit, and do not doubt but there are people enough to be had fit for your purpose, without courting any of your present acquaintance. I will consult Mrs Keck on this subject of a maid fit for you, and proper to go down to you, of which you shall have an account next post. You bid me take care of

Inform the town, this freak being over,
He would proceed, and soon discover
An art long doom'd to deep despair,
And build a castle in the air."

my health ; pray do you preserve yourself to your little ones, who are perfectly well, and your husband, who cannot be well except you are so.

I love you with all my soul, poor dear Prue, and am, for ever yours,

RICH. STEELE.

LETTER CCCLXVIII.   *To Lady Steele.*
[*Undated.**]

DEAR PRUE,—Yours lies before me, I mean that of the 14th.   I will add
two horses to your equipage.   I did not think of a strange woman, but
because you named no one of your acquaintance ; I like Madam Clark as
well as anybody, and am glad she will go, for your children heartily want
you.   I am glad you resolve to live well on the road.   As to the coldness,
on this subject I answer very sincerely, that your ladyship's coldness to me
as a woman and a wife has made me think it necessary to suppress the
expression of my heart towards you, because it could not end in the pleasures and enjoyments I ought to expect from it, and which you obliged
me to wean myself from, till I had so much money, &c., and I know not
what impertinence.   God be thanked, this whimsey has not been fatal to
our love !—It is impossible to decline going to Scotland, for ten thousand
reasons, as well as regard to honour and interest.—I am, dear Prue, ever
yours,   RICH. STEELE.

I was going to close my letter, when Betty and Moll desire their duty
to you.

LETTER CCCLXIX.   *To Lady Steele.*
St James's Street, Oct. 9, 1717.

DEAR PRUE,—Yours of October the 3d and 5th lie before me ; most part
of them are about things and persons that I can only neglect, &c.   Your
journey is a matter of consequence, and in this posture I will leave it.   I
will send you down a direction † to be sent to London with a proper direction ; and that order shall command a coach and six horses, with a discreet
woman in it, to bring you to town.   This woman shall wait upon Mrs
Keck, and have her approbation, and the whole settled with her, which is
the readiest way I can think of to follow your commands and inclinations.
—I am, Madam, your most affectionate husband, and, Prue, your faithful
servant,   RICH. STEELE.

---

* This being, as stated, in reply to one of the 14th, (probably Oct.,) should be
of the date of 19th probably.

† " So the original."

LETTER CCCLXX. *To Lady Steele.*

Oct. 15, 1717.

DEAR PRUE,—Yours of the 10th, concerning the mortgagee's refusal of his money is very surprising. All that you have to do, is to take notice of the time when he refused it, and you will from thence be liable to pay no further interest. I am giving extravagantly for money ; but my resolution is to be rid of blood-suckers, though I lose a good deal at their last draft from, dear Prue, your most affectionate husband and most humble servant,   RICH. STEELE.

LETTER CCCLXXI. *To Lady Steele.*

Oct. 17, 1717.

DEAR PRUE,—I have yours of the 12th, and have enclosed a letter to Mr Thomas. I could not write to him directly, because I did not know where his Trejendeg stands. You had best not destroy the mortgage, because it may be of use to have it in being, in defence against any other securities, till we are both wholly out of debt. But, if he insists to have it destroyed, do not delay it, but comply with him, for I shall be a clear man before New-Year's day. But, besides such considerations, while it is undestroyed, it may, by Mr Thomas's assignment of it, at any time be so much well secured for the girls. Your lesson, therefore, is, take up the mortgage, but do not tear the instrument ; but rather than not take it up, tear the instrument.—Your most obsequious husband, and most humble servant,
                                                   RICH. STEELE.

LETTER CCCLXXII. *To Lady Steele.*

Oct. 20, 1717.

DEAR PRUE,—After many resolutions and irresolutions concerning my way of going, I go, God willing, to-morrow morning by the Wakefield coach, on my way to York and Edinburgh. God of His infinite mercy preserve you, and grant us an happy meeting !

I am in too great a hurry, for I go on a sudden, but the next stage shall bring you a long letter from your most affectionate husband, and most faithful humble servant,   RICH. STEELE.

LETTER CCCLXXIII. *To Lady Steele.*

Stamford, Oct. 23, 1717.

DEAR PRUE,—I am got thus far ; and my journey, I think, does me as much good for the gout, as rocking the same way did you for the spleen.

I have ever proposed to myself to move in as useful a sphere to mankind as I was able, and have this journey taken with me Mr Majon, a French minister, (whom you have seen,) in order to speak French readily at my return ; for I find one cannot understand what passes without that language.   He lies in the same room with me on the road ; and the loquacity which is usual at his age, and inseparable from his nation, at once contributes to my purpose, and makes him very agreeable.   It is my business, while I am absent from you, to fill my leisure hours with as much innocent amusement as I can.   The children are almost always in my head at the same time with yourself ; and I hope we shall, when God blesses us in a meeting, contrive to make them a pleasure as a care.   I take very great care of myself, in hopes of that happy hour, and am, your most affectionate, obsequious husband,   RICH. STEELE.

LETTER CCCLXXIV.   *To Lady Steele.*
                                   Edinburgh, Nov. 5, 1717.

DEAR PRUE,—Five letters from you followed me to this place, which I received all at once this day.   One of the 21st approves my letter to Mr John Thomas, and desires you may do what you shall think fit by fine by way of reserving a respect from your children, and doing what you think fit with your estate* in favour of such of your children as shall please you most.   This is what I have often advised you to do, and shall never gainsay.

Another letter is without date, and has in it an enclosed note from your cousin Alexander.   What is required there shall come to you by the post of Thursday next from this place.   A third scrip, without date, says my " letters are short, and so shall yours," and concludes.   Your fourth is in a very pleasant humour, which you say you can support, provided you do not want money, and you have bespoke gossips for your next child, &c. This is as it should be ; keep up this spirit, and live and reign ; you shall want nothing on my part towards it.

That which I think must have been the last you writ is of the 28th, and speaks of an assurance or obligation that concerns my aunt Scurlock. The post here comes in and out the same day ; and I have many other letters to write, so must take till Thursday also for that.—I am, dear Prue, ever yours,   RICH. STEELE.

I shall return to London the beginning of next week, and I know the Parliament will separate some days after they meet, which time I would take to come with a coach and six horses for you, accompanied by Mrs Pugh.   If you like this, I think it would close your negotiations with a good air, and drown all impertinences about us.

---

* It descended to her eldest daughter, afterwards Lady Trevor.

LETTER CCCLXXV.   *To Lady Steele.*

Elton, in Scotland, Nov. 11, 1717.

DEAR PRUE,—Yours of October 31 came to my hand between six and seven the second morning, I should say Monday the third morning, going into the coach on my return to London. I hope, God willing, to be at London Saturday come se'nnight. I will pay off the news when I come to town, and forbid it. I desire you would answer as to my proposal of coming down for you in a coach and six with Mrs Clark, which, I think, will pin up your affairs with a good grace, and shew your power over your most obedient husband,   RICH. STEELE.

LETTER CCCLXXVI.   *To Lady Steele.*

Pearce Bridge, in the County of Durham,
Friday, Nov. 15, 1717.

DEAR PRUE,—I am now at my inn in perfect good health, with my limbs much better than usual, after seven days' journey from Edinburgh towards London. You cannot imagine the civilities and honours I had done me there, and never lay better, ate or drank better, or conversed with men of better sense than there. I grow very fond of waiting upon you, and bringing you from Wales, when the house is adjourned for a few days ; and since you hear travelling agrees with me, I hope to receive your permission to attend you. It will be a ridiculous thing for me to go down thither without you, and, when you are there, never come near the place, and I am firmly resolved to see your territories the first leisure days from Parliament. Therefore you must consider whether you will let me bring you, or come alone, and go backward and forward with me again this winter ; for, as for seasons and bad roads, I despise those considerations when I have a view for the good of my family or country.—Yours ever,

RICH. STEELE.

We shall, God willing, be at York on Friday, and London the Saturday following.

LETTER CCCLXXVII.   *To Lady Steele.*

Wednesday Night, Dec. 4, 1717.

DEAR PRUE,—Yours of Sunday was very late notice of your arrival. Willmot went to meet you that very day ; but lest you should escape him, I send Mr Evans to meet you on the day you hope to come. I write this after being in the House of Commons from one at noon to twelve at night, where King George begins to have true and real honest power.

You come in smiles, and I will sacrifice all to your good humour.—Obediently yours,   RICH. STEELE.

I am glad to find journeying agrees with you as well as me.   I hope we shall never part more.

Thursday morn.

I went to bed last night after taking only a little broth, and all the day before a little tea and bread and butter, with two glasses of rum and a piece of bread at the House of Commons.

Temperance and your company, as agreeable as you can make it, will make life tolerable, if not easy, even with the gout.   God give us a happy meeting.—Yours faithfully, tenderly, &c.,   RICH. STEELE.

CHAPTER XVII.

THE event so long discussed at length occurred—Lady
Steele returned to town from Wales—and we may reason-
ably hope that the joyful meeting, which Sir Richard
prayed for, was, notwithstanding one little recent passage
of arms between them, fully realised. Of the fact, however, we have no account, as the foregoing letters close
the correspondence with his wife, not only for the year
1717, but, with one solitary exception, finally.* From the

---

* As there will occur no opportunity of introducing in the text this final
memorial of their epistolary intercourse, it is here given as a note :—

Monday morn., June 23, 1718.

DEAR PRUE,—I send this messenger to inform you I shall not be with you till
eight o'clock to-morrow morning. At that hour, God willing, I shall reach
Hampton Court, and hasten (as soon as I have taken up you and the rest of my

same cause we are left in the dark as to the mode in which the journey was performed, whether by the stage-coach or the coach and six, with which it was proposed to astonish the natives of the principality. One thing is certain, that Steele himself did not go down to see his wife's estate, as he had proposed, nor did he succeed in carrying out that intention till he sought it as a retirement in broken health and fortune. It may seem amusing to us at this time of day, with the locomotive privileges we enjoy, to find so much made of this journey. But in those days, what between bad roads and the other appliances of travelling, we must presume equally primitive, it was rather a formidable affair. We find Steele replying to his wife's letters at an interval of five days; and though we might be disposed to attribute part of this to delay in writing, yet, besides that this inference is negatived by Steele's remarkable punctuality in that respect, this is the exact time recorded by Swift as having been occupied in his journey between Chester and London.

Before entering on the events of the year 1718, to which we are now arrived, it will be necessary to advert to those of the close of the year preceding, to which only a very general reference has been made by Steele in his letters. We cannot tell exactly the length of his stay in Edinburgh, as the date of his first letter from thence was probably some little time after his arrival, though he does not state, but we may infer, that his business arrangements, which

dear cargo) to London, where it is necessary I should be in the forenoon.—I am, dear Prue, your most affectionate, most obedient, husband and servant,

RICH. STEELE.

I was so pleased with my son from his lodging to Hampton that I shall, please God, take him with me to Scotland.

had been so long pending, might interfere with his writing
immediately. He started from town on the 21st October,
reached Stamford on the 23d, and his letter from Edin.-
burgh is dated the 5th November. However, his visit to
Scotland could not have exceeded about ten days, but into
that space he appears to have crowded a considerable
amount of incident. Though the nature of his errand
might naturally have tended to his prejudice in the
popular mind, yet the chronicles of the times record that
he was received by the higher classes with every mark of
distinction, and this is confirmed by the statement of his
letter of the 15th November, where he tells his wife she
cannot imagine the civilities and honours done him. This
led him to consider whether he might not turn this regard
to what he considered good account, by opening up the
question of perfecting the union, by extending it to a
uniformity of ecclesiastical policy north and south of the
Tweed. Not deterred from so hopeless an undertaking by
previous failures, or feeling, like Fitz-James, the danger of
the enterprise a sufficient incentive, he held communica-
tions with some of the Presbyters by way of feeling the
pulse of the ministers on the subject. Among those with
whom he conversed with that view, was a Mr Hart, whom
Sir Richard, from the reputation he had of preaching the
terrors of the law, called *the hangman of the gospel.* Notwithstanding this professional austerity of behaviour, he
was in private a very good-natured and facetious man, so
that Steele contracted a friendship for him, which he
afterwards maintained by occasional correspondence.
The project, however, in which it originated, as may be
imagined, never came to anything. In order to get an

insight into the peculiar genius of the people, and to study their character and humour where they were to be found unrestrained by conventionalities, Steele, during this visit to the Scottish metropolis, made a great feast, and, when the preparations were completed, directed his servants to gather all the poor they could find in the streets and lanes, and invite them to the entertainment. In this way Steele soon found himself surrounded by two or three score of poor and decayed people, at whose head he presided as host. After partaking of substantial fare to their satisfaction, they were supplied with punch and other beverages, under the influence of which care was soon banished, and they gave a loose to their native humours and unrestrained gaiety of heart, which, as their entertainer anticipated, produced a fund of drollery, mirth, and broad, but not the less genuine, humour. The mirth, hilarity, and ludicrous incidents of the novel scene were no doubt highly enjoyed by the entertainer, whose satisfaction in beholding so many happy human faces of his making, may be well conceived ; and he afterwards stated that, in addition to the pleasure of filling so many empty stomachs, he had been furnished with materials enough for a good comedy.*

Probably this humorous frolic may have contributed to keep Steele in popular remembrance in Scotland, as we find an anecdote which has descended in reference to the period of this visit recorded by Scott.† On a hill near Hoddom Castle, a structure dating back to the middle of the fifteenth century, and picturesquely situated on the

---

* Cibber's Lives of the Poets, vol. iv. p. 118.   † Border Minstrelsy.

river Annan, is a square building known as the *Tower of Repentance*, from a device of a serpent and a dove with that word inscribed upon it. This tower is said to have been built by a certain Lord Herries, who, like the Rhine barons, followed the " carrying" trade, and had perpetrated deeds of cruelty and blood, as a monument of his remorse. It may have been passed by Sir Richard on his road either going or returning in his journey, as his limited stay in Scotland, as well as the season of the year, and the business nature of his visit, forbid the supposition that he could have indulged his curiosity to any extent beyond the vicinity of Edinburgh in pursuit of the picturesque. The story relates that as Sir Richard rode in this neighbourhood he passed a shepherd lad reading his Bible, and inquired of him what he learned from it, to which the boy replied, " The way to heaven." " An' can you shew it to me ?" returned Sir Richard in banter. " You must go by that tower," said the shepherd lad, as he pointed to the hill and informed his querist of the name of the structure upon it.

The year 1718 was as full of incident in reference to Steele as the preceding year or two had been barren, and the only difficulty is so to dispose them as to display them in their proper lights, and without the effect of crowding. We have seen from various allusions in his correspondence the slow progress in bringing to completion his invention called the Fishpool. The aim of this project was to bring fish alive from any part of the kingdom, but with special reference to salmon from the coast of Ireland to the London market, where it then sold at the enormous price of five shillings the pound. No wonder that he should have buoyed himself up with the prospect of a handsome fortune.

A mathematician of good repute, a Mr Gilmore, to whom he had confided the construction of the machine, reported favourably, and he had obtained a patent bearing date the 10th of June this year. He at the same time published " An Account of the Fishpool," &c., which he dedicated to Sir John Ward, Lord Mayor of London. But though the project was perfectly good in theory, it failed from causes which only experience could have suggested ; for, notwithstanding an ingenious provision for supplying a constant stream of water and air in crossing the sea, yet the result proved that, in the passage, the efforts of the fish to escape from their confinement caused them to bruise themselves so much against the sides of the " pool" as seriously to deteriorate their value in the market, to such an extent, indeed, as wholly to neutralise the utility of the invention. This, however, was not discovered for some considerable time subsequently. Thus, by an accident which no human foresight could have foreseen, fell to the ground a project on which had been expended much ingenuity and considerable sums of money, and which involved in its failure the extinction of such long-cherished golden hopes. It is satisfactory at least to know, however, as we do from his letter of the 2d July preceding, that his part of the expense was by no means so ruinous as has been stated in some accounts. The project, as he admits, was the subject of some harmless ridicule, in which it only shared the fate of all failures.

In the course of the summer of this year Sir Richard, together with Bishop Hoadly and Dr Samuel Clarke, had an invitation to spend some days at Blenheim House. During his stay there the family, with the assistance of some ladies and gentlemen in the neighbourhood, got up an amateur performance of the tragedy of "All for Love," for the amusement of the Duke of Marlborough, who about this time had some lucid intervals from the complaint which ultimately reduced him to a state of second childhood. Steele, for once, appears to have been wanting in his usual gallantry.   Lady Bateman, one of the Duke's grand-daughters, vainly solicited Sir Richard for a prologue on the occasion.   The good-natured bishop, however, having procured writing materials over-night, produced the required prologue in a very satisfactory manner, which he handed to the lady the following morning at breakfast.   It was spoken by her the same evening, and it is said drew tears from the old Duke at an unexpected compliment it contained, coming from a favourite grandchild.*   Steele,

* The following prologue was the one *intended* by Steele for "All for Love," as acted at Blenheim, but withdrawn out of compliment to his friend the bishop :—

> "Since faint is praise which living merit draws,
> And always posthumous is true applause ;
> Deny not worth, far from your eyes removed,
> Its late reward to be revered and loved.
> To poetry devoted be this night,
> And kill not, with your paltry cares, delight;
> See how great Dryden could your sires surprise,
> Ere funds were given, or stocks could fall or rise,
> Ere avarice had banish'd love and truth,
> And with its vile contagion seized even youth ;
> When vice had yet no other fools to shew
> But the well-natured cully and the beau;
> 'Twas 'all for love' the world well lost of old,
> But now for money better bought and sold.
>   For shame, that's only yours, which well you give ;
> Neglect not life, only for means to live ;
> Look on yourselves, ye gaming race, with scorn,
> And see what images these scenes adorn ;
> While love and fame alternately prevail,
> As the great master works the charming tale.

who sat next Dr Hoadly, (it will be remembered they were
old friends,) having noticed with what feeling the part of
Anthony was performed by Captain Fishe, at one scene
where he was particularly sweet upon Cleopatra, Sir
Richard turned round and whispered the bishop, "I doubt
this *Fishe* is *flesh*, my lord." On taking their departure,
Sir Richard, finding that his funds were not in a state to
meet the demands of the legion of laced coats and ruffles
that met them in the hall, accosted them, saying, that
having noticed their taste and discrimination at the performance in timing their applause, he invited them all to
Drury Lane Theatre to whatever play they liked to bespeak,
and so beat his retreat under cover of this compliment.[*]

In another curious anecdote of this period the bishop
had also a part, and indeed his son, Dr John Hoadly, Chancellor of Winchester, is the authority for it. "My father," he

> Compare the generous passions he excites,
> To the fell anguish of your gaming nights,
> When round pale boards you sit with fiend-like pain,
> For base vicissitudes of loss and gain;
> When robbers, beggars, peers, with silent hate,
> And throbbing breasts, to be each other, wait.
> When thus our bard (resist him if you can)
> Has fairly from the gamester won the man;
> Raise thyself still—and the past times survey,
> Since first the age received this tow'ring play,
> Since careless luxury its force could prove
> In one consent the ' world well lost for love.'
> Reflect how care pursues her thoughtless hours,
> And fear the adder lurking in the flowers;
> Think on great William, England's shame and pride,
> And how unthank'd the toiling hero died,
> On baffled virtue, fortune vainly kind,
> Think on your conquests to your foes consign'd;
> But think, though in tempestuous seasons tost,
> While liberty is safe, the world not lost."

[*] Duncombe's Correspondence and Memoir of Hughes, vol. i. pp. 290-3.

says, "when Bishop of Bangor, was, by invitation, present at one of the Whig meetings held at the Trumpet in Shoe Lane, where Sir Richard, in his zeal, rather exposed himself, *having the double duty of the day upon him, as well to celebrate the memory of King William*, it being the 4th November, *as to drink his friend Addison up to conversation pitch, whose phlegmatic constitution was hardly warmed for society by* the time Steele was not fit for it. Two remarkable circumstances happened: John Sly, the hatter, of facetious memory, was in the house, and when pretty mellow, took it into his head to come into the company on his knees, with a tankard of ale in his hand, to drink off the immortal memory, and to retire in the same manner. Steele, sitting next my father, whispered him, 'Do laugh; it is humanity to laugh.' Sir Richard, in the evening, being too much in the same condition, was put into a chair and sent home. Nothing would serve him but being carried to the Bishop of Bangor's, late as it was. However, the chairmen carried him home, and got him up stairs, when his great complaisance would wait on them down stairs, which he did, and then was got quietly to bed. The next morning he was much ashamed, and sent the distich printed above. On such another occasion the waiters were hoisting him into a hackney coach with some labour and pains, when a Tory mob was passing, with their cry, 'Down with the Rump!' 'Up with the Rump!' cried Sir Richard, '*or I shall not be at home to-night.*'"

The pleasant lines referred to were enclosed in the following letter:—

To Bishop Hoadly.

[1718.]

My LORD,—I hope I shall be able to wait upon you at the place you

command me at three of the clock on Monday next. There is no great
danger of your assuming more power than is welcome : you never exert so
much as is voluntarily given you. Coming home the other night, after
your great condescension in liking such pleasures as I entertained your
Lordship with, I made the distich which you will find if you turn over the
leaf :—

> " Virtue with so much ease on Bangor sits,
> All faults he pardons, though he none commits."

I am, my Lord, your most obliged, most obedient humble servant,

RICHARD STEELE.

As this eminent prelate was so intimately connected with
Steele, both as a fellow-labourer in the cause of civil and
religious liberty and in private, having, among his last acts
of friendship, accepted the office of executor and guardian
of his children, a few words of notice respecting him may
not be out of place.

Dr BENJAMIN HOADLY, (1676-1761,) born at Westerham,
in Kent, after studying at Catherine Hall, Cambridge, of
which he was elected a Fellow in 1697, obtained the Rectory
of St Peter-le-Poer, in the metropolis, in 1704. Some
years subsequently he was promoted to the Rectory of
Streatham, in Surrey. Having about the same time distinguished himself in controversy with Bishops Atterbury
and Bramhall on the subject of passive obedience, he
received the thanks of the Commons for his services, on
the motion of Mr Henley, M.P. ; and at the same time an
address recommending him for preferment was presented
to the Queen, who promised compliance with the application, but owing, no doubt to the accession of her Tory
advisers shortly after, failed in the performance. Shortly
after Steele's expulsion by the Tory House of Commons, he
gave his name to a publication by Dr Hoadly, entitled
" An Account of the State of the Roman Catholic Religion

throughout the World," the dedication of which to the Pope was considered a fine piece of grave irony. Although the real authorship was very well known, the circumstance was seized on by Swift to vent his malice ; and it has been surmised by Mr Hoadly, the bishop's son and biographer, also to resent what he regarded as an invasion of his peculiar province in wit, by the reflection in the lines—

> " Steele, who own'd what others writ,
> And flourish'd by imputed wit," &c.

Early in the following reign (1716) the services of Dr Hoadly in the cause of civil and religious liberty met with the reward they merited by his receiving the appointment of King's chaplain, and being elevated to the diocese of Bangor. Not long after his elevation to the Episcopal bench occurred a memorable incident in the life of the bishop. In the year 1717 Dr Hoadly preached before the King, in the Chapel Royal, a sermon "On the Nature of the Kingdom of Christ," in which he asserted religious liberty as the right of the subject, and maintained that an established church was a mere human institution, having no divine authority to make its teachings compulsory, or to enforce them on the mind or conscience. At the next meeting of the convocation of the English clergy, they were about to vote a censure on the bishop, and to adopt other measures, when they were summarily dissolved, and this body, which from a very early period had exercised most formidable powers of a politico-theological nature, was never subsequently revived.

In 1721, Dr Hoadly was translated to the see of Hereford ; two years after to that of Salisbury ; and finally to that of Winchester, which he held nearly twenty-seven years, surviving to the advanced age of eighty-five, when he calmly expired at his palace at Chelsea. His works, with an account of his life, were published by his son, Dr John Hoadly, who was Archdeacon of Winchester.

This was about the period of Steele's connexion with Richard Savage, whose interests he espoused with characteristic zeal and generosity, little deserved by the worthlessness of him on whom they were expended. This ill-starred, but ingenious youth, in addition to the interest thrown around him by his story, (probably fictitious,) has had the advantage with posterity of having it eloquently recorded by Dr Johnson, who was thrown much into his society in his early days in London, and bound to him by the sympathy of mutual poverty. He was, as is well known, the reputed natural son of Lord Rivers and the Countess of Macclesfield, and at this time was about twenty years of age. His reputed mother always asserted that her child had died quite young, and that Savage was an impostor. He was probably in reality the son of the woman who had been employed to nurse the natural child referred to, and this woman dying suddenly, some letters of Lady Mason, the maternal grandmother of the child she had nursed, came into the possession of Savage, and may have put him upon the plan of assuming to be the child to whom they referred. He had received some education, and been afterwards apprenticed to a shoemaker. But, on making the discovery furnished by these papers, finding many to believe his story and befriend him, he enhanced his claims to public sympathy by the exercise of the talents with which he was gifted. Among the earliest and warmest of his patrons was Steele. He took every opportunity of making known his merits and the story of his misfortunes, declaring "that the inhumanity of his mother had given him a right to the friendship of every good man." It was his intention to have established him in some plan of life, and he designed to marry him to Miss Ously, an accomplished young lady, a natural daughter of his own, to whom he was much attached, and to give him a L.1000 dowry with her. But the state of his affairs not permitting him immediately to carry his design into execution, he allowed Savage an annuity in the meantime. But hearing afterwards, however, that he made it his amusement to turn his benefactor into ridicule, he withdrew from all further interference in his favour, and closed his doors against him for the future.

Whilst, therefore, the following anecdotes of Sir Richard, which rest on the authority of Savage, are here given, and are of a kind that have unfortunately a certain amount of verisimilitude, yet they have also an air of improbability and exaggeration, that, taken in connexion with the quarter from which they come, entitle them only to a very qualified confidence.

It is said that on one occasion, in the course of this year, he requested Savage, with an appearance of urgency, to be with him early the following morning. On his arrival, he found the chariot at the door, and Sir Richard waiting. The coachman was ordered to drive with the utmost expedition to Hyde Park corner, where they alighted at a second-rate tavern, and engaged a private room. Sir Richard then told Savage that he had a pamphlet to pre-

pare, and wished his assistance in writing for him.
Savage accordingly wrote from Steele's dictation till the
arrival of the dinner that had been ordered, the meanness
of which surprised the guest, (no doubt, in comparison
with what he had been accustomed to.) Savage, after
some hesitation, ventured to ask for wine, which his
entertainer, not without reluctance, ordered. Dinner
being finished, they proceeded with the pamphlet, which
was completed in the course of the afternoon. Savage
thought his task was then over, but Sir Richard undeceived
him by stating that he was without money, and that the
pamphlet must be sold before the dinner could be paid
for. Savage was therefore obliged to go and offer the
pamphlet for sale, and, after some difficulty, succeeded
in disposing of it for two guineas. Sir Richard having
paid the reckoning, for which alone he had written the
pamphlet, returned home in the evening, having spent
the day away from it for the purpose of evading his
creditors. But one would suppose that a man, wish-
ing to do this, would take a less public way than that
of starting from his door in his own chariot, and would
have gone farther out of the way than Hyde Park
corner.

On another occasion, we are told on the same authority
that Steele, having invited a large party of the first quality,
they were surprised at the array of liveries they beheld,
and after dinner, when the circulation of the wine had dissolved the frosts of ceremony, one of the guests ventured
to suggest whether they were in accordance with his circumstances? He then owned that they were retainers of
whom he would gladly be quit. Why, then, did he not

discharge them? To this he candidly confessed that they were bailiffs, who, having introduced their company with an execution for debt, he had thought it convenient, since he could not get rid of them, to turn them to account, and grace them with liveries, in order that they might do him credit during their compulsory attendance. His friends, we are told, were amused at this mode of increasing the grandeur of his establishment; and, having strongly urged him not again to place himself in a position to resort to it, enabled him to pay the debt.*

A story of a similar kind relates that Steele, Savage, and Philips having issued from a tavern in Gerrard Street, where they had supped, in a very merry mood, had their mirth spoiled by a tradesman, who, apologising for accosting them, said, that at the top of an adjoining lane, "he had seen two or three suspicious-looking fellows who appeared to be bailiffs." Immediately, it is said, without even waiting to thank their informant, all three rushed off in opposite directions, carefully avoiding, however, the locality indicated.

With regard to Savage, a few words may be added to conclude his story. A performance had been kindly got up by Wilks at Drury Lane for his benefit, and some years after his intercourse with Steele had ceased, (1723,) he himself appeared upon the boards, without much success, in the principal character of his tragedy of "Sir Thomas Overbury." By this production he realised about L.200. Four years later he enacted a real tragedy in his own person, having killed a Mr Sinclair in a brawl at a house of disrepute. He was tried and found guilty, but obtained the King's

* Johnson's Life of Savage.

pardon through the good offices of Lady Hertford.. After
this, he was taken into the house of Lord Tyrconnel, who
allowed him L.200 a year. Two years after the unfortunate
event referred to, he produced his poem of the " Wanderer."
Having quarrelled with his patron, he found himself again
without a home and without resources. His next production was the " Bastard." He soon after made a fortunate
hit in addressing a birth-day Ode to the Queen, which procured him a pension of L.50 a year, and this for some time
formed his principal maintenance ; but after the death of
the Queen, when it ceased, he sunk into a state of extreme
wretchedness. Some literary friends, however, among
whom Pope took an active part, came to the rescue, and
raised a fund for his benefit, but stipulating, in order to
remove him from the temptations of the metropolis and for
the sake of economy, that he should reside in Wales. They
found him, however, impracticable and unmanageable.
Instead of keeping faith with them, he went to Bristol,
where he not only squandered the money, but got
into debt, for which he was arrested. From the county
jail he was ultimately removed to Newgate, and there
died in 1743. Such was the chequered story of Richard
Savage, who created an interest, and had chances in
life greater than his personal merits warranted. His
poetical pretensions were of no high order, and in most
instances his productions were only redeemed by a few
vigorous lines.

To Steele this year closed, as the following opened, in
darkness and disaster. No merry Christmas or happy
New-Year awaited him. On the day succeeding the first
of these festive occasions, Dec. 26, 1718, he received an

irreparable blow in the fatal termination of the illness from
which Lady Steele appears to have suffered for a considerable time. She was in her fortieth year, and her remains
were interred in Westminster Abbey.*

The following letter, communicating the melancholy
event to her friends, was written immediately after :—

LETTER CCCLXXVII.   *To Mr Alexander Scurlock.*

Dec. 27, 1718.

DEAR COUSIN,—This is to let you know that my dear and honoured
wife departed this life last night.

I desire my aunt Scurlock, and Mrs Bevan, and you yourself, would
immediately go into mourning, and place the charge for such mourning of
those two ladies and your own to the account of, Sir, your most affectionate
kinsman and most humble servant,

RICH. STEELE.

Thus was prematurely severed to Steele the dearest
earthly tie, which, with whatever of the alloy of infirmity,
which is the condition of all things human, it may have
been accompanied, was, in the main, a happy one, we cannot doubt. He has left us too many proofs under his own
hand to admit of that. And now, at a most critical time,
when so much needed, that presence which had lightened the darkest clouds, and lent additional brightness to
the sunshine for better than ten years, was withdrawn for
ever; and that the dreary blank was keenly felt during the
remaining ten we cannot doubt from his affectionate and
social nature.

* With this inscription : " Dame Mary Steele, wife of Sir Richard Steele,
Knight, daughter and sole heiress of Jonathan Scurlock, Esq., of the county of
Carmarthen, died Dec. 26, 1718, aged 40 years, leaving issue, one son and two
daughters, Eugene, Elizabeth, and Mary."

In considering the attributed weaknesses of her character, which consisted chiefly in her conduct as a capricious beauty and the undue love of money, which was with him a frequent subject of pleasant banter, we must not forget the probability that these shortcomings were, at the least, greatly aggravated by his culpable improvidence. But his correspondence is full of testimonies to his appreciation of her worth ; and in a beautiful letter in which he dedicates to her the third volume of the " Ladies' Library," (which may probably have suggested to Charles Lamb the dedication to his sister, where he speaks of the " monotony of the affection" which is apt to exist with people living much together, so that it is sometimes necessary " to call to our aid the trickery of surprise,") he dwells upon her wit, her beauty, and her numerous amiable qualities, as well as his many obligations to her for her ministrations to him, in a strain of courtly compliment which, though we made some allowance for colouring in an epistle dedicatory, yet there could be no reason to doubt of its being sincere and well founded. He there winds up with this climax : " If there are such beings as guardian angels, thus are they employed. I will no more believe one of them more good in its inclinations than I can conceive it more charming in its form than my wife." And on a subsequent occasion, when her loss had made the preceding allusion still more literal, he says, " The best woman that ever man had cannot now lament and pine at his neglect of himself." *

Though we might infer that she was not ordinarily demonstrative in her affection, yet we might be disposed to

* *The Theatre,* No. 12.

retract even that impression on reading the following
lines addressed to her husband during some period of their
early married life :—

> " Ah ! Dick Steele, that I were sure
> · Your love, like mine, would still endure ;
> That time nor absence, which destroys
> The cares of lovers, and their joys,
> May never rob me of that part
> Which you have given me of your heart :
> Others, unenvied, may possess
> Whatever they think happiness.
> Grant this, O God, my great request,
> In his dear arms may I for ever rest."

Having mentioned the private theatricals at Blenheim,
those which took place at Hampton Court about this time
may be here referred to. These, however, were not
private theatricals, in the sense of being performed by
amateurs. By direction of the King, the great old hall at
Hampton was fitted up as a theatre, with the intention of
having plays performed twice a week during the summer
season. The arrangements, however, occupied so much
time that only seven performances took place before the
return of the Court to town. The services of the actors
from Drury Lane were engaged on the occasion. Among
the plays performed was " Henry VIII.," and Cibber, who
gives an account of the matter,* mentions a pleasantry of
Steele in reference to this performance. Being asked by
a grave nobleman, shortly after, how the King liked it, he
replied, in reference to his office of governor of the company, " So well, my lord, that I was afraid we should have
lost all the actors ; for I was not sure the King would not

* Cibber's Apology, chap. xvi.

keep them to fill the posts at Court that he saw them so
fit for in the play."

The following prologue was written for these theatricals
by Steele :—

" Howe'er we 're wont to feign, we now appear
With true concern and undissembled fear ;
Our disadvantage, too, too well we know,
And here dare only comic humour show ;
Our tragic pomps are for the world below.
They know not sentiment from empty rage,
When the theatric monarch shakes the stage ;
Strides o'er his realms with sceptre in his hand,
By hat and feather raising his high stand,
Mantle and train half covering his command ;
But audiences who weigh the source of things,
The rise of nations, and the fate of kings,
Detest an inexperienced, wild essay,
And close examine by the life a play.
By such, stage heroes with contempt are seen
Who swell with rage, to form a princely mien.
The counterfeit abhors a nearer view,
The mimic greatness dreads to approach the true—
With easy, kind, familiar power that reigns,
As life informs our frame, as blood our veins :
Terror and noise spring from erroneous force :
Thunder is an offence in nature's course—
That bursts around, an empty meteor forms,
It mounts in vapours and descends in storms.
Nature's true force is in calm order seen ;
Small power is rough, consummate is serene.
True majesty 's by smiling virtue known,
Mix'd in a crowd, attended, or alone.
With conscious goodness raised above its throne,
Homage it loathes, delights to make men free,
And raise the bended suppliant from the knee ;
Rules not by stupid pomp, but human arts,
And with the social virtues glads our hearts ;
Smiles at our follies, steals our souls away,
And with our wills has arbitrary sway ;
Neglected want and friendless merit trace,
In tender features of a gracious face ;

Not fierce the lord, but friend of human race.
As grace and favour heaven itself employs,
But, by its angels' ministering, destroys;
In gentle acts of every passing hour,
The King diffuses through the land his power;
While conquering arms and dreaded fleets restrain
Rash distant powers, and vindicate the main." *

* *The Theatre*, No. 13.

CHAPTER XVIII.

THE visits of misfortune, unlike those of angels, are proverbially said to be often not far between. Scarcely had Steele had time to recover from the first shock of that most overwhelming calamity, which had left his home and hearth desolate, than an unfortunate controversy on a public question, arising out of a strong sense of what he deemed his public duty, led to coldness and estrangement with his dearest remaining earthly friend. Nor was this all; for a thunderbolt was at the same time, and owing to the same causes, hurled at his head, charged with loss and damage to his pecuniary interests. About the beginning of the year 1719 a bill was proposed by the Earl of Sunderland, a member of the ministry, for the purpose of fixing permanently the number of the House of Peers, and preventing, for the future, any fresh creations, except when an existing one had become extinct. The lords, of course,

highly approved a measure which enhanced the value of
their privileges, and the King, who, as Johnson states,
" was yet little acquainted with his own prerogative, and,
as is now well known, almost indifferent to the possession
of the Crown, had been persuaded to consent." The Commons, however, as was natural to expect, were not disposed to recognise the permanent exclusion of themselves
and their posterity from the chances of the dignity whatever it was worth.   The professed ground of the proposed
measure was the abuse of the prerogative in the last reign,
by the creation of twelve new peers at one time for party
purposes, and to prevent a like abuse for the future ; yet,
by a glaring inconsistency, it was proposed now to make
a still greater addition, which would of course have been
from the friends of the party in power, and then to close
the door for ever.   It was, therefore, obviously a party
measure—but though that party was his own, Steele so
strongly objected to it that, not satisfied with the prospect
of opposing it in his place in Parliament, he endeavoured
to stifle it by bringing to bear against it the powerful
influence of public opinion.   With this view he started a
paper called the *Plebeian*, the first number of which appeared on the 14th of March 1719.   He there insisted that
the tendency of such a stereotyped aristocracy was the
introduction of that worst form of government, an oligarchy, and adduced numerous examples, both ancient
and modern, to shew that where the prerogative was not
excessive the reduction of it had invariably proved the
prelude to the assumption of proportionate power on the
part of the nobles, when there ceased to be any check
upon them by the Crown.   He maintained that the in-

creasing the number of peers is always to be wished for by
the Commons, because, the greater their number, the less
considerable they become, and the less within the influence
of Court favours ; that since the Habeas Corpus Act, and
the many restraints upon the power of the Crown in King
William's time, the prerogative was now so reduced that
the Commons had nothing to fear from it ; that the proposed measure was an important innovation on the constitution, as well as an infringement of the privileges
guaranteed by the articles of union, in the case of the
Scottish peers, and concluded by denouncing, in the
strongest terms, those who should support such a measure
by having in their pocket the assurance of being made a
peer as the reward of their advocacy.

To this, Addison, on the 19th of the same month, replied
in a paper or pamphlet entitled the *Old Whig.* He
argued that it was desirable to reduce the prerogative from
the example of its abuse in the late reign, and that the
prerogative of the veto was enough for the Crown. That,
so long as the Crown had the power of filling the House
of Lords with its creatures, there were virtually only two
branches in the Legislature ; that it was as legitimate to
fix permanently the number of the Peers as of the Commons,* and that the additions which the Crown would
still retain the power of making, in order to supply the
place of those which had lapsed, would be quite sufficient
new creations for all necessary purposes.   Although Addi-

---

* It is obvious that the cases are not analogous except in a merely literal sense
of fixed numbers, for no one in the state was precluded from aiming at admission
to the House of Commons, nor was the honour hereditary.   The argument of
Steele, that the greater the number of the Peers the more inconsiderable they
became, appears much more solid.

son advocated the side tending to the aggrandisement of
the Peers, he does not by any means take an exalted tone
in reference to that body, but speaks almost with ridicule
similar to Sydney Smith in reference to their opposition to
the Reform Bill, at the notion of the Commons having
anything to fear from them; and this was in fact the point
of that remark so long erroneously supposed to be personally disrespectful to Steele.

The personalities which too generally accompany the
discussion of public questions of exciting interest were
unfortunately not wanting on this occasion, but they have
not been quite accurately stated in the general accounts of
the affair. The statement of Dr Johnson has been generally
followed by subsequent writers. His account of the origin
and progress of the controversy is remarkably succinct and
lucid, but he admits that he had his information second-
hand, (the *Old Whig* not having been inserted in the
original editions of Addison,) and has been mistaken as to
the exact phraseology employed. He attributes to Addison
a contemptuous allusion to Steele as " Little Dicky, whose
trade was to write pamphlets." Now, no such single
sentence occurs. The expression " Little Dicky" occurs
in a reference which he makes to a passage in the "Spanish
Friar" of Dryden by way of illustration ; and though the
exact meaning of the allusion would not be obvious to the
general reader, it would be a natural supposition that the
diminutive epithet could not have applied to one who had
been a guardsman. This imputation was for the first time
satisfactorily refuted, however, by the explanation of Lord
Macaulay, who states that " Little Dicky" was the nick-
name of Henry Norris, an actor of remarkably small

stature, but of great humour, who played the usurer Gomez, then a most popular part, in Dryden's " Spanish Friar." *
In this case the reference to the diminutive stature of the actor heightened the humour of the allusion to the passage of the play referred to. Nor is the other part of the re- flection put in so pointed a form as that so often quoted, though scarcely sufficient to exonerate him, as Lord Macaulay has done, of stepping wide of the rules of good taste and good breeding. On the contrary, he was the first to introduce the element of direct personality by com- mencing his second *Old Whig* with the remark that "the author of the *Plebeian*, to shew himself a perfect master in the vocation of pamphlet-writing, begins like a son of Grub Street," &c. Of course, both writers were anonymous, and therefore it may be said he was not applying this to his friend ; neither is the remark tantamount to saying that his opponent *was* a Grub Street writer, but it certainly savours of the offensive. It is true Lord Macaulay says, " Steele so far forgot himself as to throw an odious impu- tation on the morals of the chiefs of the administration." If so, it must have been a far-fetched inference from some historical allusions he makes. The oft-repeated statement founded on Johnson's account gives Steele credit for humility and moderation, and not forgetting even under provocation his settled veneration for his friend, but merely conveying his reproof in a quotation from Cato. Lord Macaulay, on the contrary, says he replied " with great acrimony." We think neither account is exactly accurate. He certainly makes use of the terms " mean" and " inso- lent," but he does so apparently rather in sorrow than in

* Macaulay on Life and Writings of Addison.

anger, and without excitement. The "kind and courteous
expressions" with which Lord Macaulay says Addison
"softened" his personalities must refer to the conclusion
of his paper, and appear to savour rather of a patronising
air, or the trick of a controversialist who pays a compliment
to his opponent at the expense of his cause : " I must own,
however, that the writer of the 'Plebeian' has made the
best of a weak cause, and do believe that a good one
would shine in his hands," &c. Lord Macaulay has taken
his usual depreciating view in reference to Steele. Without stating what the error was, he says, " It seems to us
that the premises of both controversialists were unsound ;
that on those premises Addison reasoned well and Steele
ill; and that consequently Addison brought out a false
conclusion, while Steele blundered upon the truth." That
at least was something to do, and this ingenious way of
accounting for Steele's success is the only credit he gives
him for opposing a measure which he admits he considers
" was most pernicious;" but it is quite in keeping with the
ungracious way in which this distinguished writer ever
allows a shadow of credit to Steele. As an illustration of
the old proverb how doctors differ, we may add that Mr.
Forster expresses the opinion " that both in the argument
and the conclusion Steele had the advantage." The remarks of Johnson on this unhappy controversy are too
admirable to be omitted : " Every reader surely," he says,
" must regret that these two illustrious friends, after so
many years passed in confidence and endearment, in unity
of interest, conformity of opinion, and fellowship of study,
should finally part in acrimonious opposition. Such a controversy was *Bellum plusquam civile*, as Lucan expresses it.

Why could not faction find other advocates? But, among the uncertainties of the human state, we are doomed to number the instability of friendship."* In consequence of the opposition offered to the bill, it was dropt during that session, and when introduced again in December following, was thrown out. In the interim, Addison was no more.

On the same day in which the bill was reported in the House of Lords, namely April 6th, appeared the fourth and last *Plebeian*. On the 7th of December following, when, after the second reading, a motion was made for committing the bill, Steele was the first to speak in opposition, making use of the same arguments as he had already done in his pamphlets and in a letter which he had addressed the same day to the Earl of Oxford. He was succeeded, among others, by Mr Pitt, Horatio Walpole, and Sir John Pakington. The latter spoke eloquently on the occasion. He acknowledged the reason they all had to be sensible of the good intentions his Majesty had been pleased to express in his speech towards his subjects, but "that, in his opinion, his Majesty was not rightly informed of the manner of making his subjects feel the effects of those gracious intentions; and that, in particular, the bill before them was a very improper return for all the demonstrations of duty, zeal, and affection which his faithful Commons had given since his Majesty's happy accession to the throne." After referring to several examples, he added, "But after all these, and several other, instances of obsequiousness and complaisance which the Commons had shewn for the ministers, it was matter of wonder that they should at last be no better rewarded

* Lives of the Poets.

than by a bill which was visibly calculated to exclude them
from titles of honour, and to raise the dignity and power
of the peers. That, for his own part, he never desired to
be a lord, but that he had a son who might one day have
that ambition : that it was indeed an extraordinary and
unexampled condescension in his Majesty to part with so
valuable a branch of his royal prerogative. However, considering what equivalent was given by this bill to his
Majesty, nobody would wonder at this concession, if it
reached no further than his Majesty. But he hoped this
House would never concur in depriving of so bright a jewel
of the crown the Prince who, in his proper turn, was to
wear it." He was replied to by Mr Hampden and Mr
Secretary Craggs. The former, referring to the argument
of the increased importance of the peers, endeavoured to
show, as Addison had done in the *Old Whig*, that its
tendency would be the reverse, by retaining the great
fortunes among the Commons. The latter, referring to
the abuse of the prerogative in the previous reign, said,
"That it was only in the reigns of good princes that
legislators had opportunities to remedy and amend the
defects to which all human institutions are subject ; and
that if the present occasion of rectifying that flaw in our
constitution was lost, it might never be retrieved." Mr
Methuen, a former Secretary of State, replied, urging the
danger of attempting alterations in the ancient fabric of the
constitution, the removing of one stone in the foundation
of which might endanger the whole edifice. After some
others had spoken on the same side, Mr Attorney-General
spoke in defence of the measure. Though he owned he
did not like the bill as it stood, " yet he did not doubt but

it might be made a good one, provided the Lords would give the Commons an equivalent, and share with them several privileges and advantages which their lordships enjoy. Therefore he insisted on the committing the bill, that they might make proper amendments to it; and as to the objection, that it was dangerous to make any innovations in the constitution, the Act for limiting the succession and the Act of Union had altered, but had rather improved and strengthened, than prejudiced the original constitution." Mr Walpole, the afterwards eminent minister, followed, and spoke against the measure with his usual force and eloquence. Among other arguments, he stated, "That among the Romans, the wisest people on earth, the Temple of Fame was placed behind the Temple of Virtue, to denote that there was no coming to the former, without going through the other : but that, if this bill passed into a law, one of the most powerful incentives to virtue would be taken away, since there would be no coming to honour but through the winding-sheet of an old decrepit lord, and the grave of an extinct noble family. That it was matter of just surprise that a bill of this nature should either have been projected, or at least promoted, by a gentleman who not long ago sat amongst them, and who having now got into the House of Peers, would shut up the door after him. That this bill would not only be a discouragement to virtue and merit, but also endanger our excellent constitution ; for as there was a due balance between the three branches of the legislature, if any more weight were thrown into any one of these branches, it would destroy that balance, and consequently subvert the whole constitution. That the peers were already possessed of many valuable privileges, and to give them more power and authority, by limiting their number, would in time put the Commons again into that state of servile dependency they were in when they wore the badges of the Lords. That he could not but wonder that the Lords would send such a bill to the Commons ; for how could they expect that they would give their concurrence to so injurious a law, by which they and their posterities are to be excluded from the peerage ? And how would the Lords receive a bill by which it should be enacted that a baron should not be made a viscount, nor a viscount be made an earl, and so on ? That besides all this, that part of the bill which related to the peerage of Scotland would be a manifest violation of the Act of Union on the part of England, and a dishonourable breach of trust in those who represented the Scotch nobility. That such an infringement of the union would endanger the entire dissolution of it, by disgusting so great a number of the Scotch peers as should be excluded from sitting in the British Parliament. For, as it was well known that the Revolution Settlement stood upon the principle of a mutual compact, if we should break first the articles of union, it would be natural for the Scots to think themselves thereby freed from all allegiance. And as for what had been suggested, that the election of the sixteen Scotch peers was no less expensive to the crown than injurious to the peerage of Scotland, it might be answered, that the making twenty-five hereditary sitting Scotch peers would still increase the discontents of the electing peers, who thereby would be cut off of a valuable consideration for not being chosen."

After Mr Aislabie, the Chancellor of the Exchequer, Mr

Sergeant Pengelly, and one or two other members had
spoken, the question was put, on the motion of Lord
William Powlett, and carried in the negative by 269 to
177, so that the bill was lost.*

On the same day on which the bill was introduced,
Steele had, by anticipation, addressed an able letter on
the subject to his former antagonist, Lord Oxford, in which
he at the same time took occasion to make a frank and
manly avowal of the excess to which he had been led by
the ardour of his zeal in reference to him in his former
writings, and of the pain which the consciousness of this had
since caused him. It was occasioned by the coincidence
of their views with regard to the bill. In reference to the
sentiments of a personal nature, it will be remembered
that Steele had formerly been under obligations to Oxford,
and, in his letter resigning his Commissionership of Stamps,
had expressed his personal good feeling. The arguments
in this letter formed the substance of Steele's speech
against the bill the same day in the House :—

December 7, 1719.

"My Lord,—I am very glad of an occasion wherein I have the good
fortune to think the same way with your lordship, because I have very
long suffered a great deal of pain in reflecting upon a certain virulence
with which my zeal has heretofore transported me to treat your lordship's
person and character. I do protest to you, excepting in the first smart of
my disgrace and expulsion out of the House of Commons, I never wrote
anything that ought to displease you, but with a reluctant heart, and in
opposition to much good will and esteem for your many great and uncommon talents. And I take the liberty to say, thus publicly to yourself,
what I have often said to others on the subject of my behaviour to you ;
I never had any other reason to lessen, my Lord of Oxford—than Brutus
had to stab Cæsar—the love of my country. Your lordship will, I hope,

---

* See the *Political State*, December 1719.

believe there cannot be a more voluntary unrestrained reparation made to a man than that I make to you, in begging your pardon thus publicly, for everything I have written to your disadvantage foreign to the argument and cause which I was then labouring to support. You will please to believe, that I could not be so insensible as not to be touched with the generosity of part of your conduct towards me, or have omitted to acknowledge it accordingly, if I had not thought that your very virtue was dangerous ; that it was, as the world then stood, absolutely necessary to depreciate so adventurous a genius, surrounded by so much power as your lordship then had. I transgressed, my lord, against you when you could make twelve peers in a day ; I ask your pardon when you are a private nobleman ; and, as I told you, when I resigned the stamp office, I wished you all prosperity consistent with the public good, so now I congratulate you upon the pleasure you must needs have in looking back upon the true fortitude with which you have passed through the dangers arising from the rage of the people and the envy of the rest of the world. If to have rightly judged of men's passions and prejudices, vices and virtues, interests and inclinations, and to have waited with skill and courage for proper seasons and incidents to make use of them for a man's safety and honour, can administer pleasure to a man of sense and spirit, your lordship has abundant cause of satisfaction."

The spirit displayed in these introductory remarks affords a striking proof of the tenderness of Steele's conscience and feelings. He was not at ease until he had made amend for his former severity, which, though it might have been undue, was committed in a time of war, and which, whether before or after his unjustifiable expulsion from the House of Commons, most men would have considered as cancelled by that act. Steele, however, forgetting his own grievance, thought only of the offence against his former antagonist, instead, as might have been supposed, of rejoicing in his humiliation since the time when, in his day of power, he was so injuriously treated at his bidding.

After this graceful *amende,* he enters on a review of the various provisions of the obnoxious bill, which might, he

said, change this free state into the worst of all tyrannies
—that of an aristocracy.   He notices that no allusion was
made in the bill to the only plausible reason for it, in the
late abuse of the prerogative by the nobleman he addressed.   After referring to the part relating to the peers
of Scotland, from whom it was proposed to remove the
representative element, and to raise their number from
sixteen to twenty-five hereditary peers, as a breach of the
terms of the union, which might lead to the most dangerous
consequences, he proceeds to urge that we are safer under
the prerogative than under an aristocracy.   That the
animosities and quarrels of the time should not deprive
the sovereign of a power which was proper to him, and
which would be so felt a hundred years hence.   Any
sudden and surprising way of creation, he said, was open to
the legislature for censure ; and the great diminution
which all creations bring upon the King's authority is a
sufficient defence against the abuse of that authority: for
when the King makes peers, he makes perpetual opponents
of his will and power, if they shall think fit.   But in case
this should not be deemed sufficient, he proposed, that to
prevent the sudden occasional increase of peers, an easy
and obvious method would be that new peers should be
prohibited to sit or vote in Parliament till after a convenient time from their creation.   He spoke not this
that he approved of such a remedy, but named that expedient only to show that more is asked than is needed.
There was no part of society, he said, considered in this
bill but the peers.   Though a commoner was not to be
admitted to the ranks of the peerage, yet the power of
making promotions within the body was not removed, nor

was the crown prohibited from making peers from the members of the royal family, who were not to count in the fixed number. The restraint of the peers to a certain number would, he said, render the House useless, because it is well known that the great business is always carried on by men created first in their own persons. The Lords exercise a power in the last resource of justice, and an appeal, they say, lies to them from the courts of Westminster Hall, for determining all the property in Great Britain, yet they are willing to have a law which must disable them from being a capable court of justice for the future. When they were confined to a number, the most powerful of them would have the rest under their direction, and all the property disputed before them liable to be bestowed, not by judgment, but by vote and humour or worse. Judges made by the blind order of birth will be capable of no other way of decision. It is said, he remarked, that power attends property; it is as true that power will command property, and according to the degeneracy of human nature the Lords may as well grow corrupt as other men. Shall we, then, expose ourselves to probable evils with the prospect of impossible remedies against them?

With relation to the Scottish peers, the bill was a violation of justice and common right; and the principles of the union once broken, it would exist only on sufferance or by force, not by law. With regard to the King's prerogative, this law would diminish it to an irreparable degree, and at a time when in possession of a prince so moderate as to be willing to resign it. It was a part of the estate of the crown which they should not consent to remove without just occasion. The prerogative can do no hurt when ministers do their duty; but a certain number of peers may abuse their power, when no man is answerable for them. He knew it was said the manner of their power would be the same as now, but then the application of it may be altered when they are an unchangeable body.

He had always asserted, he said, that if there had been any outrage in the case of the twelve simultaneous creations, the peers should have then withstood the receiving of them, or done what they thought fit for their satisfaction, and not, when it is too late, instead of asserting their liberties, seek their future security in unreasonable concessions from the crown and discouragements of the merit of the Commons. As to the provisions of the bill respecting the order and economy of the nobility, plain men and commoners would not dispute about things merely trifling and ornamental; and if they would be satisfied with their present power as peers, they should be dukes, marquises, earls, or what other words they pleased, without envy or opposition. But as it was the last time it might be in their power to make a stand for themselves and their posterity, they should be very zealous. At the same time, they could not be more exorbitant in their use of this bill if successful, than in the circumstances under which they send it for acceptance; and it was not thirst of power, but moderation in the use of it, could recommend men to further trust: it was to be apprehended that what was founded in usurpation would be exerted in tyranny. It was a melancholy consideration that, under the pressure of debts, the necessities of a war, the perplexities of trade, and the calamities of the poor, the legislature should thus be taken up and employed in schemes for the advancement of the power, pride, and luxury of the rich and noble. He spoke not thus, he said, to spread discontents or sow divisions, but to heal them, and in charity to all men. If this bill was necessary to prevent the creation of occasional peers, why at the same time are an unprecedented number to be made now? Is it not the same as saying, if you will let us make so many this one time under the sanction of a law, we will make no more, for we shall have no occasion for any more. The former conduct of the House of Peers, of admitting or opposing creations of the crown, shows that they well knew that they have a power of so doing, when the reason of the thing gives them authority for it. The latter end of the bill, he says, seems to have some compassion towards the prerogative, and enacts something gracious towards the descendants of the sovereign before the commencement of the aristocracy, laying no restraint upon the " advancing or promoting any peer, having vote and seat in Parliament, to any higher rank or degree of dignity or nobility; nor from creating any of the princes of the blood peers of Great Britain or lords of Parliament; such princes, so created, not to be esteemed any part of the number to which the peers are by this Act restrained." He concludes by applauding those who had taken an active part in opposing the bill, especially one young nobleman, probably the son of his correspondent, to whom he alludes,—speaking of himself as "a poor plebeian who, from the love of justice and virtue, had, at the entrance into old age, but just lifted his head out of obscurity into noise, clamour, and envy,"—a singular and characteristic proof of modesty in one who had previously raised to himself a monument more lasting than the fleeting interests of politics could confer.

Having thus endeavoured to give the substance of this letter as nearly in Steele's own words as was consistent with brevity, it may not be out of place here, where his name occurs for the last time, to glance at the nobleman to whom it was addressed, who acted so conspicuous a part in the memorable transactions of the preceding reign.

ROBERT HARLEY, (1661–1724,) who became Earl of Oxford and Mortimer, was the elder son of Sir Edward Harley, a Hertfordshire baronet, who had been an active partisan of the Parliament in the civil war, and at the Revolution, in conjunction with his son, raised a troop of horse, and joined the Prince of Orange. After receiving an excellent private education, young Harley had been destined for the military profession, but, in accordance with the evident tendency of his talents and inclinations, which clearly pointed to civil life, the original intention was relinquished. Shortly after the Revolution, Mr Harley entered Parliament as member for Tregony. He afterwards sat for Radnor, which he represented till removed to the Upper House. His family being Presbyterians and Whigs, he commenced life professing his hereditary principles. From whatever cause, however, whether dissatisfaction, or more probably from what he regarded as his interest, (for he still had a leaning to his old principles,) he soon enlisted himself among the opposition party. Marlborough had not then joined the Whigs, and with him Harley formed an intimate connexion. Having established a character for ability by his address in debate, the know-

ledge he displayed on financial questions, and his management of a bill for the more frequent summoning of parliaments, he was chosen Speaker in the fifth Parliament of
William (1701,) as he was again at the commencement of
the following year, and a third time in the first Parliament
of Queen Anne. This important office, which did not then
preclude the active participation in the strife of party, he
was considered to have filled with credit. A curious
example of chicanery over-reaching itself occurred in the
discussions on the Act of Settlement, when Harley, in the
interest of his adopted party, which could not openly
oppose a measure which was only the sequel of the Revolution, suggested, among other expedients of obstruc-
tion, certain restrictions of the prerogative which, he said,
had been overlooked from haste in the existing Government. These were actually adopted by the promoters of
the bill and passed along with it. So that a prominent
leader of the party assuming to be the special friends of
the crown and its prerogatives, and the man who afterwards made his way to power by fostering the Queen's
prejudices against the Whigs, and representing them as
actuated by a desire to curtail the prerogative, was the
means of permanently reducing it beyond what it had ever
previously been. In the administration of Marlborough
and Godolphin, they attempted the same policy of a coalition of the moderate of both parties, which he afterwards
endeavoured to carry out. Through their influence he
was appointed to the office of Secretary of State in 1704,
and Henry St John, afterwards Lord Bolingbroke, was
nominated Secretary-at-War. He was not long in office,
however, when, by the agency of Mrs Masham, a lady of

the Queen's household, who had been appointed through the influence of Lady Marlborough, to whom, as well as to Harley, she was related, he began that system of intrigue and duplicity against his patrons which has given him a pre-eminence, in an unscrupulous age, as the most unscrupulous of politicians and perfidious of friends. The particulars have been previously referred to, and need not here be repeated. Suffice it to say that, with the aid of his friend, and taking advantage of his official position, he succeeded in ingratiating himself with the Queen, and ultimately, by those insinuating arts of which he was master, and by flattering her prejudices, acquired an ascendancy over her greater than that of any other of her ministers. The aim of the compact between Harley and Mrs Masham was nothing less than to promote their ambitious views by undermining the influence of the present Ministry, and the formation of another on its ruins, of which he should be head. The lady had already succeeded in supplanting her patron, and by assisting the Secretary to follow her example, she would be able to serve herself and the husband who had recently married her without a dower. The great means employed to this end was the peace policy, which had begun to find favour with the Queen, and even with the nation, which now began to wince under the burden of the war. During all this time he had been making the most plausible professions of attachment to the interests of his chiefs. But these intrigues and clandestine interviews becoming known before Harley's plans were ripe, Godolphin and Marlborough insisted on his dismissal. With this the Queen refused compliance ; but the affair of Greg's treasonable correspondence emanating from his office, though there was no evidence implicating the Secretary, yet occurring at the same time with his own treachery and duplicity, with which it seemed to have so suspicious a family likeness, its effect was so damaging as to induce him voluntarily to resign.   He was followed by St John, Harcourt, and others of the party he had been organising.   This was the first instance of his crooked policy recoiling on himself, which did not, however, make him despair of employing it successfully on a future occasion.   For about two years and a half he remained out of office, though still enjoying the confidence of the Queen, watching his opportunity and employing the interim in sowing dissensions and jealousies among the opposing parties.   At length the opportunity for which he waited arrived.   In an ill-fated hour the Ministers, despite the advice of Somers, determined on impeaching a foolish parson for some violent rhodomontade of a political nature in the pulpit.   The opportunity was seized on by the opposite party to set up the cry of "The Church in danger," and the furious and wide-spread display of High Church popular enthusiasm proved a storm too violent for the Whig pilots to weather.   The Queen, seeing that she had now a favourable pretext for following her inclinations, lost no time in clearing the way for her favourite.   The Chamberlain was first dismissed to make way for the Earl of Shrewsbury, without consulting Godolphin; Sunderland followed, being a connexion of Marlborough, as if to intimate that that interest was shaken. Whether this was intended to pique him into a resignation, or any overtures were made him with the view of a compromise, is uncertain.   But early in August 1710, Godol-

phin, the Lord Treasurer, was dismissed. The probability
is that Harley calculated on the others being induced to
remain in office, according to his favourite theory of uniting
the talents and experience of both parties. Indeed, according to his own acknowledgment, this was not merely
a matter of policy, but almost of necessity, the Tories
having no men of business ability or experience among
them. The remainder of the Ministers, however, at once
gave in their resignation.

The new Tory Ministry was duly inaugurated in August
1710, Harley himself holding the offices of Chancellor
of the Exchequer and one of the Commissioners of the
Treasury ; the Earl of Rochester, the Queen's uncle, being
Lord President of the Council. The other offices were
not hastily filled, Harley, as virtual, though not nominal, chief of the Cabinet, hoping to lure some Whigs
of experience and influence to join them. Not only by
his personal exertions, but by means of a pamphlet designed to show the folly of party distinctions, and that
they were more imaginary than real, did he endeavour to
compass his design of the fusion of rival interests. In
this scheme, the theory of which might be very good if it
could be honestly carried out, he was unsuccessful. His
own party, meantime, were much disappointed. It was
not until St John and Harcourt had threatened to retire
and leave him to his fate, that they succeeded in their
wishes. The former then became Secretary of State, and
by his great eloquence, both in speech and writing, became the great champion of the Administration. At the
elections, owing to the extraordinary outburst of High
Church zeal, the interest of the new Government carried

all before it. But it was internally weak. Heart-burnings and jealousies manifested themselves from the very outset. Harley's professedly moderate, or, as they termed it, trimming policy, was displeasing to his colleagues, and there were various contending claimants struggling for precedence in the Cabinet. The bickerings between Rochester and Harley were matter of notoriety. The former founded his claim to precedence on his long experience and his affinity to the Queen, while the ambition of St John, with his towering abilities, ill brooked a superior. A foreboding of a speedy break-up led both Harley and St John to pay court to the Whigs.

An event of a startling nature finally decided this question, and, by the shock which it gave, tended to stifle for a time the suicidal contentions in the Cabinet. A French adventurer, the Abbé de Bourlie, better known as the Marquis de Guiscard, who pretended some claims on the ground of services rendered to the allies, had, after much importunity, succeeded in obtaining the sanction of the Queen to the grant of a pension, the amount of which Harley had reduced. In his indignation at this, Guiscard had sought to revenge himself, and make his peace with his own government by a treasonable correspondence, for which he had been brought before the Privy Council on a secretary's warrant. He was very violent under examination, and after requesting a private interview with Mr St John, with whom he had formerly been intimate, and who had signed the warrant, which was refused him, approached the table and stabbed Mr Harley twice with a pen-knife. Mr St John, seeing Harley fall, drew his sword, and with others inflicted on the assassin a number of

wounds, of which he died in prison. The sensation produced by an event so shocking was of course very great, and
tended to fix universal attention and interest on the
victim.   Addresses of condolence and sympathy on his
behalf were presented to the Queen by both Houses of
Parliament.   Constant messages of inquiry were sent
during his confinement by the most distinguished persons,
including the sovereign herself, and on his convalescence
he received a congratulatory address from the Commons
couched in the most flattering terms. The regret expressed by Harley at the death of Guiscard, mentioned by
Swift,* although his living could not have been much to
his advantage after such a deed, was, if sincere, a remarkable proof of his amiability.

On his recovery, the recognition of his precedence in
the Cabinet immediately followed.   Two months after, he
was raised to the peerage by the title of Earl of Oxford
and Mortimer, and a few weeks later promoted to the
office of Lord Treasurer. This extraordinary accession of
popularity caused his great financial scheme for the payment of the national debt, which he introduced shortly
after his return to the House, to be received with general
acceptance, though not quite approved by some of his
colleagues.   By his admirers, indeed, it was extravagantly
extolled. Yet the leading provisions of the measure were
for the establishment of a lottery and the formation of
that delusive South Sea Company which, in the following
reign, terminated in most disastrous results. He was the
first governor of the company.

The two most notable acts of the Oxford Administration

* Journal to Stella, April 13, 1711.

were the creation of twelve new peers in one day at the close of 1711, and the treaty of peace (Utrecht) in 1713, which terminated a ten years' war. With regard to the former, though the politico-theological fanaticism existing when they entered upon office enabled the Tories to return an overwhelming majority in the Commons, the Lords had still remained a stronghold of the Whig interest, and had proved on various occasions a thorn in the side of the Administration. It was to obviate this constantly-recurring difficulty, the last of which was in the discussion relative to the proposed treaty of peace, when they were in a minority,* that the Lord Treasurer proposed to the Queen an exercise of the prerogative, which, though there was no legal impediment to it, was an unprecedented straining of the power of the Crown for party purposes, and so far unconstitutional in spirit that its direct aim was to interfere with the freedom of Parliament. The treaty which after tedious negotiations was at length concluded at Utrecht, in the early part of 1713, between Great Britain, Holland, and France, was assailed by the Whigs with a storm of opposition which had such an effect upon the public mind

---

* This produced a great panic among the Tories, which was increased by their fears that the Queen was wavering. Mrs Masham, after having supplanted her patron, Lady Marlborough, was now in a great measure supplanted in turn by the Duchess of Somerset. "I immediately told Mrs Masham that either she and the Lord Treasurer had joined with the Queen to betray us, or that they two were betrayed by the Queen. She protested solemnly it was not the former, and I believed her; but she gave me some lights to suspect the Queen is changed. For yesterday, when the Queen was going from the House, where she sat to hear the debate, the Duke of Shrewsbury, Lord Chamberlain, asked her 'whether he or the Great Chamberlain, Lindsay, ought to lead her out,' she answered shortly, 'Neither of you,' and gave her hand to the Duke of Somerset, who was louder than any in the House for the clause against peace. She gave me one or two more instances of this sort, which convince me that the Queen is false, or at least very much wavering."—*Swift's Journal to Stella*, Dec. 8, 1711.

as to make the Ministry dread a reaction in public opinion, and led to the most stringent and arbitrary measures against the freedom of the press.   At the close of the previous year there were no less than twelve prosecutions for seditious pamphlets on the first day of term in the Queen's Bench.   The portion of the treaty which related to commerce, in which the interests of the country were considered as sacrificed to the incompetence or treachery of the Ministers, was attacked with special severity. Among the assailants were Addison, Maynwaring, and Martyn.   The only advantage the country derived from the lavish expenditure of its blood and treasure in a ten years' war was the cession of Gibraltar and Minorca, and what was called the assiento contract, by which the exclusive privilege of the carrying trade in reference to the slaves to the Spanish West Indies, was guaranteed to this country.   Philip V. retained the crown of Spain and its West Indian possessions, but it was stipulated that his descendants should be incompetent to inherit the French crown, or the Kings of France that of Spain.   The French at the same time relinquished their pretensions in the Netherlands.   Thus the Spanish crown, the usurpation of which, contrary to the barrier treaty, had been one of the principal causes of the war, remained as before.   In addition to the advantages being wholly inadequate to the success of the war by British instrumentality, it was a stigma upon the national honour that we should have deserted our ally the Emperor of Germany and have stooped to a separate treaty, leaving him to struggle single-handed.

The execution of the treaty was chiefly the work of Bolingbroke, though in pursuance of the policy of Harley, among other reasons from his accomplishments as a linguist, in which he had so great a talent that he boasted of having acquired Spanish in a fortnight. But in the midst of the triumph of Oxford and his colleagues at having, as it were, taken the ground from under the feet of the Whigs, a retributive vengeance pursued him. What Steele foretold came to pass, that "he would raise up powers he would be unable to control, and which would tear him to pieces." The Duke of Somerset, whom his arts, probably, had seduced, along with others, on some ground of disgust, from his allegiance to the Whigs, was soon dissatisfied with his new allies, and was supposed to be fraternising with his old friends. His duchess, who had succeeded Lady Marlborough at court, and whose insinuating manners had firmly established her in the favour of the Queen, was also a thorn in the side of the Ministers. The extreme section of the treasurer's own party, moreover, known as the October Club, irritated with his professed moderation and trimming policy, had on the treaty of commerce risen in open rebellion against him ; his colleague Bolingbroke had placed himself at the head of an independent party, and galled him on every opportunity. Nor was this all. Through the very agency by which Harley had supplanted his predecessor and patron Godolphin, and by the same wily arts, he found that Bolingbroke had succeeded in supplanting him. The secretary had done the favourite, now Lady Masham, a service which Oxford had failed to do, and she consequently employed her influence for him as she had formerly done for the other. There is reason to believe that Bolingbroke's Jacobite tendencies had also as much to do with his advancement to favour as his talents and in-

sinuating address.   Harley had played with the Jacobites,
and wished to be thought by them as favourable to their
views, but he also wished to be thought not by the opposite
party.   They probably saw through him, and this most
likely was the cause of his fall.   Then commenced a scene
of recrimination of unprecedented acrimony, which neither
the respect due to the presence of the sovereign, nor her
sex, nor the feebleness of her health, could restrain.   The
meeting was prolonged till two in the morning, and the
Queen is said to have declared, that she never would
recover the effect of the perturbation into which she was
thrown by such an unseemly altercation.   On the 27th of
July 1714, the treasurer's staff was demanded, and placed
in the hands of Shrewsbury by the dying Queen, who, after
remaining in a lethargic condition, expired on the 1st of
August.

By the publication of the memoirs of the Duke of Ber-
wick, who was a natural son of James II., it appears that
the disgrace of Harley was the result of an intrigue between
him, Bolingbroke, and Mrs Masham, and that the sudden-
ness of the Queen's demise prevented the measures that
were intended to be concerted subsequently.   As it was, it
is said that Bishop Atterbury offered to proclaim the Pretender in full canonicals if he were only allowed a troop of
guards to protect him.   On the day following the dismissal
of Oxford, Bolingbroke entertained a party of the leading
Whigs, possibly with the double design of celebrating his
triumph, and as a cover to his designs; but he was not destined to realise the hopes of promotion he had founded on
it.   He had also invited the Duke of Marlborough to return,
and Oxford is even stated to have attempted a reconcilia-

tion by the same means. It is certain that the duke did proceed on his return previous to the Queen's decease, and was only detained by contrary winds.

On the arrival of the King on the 18th of August, Bolingbroke was dismissed, and shortly after fled. Articles of impeachment were prepared against both him and Oxford; but the latter, with the courage he had displayed under the most critical circumstances on former occasions, stood his ground. He was committed to the Tower, where, in consequence of the prorogation of Parliament, he remained upwards of two years. On his petition, May 22, 1717, that the House of Peers would take his case into consideration, " being assured it was not their Lordships' intention that his confinement should be indefinite," the day for the trial was fixed for the 24th of June. On his appearing, however, some difference arose on a point of form between the two Houses, and the Commons declining to appear on the terms proposed, the Lords acquitted Oxford. The Whigs were so implacable against him that the Commons proposed to try him in a different form, and addressed the King on the subject, but the matter ultimately fell to the ground without any further proceedings.

The remainder of the life of Lord Oxford was spent in retirement, and devoted to art and literature, of which he had ever been an admirer, patron, and cultivator, from something more than policy. Although his personal attainments did not rise above mediocrity, he was a persevering student, and the uniform and liberal patron of men of letters. Among others, Defoe was indebted to his liberality, and for his release from the long incarceration he had suffered in consequence of the intolerance of the times. We find Steele acknowledging his generosity in the letter in which he resigned his office. The completion of that noble collection of books and MSS. which bears his name, and now forms one of the most valuable portions of the treasure of the nation in the British Museum, was the work of his latter years. And, to compare great things with small, as in the cases of Milton, Bacon, and others, whose brightest, best, and no doubt happiest days, which have made the world their debtors, were those of their retirement, consequent on what the world calls disgrace, it may be questioned if, in the society of the living ornaments of letters, Pope, Prior, Gay, Arbuthnot, and others, and the brightest part of those departed enshrined in books, Harley had not a truer enjoyment of life than when, in the fickle sunshine of a court, he intrigued against his friends, or was intrigued against by others of them in turn.

Mr Lewis, an official favourite of Lord Oxford, in a letter to Swift, written some years later, remarked in reference to his " History of the Four Last Years of Queen Anne," which was only published posthumously, that the true monument of Oxford was the treaty of Utrecht. But it is no bad test of the difficulties that stood in the way of his predecessors in making an honourable peace, that he should have been so long after entering upon office in carrying out the very measure on the strength of which he attained to power, that it was conducted in a clandestine. manner, and that it was finally concluded by a partial and unsatisfactory measure, and by the desertion of the German allies. When the Duke of Marlborough proposed peace, the French Court construed it into weakness, and treated it accordingly. Several years previously the Whigs

had all but settled a peace, which would not have left the
Spanish Crown in possession of the Bourbons, but for the
difficulty of obtaining satisfactory guarantees for the ful-
filment of the conditions, considering that the war was
occasioned by the breach of a former treaty.

Swift, with whom he agreed in fondness for *la bagatelle,*
and would trifle like a schoolboy, has drawn his portrait.
He represents him as unaffected by the possession of
power in a remarkable degree; as abounding in good-
nature and good-humour ; as having the greatest variety
of knowledge he had ever met with ; as a perfect master
of the learned languages, and well skilled in divinity; as
possessing a prodigious memory and most exact judgment;
as a great favourer of men of wit and learning ; of the
greatest liberality and contempt of money; as an utter
stranger to fear ; as reading the libels and pamphlets
against himself with a most unaffected indifference;
and possessing as much virtue as could consist with
the love of power. He might have said with power so
attained.

The reputation of Lord Oxford was first acquired by
his financial and constitutional knowledge, and his tact in
debate, but did not keep pace with his advancement. As
the world, whether justly or not, recognises a difference
between.public and private character and honour, in the
latter Lord Oxford was of unblemished reputation. Bolingbroke is said to have been exceedingly jealous of those
beautiful but extravagant lines addressed to him by Pope,
in his dedication to " Parnell's Poems :"—

> " And sure, if aught below the seats divine
> Can touch immortality, 'tis a soul like thine ;

A soul supreme, in each hard instance tried,
Above all pain, all passion, and all pride,
The rage of power, the blast of public breath,
The lust of lucre, and the dread of death."

In the autumn of this year Steele received a complimentary dedication from Mr. Colley Cibber of his tragedy
of "Zimenes, or the Heroic Daughter," in which, after
dwelling upon the obligations the drama was under to him,
and the improvement and reformation of the stage by his
criticisms, he refers to the depreciation of his literary fame
by his political enemies, and the invidious comparisons by
which Addison was allowed the lion's share, which have
unhappily survived :—

"How long and happily did *old Isaac* (Bickerstaff) triumph in the
universal love and favour of his readers? The grave, the cheerful, the
wise, the witty, old, young, rich and poor, all sorts, though ever so opposite
in character, whether beaux or bishops, rakes or men of business, coquettes
or statesmen, Whigs or Tories,—all were equally his friends, and thought
their tea in a morning had not its taste without him. Thus, while you appeared the *agreeable philosopher* only, mankind, by a general assent, came
into your applause and service. And yet, how in a moment was this
calm and unrivalled enjoyment blown into the air, when the apprehension of your country's being in a flame called upon you to resign it . . . .
in the restless office of a *Patriot !* for no sooner did you rise the champion
of our insulted constitution, than one-half of the nation (that had just
before allowed you the proper censor of our morals) in an instant denied
you to have wit, sense, or genius. The column they had been two years
jointly raising to your reputation, was then, in a few days, thrown down by
the implacable hands that raised it. But when they found that no attacks
of prejudice could deface the real beauty of your writings, and that they
still recovered from the blow, their malice was then indeed driven to its
last hold, of giving the chief merit of them to another great author, who,
they allowed, had never so audaciously provoked them. This was, indeed,
turning your own cannon upon you, and making use of your private
virtue to depreciate your character ; for had not the diffusive benevolence
of your heart thought even fame too great a good to be possessed alone,
you would never (as you confessed in the preface to those works) have

taken your nearest friend into a share of it. . . . . Your enemies, there-fore, thus knowing that your own consent had partly justified their in-sinuations, saved a great deal of their malice from being ridiculous."

He concluded with a quotation from Shakespeare which, by inference,—which none would more have deprecated than Steele himself—placed him above his illustrious friend. The following compose his correspondence in 1719 :—

LETTER CCCLXXXI.   *To Mr Alexander Scurlock.*
> *Villiers Street, York Buildings,*
> *Feb.* 19, 1718–19.

DEAR COUSIN,—I believe this will come to Carmarthen about the time of your arrival there : and I send it to signify to you, that I foresaw many inconveniences which might arise from making any assignment on the playhouse ; and, therefore, instead of giving Mrs Roach any order on that part of my income, I gave her another letter of attorney for a hundred a year to be paid by you—that is, a further hundred ; in all, two hundred. I shall take care, God willing, to appropriate all arising from the estate to the service of the children ; but, at the same time, I must make it pay all funeral charges of the late possessors of it, my honoured mother and dear wife : therefore I entreat you to have your thoughts upon supplying those proper charges with the greatest expedition that may be proper. I have ordered all the tradesmen to bring in their bills, and shall transmit the sums to you, and desire thereupon that you may tell me what they are to trust to as to time of payment.—I am, dear Sandy, your faithful friend and humble servant,   RICH. STEELE.

LETTER CCCLXXXII.   *To Mr Law,* at Paris.*
> *Aug.* 12, 1719.

SIR,—I believe you may have heard my name mentioned since I had the honour to converse with you, and therefore will not suppose you have

---

* "John Law, Esq., (one of the early friends and companions of Captain Steele,) was memorable for a fatal duel, in 1694, with Beau Wilson, for which he was tried at the Old Bailey, and, being convicted, received a pardon from the Crown, but was detained in prison by the relations of Mr Wilson under an appeal. He found means, however, to escape ; and, going to France, became the founder of the famous Mississippi scheme. In 1721 (having pacified the surviving relations of Mr Wilson with L.100,000) he returned to England, where he continued to

wholly forgot me. With this hope I enter upon the business of this letter with the less preface, and at once inform you that the King has given me his letters patent for the sole use of an invention for bringing fish alive and in good health, wherever taken, to any other part however distant. It is well known how ill Paris and other parts of France are supplied with that commodity; and it will soon occur to you what great advantage may be made of such a privilege given by the King of France for his dominions.

You have, enclosed, an examplar of the letters patent in print; and you shall join your own, that of your brother, or any other name, in partnership with me in such patent.

The thing pretended is done to all intents and purposes; and I have, under a great deal of ridicule and contempt of the greater, the unthinking, part of the world, worked it up to an undoubted experiment in a sloop of sixty-one tons. Farther I am not able to carry it of myself; but, now the truth of the design is evident, I doubt not but I shall find means to carry it on from a partnership from the profits that may very visibly arise from it. The thing itself is a service to the world in general, and a merit to the whole species of men, and not only to this or any other nation; and therefore I presume it is a request grounded upon the law of nature, that every country should distinguish those from whom they receive benefit, without regard to the places of abode or nativity, or the soil to which they are born subjects. You have too enlarged a view, and the prince whom you serve has too well shown (by his just regard and favour to you) the same magnanimity, to need much discourse on this occasion.

---

reside till he received the mortifying intelligence of the confiscation of his whole property in France; but, being conscious of the rectitude of his conduct in the management of the finances, and that the balance would, upon examination, be found considerably in his favour, he had good reason to flatter himself with the hopes of receiving a large sum, especially as the Regent always professed a more than ordinary regard for him, and continued punctually to remit his official salary of 20,000 livres a year. But the death of his Royal Highness, December 2, 1723, was a fatal blow to the hopes of Mr Law, who, in a memorial to the Duke of Bourbon, dated October 15, 1724, states himself as 'bankrupt, not only in France, but also in other countries,' and 'his children counted by the most considerable families in France as destitute of fortune and establishment.' 'I had in my power,' he says, 'to have settled my daughter in marriage in the first houses in Italy, Germany, and England; but I refused all offers of that nature, thinking it inconsistent with my duty to, and my affection for, the state in whose service I had the honour to be engaged.' He bade a final adieu to Britain in 1725, and fixed his residence at Venice, where he concluded the chequered course of his life, in a state but little removed from indigence, March 21, 1729, in the fifty-eighth year of his age."

But whatever befalls this application, I wish your great and noble genius the continuance of prosperous adventures, and am, sir, your most obedient and most humble servant,   RICH. STEELE.

LETTER CCCLXXXIII. . *From Mr Dennis,*
Declaring the reasons for which he published the two volumes of "Select Works."

Sept. 4, 1719.

SIR,—I here send you, by the bearer, several pieces in verse and prose, written formerly by me, and lately printed in two volumes; but I send them not without a double design on you. For, first, I desire that you would have the goodness to oblige your managers to make me some recompense this winter for the wrong which they did me the last. Secondly, I desire that you will give me leave to say something concerning the pieces contained in these two volumes, and more particularly concerning the motive which obliged me to write the chief of them at the first, and to publish them lately together; which I shall do with pleasure to one who has done so much good in the same cause in which most of them were written.

Several of the pieces in verse and prose, and three of the plays, were written in the cause of liberty. The narrative poems of greater length were all of them written upon great and public occasions; and were designed as so many panegyrics upon those illustrious persons whose great and heroic actions had made them benefactors to Great Britain and liberty.

It has always been my opinion that a free nation can never be too zealous in maintaining their liberties, because we have been taught by too many fatal events, that they have at last been often lost by the security and corruptions of those who had for several centuries enjoyed them. Witness the ancient Grecians and Romans, and the ancient and modern Spaniards and French. But whenever the liberties of a great nation are in manifest danger, there all the several members of it, who are not abjectly base, will use their utmost efforts in defending them. The liberties of Great Britain have in our own memory been in so much danger, that they have been twice in thirty years retrieved from immediate ruin, first, by the Revolution, and, secondly, by the accession of King George to the imperial crown of this island; but even now they by no means appear to me to be entirely secured.

Since the Revolution things appear to have been strangely reversed in Great Britain with regard to liberty. In four or five reigns immediately preceding the arrival of King William, of immortal memory, the court was for arbitrary power, and the people appeared strenuous for liberty. But since that time the court has for the most part contended for liberty, and the people, I mean too great a part of them, have declared for slavery. Now, if ever we should come to be under a king who would sacrifice his Protestant Dissenting subjects to the High Church clergy, we should quickly see whether the liberties of a nation are most secure when a considerable part of the people (who are their natural guardians) are resolved to defend or determined to resign them. In the meantime, sir, it must be acknowledged, to the immortal honour of the present King, that, by endeavouring to secure the Dissenters from such treatment in time to come, he is taking the most effectual method to immortalise liberty.

Thus, sir, I have acquainted you with the only motive of writing the chief of these poems, which was the apprehension I had of the danger which the liberties of my country were in, and consequently the liberties of the Christian world, of which ours are the strongest bulwark. I wrote them not then as one who espoused a party, but as a lover of my country, and one zealous to promote the happiness of Great Britain. I have been so far from having any ambitious aims or sordid views of interest, that I have been contented to see several of the public rewards engrossed by some who are lukewarm, and by others who are Jacobites in Whig clothing, while I have remained very poor in a very advanced age. But one thing, indeed, I have sometimes been apt to think exceeding hard ; and that is, that these lukewarm persons, and these Jacobites in Whig clothing, should be suffered to make use of the power which they have acquired by their falsehood, to the utter ruin of one who has behaved himself all along with the utmost sincerity in the noblest cause of liberty.

Thus, sir, have I laid before you the motive which engaged me to write the greater part of the pieces which are contained in the two volumes. I shall now show you how the same motive obliged me to use my endeavours to preserve them, if they should appear worthy of it, and consequently to publish them in the two forementioned volumes.

It was in October 1716 that I desired a bookseller to collect them for me. I thought that, after so much time had passed since the writing them, I should be capable of forming as true a judgment myself of them as any other person whatsoever, who has no better judgment in poetical matters than I have, or that the precept of Horace, *nonum prematur in annum*, must be false and vain.

Upon a very slow and deliberate perusal of them, I could not but conclude that, with all their faults, they were not altogether deprived of that noble fire which alone can make them pleasing, nor of that justness and solidity which alone can make them lasting. I believed that, if they were published together, they might be able one day to do some good to the public, and no discredit to me.

And I was the more encouraged to venture on this publication, because,

sir, you may be pleased to remember that they had been favourably received
by the most illustrious persons of both parties for their judgment in poetry,
and their knowledge of the *Belles Lettres,* by the late Earls of Godolphin
and Halifax, Mr Maynwaring, and others, among the Whigs ; and by the
present Duke of Buckingham and my Lord Lansdowne, among the Tories.
And if any temptation could make me vain, it would be the favourable
opinions of the last two noble persons, because, as their judgments in
matters of poetry are unquestioned, they can never be supposed to be
partial to one who has all his lifetime appeared very zealous in contrary
principles to those of a party which they by some means have been supposed to favour.   My Lord Lansdowne, by making me a present so noble
as has never been made by a subject to any author now living, sufficiently
declared that what I had written had not been altogether displeasing to
him.   And it is to the warm approbation which the Duke of Buckingham
gave to the poem, " On the Battle of Blenheim," that I owe the honour of
being first known to the late illustrious Earl of Godolphin, whose good and
great qualities, and the benefits which Great Britain received from his
good and his wise administration, make me proud to own for the first and
greatest of my benefactors.

Thus, sir, I found encouragement to preserve these pieces, and especially
the poems written in the cause of liberty.   But I was convinced, at the
same time, that the only way to preserve them would be to publish them
together.   They were in a great many different hands, and some of them
in the hands of such as were mortal enemies to the cause in which they
were written.   Some of them had been very incorrectly printed.   The
very subject which ought to recommend them to all Englishmen, as well
as the harmony without rhyme in several of the poems, made some of
them for the present less pleasing to above half the readers of poetry.
Some of them that had once appeared with applause seemed to have been
forgotten.   For all things of late days have been managed by cabal and
party ; and there seems to have been a conspiracy in the commonwealth
of learning, among fools of all sorts, to exalt folly at the expense of common-sense, and make stupidity triumph over merit in the dominions of wit,
which has been one of the causes why things are reduced to that deplorable
state upon our British Parnassus.   Apollo and the Muses seem to have
abandoned it, disdaining that their divinities should honour a place with
their songs, where fools and pedants, buffoons, eunuchs, and tumblers,
have so often met with applause.

Who could have thought, if he had been told twenty years ago, that he
should outlive tragedy and comedy, that he had been promised a life of
not quite twenty years ?   Yet it is very plain that the promise had extended no further, such is the power of cabal and party.

I have all along had a great aversion to the making a party, or the entering into a cabal; and have sometimes looked upon it with horror, and sometimes with contempt.   Who that has common-sense can forbear laughing, when he sees a parcel of fellows who call themselves wits, sit in combination round a coffee-table, as sharpers do round a hazard table, to trick honest gentlemen into an approbation of their works, and bubble them of their understanding !

And yet I have all along known that nothing in the greater poetry can grow immediately popular without a cabal or party.   I have long been convinced that the more sublimely anything is written in poetry, and the nearer it comes to perfection, the longer it will be before it grows popular without such a cabal : because the more sublimely it is written, and the nearer it comes to perfection, the more it is raised above the apprehension of the vulgar.   And yet, notwithstanding this knowledge, I have all along resolved to have no reputation, or to owe it to my writings.

Thus, sir, you see the reasons why the writings that make up these two volumes, or at least the greater part of them, had been in danger of being lost, if I had not taken pains during my lifetime to correct and publish them together.   There is one more reason remaining, and that is, the malice of those people whom the world calls poets, whose hatred I have been proud to incur, by speaking bold and necessary truths in the behalf of a noble art, which they have miserably abused by their vile poems, and their more vile criticisms.

And yet it is from these people that the foolish readers of poetry, which are nine parts in ten, take their opinion of poets and their works ; little believing, or once imagining, that these persons are, of all mankind, the very worst qualified to judge of their own art, as having neither the capacity nor the impartiality which are requisite for the judging truly ; for it will be found, generally speaking, that poets, painters, and musicians are capacitated less than other men to judge of poetry, painting, and music. This, I must confess, may appear to some to be so bold a paradox, that I shall endeavour to make it out both by reason and authority, though I know very well, at the same time, that you can make no doubt of it.   The generality of poets, painters, and musicians are such by the mere power of a warm imagination ; and it is very rarely that a strong imagination and a penetrating judgment are found in the same subject.   We need go no further than Boileau to hear that a celebrated poet is often a contemptible judge :—

> *Tel excelle à rimer qui juge sottement,*
> *Et tel s'est fait par ses vers distinguer par la ville,*
> *Qui jamais du Lucain n'a distingué Virgile.*

As for what relates to painters, I shall content myself with the citation of a remark from the ingenious and judicious author of " Observations upon

Fresnoy's Art of Painting," translated by Mr Dryden. It is the fiftieth remark upon these words of Mr Dryden's translation, " as being the sovereign judge of his own art."

" This word, Sovereign Judge or Arbiter of his own art, presupposes a painter to be fully instructed in all the parts of painting ; so that, being set, as it were, above his art, he may be the master and sovereign of it, which is no easy matter. Those of that profession are so seldom endowed with that supreme capacity, that few of them arrive to be good judges of painting ; and I should many times make more account of their judgment who are men of sense, and yet have never touched a pencil, than of the opinions which are given by the greatest part of painters. All painters, therefore, may be called arbiters of their own art, but to be sovereign arbiters belongs only to knowing painters."

What is said by this ingenious gentleman of painters is exactly true of musicians, for which I have the opinion of more than one master among them ; and as to the truth of this observation with relation to poets, I have said enough above.

But as poets are not capable, neither are they impartial judges. I speak of those who are only rhymesters. For a great master is for the most part as impartial as he is knowing ; but for the rest the readers of poetry would do well to consider, that if a mistress who is courted by a great many passionate rivals should ask any one of them his opinion of the rest, it is ten to one that he would prefer him most whom he esteemed least, and whom he believed least capable of getting that mistress from him.

Thus, Sir, have I acquainted you with the motives which obliged me to write the greater part of these treatises, and which afterwards engaged me to publish them in the two volumes which you will receive with this. I hope I shall not be thought troublesome if, in a second letter, I say something in particular of the pieces both in verse and prose. However, these two letters will convince you of the good opinion I have a long time entertained both of your discernment and your impartiality.—I am, Sir, your most humble and most obedient servant,   JOHN DENNIS.

LETTER CCCLXXXIV.   *To Mrs Elizabeth Steele.**

MY DEAR CHILD, MISS BETTY,—One matter of moment or other has detained me all this day ; nor can I see you to-night. I thank you for your purse ; and, if you and I live till this day twelvemonth, you are to ask me for it again full of gold. God bless you. Remember me to Molly. Be observant of the good guardian God has raised for you.

RICH. STEELE.

---

*Afterwards Lady Trevor.

LETTER CCCLXXXV. *To Mrs Elizabeth Steele.*

DEAR BETTY,—If you have a letter from Mrs Keck to me, pray send it me by the bearer, sealed up. You may remember you sent me one open by him. He is a very faithful servant, but he might have been otherwise for aught you knew, not to say that it is also respect to me to have a letter from you when I send you one.

Give my most humble service to Mrs Snow when you see her, and beg her favour to visit you. You are at your new lodgings, and always preserve the highest respect to her being willing to receive you.

But it is impossible for me to be easy without seeing you every moment I have leisure.—I am, most affectionately, your father,

RICH. STEELE.

My service to Molly.

I had business kept me at home all day.

LETTER CCCLXXXVI. *To Dear Betty Steele.*

May 21, 1719.

DEAR CHILD,—I have your pretty letter, and have sent to know whether I can have any tickets* or not, or whether there will be room, but have not yet an answer. Be grateful, obedient, and respectful to Mrs Keck, and you will oblige your most affectionate father, RICH. STEELE.

Service to Molly.

LETTER CCCLXXXVII. *To Mrs Elizabeth Steele.*

August 21, 1719.

MY DEAR CHILD,—I have your letter, and am very much pleased with the improvement of your hand. I earnestly desire you to be careful of obeying whatever your good guardian† and kind mistress‡ direct. I have been taken up with cares, which, I hope, will make my children easy after me. I pray for you and your sister, and am, your affectionate father,

RICH. STEELE.

---

* "This possibly might be to a splendid ball which was given to the young Princesses in the Greenhouse at Kensington Gardens on the king's birthday, May 28, the day on which their household establishment was formed."

† Mrs Keck. ‡ Mrs Nazercan.

CHAPTER XIX.

THE satisfaction and triumph of Steele at the failure of the attempted innovation on the constitution, which had called forth his spirited opposition, was very far indeed from being unalloyed. He was soon made to feel that courts were not to be thwarted with impunity by those in their power, and the meanness and injustice of the revenge to which it condescended was for some years most disastrous to his interests. It is true that when the Duke of Newcastle, the then Lord Chamberlain, had entered upon his office three years previously, notwithstanding the marked favour he had formerly shown to Steele, he had, apparently from officiousness or jealousy that anything connected with his office should be out of his power, or as Steele expressed it to himself, "a dangerous design of making every office and authority the better for his wearing," requested a resignation of his patent, and offering a licence in return. This modest request Steele had thought proper to decline, and petitioned his Majesty for his protection in the grant formerly made him. This setting at nought his authority must naturally have nettled the Lord Chamberlain, who told Sir Richard that his patent should be invalidated by process of law. Thus the matter had rested for a considerable time ; but when he had afterwards incurred the displeasure not merely of a great officer of the household but of the Government, by daring to oppose their unconstitutional efforts, the weapon which had been so long suspended over his head descended, and inflicted a damaging blow to his personal interests. It was all the more cruel as it came from a hand which had formerly conferred benefits ; and to add to the hopelessness of any opposition, his steady friend Walpole was now out of office, the Duke of Marlborough invalided, and every avenue to the royal ear closed by his powerful adversary. He could not submit, however, to be beggared without exerting every possible effort to prevent it ; he therefore had recourse to that engine which had stood him in such good stead on so many occasions, and determined to make his appeal to the public through the press. Accordingly he started a periodical paper entitled *The Theatre*, with the ostensible design to advocate the utility of the stage and the merit of deserving performers, but in reality chiefly to vindicate himself and the managers, and to deprecate the threatened injury and injustice. The first number appeared on the 2d of January 1720, and it was continued twice a week for some months. The effort served as a diversion of his spirits, but failed of any successful result. Not many weeks had elapsed from its commencement when the preparatory blow was struck by an order for the dismissal of Mr Colley Cibber, one of the managers and a principal performer. Steele immediately took 'up his vindication in the paper, and wrote a letter of expostulation on the subject to the Lord Chamberlain. This produced only a very haughty and arrogant message to Sir Richard through the Chamberlain's secretary, telling him that his patent should be prosecuted by law, and forbidding him all further personal intercourse by word or writing. Such a result, of course, in reference to one from whom he had formerly received high favours, must have produced a very painful struggle in the mind of such a man as Steele, between sorrow and indignation. After expressing to the bearer, in remembrance of the past, his unfeigned regret, he added, " At the same time, you may very truly say, that if any other man were Chamberlain, and should send me such a message, my reply should be as haughty as it is now humble." The fatal blow soon followed, by an order revoking his patent, accompanied by a signed manual. Steele then addressed an expostulatory letter to the Chamberlain through the medium of the paper, as he was forbidden any other channel. He therein, after expressing his sorrow at seeing the signature at the bottom of the order he had received, that he had believed it impossible for him to have been prevailed upon to take such a step, and that he made him allowance for the disadvantages of youth and prosperity, adds his conviction that his patent could not legally be hurt unless it could be shown that it was obtained *per deceptionem*, and that if the matter had been fairly represented, it had been impossible to destroy by a signed manual what had been granted by the great seal. The greatest malefactor was permitted what was denied to him, an unprejudiced trial by due course of law, as the signed manual must necessarily disable him as to his defence. When he represented his case by petition, he knew not, he said, by what accident his petition was never read, but the next news he heard was the order of revocation. After referring to the careful wording of the signed manual, "as much as in us lies, and as by law we may," and regretting that the Chamberlain had not been as careful in leaving him to the law, he concludes by requesting to be made acquainted with the name of his legal adviser in this affair, on whom he vents all the vials of his indignation in as strong terms as language would permit. "When I know who has made your grace thus injure the best master and the best servant that ever man had," that is, the king and himself, "I will teach him the difference between law and justice: he shall soon understand, that he who advises how to escape the law and do injustice to his fellow-subject is an agent of hell; such a man, for a larger fee, would lend a dark lanthorn·to a murderer." It could not escape him, though, as he had previously stated, the prince is presumed to be the author only of favour to his subjects, and the minister who subscribes the document is answerable for what he writes, yet whatever censure applies to a lawyer for giving any specific advice, is at least equally applicable to him who asks and acts upon it. He concluded by reminding the Chamberlain that it was not alone himself and his family that were concerned, and that his obligations to him could not discharge those he was under to the rest of the world. He could not, he said, consign to distress and poverty above sixty families, who all lived comfortably, many of them plentifully, under his present jurisdiction. "When I resign them, they may be governed by your grace's successor in your office, as they have been by your predecessor, according to humour and caprice, and not reason and justice. In their defence and my own, I deny all allegations of voluntary neglect imputed to me or them; or undue demands made upon the subject by me or them."*

Finding this appeal, as might have been anticipated, without effect, Steele drew up a pamphlet, which he then published, under the title of "The State of the Case between the Lord Chamberlain of his Majesty's Household and the Governor of the Royal Company of Comedians," accompanied with the opinion of three eminent lawyers on the question. He considers L.6000 a moderate estimate of the value of L.600 a year, which was his salary, which, with three years' income after his death (which was the terms of his patent) making L.1800 more; and taking his interest in the property of the company at L.1000, and the profits arising from his own plays at a similar sum, would make his total loss amount to L.9800. He protests against having done one single act to justify the proceedings against him, and accuses the Chamberlain of openly stating that he would ruin him; "which," says Steele, "in a man in

* *The Theatre*, No. 8.

his circumstances against one in mine, is as great as the humour of Malagine in the comedy, who valued himself upon his activity in tripping up cripples." " All this," he adds, " is done against a man to whom Whig, Tory, Roman Catholic, Dissenter, native, foreigner, owe zeal and good-will for good offices endeavoured towards every one of them in their civil rights, and their kind wishes for him are but a just return. But what ought to weigh most with his Lordship the Chamberlain is my zeal for his Master, of which I shall at present say no more than that his Lord-ship, and many others, may perhaps have done more for the House of Hanover than I have, but I am the only man in his Majesty's dominions who did all he could." *

Steele had learned by bitter experience the justice of that admonition, " Put not your trust in princes," and his only hope was in the removal or retirement of the existing Chamberlain, on whose advice he acted. Though it is scarcely matter of surprise, from what we know of the Duke of Newcastle, that Steele should have experienced such treatment at his hands, after having thwarted him by not relinquishing his property at his bidding, and subse-quently given offence to the Government by his opposition ; yet it is painful to think that he should have been at the mercy of such a man, " dressed in a little brief authority." For grasping greediness of power, jobbery, and perfidy, combined with mental imbecility, considering the high offices he held by such a lengthened tenure, he transcended all example. The honours and emoluments showered on such a man give anything but an exalted notion of courts or court favours.

* State of the Case, p. 30.

THOMAS PELHAM, Duke of Newcastle (1694-1768), who succeeded his father as Lord Pelham in 1712, and was the adopted heir of his uncle, John Holles, Duke of Newcastle, was now in his seven-and-twentieth year, having already ascended through all the steps of the peerage, and being subsequently destined to honours and rewards that could not have been exceeded in the case of the highest merit. At the close of Queen Anne's reign, and on the accession of George I., he had distinguished himself by his zeal in the cause of the House of Hanover. On the new settlement of the Crown, the Tories being driven to despair by the policy pursued towards them, which indicated a permanent exclusion from all offices of honour or emolument, were led into a union with the Jacobites; and under their joint auspices, serious and extensive riots, under the convenient watchword of the Church, had taken place by an organised system of mobs in various parts of the provinces, as well as in the metropolis. The interposition of the military was not considered politic by the new Government, except in extreme cases. On this occasion, Lord Pelham displayed his zeal in the cause of loyalty and order by the very questionable, but, as it proved, effective method of resorting to a counter mob, which bore his name. He had not established any claim to ministerial place, and there were too many claimants of tried ability and experience for those offices; but having succeeded in obtaining high favour with the King, his assiduity in promoting the cause of loyalty was amply rewarded with other honours and emoluments. In October 1714, he was created Earl of Clare and Viscount Pelham of Haughton, and appointed Lord-Lieutenant and *Custos-rotulorum* of Nottingham

county.   In the following month he was appointed to the
same offices for Middlesex and the liberties of Westminster,
and before the close of the year made Steward of Sher-
wood Forest.   In the course of the following year he was
created Marquis, and Duke of Newcastle-under-Line.

Two years after (1717), on the promotion of the Duke of
Bolton to the Vice-royalty of Ireland, Newcastle succeeded
him as Lord Chamberlain of the Household.   The next
year he was honoured with a vacant Garter, and in 1719
was one of the Lords Justices during the King's absence in
Hanover, an office which he subsequently held at different
times in that and the following reign.   In 1724, he resigned
the Chamberlainship, having succeeded as one of the principal Secretaries of State on the appointment of Lord
Carteret as Lord-Lieutenant of Ireland.   His brother, the
Hon. Henry Pelham, who possessed considerable ability,
succeeded at the same time as Secretary at War, and then
commenced that long, combined, and eager pursuit of self-
aggrandisement on the part of the two brothers, which has
rendered their names pre-eminent in that respect.   Two
years subsequently, the Duke became Recorder of Nottingham, in which county his interest chiefly lay.

The next year (1727), George II. succeeded, when a
change in the Cabinet was anticipated by the Tories, the
prince and Walpole not having been on good terms, but the
Minister brought the interest of the Queen to his aid by
offering her a larger allowance than his opponents.   Walpole's power continued firmly established, and as long as
it remained so, the Pelhams were his strenuous supporters.

In 1742, Walpole was obliged to succumb to a violent
combined opposition, under the title of patriots, who

brought that name into derision and contempt on coming into power, both by their omissions and commissions, repudiating the measures they had previously clamoured for, and shamefully transcending what they had formerly denounced and thundered against. A coalition Ministry of discordant materials was then formed, in which Henry Pelham, in the following year, became First Lord of the Treasury, and Newcastle second in authority. The times being favourable, some excellent measures were passed by that administration, particularly that for the reduction of the interest on the national debt, and another which effected the change from the old to the new style of marking the year. But the present notice is only concerned with what is personal to the Duke of Newcastle, of whom we have a sketch by Lord Macaulay, too graphic to be omitted :—

"If," he says, "the fate of Walpole's colleagues had been inseparably bound up with his, he probably would, even after the unfavourable elections of 1741, have been able to weather the storm. But as soon as it was understood that the attack was directed against him alone, and that, if he were sacrificed, his associates might expect advantageous and honourable terms, the Ministerial ranks began to waver, and the murmur of *sauve qui peut* was heard. That Walpole had foul play is almost certain, but to what extent it is difficult to say. Lord Islay was suspected ; the Duke of Newcastle something more than suspected. It would have been strange indeed if his grace had been idle when treason was hatching. 'His name,' said Sir Robert, 'is perfidy.' . . . It would have been a busy time indeed in which the Pelhams wanted leisure for jobbing ; and to the Pelhams the whole cry of place-hunters and pension-hunters resorted. The parliamentary influence of the two brothers became stronger every day, till at length they were at the head of a decided majority in the House of Commons.

"We wonder that Sir Walter Scott never tried his hand on the Duke of Newcastle. An interview between his grace and Jeanie Deans would have been delightful and by no means unnatural. There is scarcely a public man in our history of whose manners and conversation so many particulars have been preserved. Single stories may be unfounded or exaggerated. But all the stories about him . . . are of the same character. Horace Walpole and Smollett differed in their tastes and opinions as much as any two human beings could differ. . . . Yet Walpole's duke and Smollett's duke are as like as if they were both from one hand. Smollett's Newcastle runs out of his dressing-room, with his face covered with soapsuds, to embrace the Moorish envoy. Walpole's Newcastle pushes his way into the Duke of Grafton's sick-room to kiss the old nobleman's plasters. No man was so unmercifully satirised. But, in truth, he was a satire ready made. All that the art of the satirist does for other men, nature had done for him. Whatever was absurd about him stood out with grotesque prominence from the rest of the character. He was a living, moving, talking caricature. His gait was a shuffling trot; his utterance a rapid stutter; he was always in a hurry; he was never in time; he abounded in fulsome caresses and hysterical tears. His oratory resembled that of Justice Shallow. It was nonsense effervescent with animal spirits and impertinence. Of his ignorance many anecdotes remain, some well authenticated, some probably invented at coffee-houses, but all exquisitely characteristic. ' Oh, yes, yes, to be sure ; Annapolis must be defended ; troops must be sent to Annapolis. Pray, where is Annapolis ?' ' Cape Breton, an island ! wonderful ! Show it me in the map. So it is, sure enough. My dear sir, you always bring us good news. I must go and tell the king Cape Breton is an island.'

" And this man was during near thirty years Secretary of State, and during near ten years First Lord of the Treasury ! His large fortune, his strong, hereditary connexion, his great parliamentary interest, will not alone explain this extraordinary fact. His success is a signal instance of what may be effected by a man who devotes his whole heart and soul, without reserve, to one object. He was eaten up by ambition. His love of influence and authority resembled the avarice of the old usurer in the 'Fortunes of Nigel.' It was so intense a passion that it supplied the place of talents, that it supplied even fatuity with cunning. ' Have no money dealings with my father,' says Martha to Lord Glenvarloch, 'for, dotard as he is, he will make an ass of you.' It was as dangerous to have any political connexion with Newcastle as to buy and sell with old Trapbois. He was greedy after power with a greediness all his own. He was jealous of all his colleagues, and even of his own brother. Under the disguise of levity, he was false beyond all example of political falsehood. All the able men of his time ridiculed him as a dunce, a driveller, a child, who never knew his own mind for an hour together, and he over-reached them all round.

"   .   .   But the inauspicious commencement of the Seven Years' War brought on a crisis to which Newcastle was altogether unequal. After a calm of fifteen years, the spirit of the nation was again stirred to its inmost depths. In a few days the whole aspect of the political world was changed." *

It was the fate of Steele to experience ingratitude and meanness in another quarter, where he should least have expected it, from a man of some pretensions in literature, but unfortunately combined with those qualities which have tended to degrade and render contemptible the profession of letters. John Dennis (1657-1734) was the friend of no man, and least of all of his own order. The son of a London citizen, he had studied at Cambridge, and, after making the tour of France and Italy, produced some dramatic pieces of little merit. His want of success probably tended to sour his disposition, and was aggravated by straitened circumstances. He became a critic, and attacked with severity, though not without acuteness, all merit greater than his own. Addison and Pope were among his victims, and the latter, who, without the extenuating circumstances in his case, resembled him in his malignity and vindictiveness, gave him a prominent place in the *Dunciad.* He survived to a great age ; and having outlived his fortune and his sight, and disposed of an employment he had obtained from the Duke of Marlborough, a benefit was given him at the Haymarket Theatre, when his former antagonist Pope, to his honour, contributed the prologue. Whether at this time he was hired by the Lord Chamberlain to make this dastardly attack, which was the second he had made upon Steele, in both cases when he was involved in his circumstances, and suffering persecution from those in authority, may admit of doubt. He evidently enjoyed a malignant pleasure in endeavouring to

* Essay on Horace Walpole.

embitter the cup of adversity, and to make it overflow.
What intensified the baseness of his conduct was the fact
that he was under personal obligations to Steele, who had
actually suffered arrest by having gone security for him.
On hearing it, " S'death," said he, " why did he not keep
out of the way, as I did." Dennis at this time published a
pamphlet entitled " The Character and Conduct of Sir
John Edgar, called by himself sole monarch of the Stage in
Drury Lane, and his three Deputy-Governors. In two
Letters to Sir John Edgar."* This was the feigned name
under which Steele conducted the periodical paper, *The
Theatre.* The two points of the scurrilous and impotent
attack, which would have been simply ludicrous if it had
been nothing worse, were his country and his personal
appearance. He gave a vulgar caricature implying that
Steele was ugly and ill-made, and that he had the vanity to
think otherwise. The mirth with which Steele very properly met this low attack must not only have had a salutary
effect upon his mind by acting as a diversion to the depressing thoughts which the state of his affairs must have forced
upon him, but have proved to his insulter that he had provoked one that was more than his match at his own weapons. It brought home to him the proverb about those
who live in glass-houses, and sent him away covered with
ridicule and contempt. Mr Bickerstaff is himself again.
" The defamer," he says, speaking in his assumed character

---

* " His pamphlet is so cruel," says Steele, " that it could not be writ by anything but a coward, indulging, sating, and wreaking his malice upon an object
wholly in his power, which he could *stab* without resistance." In a note to
Nichol's edition of *The Theatre*, &c., it is stated " Dennis was expelled from his
college for stabbing a man in the dark, (see ' Farmer's Essay on Shakespeare,'
p. 6,) but it is doubtful if Steele knew this."

of Sir John Edgar, " has this phrase in his first page,
' Your black peruke and your dusky countenance.' This
treatment of a visage so well known is an impudence that
transcends all example, and I have ordered new editions
of his face after Kneller, Thornhill, and Richardson, to
disabuse mankind in this particular. He is painted by the
first *resolute*, by the second *thoughtful*, by the third *indolent*.
Sir Godfrey bewailed that Caraccio was not living when he
sat to him, and when he took pencil in hand repeated this
sentence out of Mr Steele's epistle to the bailiff of Stockbridge : ' *He is gone but a little way in the course of virtue,
who cannot bear reproach for her sake.*' You may observe
a roughness in the portraiture from the rigour of that
thought, which has occasioned that most ladies choose Mr
Richardson's work rather than Sir Godfrey's."* In a
subsequent number he followed up the subject in the same
strain of humour :—" An eminent Turkey merchant and
an ingenious foreigner do hereby give notice, that if any
person will discover the libeller or libellers who has and
have falsely and maliciously insinuated in their writings
that Sir R—d St—le is ugly, so that they may be prosecuted
by law, he shall have all fitting encouragement, the said
gentlemen having lost considerable matches by reason of
the similitude of their persons to the said injured knight."†

Nor did he let his antagonist go until he had visited
him with ridicule of a sharper and severer kind, and carried the war into the enemy's country. "Thou never
didst let the sun into thy garret for fear he should bring a
bailiff along with him. . . . . Your years are about sixty-

* *The Theatre*, No. 10.   † *Ibid.*, No. 18.

five, an ugly vinegar face, that, if you had any command, you would be obeyed out of fear, from your ill-nature pictured there ; not from any other motive. Your height is about some five feet five inches. You see I can give your exact measure as well as if I had taken your dimensions with a good cudgel, which I promise you to do as soon as ever I have the good fortune to meet you. . . . .

"Thy works are libels upon others, and satires upon thyself ; and while they bark at men of sense, call him knave and fool that wrote them. Thou hast a great antipathy to thy own species, and hatest the sight of a fool but in thy glass."

Cibber having offered ten pounds for the discovery of the author—

"I am only sorry," says Steele, " he has offered so much, because the twentieth part would have over-valued his whole carcase." He concludes by a ludicrous account of the precautions he took for his personal safety. "It takes him up half an hour every night to fortify himself with his old hair trunk, two or three joint-stools, and some other lumber, which he ties together with cords so fast that it takes him up the same time in the morning to release himself." *

The encounter with this ferocious literary Ishmael, whose hand was against every man and every man's hand against him, though it left the assailant little to boast of, yet what could hurt such a man, or what honour could be derived from an encounter with such a one ? And this consideration is probably the source of the temerity in such cases.

The periodical paper, *The Theatre,* which had served

* " Answer to a whimsical pamphlet called the ' Character of Sir John Edgar.' "

Steele as the organ of his vindication both in this encounter
with an unworthy antagonist and in his unequal contest
with power in hands scarcely less contemptible, had now
done its work. It had made a brave fight, but it had unfortunately not been successful in the object for which it had
been started, and it was relinquished on the 5th of April,
after an existence of about three months, and the completion
of twenty-eight numbers. Its special aim, and the anxieties
connected with his affairs which oppressed his mind at the
time, tended to limit the range of its literature, but it was not
wholly devoid of general interest, and its miscellaneous con-
tents include some of Steele's poetical effusions. But it is
much to be regretted that in the full maturity of his powers,
and ere their vigour had suffered decay, he had not concentrated his mental energies in the elaboration of one more
serial which might have descended to us with his early
labours, and contested the palm with the delightful phan-
tasies of the immortal Bickerstaff or De Coverley. If he
had, the result might have enabled him to laugh to scorn
the meanness of chamberlains or the patronage of courts.
No doubt other engagements, anxiety perhaps, and failing
health, may have interfered to prevent it. He was no
doubt about this time engaged upon his next comedy, and
may have been anxious to insure its completion. But we
doubt if even that, admirable as it was, repaid him, either
as regarded the present or the future, at all in comparison
with what he might have effected,. after his mind had so
long lain fallow, by a resumption of his former pursuits.

One subject which he had taken up in the columns of
The Theatre, and which was at this time a topic of intensely
exciting public interest, the South-Sea scheme, he resumed

in a distinct form. The way in which this pamphlet was first announced to the public is too amusing to be omitted. He represents the feigned Sir John Edgar as paying a visit to himself, which he describes in the pages of *The Theatre.* After some discourse, he asks the subject of a bundle of writings he observes on the table, and being informed by Sir Richard that it was a calculation of his for paying the debts of the nation, founded on what he termed his first rule in politics, to wit, a nation a family; Sir John gravely made answer, "People would expect great things of him indeed on that foundation, he had such a reputation for economy." He is then represented as leaving in rather a testy humour, and heading the paper in *The Theatre,* in which he describes the interview, with the extempore distich—

> "To make his public spirit better known,
> He to the public debts postpones his own."

The publication thus curiously announced made its appearance on the 1st of February, entitled " The Crisis of Property; an argument proving that the annuitants for ninety-nine years, as such, are not in the condition of other subjects of Great Britain, but, by a compact with the Legislature, are exempt from any direction relating to the said estates." This was followed at the latter end of the same month by " A Nation a Family; being the Sequel of the Crisis of Property; or, a Plan for the Improvement of the South-Sea Proposals."

This scheme had been originally projected, as previously stated, by Harley, Lord Oxford, in 1711. His design was the incorporation of a company of merchants, who, in con-

sideration of certain commercial privileges, should buy up
the debts of the nation from the present holders of Government stock, and retain them on more favourable terms to
the country. The depreciation of public credit by the
removal of the Whig ministry had been foretold by all the
great monied interests, and the prediction seems to have
been realised. Swift, in his Journal, attributes the mone-
tary difficulties of the Tory Ministry, and the depreciation
of credit, to the fact that the great Whig capitalists would
not lend to them. If this was so, they probably contemplated that, by means of this company, they would have a
grand monied corporation of their own, but it would not
appear to have progressed much in its object under their
auspices. Extravagant rumours were set afloat of the
Spaniards opening a free trade, or rather giving them a
monopoly of trade, to their South American possessions
and golden visions were conjured up of the rich harvest to
be reaped by the exchange of British manufactures for the
produce of the mines of Mexico and Peru. But the only
real concession which the King of Spain could be induced
to make was to permit one annual ship, of a certain pre-
scribed tonnage, to trade with his South American possessions, in consideration of a considerable portion of the profits to himself, and an additional per centage in duty. Even
of this slender privilege they do not seem to have been in
any hurry to avail themselves, for it was not till 1717 that
the ship made its first annual voyage, and the intercourse
was subsequently interrupted by the rupture with Spain.
In the same year, the King's speech at the opening of Parliament contained a recommendation of some measure for
the reduction of the debt of the nation. In the following

May, the South-Sea Company made proposals on the subject. But it was not till the beginning of 1720, after a similar recommendation from the throne, that the House resolved itself into a committee for the consideration of the question. The national debt was then nearly thirty-one millions, and this the South-Sea Company proposed to take upon themselves at the rate of five per annum, till 1727, when it was to be reduced to four, and the whole to be redeemable at the option of the Legislature in four years. At the beginning of February the company's proposals were agreed to in preference to those of the bank, and a bill was prepared on the subject. Walpole alone opposed it in the Lower House, and predicted in strong and eloquent terms the pernicious results of the scheme, as countenancing the dangerous practice of stock-jobbing, and tending to divert the resources of the nation from trade and industry, and to lure the people to part with the earnings of their labour for an imaginary wealth. He prophetically foretold that the result would be general discontent and ruin, and that people would start up as from a dream, and ask if such things could be true. Such language, in view of the actual result, would appear little short of inspiration, were it not that an example of a similar kind had just occurred in France, in the disastrous results of the Mississippi scheme set on foot by the famous John Law, who had been comptroller-general in that country. Walpole was usually listened to with the greatest attention, but now, such was the mania that seemed to prevail, his warnings were unheeded or scoffed at.

On the acceptance of their proposals, the company petitioned to be allowed to increase their original stock of

ten millions, and books were opened for receiving fresh
subscriptions and shareholders. Again those delusive
stories of participating in the wealth of the Mexican and
Peruvian mines were put in circulation. It was stated
that proposals had been made for the cession of Gibraltar
and Minorca to Spain, in consideration of a monopoly of
this trade. The various means employed to raise the
stock to a fictitious value were successful. The subscription filled up rapidly. Cornhill and Exchange Alley were
blocked up with carriages. All classes were in a fever of
avaricious excitement. The shares which had previously
been at L.130 rapidly rose to L.400, and, after some
fluctuations, continued to advance. By the beginning of
August they had reached the astonishing height of L.1000
the share. After attaining that culminating point, and
oscillating for a little, they receded and continued to decline
still more rapidly than they had risen, having in the following month fallen to L.700, and soon after to L.400. A
panic then ensued. The Government became alarmed
and called in the aid of the bank, but, after an unwilling
and ineffectual effort, they withdrew from all interference,
fearing to be swept away in the torrent. The advice of
all persons of financial abilities was called for by the
Ministers. In this extremity Walpole submitted a draft
of a scheme which was ultimately adopted as the groundwork of a plan to meet the case, and the public excitement was in some degree allayed. The proposal of
Walpole was to incorporate nine millions of the stock
with that of the East India Company. Still, notwithstanding all the efforts that could be made to restore
public confidence, by the end of September the stock

had fallen to about L.135. The crisis was such that the King, who had been absent in Hanover, hastened his return, and a parliamentary inquiry into the conduct of the directors was commenced early in December. The treasurer of the company, named Knight, had however absconded, taking with him all the books and papers he could conveniently. The chairman and directors were committed to custody, and those who were members of Parliament were expelled. Cries of vengeance were everywhere heard, and petitions to that effect were forwarded from all parts of the kingdom. No one seemed to attach any blame to the sufferers who had been duped and over-reached by their own grasping avariciousness. Very exciting discussions occurred in both Houses of Parliament, and insinuations thrown out implicating Ministers, inuendoes being directed particularly against Mr Craggs and Earl Stanhope, two of the Secretaries of State. The former met them with defiance; and the latter, in his vehemence and excitement, caused a rush of blood to the head which, though remedies were immediately applied, proved fatal on the following day. The other also died suddenly shortly after, not without suspicions of violence. But he was also said to have been suffering from gout, and his decease to have been accelerated by grief for the loss of his son, who had been one of the Secretaries of the Treasury, and had died recently.[*]

* See, in a note to a paper in Lady Montagu's works, (Bohn's edit. vol. i. p. 130,) entitled "An Account of the Court of George I.," which is one continued tissue of scandal and gossip, a repudiation of the family history of this statesman which had been current, which is not only given by Lady Mary, but has found a place in Lord Macaulay's history. Its origin is here traced to some scandalous and libellous pamphlet of the time.

By the report of the committee of secrecy, it appeared that in the books produced there were false and fictitious entries, and in other cases blanks were left for the names of the stockholders. In some instances there were erasures and alterations, and in others leaves were altogether torn out. Among other revelations, it appeared that previous to the passing of the act in favour of the company, an assignment of stock to a large amount had been made to various persons connected with the Government, for which no consideration had been given—including the amount of L.50,000 to the Earl of Sunderland, (the Premier,) to Mr Charles Stanhope, (one of the Secretaries of the Treasury,) L.10,000 — in addition to the immense sum of L.250,000 to the latter, being the difference in the price of stock. His name had, however, been altered. Mr Aislabie, the Chancellor of the Exchequer, had an account with a firm, who, being also South-Sea directors, may be presumed to have been the confidential brokers of the company, to the amount of L.794,451, and had not only sanctioned, but advised the exceeding by the company in their second subscription the amount for which they had authority by half a million. In their third subscription his name was down for L.70,000; Mr Craggs, senior, for L.659,000; the Earl of Sunderland for L.160,000, and Mr Stanhope's for L.47,000.

Mr Charles Stanhope was the first who was called to account by the House, but he, as well as the Earl of Sunderland, by plausible pleas, and the active exertions of his personal friends, was acquitted by a small majority. But the public voice was vociferous in demanding a victim, and Mr Aislabie, the Chancellor of the Exchequer, was given to them. He was found guilty, without a dissentient voice, of complicity in the infamous practices of the directors, was expelled the House, and committed to the Tower, amid the most extravagant demonstrations of joy by the public.

Among the resolutions adopted, was one to the effect that the delinquents ought all to be required to make satisfaction out of their estates to those whom they had injured, and a bill was ordered to be brought in for the relief of the sufferers. A sum of upwards of two millions was ultimately confiscated from the property of the directors,[*] who were each allowed only a few thousands out of fortunes which, in many cases, had amounted to hundreds. In addition to this, a sum of upwards of eight millions was deducted from the capital of the company, and similarly appropriated.[†]

The reputation acquired by Steele as a patriot, by his opposition to the Peerage Bill and this nefarious scheme, was no inconsiderable indemnity for the pecuniary loss he sustained by the disgraceful persecution of the court. Yet notwithstanding his zeal in exposing the system, he was one of the few opposed to unduly vindictive proceedings against the perpetrators, and was subjected to reflections for inconsistency by Whiston, just as he had been with regard to the rebels in 1715—as if there were any inconsistency in denouncing a crime, and yet objecting to a blind and furious vindictiveness to the offender.

---

[*] One of these was Mr Edward Gibbon, grandfather of the historian, who in his autobiography enters his protest against this arbitrary system of *post facto* legislation, or rather its retrospective operation, and asserts that his progenitor had previously amassed a considerable fortune, as he did subsequently.

[†] See Dr Mackay's " Memoirs of Popular Delusions."

The following is Steele's correspondence for 1720 :—

LETTER CCCLXXXVIII.   *To the Lord Chancellor.**

Jan. 17, 1719-20.

MY LORD,—That you were Lord Chief-Justice, was a consideration which gave me much resolution in the last reign ; that you are Chancellor, is a comfort to me under much hardships in this. I have, my lord, a . . . by letters patent from his majesty, to keep and govern a company of comedians ; the tenure is for my life, and three years after my death. My Lord Chamberlain thinks his office injured in this grant, and disturbs me in it. His grace has already sent an order to silence one of the chief actors ; upon which I wrote to him, and complained of the oppression, which I took the liberty of [calling] it. Upon this, I received a message by his secretary, never to write or speak to him more during our natural lives. His grace has since declared, he will obtain a sign manual to silence the theatre. I cannot, by his own order, expostulate with him ; therefore am obliged to apply to other Lords of the Council to prevent the grant of such an instrument. My lord has acquainted me that this patent of mine shall be disputed in Westminster Hall ; which I am very glad of, and am ready to defend myself ; but cannot do so if my means of doing it are taken from me, and the cause is in effect to begin at the latter end of it, and, by the interposition of the King's name and authority, I am to be bereaved in a summary and arbitrary way of what I am to dispute according to the rules of justice.

I presume to write to the other great officers of the crown on this subject ; and hope I shall not be distinguished by receiving injustice with relation to the playhouse, as I have been by right justice in case of omission of duty in the Commission of Forfeitures.†—I am, my lord, your lordship's most obedient and most humble servant,

RICH. STEELE.

LETTER CCCLXXXIX.   *To the Duke of Argyle.‡*

Jan. 17, 1719-20.

MY LORD,—I am necessitated to be guilty of this presumption, from a menace of my Lord Chamberlain, that he would silence the theatre under my government by a sign manual, though at the same time he sent me word by his secretary that he will prosecute my patent according to law.

---

* "Thomas, Lord Parker ; Lord Chief-Justice of the King's Bench, 1710 ; Lord Chancellor, 1716 ; created Earl of Macclesfield, 1721."

† "For which he incurred and paid a penalty of L.500."

‡ "John Campbell, Duke of Argyle and Greenwich."

I have not the honour of your grace's friendship, and therefore want a powerful man who knows superiority is maintained only by benefaction, and that no man is truly above a gentleman of England, but merely in a ceremonial and insipid way, but he who is ready to favour, protect, and defend him.

This, my lord, is what you are well known to understand and perform with a frankness and beauty which very few are capable of imitating. But as I have no pretension to such protection and patronage from you, I only apply to you, as you are a Privy Councillor, for justice; and humbly beg of you to grant me so far your observation (as it may come before you either in business or conversation) should a step be made; but I shall not omit to tell you, who know human life, and have reason about you, in spite of being a man of immense fortune, and the highest title I can say to you, that this attack at the playhouse, and taking from me the penalty of L.500 for my absence from Scotland, has extremely reduced my finances and credit.

Forgive me, my lord, for this application to you, which proceeds from a deep sense of your many noble qualities, which make me, (though I speak it when I am a petitioner,) my lord, with great truth, your grace's most obedient and most humble servant,   RICH. STEELE.

LETTER CCCXC.   *To James Craggs, Esq.*[*]

Jan. 17, 1719-20.

SIR,—I presume to give you this trouble in hopes of your protection, as you are a Privy Councillor, against what his grace, my Lord Chamberlain, is pleased to threaten, contrary to the rules of justice. My lord is instigated to dispute the King's authority in giving me a patent for the government of the playhouse, and has sent me word that he will go to law with me on that subject, but at the same time menaces to silence the house by his Majesty's sign manual. I insist upon it that it will be an arbitrary application of the sign manual, and doubt not but you will, in duty to your sovereign and justice to your fellow-subjects, if it should fall to your province to be consulted, avert this calamity from, sir, your most obedient and most humble servant,   RICH. STEELE.

---

[*] "This was the 'statesman, yet friend to truth,' who is so justly complimented by Mr Pope. He was made Secretary of State in 1718, and died Feb. 14, 1720." He was the friend and successor of Addison, who dedicated to him the collected edition of his works.

LETTER CCCXCI.   *To Earl Stanhope.**

Jan. 17, 1719–20.

MY LORD,—I am obliged to give your lordship this trouble on occasion of a menace from my Lord Chamberlain, that he will silence the actors under my government by his Majesty's letters patent, though, at the same time, he has notified to me by his secretary that he will proceed against this little theatrical authority according to law. I presume to assert that a sign manual on such an occasion is illegal and arbitrary; and humbly desire your lordship will, in a ministerial capacity, protest against such an insult upon the property of, sir, your most obedient and most humble servant,   RICH. STEELE.

Mr Dennis, finding he took so little by the experiment of his low, personal attack upon Steele, modestly assumed a tone of injured innocence, and addressed one of his long-winded letters with his ground of complaint to Sir Richard :—

LETTER CCCXCII.   *From Mr Dennis.* †

March 4, 1719–20.

SIR,—Though, at the time of writing this, I am almost overwhelmed both with sickness and grief, yet I cannot forbear making a just complaint to you, for your being the occasion of both these, either by your actually breaking your word with me, or being perfectly passive while your managers broke it; which, if it has not reduced me to immediate necessity, yet has brought me within the danger of it, and consequently within the apprehension of it, which is as grievous almost as the thing. And that this complaint is but too justly grounded, you yourself will acknowledge when I have laid my case before you, which I shall do in as few words as I can.

It was upon the 27th of February 1717–18, that I received a letter from Mr Booth, by your direction, and the direction of the managers under you, desiring me to dine at your house on the 28th, and after dinner to read the tradegy of "Coriolanus" to you, which I had altered from Shakespeare.

---

* Who was one of Steele's supporters in 1714, when he made his defence at the bar of the Commons, and to whom (then General Stanhope) he dedicated the first volume of the *Englishman.*

† "Directed, 'To Sir Richard Steele, Patentee of the Theatre in Drury Lane.'"

You cannot but remember, sir, that, upon reading it, the play, with the alterations, was approved of, nay, and warmly approved of, by yourself, Mr Cibber, and Mr Booth, (the other manager was not there;) and that resolutions were taken for the acting of it in the beginning of this winter. Now, I appeal to yourself if any dramatic performance could be more seasonable in the beginning of a winter, when we were threatened with an invasion from Sweden on the north, and from Spain on the west, than a tradegy whose moral is thus expressed in the last lines of the play :—

> " ——— They who, through ambition or revenge,
> Or impious interest, join with foreign foes,
> T' oppress or to destroy their native country ;
> Shall find, like Coriolanus, soon or late,
> From their perfidious foreign friends their fate."

I am sure, sir, I need not tell one of your understanding, that this moral is so apparently the foundation of the dramatic action, and must appear to every spectator and reader to be so truly the genuine result of it, that if I had not said one word of it, every reader and spectator would have been able to have suggested so much to himself.

Well, sir, when the winter came on, what was done by your deputies? Why, instead of keeping their word with me, they spent above two months of the season in getting up " All for Love ; or, The World Well Lost," a play which has indeed a noble first act, an act which ends with a scene becoming of the dignity of the tragic stage. But if Horace had been now alive, and been either a reader or spectator of that entertainment, he would have passed his old sentence upon the author,—

> " Infelix operis summâ, quia ponere totum
> Nesciet." *

For, was ever anything so pernicious, so immoral, so criminal, as the design of that play? I have mentioned the title of it, give me leave to set before you the last two lines :—

> " And fame to late posterity shall tell,
> No lovers lived so great, or died so well."

And this encomium of the conduct and death of Anthony and Cleopatra— a conduct so immoral, and a self-murder so criminal—is to give it more force, put into the mouth of the high priest of Isis ; though that priest could not but know that what he thus commended would cause imme-

---

* " Unhappy in the whole, because unskill'd
    To join the parts, and make them harmonise."—*Duncombe.*

diately the utter destruction of his country, and make it become a con-
quered and a Roman province. Certainly, never could the design of an
author square more exactly with the design of Whitehall at the time when
it was written, which was, by debauching the people, absolutely to enslave them.

For pray, sir, what do the title and the last two lines of the play amount
to in plain English? Why, to this, that if any person of quality, or other,
shall turn away his wife, his young, affectionate, virtuous, charming wife,
(for all these Octavia was,) to take to his bed a loose abandoned prostitute,
and shall in her arms exhaust his patrimony, destroy his health, emas-
culate his mind, and lose his reputation and all his friends; why all this
is well and greatly done, his ruin is his commendation. And if afterwards, in despair, he either hangs or drowns himself, or goes out of the
world, like a rat, with a dose of arsenic or sublimate, why it is a great and
envied fate, he does nobly and heroically.

It is, sir, with extreme reluctance that I have said all this; for I would
not be thought to affront the memory of Mr Dryden, for whose extraordinary qualities no man has a greater veneration than myself. But that
all considerations ought to give place to the public good, is a truth of
which you and all men, I am sure, can never doubt.

And can you believe then, after having recommended virtue and public
spirit for so many years to the world, that you can give your subalterns
authority to preach up adultery to a town which stands so little in need
of their doctrine? Is not the chastity of the marriage bed one of the chief
incendiaries of public spirit, and the frequency of adulteries one of the chief
extinguishers of it? according to that of Horace: *—

> " Fœcunda culpœ secula, nuptias
> Primum inquinavere, et genus, et domos.
> Hoc fonte derivata clades
> In patriam populumque fluxit." †

For when adultery is become so frequent, especially among persons of condition, upon whose sentiments all public spirit chiefly depends, that a
great many husbands begin to believe, or perhaps but to suspect, that

---

* 3 Od. vi. 17.
† " Fruitful of crimes, this age first stain'd
  Their hapless offspring, and profaned
  The nuptial bed, from whence the woes,
  That various and unnumber'd rose
  From this polluted fountainhead,
  O'er Rome, and o'er the nations spread."

they who are called their children are not their own ; I appeal to you,
sir, if that belief, or that suspicion, must not exceedingly cool their zeal
for the welfare of those children, and consequently for the welfare of
posterity.

As I had infinitely the advantage of " All for Love" in the moral of
" Coriolanus," I had it by consequence in the whole tragedy ; for the
" Coriolanus," as I have altered it, having a just moral, and, by consequence, at the bottom a general and allegorical action, and universal and
allegorical characters, and for that very reason a fable, is therefore a true
tragedy, if it be not a just and regular one ; but it is as just and as regular
as I could make it, upon so irregular a plan as Shakspeare's ; whereas,
" All for Love" having no moral, and consequently no general and allegorical action, nor general and allegorical characters, can for that reason
have no fable, and therefore can be no tragedy. It is indeed only a particular account of what happened formerly to Anthony and Cleopatra, and
a most pernicious amusement.

And as I had the advantage in the merit of " Coriolanus," I had it likewise in the world's opinion of the merit and reputation of Shakspeare in
tragedy above that of Mr Dryden. For, let Mr Dryden's genius for tragedy
be what it will, he has more than once publicly owned that it was much
inferior to Shakspeare's, and particularly in those two remarkable lines in
his Prologue to Aurenge-Zebe :—

> " And when he hears his god-like Romans rage,
> He in a just despair would quit the stage."

And in the verses to Sir Godfrey Kneller—

> " Shakspeare, thy gift, I place before my sight ;
> With awe I ask his blessing ere I write ;
> With reverence look on his majestic face,
> Proud to be less, but of his godlike race."

And the same Mr Dryden has more than once declared to me that there
was something in this very tragedy of " Coriolanus," as it was written by
Shakspeare, that is truly great and truly Roman, and I more than once
answered him that it had always been my own opinion. Now, I appeal to
you and your managers if it has lost anything under my hands.

But what is more considerable than all this, your deputy-lieutenants for
the stage have ten times the opinion of the advantage which Shakspeare
has over Mr Dryden in tragedy than either I or the rest of the world have.
Ever since I was capable of reading Shakspeare, I have always had, and
have always expressed that veneration for him which is justly his due, of
which I believe no one can doubt who has read the essay which I pub-

lished some years ago upon his genius and writings. But what they express upon all occasions is not esteem, is not admiration, but flat idolatry.

And lastly, I had the advantage of the very opinion which those people had of their own interest in the case. They knew very well that it was but twelve years since " All for Love " had been acted. And they were likewise satisfied that from its first run, as they call it, to the beginning of this last winter, it had never brought four audiences together. At the same time, there was no occasion to tell them that the " Coriolanus" of Shakspeare had not been acted in twenty years, and that, when it was brought upon the stage twenty years ago, it was acted twenty nights together.

And now, sir, I shall be obliged to you if you will acquaint me for what mighty and unknown reason the " Coriolanus," notwithstanding your words solemnly given to act it as soon as it could conveniently be brought upon the stage this winter, notwithstanding the merit of the play itself—I speak of Shakspeare's part of it—notwithstanding the world's and their own opinion of the superior merit of Shakspeare to Mr Dryden in tragedy, and their very opinion of their own interest in the case ; nay, notwithstanding the exact seasonableness of the moral for the service of King George and of Great Britain, which above all things ought to have been considered by those who call themselves the king's servants, and who act under his authority; I say, sir, I should be extremely obliged to you if you would tell me what powerful reason could so far prevail over all those I have mentioned as to engage them to postpone the " Coriolanus," not only for " All for Love," but likewise for that lamentable tragic farce, " Cæsar Borgia," * from which nobody expected anything but themselves ; and a comedy after it called " The Masquerade,"† from which they themselves declared they expected nothing.—I am, &c.   JOHN DENNIS.

LETTER CCCXCIII.   *To Mrs Elizabeth Steele, at Mrs Nazereau's,*
                              at Chelsea.

                                           Edinburgh, Sept. 17, 1720.

MY DEAR CHILD,—I keep your letters safely tied together, in order to observe your improvement, which I take notice of with great pleasure. Mrs Mary's mark is no less a satisfaction to me, because it denotes that she is well, and shows her endeavours to converse with me. But I hope you

---

* " A tragedy, by Nat. Lee."
† " A farce, by Benjamin Griffin, performed in 1717, at Lincolns-Inn-Fields, with some success."—*Biog. Dram.*

will now make her begin to sign the first letters of her name. Be pleased to write every other letter in English. To make this easy, I will be contented that what is written in your mother tongue one post may be in French the next.

Be very dutiful and obedient to Mrs Keck, and believe me to be the most affectionate of fathers,   RICH. STEELE.

Remember me to Molly.

LETTER CCCXCIV.   *To Mrs Elizabeth Steele.*

Edinburgh, Oct. 7, 1720.

MY DEAR CHILD,—I have yours of the 30th of the last month ; and, from your diligence and improvement, conceive hopes of your being as excellent a person as your mother. You have great opportunities of becoming such a one by observing the maxims and sentiments of her bosom friend, Mrs Keck, who has condescended to take upon her the care of you and your sister, for which you are always to pay her the same respect as if she were your mother.

I have observed that your sister has, for the first time, written the *initial* or first letters of her name. Tell her I am highly delighted to see her subscription in such fair, fair letters, and how many fine things those two letters stand for when she writes them. M. S. is *milk* and *sugar*, *mirth* and *safety*, *music* and *songs*, *meat* and *sauce*, as well as *Molly*, and *Spot*, and *Mary Steele*.

You see I take pleasure in conversing with you by prattling anything to divert you. I hope we shall next month have a happy meeting, when I will entertain you with something that may be as good for the father as the children, and consequently please us.—I am, madam, your affectionate father and most humble servant,   RICH. STEELE.

LETTER CCCXCV.   *To Mr Brookesby.**

Dec. 1, 1720.

SIR,—I thank you for your intended favour of communicating to me discoveries in *Alchemy*, but I have long resolved never to concern myself in inquiries of that sort.—I am, sir, your most humble servant,

RICH. STEELE.

---

* Directed, " At his house, the first door on the right hand in the Little Almonry, by the Dutch Envoy's, near Dean's Yard."

LETTER CCCXCVI. *Copy of a Letter, written in a cipher, " To Mr Gilmore, at his house at Poplar, near the Church."*

Dec. 10, 1720.

SIR,—I have great reason of complaint against Mr Dale for his conduct in relation to the Fish-pool. The way in which he has acted, and now proceeds, can lead to nothing but ruin of that invention, and dishonour to you and myself, who brought it into the world. I will, with the blessing of God, take the most just and effectual methods to obtain satisfaction to all innocent persons concerned for the affair, beginning with you, and ending with myself. In the meantime, I must conjure and charge you at your peril not to finish the tender, or let him into the secret of the structure thereof, without notice and consent of, Sir, your most obedient humble servant,   RICH. STEELE.

Perhaps the reader will not be displeased if the notice of this period close with some lines addressed to Steele, by a lady, on the death of Addison, and upbraiding his silence on the subject :—

March 1, 1720

If I, O Steele, presumptuous shall appear,
And these unskilful notes offend thine ear,
Forbear to censure what I've artless writ,
No well-bred man e'er damn'd a woman's wit.
But sure there's none of all the inspired train
Who do not of thy indolence complain.
Ingrate, or indolent; or why thus long
Should Addison require his funeral song ?*
When a loved monarch quits his cares below,
The meanest subjects join the common woe ;
But from the favourite who his worth best knew
A tribute of superior grief is due.
Shall Ramsey, and Melissa, lays produce,
(That a mechanic's, this a woman's muse,)
While *thou*, wit's sole surviving hope ! supine,
The melancholy theme dost still decline ?

---

* The death of Addison, which occurred June 17, 1719, was lamented in an elegy by Tickell, his literary executor, which has been much admired, though Steele did not do justice to it, and appears to have contemplated some memorial of his friend, which it is much to be regretted should never have been executed.

Exert that fire which glows within your breast,
Nor longer thus in lazy silence rest ;
Aloft your skilful muse can wing her flight,
And emulate his strains whose praise you write.

For me, the meanest of the tuneful train,
T' attempt th' unequal task were fond and vain ;
But, could I sing, O sacred shade ! thy praise
Alone should claim, alone inspire my lays.
Thou kind preceptor of the tender fair !
Great was the charge, and generous the care.
You show'd us virtue, so celestial bright,
So amiable, in so divine a light ;
Ashamed at last, false glories we resign'd,
By thee instructed to improve the mind.
How oft, reclined beneath a sylvan shade,
Have I thy Marcia read, thy matchless maid !
In her superior worth and virtue shine,
Her wisdom, manners, her whole self divine.
A great exalted mind in her appears ;
And gentle Lucia melts my soul to tears.

Here, O ye fair ! in this bright mirror learn,
Your minds with never-fading charms t' adorn !
On these accomplishments bestow some care,
'Tis no great merit to be only fair.

His Rosamonda shall for ever prove
A mark to keep us safe from guilty love.
Beauty 's a snare, unless with virtue join'd,
An angel form should have an angel mind.
But when the bard displays the artful scene,
The suppliant beauty, and the furious queen,
In melting notes sings her disastrous love,
With tears we pity what we can't approve.

How learn'd he was, O Steele, do thou declare,
For that 's a task beyond a woman's sphere.
Some works I 've seen, wrought up by rules of art,
Where poor excluded nature had no part ;
But he, the Stagyrite's strict axioms knew,
Yet still to nature, as to art, was true.
He touch'd the heart, the passions could command,
'Twas nature all but mended by his hand.
His style is noble, sentiments refined,
Full of benevolence to all mankind.
In more than theory he religion knew,

And kept the heav'nly still in view ;
Rapt on her wings, his soul ecstatic soars,
Leaves our dull orb, a better world explores,
And now he's reach'd th' ethereal plains above,
Th' eternal seat of harmony and love ;
Blest harmony and love anew inspire,
With hymns, like theirs, he joins th' angelic quire.
　He's gone ! oh, never, never to return !
Around his tomb, ye sacred Muses, mourn ;
Your pious tears on the cold marble shed ;
You loved him living, now lament him dead !
Cold is that breast, where glow'd your hallow'd fire ;
Silent that voice whose notes you did inspire ;
Still lies that hand th' harmonious lyre best strung,
Unmoved the gen'rous heart, and mute the tuneful tongue !
That dome, where his remains now lie confined,
Holds not the clay that held a nobler mind.
Here peaceful rest, to wait Heaven's great decree,
Soft be thy slumbers, sweet thy waking be !
　Who can his Warwick's anxious woes express,
The bitter anguish, and the deep distress ?
The lonely mourner does not grieve alone,
And distant Cambria echoes to each groan ;
Her native country lends this poor relief.
We weep, we sigh, with sympathetic grief.
Ev'n I, oppress'd with sorrows of my own,
Suspend them all, to mourn her Addison.
Oh, will she deign to accept these lowly lays
My humble Muse thus offers to his praise !
　Oh, may the lovely child, the budding fair,
Soothe all her griefs, and sweeten every care !
Still grow in virtue, as she grows in years,
Till she in full-blown excellence appears ;
May she be perfect, as his fancy wrought,
The poet's race excel the poet's thought !
Let charms united blooming Marcia grace,
Her sire's exalted wit, her mother's beauteous face.

CHAPTER XX.

THE alternation of sunshine and clouds by which the career
of Steele was so remarkably chequered, received at this
time a fresh illustration by another turn in the wheel of
fortune. The quiet magnanimity with which he had borne
the long and cruel adversity inflicted on him by his unprincipled adversary was above all praise. He had now
fathomed the lowest depth of his fortune. But the darkest
hour of the night is that which precedes the dawn. The
continuance of his steady friend, Mr Walpole, in power
would no doubt have saved him from his recent misfortunes,
but unluckily he had resigned his office of First Lord of the
Treasury in 1717, about the same time that that uncertain
and selfish patron, the Duke of Newcastle, became Lord
Chamberlain. Walpole—who, since the previous June had
held the lucrative but minor office of Paymaster of the
Forces, on the 2d of April 1721, in consequence of the
retirement of the Earl of Sunderland, as previously stated—
once more resumed his place at the head of the Treasury.

As this eminent statesman was so intimately connected
with Steele in his political capacity, and exerted so favourable an influence on his fortune, a few words respecting him
may here be added. ROBERT WALPOLE, afterwards Earl of
Orford, (1676-1745,) was of a good old Norfolk family.
Being a younger son he had, in consequence, been originally designed for the Church, and always asserted that he
would have risen to the Primacy. After a preparatory
education in a private school at Massingham, in his native
county, he proceeded to Eton, and thence to King's College,
Cambridge, where in 1696 he obtained a scholarship. This
he resigned, after two years, in consequence of the death
of his elder brother, and having himself suffered serious
indisposition. He then returned to reside on the estate of
which he was now heir, along with his father, who was one
of the representatives of the borough of Castle Rising.

At the close of 1700, Mr Walpole succeeded to the property—about L.2000 a year—by the death of his father,
having in the course of the previous summer married the
daughter of Sir John Shorter, Lord Mayor of London. At
the same time he also succeeded his father in the representation of Castle Rising, the two seats of which, as well
as one of King's Lynn, were in the interest of his family.
In the last year of King William, when his parliamentary
career commenced, though the Tory party was in the
ascendant, he became an active supporter of the Whig interest. He seconded the motion for extending the Oath of
Abjuration to members of the Church and the universities.
His merit did not fail to attract the attention of Godolphin
and Marlborough ; and when they were strengthening the
Whig interest in the then mixed cabinet, he received the

appointment of a member of the council of the Prince Consort, George of Denmark, as Lord High Admiral, in 1705 ; and on the retirement of Harley and his party, three years after, succeeded St John as Secretary at War, and became afterwards Treasurer of the Navy. When that Whig folly, for which they paid so dearly—the impeachment of Sacheverell—was proposed, he did all he could to prevent it ; but when it was determined on he was appointed one of the managers. On the dismissal of Godolphin, to make way for the Tory favourites of the Queen, disdaining the overtures of the new dispensers of power, he resolutely followed the fortunes of his chiefs. As he would not be one of them, he was to be ruined. His offence was aggravated by subsequently entering the lists against the assailants of Marlborough, who had also been vainly tampered with, and was similarly treated. In the course of the following year he was expelled the House by a small majority of that Tory parliament, and committed to the Tower on the charge of corruption in his office of Secretary at War, in having received two notes of L.500 each from a contractor. Walpole drew up a pamphlet on the subject. His plea was, that the pecuniary advantage was not for himself. In the terms of agreement a certain proportion of the contract had been reserved for the benefit of a friend whom he should name. This friend, since dead, was Mr Mann, of whose name the other contractors not being aware, the notes were drawn in favour of Walpole. However dubious the transaction may be, it is remarkable that they never ventured to impeach or prosecute him. So much was he regarded as the victim of party malice, that some of the ministerial party had voted in his favour, and others had declined to vote. Being re-elected, he was declared ineligible to sit in the same parliament.

During the few remaining years that the Queen survived, he devoted himself to the most energetic opposition, and for the time rather involved his means by the splendour of his hospitality at Houghton, and in other ways in the interest of his party. It is a curious fact in the history of party, that on Oxford's dismissal Bolingbroke made it a day of rejoicing by entertaining Walpole and some of the other leading Whigs. This was probably done with the double object to mortify his hated rival, and as a blind to his real designs, and possibly with the hope of making friends on the opposite side in case of the game going against him.

On the accession of George I., which almost immediately followed that event, the Whigs were again in the ascendant, and Walpole was appointed, in the first instance, Paymaster of the Forces, Treasurer of Chelsea Hospital, and a Privy Councillor, (Sept. 1714,) and in October of the following year First Lord of the Treasury and Chancellor of the Exchequer. He was also elected Chairman of the Committee of Secrecy to inquire into the conduct of the previous ministers, and drew up and moved the impeachment of Bolingbroke and Oxford. An illness succeeded, probably caused by the anxieties and exertions of the year of the rebellion in favour of the Pretender, and during his absence the Septennial Bill, a measure in the preparation of which he is supposed to have had a principal hand, was introduced by his brother-in-law, Lord Townshend, who was nominally chief of the Cabinet. During the King's visit to his Hanoverian dominions in 1716, he was accompanied by the Earl of Sunderland, one of the Secretaries of State, who succeeded on that occasion in establishing himself in a position of great personal influence. As the ambition of Sunderland had always aimed at the premiership, his increased influence led to differences in the cabinet, which induced Townshend to exchange his Secretaryship for the Vice-royalty of Ireland ; and Walpole, not finding his position satisfactory, tendered his resignation in March 1717. The King is said to have playfully thrown back the seals to him many times before he would accept them from him.

On the day of his resignation Walpole brought in his Sinking Fund Bill for reducing the debt of the nation. He is supposed to have subsequently arrived at a similar opinion of the fallacy of the principle of a sinking fund now entertained—but as no doubt was then entertained on the subject, it answered the practical purpose of enabling the Government to borrow money at a greatly reduced rate of interest. Walpole soon established himself in a position of such strength in opposition as to oblige the selfish rival, who, on the strength of the royal favour, seemed bent upon reigning alone, to come to terms. He consequently resumed office in June 1720 in a place he had formerly held, that of Paymaster of the Forces. On the bursting of the South Sea Bubble in that year, the King, the legislature, and the nation displayed their confidence in the prophet whose warnings had been despised or unheeded, and seemed to regard him as the only man equal to the occasion. When it was known he had taken the matter in hand, the popular excitement sensibly abated, and the stock rose from its excessive depreciation. On the reluctant, but almost compulsory retirement of Sunderland, as something more than suspected of participation in the practices of the company, though acquitted by the House, Walpole again resumed his place, in the beginning of April, at the head of the Treasury. He displayed his generosity towards the man who, in the day of his triumph, had been chiefly instrumental in driving him from power, by shielding him in the hour of his extremity, when angry cries for vengeance rung through the land. Though these were chiefly aimed at the directors of the company, yet Sunderland's conduct was greatly aggravated by his responsible and elevated position. Though Walpole suffered some diminution of popularity in consequence, he failed of receiving in return the gratitude of him he had so materially contributed to save. In the re-adjustment of the cabinet, Walpole's brother-in-law, Lord Townshend, became again the nominal chief.

In the following year the disclosure of a Jacobite conspiracy, in which the celebrated Atterbury was implicated, resulted in the exile of that intriguing prelate, the evidence against whom was only circumstantial, but has been fully confirmed by the subsequent publication of his correspondence. Indeed, he justified the suspicions against him, like Bolingbroke, by his own act in immediately taking office under the Pretender; and, like him, too, was fated to meet with an ungrateful reward of his zeal in being discarded. At the same time Walpole gave proof of his moderation and freedom from vindictiveness in withdrawing the proceedings against Bolingbroke, to the extent of permitting him to return according to his wish, but without restoring to him either his property or title. But if he anticipated any services or gratitude in return, he was fated to be disappointed, for that arch intriguer fully realised the definition of the latter quality as "a lively sense of favours to come," and considering nothing done so long as anything remained undone, became one of the most bitter and violent of the opponents of his benefactor.

In the same year (1723) Walpole was one of the Lords Justices, and sole Secretary of State, in the absence of Lords Townshend and Carteret with the king in Hanover, and in the next had the Order of the Bath conferred upon him. A peerage, which he had himself declined, was granted to his son ; and, after having in the previous year again filled the office of one of the Lords Justices, in 1726 he received the Order of the Garter, an honour which, with one exception, had previously been confined to the peerage.

The opposition to the minister, the nucleus of which his predecessor had fostered and left behind him in revenge for having been supplanted by him, found a powerful ally in Ireland in another disappointed politician. Swift, on the break up of the Tory Cabinet of Queen Anne, of whose members he had been the friend and adviser, retired to his deanery—the first promotion he had received from them, and only just in time—and devoted himself for some years, in sullen disappointment and chagrin, to the exemplary discharge of its duties. On his first arrival he had been very unpopular, and had even been subjected to insults in the streets as a Jacobite. But it was not possible that such energies and such passions should remain for ever unemployed. After having published a " Proposal for the Universal Use of Irish Manufactures," which had turned the tide of popularity very strongly in his favour, in the year 1724 an opportunity occurred for striking a memorable blow at the Government. A patent having been granted to a person of the name of Wood for a copper coinage for Ireland, Swift, in a series of letters, written with great plausibility in the character of a man of plain sense, under the signature of " M. B. Drapier," denounced the affair as a scandalous job, and successfully persuaded the people to reject it, or that they would be ruined by the worthless coin. It can scarcely be believed, even if the coin had been as bad as he represented, that any one could have been injured by it, unless on the supposition of any one having a large amount of it, and that it had ceased to be a legal tender. But so far was his representation from being justified that, after the outcry against it, it was tested by the Master of the Mint, no less a person than Sir Isaac Newton, and found to be satisfactory. At the same time that he had shown his power in thus successfully opposing one of the measures of the Government, he prudently avoided closing the door of hope against himself, by exonerating the minister personally of blame. It may also be stated, in Swift's behalf, that there was much more justice in his statement of the general grievances of Ireland, of which this was the prelude. So effective was the opposition that the patent was ultimately withdrawn. Walpole took the opportunity also to avail himself of the remarkable talents of Lord Carteret, afterwards Earl Granville, by sending him to Ireland as Lord-Lieutenant to allay the agitation on the subject, at the same time that he rid himself of a formidable rival.

Two years after, Swift spent some months of the summer with Pope, and took the opportunity of waiting upon Walpole, with the ostensible view of laying before the minister a just representation of the affairs of Ireland. If there was only one visit, his reception and the result have been variously stated, but his failure has been attributed to the minister having previously had intimation of a letter of his to Arbuthnot, in which he had expressed his design of stealing a march upon him, and his opinion of the amount of flattery he would bear. The accounts of Dr Rundle, Bishop of Derry, and Horace Walpole, in his "Reminiscences," have a general resemblance. The former represents him as saying to the minister, "For God's sake, Sir Robert, take me out of that cursed country, and place me somewhere in England." "Mr Dean," replied Sir Robert, "I should be glad to oblige you, but I fear removing you would spoil your wit. I transplanted that tree (pointing to one under the window) from the hungry soil of Houghton to the Thames side, but it is good for nothing here." Swift is said to have hastened his departure much chagrined; and to this his subsequent acrimonious treatment of the minister, both in prose and verse, has been attributed. In the "Rhapsody" on poetry, one of the most elaborate of his poetical pieces, Walpole comes in for his full share of the satire :—

> " Now sing the minister of state,
>   Who shines alone without a mate.
>   Observe with what majestic port
>   This Atlas stands to prop the court,
>   Intent the public debts to pay,
>   Like prudent Fabius, by delay.
>
>   .   .   .   .   .   .
>   St George beheld thee with delight
>   Vouchsafe to be an azure knight,
>   When on thy breast and sides herculean
>   He fixed the star and string cerulean."

To enter into the details of the public life of Walpole

would be to write the history of the country for twenty years. On the accession of George II., in 1727, he retained his places, though he had been necessarily involved in the differences between the father and son in the preceding reign, and the Opposition eagerly looked for his dismissal. Differences between him and Townshend led to the retirement of the later, from which time Walpole reigned alone. In 1733 his celebrated excise scheme called forth the strenuous opposition of Pulteney, afterwards Earl of Bath, who, from his immense wealth and great talents in debate, was a powerful leader of the Opposition. That party, already strong, received an accession, two years later, of incalculable importance in the surpassing abilities of the elder Pitt. He was then a young officer in a cavalry regiment, and Walpole made the fatal, and with him unusual, mistake of making an enemy for life, and in addition concentrating his energies on politics, by depriving him of his commission. This eminent man lived to see and openly to confess his mistake in his violent opposition to Walpole. The Opposition, in the House and out of the House, was composed of such incongruous materials as to resemble Ovid's description of chaos, having no principle of cohesion but hatred of the minister. It was headed by the Prince of Wales, and composed of Jacobites, Tories, disappointed Whigs, and unpatronised authors.

The great blot upon the administration of Walpole was his allowing himself to be driven into an unjustifiable war with Spain in 1739, by the clamour of the Opposition and the popular feeling, contrary to his own judgment, for the sake of retaining power. It must, however, be admitted that Walpole tendered his resignation, and was only retained in office by the urgent intreaties and commands of the King. With another foolish war, entered into a few years later, against France and in favour of Hungary, in compliance with the wishes of the King and the people, he declined to be identified, and allowed himself to be driven from power in the beginning of 1742. On his retirement he was created Baron Houghton, Viscount Walpole, and Earl of Orford. The old veteran had maintained the fight gallantly to the last, nor would submit to a compromise by the division of power for the sake of retaining it—"leaving," in the words of Macaulay, "to those who had overthrown him shame, discord, and ruin."

It is a remarkable example of the vitality of prejudice and injustice, notwithstanding the trite sentiment about "veritas prevalebit," that the reputation which an Opposition, unprecedented in political warfare for its duration and violence, succeeded in attaching to the name of Walpole, as a monster of corruption, should have survived in popular estimation, perhaps somewhat modified, to the present time.*

---

* Two very striking vindications of him have appeared within the last twenty or thirty years by two eminent individuals, who united political experience with the highest literary merit, and who were little likely to sympathise with corruption—Brougham and Macaulay. The former says, "Few men have over reached and maintained for so many years the highest station which the citizen of a free state can hold, who have enjoyed more power than Sir Robert Walpole, and have left behind them less just cause of blame, or more monuments of the wisdom and virtue for which his country has to thank him. . . . We may now distinctly perceive the merits of this great statesman, and we shall easily admit that he was one of the ablest, wisest, safest rulers who ever bore sway in this country. . . . Walpole yet ranks in the very highest class of those whose unvarying prudence, clear apprehension, fertility of resource to meet unexpected difficulties, firmness of purpose, just and not seemingly exaggerated self-confidence, point them out by common consent as the men qualified to guide the

After successfully endeavouring to sow divisions and jealousies among his rivals and successors, the remainder of his life was spent in a very retired manner, though frequently consulted by the King, whose esteem and confidence he retained.   His pictures, his garden, and the sweets of private friendship divided his closing years.   His own hospitality had ever been rather in excess.   In general society, his frank, unreserved and generous nature, his heartiness and constant good humour, made him an

course of human affairs, to ward off public dangers, and to watch over the peace of empires. . . . It was this general tide of public opinion, as well as the undercurrent of royal and courtly inclination, that Walpole had to stem for many a long year.   He did stem it; gallantly he kept the vessel to her course; and he was not driven from the helm by the combined clamours of the mob and intrigues of party, until after he had secured the incalculable blessings of a repose, without example, for all the great interests committed to his charge."—*Hist. Sketches of Statesmen*, vol. iii.

Lord Macaulay, in the latter part of one of his essays, says, " We have no reverence for the memory of those who were then called the patriots.   We are for the principles of good government against Walpole, and for Walpole against the Opposition. . . . They held up a single man as the sole cause of all the vices of a bad system which had been in full operation before his entrance into public life, and continued to be in full operation when some of these very brawlers had succeeded to his power."   And, again, " The government could not go on unless the Parliament could be kept in order. . . . The Parliament had shaken off the control of the royal prerogative.   It had not yet fallen under the control of public opinion. . . . Under these circumstances the country could be governed only by corruption.   Bolingbroke, who was the ablest and most vehement of those who raised the clamour against corruption, had no better remedy than that the royal prerogative should be strengthened.   The remedy would no doubt have been effective.   The only question is, whether it would not have been worse than the disease.   The fault was in the constitution of the legislature; and to blame those ministers who managed the legislature in the only way in which it could be managed, is gross injustice.   They submitted to extortion because they could not help themselves.   We might as well accuse the poor lowland farmer, who paid black mail to Rob Roy, of corrupting the virtue of the Highlanders, as accuse Sir R. Walpole of corrupting the virtue of Parliament.   His crime was merely this, that he employed his money more dexterously, and got more support in return for it than any of those who preceded or followed him.   He was himself incorruptable."—*Essay on Horace Walpole.*

eminent favourite. It is remarkable that Pope, though
professing to think it his vocation to satirise corruption,
never ventured to attack him whom his enemies represented as its very fountain head. On the contrary,
he noticed him in the most flattering manner, describing
him in private in a way in which all his contemporaries
concur :—

> " Seen him I have, but in his happier hour
>   Of social pleasure, ill-exchanged for power ;
>   Seen him, uncumber'd with a venal tribe,
>   Smile without art, and win without a bribe."—*Epilog to Sat.*

A painful complaint, from which he had long suffered,
proved fatal in the year 1745, in his sixty-ninth year.

The restoration of Walpole to power was an event so
favourable to Steele that his hopes were raised accordingly,
and stimulated him to fresh exertions for the restoration
of the rights of which he had long been so unjustly and
cruelly deprived. Before, however, anticipating the result,
some fragments of a diary which Steele commenced about
this time may be here presented to the reader. It is much to
be regretted that he did not sooner commence this practice
of noting down passing events and feelings, and continue
it longer. Of the value and interest that might have been
attached to the result, we may judge from Swift's journal
to Stella, which is certainly among the most valuable and
interesting of his productions, though merely recording
his unpremeditated remarks upon passing events. The
present fragment of a diary was begun by Steele just two
days after the resumption of office by his powerful and
consistent friend, Mr Walpole. We find him stating distinctly his impression of the secret cause of the depriva-

tion of his rights, in a way to exonerate the Duke of Newcastle, at least of the exclusive blame.

FRAGMENT OF A DIARY.

April 4, 1721.—I have lately had a fit of sickness, which has awakened in me, among other things, a sense of the little care I have taken of my own family. And as it is natural for men to be more affected with the actions and sufferings and observations upon the rest of the world, set down by their predecessors, than by what they receive from other men; I have taken a resolution to write down in this book, as in times of leisure I may have opportunity, things past, or things that may occur hereafter, for the perusal and consideration of my son, Eugene Steele, and his sisters Elizabeth Steele and Mary Steele, my beloved children.

Easter Sunday, April 9, 1721.—After the repeated perusal of Dr Tillotson's seventh sermon, in the third volume of the small edition of his admirable and comfortable writings, and after having done certain acts of benevolence and charity to some needy persons of merit, I went this day to the holy sacrament. In addition to the proper prayers of the Church, I framed for my private use on this occasion the following prayer :—

" O Almighty Lord God, I prostrate myself before thy divine majesty, in hopes of mercy for all my former transgressions, through the merits of Thy Son, Jesus Christ.

" Thou art my Maker, and knowest my infirmities, appetites, and passions, and the miserable habit of mind which I have contracted through a guilty indulgence of them. Pardon me, O Lord, in that I permitted them to grow upon me ; and allow the moments for retrospect and repentance ; or afford me Thy mercy, if Thou shalt please to take me away in the course of a faithful endeavour. I bow down to Thee with a firm resolution to resist all perverse and sensual inclinations for the future. I beg Thy grace and assistance, for the sake of our Lord Jesus, who has instituted this means of salvation, to which I approach with faith. Lord, O Lord, receive a broken and contrite heart. Amen."

April 9, (10?) 1721.—I have this morning resolved to pursue very warmly my being restored to my government of the Theatre Royal, which is my right, under the title of the Governor of the Royal Company of Comedians, and from which I have been violently dispossessed by the Duke of Newcastle, Lord Chamberlain of his Majesty's Household, upon a frivolous pretence of jurisdiction in his office, which he has been persuaded to assert against the force of the King's patent to me. This violation of property I take to have been instigated by the late Secretaries Stanhope and Craggs, for my opposition to the Peerage Bill, by speeches in the House and printed pamphlets.

The Duke of Newcastle brought me into this present Parliament for the town of Burroughbridge, upon which consideration I attempt all manner of fair methods to bring his grace to reason without a public trial in a court of justice : and, therefore, after applying to my Lord Sunderland *

---

* Son-in-law to the Duke of Marlborough, and the Secretary of State, with whom Steele was early connected as gazetteer. "The following dialogue, which is said to have passed, in or about 1719, between Sir Richard Steele and the Earl of Sunderland, first Lord Commissioner of the Treasury from 1718 to 1721, (whether genuine or not,) is characteristic, and is here transcribed from Ralph's 'Case of Authors by Profession : '—

"STEELE.—I beg your pardon, my lord, though such as you seldom remember, such as I seldom forget. And I must now beg leave to put you in mind of what you have told me over and over again, that you thought Dick Steele had almost as good pretensions as Bob Walpole ; that it was unpardonable in one who had been my right-hand man at the bar of the House, to turn his back upon me when at the head of the Treasury ; and that, when you came to be minister, all should be made up to me.

"LORD SUNDERLAND.—I did, I did, sure enough. But, my dear Sir Richard—

"STEELE.—My lord, my lord, I know what you would say ; and I will save you the trouble of saying it. I am of the miller's mind. The fault is in the mill, in more senses than one.

"LORD SUNDERLAND.—What mill? I do not understand you.

"STEELE.—Afford me a little patience, my lord, and I will make you understand me. A poor country fellow, coming too late of a Saturday evening to the mill with his corn to be ground, found the miller had shut up, and was jogging home. This was a sorry sight, as Macbeth says. Bread for himself and family for the next week was the point in question : the miller was a churl, and not easy to be talked into anything. However, he did his best, scratched his ears, told his tale, and so far with success, that he obtained the custody of the mill, with leave to grind for himself, on condition he did justice to the crib, and paid the same toll as if the miller had done the job himself. The fellow promised, like any minister, my lord, and performed accordingly ; for going to the till, with an honest purpose, he thought, to pay the miller his due, he found such a quantity of grist lodged there already, that he could not resist the temptation which assailed him to take twice as much away as he had been enjoined to add. But here the parallel fails, my lord : for on his return home his heart smote him. He could not sleep all night ; he could not eat all day ; and at last, he found himself under an irresistible impulse to make restitution. The miller, in the meantime, having examined his crib, and seeing him approach with a sack on his back as before, took it for granted he was come to repeat his experiment, and resolved to give him a suitable reception ; but was not allowed time enough. For the poor

and Walpole for their good offices, I writ the following letter to his
grace's brother, Mr Henry Pelham, lately appointed one of the Lords of
the Treasury :—

(LETTER CCCXCVII.)—"SIR,—I presume to address myself to you for
your favour and patronage with your brother, the Duke of Newcastle. The
matter is too public, and necessarily made so even in print, by a command
to me from his grace to apply to him neither by friends, speech, or letter,
and consequently leaving me no other way to represent my condition.   It
is my misfortune to do exactly as the question lies before me in a certain
House, where, I am glad to see, you are growing eminent.

"By this means good-will towards me is tossed from one interest into
another, as the point which I vote for is respectively acceptable or ungrateful. At present I am wholly friendless, for no one is obliged to one
who will do nothing but what he thinks just, because his suffrage never
attends persons or parties. However, sir, your quality and time of life
make me hope you have the disinterested magnanimity to espouse an unhappy man, to the dissuasion even of your brother from prolonging a
mortification, which unhappy incidents (without any particular provocation from me, or personal resentment in his grace) brought upon me, to
the suffering of a long series of time all the evils and sorrows that this
life can afford.—I am, sir, your most obedient and most humble servant,

"RICH. STEELE.

"To the Right Hon. Henry Pelham, Esq.,
   one of the Lords of the Treasury, &c.,
      April 5, 1721."

April 29, 1721.—I purchased this day fifteen assignments in the Fish-

---

penitent made all the haste he could to confess the fraud, and, with tears of contrition, discharged the load at his feet.   This melted the miller into another
mood; and, having paused upon the matter a moment or two, 'Gum, gum,' said
he, 'tak hart, mun, tak hart ! The vaate's in the mill. I do knau it is. Why,
mun, I was as honest as the day, when I com'd into it vurst. And now—sha't
ha' the grist—sha't ! For, mun, wur I to do as thee hast done, I should not ha'
a bed to lie on.'

"LORD SUNDERLAND.—Ha, ha, ha ! You were always a wag, Sir Richard,—ha,
ha, ha !

"STEELE.—To be serious, then, for once, my lord,—Knaves take care of themselves, and fools are undone by relying on other people's promises.

"'Addison,' Mr Ralph adds, 'and his advancement, hardly need to be mentioned, the instance is so notorious; but everybody may not so readily recollect
that his party services contributed more to it than all his laudable efforts to
refine our manners and perfect our taste.'"

pool undertaking, with a promissory note to deliver to Mr Robert Wilks (who sold them to me) a bond of five hundred pounds upon demand;* the said bond to be payable within two years after this day.

These entries, with another small fragment at a later date, constitute the whole of the diary; and comparatively trifling as they are, these few items but make us regret the more what we might have had if the plan which he thus late and fitfully took up had been sooner adopted, and he had given us the spirit of those Attic nights which he enjoyed in the company of Addison, Congreve, and the other wits, as well as notices and anecdotes of the leading men and events of the time.

With regard to the foregoing application, we may imagine it was about as successful as the numerous others which he had thought it his duty to make, and for which, however hopeless, he cannot be blamed. Within a month or six weeks, however, namely, on the 18th of May following, he was once more restored to his office and emoluments, through the good offices of Mr Walpole, now the most rising statesman of the time, or more properly speaking, perhaps, one of the few of the then public men deserving of the name. Of his engagements immediately subsequent to that happy event, we have no note; but as no news is commonly said to be good news, we may presume that he was getting on as tranquilly and satisfactorily as was consistent with that great deficit which the prolonged lapse of the income arising from his office must necessarily have created. As he produced nothing this year, we may suppose he was engaged, now that he was restored to case of

* "June 6, 1721.—I purpose to carry the above-mentioned bond to Mr Wilks this morning."

mind, upon the comedy he had so long had on hands. In this dearth of information, it only remains, after a brief entry in continuation of his diary, to furnish his correspondence for the year, as the only source from which anything is to be gleaned. The only thing noticeable about it is, that it affords indications of that difference with the managers which unhappily led to subsequent litigation.

Sunday, Sept. 17, 1721.—I am going this morning to the Lord Bishop of Bangor,* now nominated Bishop of Hereford, with a design to leave with his lordship my last will, whereby he is my executor and guardian to my son ; and (humbly resigning myself to Providence, whether I shall live to do anything I design,) I purpose to leave all my papers in as good order as I can for his perusal before I go to Scotland.

The following is his correspondence for this year :—

LETTER CCCXCVIII.   *To Mrs Elizabeth Steele.*

March 29, 1721.

DEAR CHILD,—I have yours, and beg your pardon that I did not, as I designed, visit you with your brother ; but he was so dirty that I was ashamed to bring him to your school. I beseech you to continue in the good and diligent way you are in, and you will be an unspeakable delight and satisfaction to, madam, your most affectionate father and most humble servant,   RICH. STEELE.

LETTER CCCXCIX.   *To Mrs Elizabeth Steele.*

April 5, 1721.

MY DEAR CHILD,—I have received your letter by the penny post, and read it with great pleasure and comfort, though I was then a little discomposed.

I have to-day had a tooth drawn, and am disordered also with a cold ; but, as soon as I go out, I will not fail to visit Mrs Keck and my dear little ones.

Service to Miss Molly, but tell her I am sorry she has forgot the charms I find in *M. S.*—Your affectionate father,   RICH. STEELE.

---

* Dr Benjamin Hoadly.

LETTER CCCC.   *To Mrs Elizabeth Steele.*

April 5, 1721.

MY DEAR DAUGHTER,—I thank you for your kindness, which makes you attempt to draw your father's picture, but I hope and am confident you are still better employed in imitating the life of your excellent mother. Her friendship is the best example and help you can have in pursuing that amiable and worthy pattern. I am this morning much better, and purpose, God willing, to go and bring home your brother, but I shall not adventure to introduce him to such fine ladies as his sisters are till he has got his new clothes.—I am, dear child, most affectionately yours,

RICH. STEELE.   .

My thanks and service to *M. S.*

LETTER CCCCI.   *To Mrs Elizabeth Steele.*

April 12, 1721.

MY DEAR BETTY,—Write this carefully over again, with the amendment of a large letter beginning every line, as likewise the stops as pointed to you, and send both this and what you write again to, madam, your most affectionate father and most humble servant,   RICH. STEELE.

LETTER CCCCII.   *To Mrs Elizabeth Steele.*

April 14, 1721.

MY DEAR CHILD,—I have received yours of this day, with the corrected copy, in which there are still some faults, and which I will shew you when I see you. In the meantime, as I take pleasure in instructing you from the diligence I see in you, I remark to you, that you are apt to add flourishes to your writing. To this you must by no means accustom yourself, but remember that plainness and simplicity are the chief beauties in all works and performances whatsoever. Be pleased to forbear adding at the end of a verse a line as thus——. You have done so to every line of this last copy. In the main, you have done it very well, and to the satisfaction of, madam, your most affectionate father and most humble servant,

RICH. STEELE.

LETTER CCCCIII.   *To Mr Alexander Scurlock.*

Aug. 13, 1721.

COUSIN SANDY,—I had a letter from you last post, without date of the month, and bearing only the year. Your four twenty pounds are well paid to me, and entered in my day-book.

I observe you cannot understand that you may with safety comply with my request, of sending me your note or money for what is already due. That matter is so plain, that I know it cannot be for want of apprehension that you do not come into it. All I shall say on that subject is, that people do not their duty in life who will not readily execute anything consistent with their own interest and safety that is conducive to the ease and prosperity of their friends.—Your humble servant,

RICH. STEELE.

LETTER CCCCIV.   *To Mr Alexander Scurlock.*

Aug. 29, 1721.

COUSIN SANDY,—This is to acquaint you that I am applied to by eminent persons who deal in mines in order to work that near Llangmmor. I desire you would ask Mr Morgan Davies whether the persons who had a lease of it, to wit, Caresbrook, Batchelor, and Harry Owen, were not ejected regularly and by formal course of law ; if not, I am to consider and advise whether, for default of working or other failure, their pretensions are not extinct. I shall be very cautious in this matter, and go no hazard myself, or entail any on my successors, on this head, but be as circumspect as possible. Please to give me the best intelligence you can get in the history of this transaction, in which you will oblige, sir, your most humble servant,

RICH. STEELE.

LETTER CCCCV.   *To Mr Wilks.*

Dec. 7, 1721.

SIR,—I have great acknowledgments to make to you for putting me in the head at first of being concerned at the playhouse, and I have ever endeavoured to shew you very particular instances of my esteem and affection during the time we have been together.

I am sorry that the gift of L.1400, for what was mine before, could not prevail so much as to let what I had stand as a deposit, for a contingent, in case an impudent cheat is not determined to be such in Wilbraham, who detains my writings contrary to the order of Minshall, to which he is obliged under his hand to deliver them.

But the business of this letter is in particular to speak to you, not to persist in so unreasonable a thing as the denial of payment of the sum which remains above what there is any claim or pretence against my receiving.

It is hardly in your power to make me other than, sir, your most affectionate friend and most humble servant,   RICH. STEELE.

LETTER CCCCVI.   *To Mr Cibber.*

York Buildings, Dec. 7, 1721.

SIR,—When you came to me with the modest request of desiring I would repurchase my share in the scenes and the stock, I did not doubt but you had sentiments of great kindness towards me in general ; and that all the chapter, as I have taken the liberty to call us in conjunction, had as much terror of doing as receiving a hardship. But, if it could have entered into my thoughts that it was possible men could fail of placing the same value (as a security against a contingent demand) which I gave for it, your answer had not been at all like what it was.

You have been the chief engine in ensnaring me into a concession which I should have been ashamed to own, before you had the resolution to deny so equitable a demand as I made to you. But, as it now is, besides the folly of giving to men richer than myself, I have done it to those who have no regard for me, but as a tool and a screen against others, who want to treat you ill, and forbear only because of my relation to you, which shall not be very long, for I have it in my power to get rid of my enemies much more easily than I can have common justice of my friends. This is evident in the monstrous hardiness of denying the governor of your house, as you shall find I am, the superfluity of his income, which is liable to no demand or pretence but that of, sir, your most humble servant,

RICH. STEELE.

LETTER CCCCVII.   *To Mr Booth.*

Dec. 7, 1721.

SIR,—It has not happened to me to be so conversant with you as I have been with Mr Wilks and Mr Cibber, and therefore could not expect that concern and tenderness for me as I hoped from them. But as you are affected by my late concession of a large sum of money greatly to your advantage, I hoped the justice of letting that value secure me against pretences to it elsewhere. But, since you have not thought that reasonable, and have taken counsel whether a partner who has paid the mortgage off of his part of the effects, and given the partners, in pure benevolence, a thousand pounds as a title to their taking his share of the estate, security against the mortgage-deeds unjustly detained from him—I say, since this is the disposition you are in towards me, I expect you, for your own sakes as well as mine, not to detain the fifth of the fourth heretofore demanded, and to which there is no claim.—I am, sir, your most obedient and most humble servant,   RICH. STEELE.

The ease and freedom of mind resulting from the restoration of his rights and emoluments by the removal of the suspension of his patent, had enabled him to put the finish-ing hand upon the comedy which the infirm state of his health, and the harassing anxiety connected with his affairs, had kept so long in abeyance. The " Conscious Lover" was this year (1722) brought upon the stage. After having for such a long series of years relinquished his dramatic pursuits, in consequence of the undeserved recep-tion of one of his last efforts in that line, he had once more reverted to them in the full maturity of his powers with renewed and heightened brilliancy in the result, and a reward in the reception which must have equalled, if it did not surpass, his most sanguine expectations. The success of this celebrated comedy was immense, but not beyond its merit. The scenes in some parts trench so much on the province of tragedy as rather to entitle it a melodrama than a comedy. It is confessedly an adaptation from Terence. A lyrical ballad, descriptive of the distress of a love-sick maid, which Steele tells us was omitted in the performance for want of a singer, may here be introduced as a pleasing specimen of his versification :—

> " From place to place forlorn I go,
>   With downcast eyes a silent shade ;
> Forbidden to declare my woe,
>   To speak, till spoken to, afraid.

> " My inward pangs, my secret grief,
>   My soft consenting looks betray ;
> He loves, but gives me no relief ;
>   Why speaks not he who may ? "

In a pecuniary point of view, the harvest he reaped on this occasion must have been very considerable, if we in-clude the receipts from the representation, the sale of the copy, and the sum of L.500 presented him by the King, to whom it was dedicated. The probability is, however, that it was all absorbed in meeting the deficiency of the preceding years, if indeed it sufficed to fill the gap, and, as in the dream of the eastern monarch, the lean and blasted ears swallowed up the rank and full ones.

There are few remaining incidents to notice of this year, except a very complimentary dedication of a work on the " Antiquities of Westminster Abbey," which Steele received, and the recrimination to which the oblique reflections and latent depreciation of Mr Tickell, in the preface to the writings of Addison, led him. His appeal from Mr Tickell was made in a letter to Congreve, forming a sort of epistle dedicatory to a new edition of the " Drummer." It is undeniable that there had existed no very good feeling between Steele and Tickell at any time, and that the ardour of his love and friendship for Addison made him jealous and resentful of what he regarded as being supplanted in some degree by an attachment which had not been cemented by early ties and nurtured by the early dews; and but for the sensitiveness arising from this cause, the remarks of Addison's editor, though not strictly correct, might have passed unnoticed. Steele had stated that he owed "some of the most applauded strokes" in his comedy of the "Tender Husband" to the friend, whose praise he was never tired of sounding, and the remark might have applied to an occasional suggested word or line; but Tickell, in referring to this acknowledgment, gives it a more wholesale application, and makes it "some of the most taking scenes." After referring to Addison's occasional assistance in the *Tatler*, he adds, that it " was dropped at last, as it had been taken up without his participation," in which there seems nothing particularly to find fault with, yet the sensitiveness of Steele seemed to detect a latent reflection. Addison's editor then proceeds to say that, though Steele handsomely acknowledged this assistance in the preface to the collected papers, yet that being only in general terms, in the subsequent work, the *Spectator*, Mr Addison, "who was content with the praise arising from his own works," thought fit to affix to his writings certain distinguishing marks. To this Steele replied by stating that he had been prohibited mentioning his friend by name, but shewed by a reference to the preface that he had indicated the principal of his papers by their subject-matter, and that with reference to the papers in the *Spectator* and *Guardian*, he had himself, as stated in the preface, inserted those distinguishing marks, which Mr Tickell had ascribed to Addison, as a precaution against him. Steele's exception to Mr Tickell's way of accounting for Addison's not taking orders, which he attributes to his modesty and overpowering sense of the responsibilities of the priesthood, seems too minute and critical ; for, though it is true that Lord Halifax did use his influence with the heads of his college not to insist on his taking orders, yet it is quite certain that, before that event, he had not exhibited any haste to take that irrevocable step.

Among many interesting remarks in this letter, he says, "He could shew under the Dean's (Addison's father) own hand, in the warmest terms, his blessings on the friendship between his son and him; nor had he a child who did not prefer him in the first place of kindness and esteem, as their father loved him like one of them." It is here also that he makes that allusion to Addison that he had "often reflected after a night spent with him apart from all the world, that he had had the pleasure of conversing with an intimate acquaintance of Terence and Catullus, who had all their wit and nature, heightened with humour more exquisite and delightful than any other man ever possessed;" and that other remark respecting his singular bashfulness in mixed company. Speaking of the comedy of the "Drummer," he says, "Here is that smiling mirth, that delicate satire, and genteel raillery, which appeared in Mr Addison when he was free among intimates: I say, when he was free from *his remarkable* bashfulness, which is a cloak that hides and muffles merit." He also makes an interesting allusion to his facility of composition, in reference to Mr Tickell's statement of the many years he was engaged on "Cato," and which is contrary to the popular impression: "If I remember right, the fifth act was written in less than a week's time; for . . . when he had taken his resolution, or made his plan for what he had designed to write, he would walk about the room, and dictate it into language with as much freedom and ease as any one could write it down."

After stating his belief, and his reasons for it, that the comedy of the "Drummer," which Addison had handed him to dispose of for a gentleman he did not name, was the production of his friend, though Mr Tickell had not included it in his works, he concludes by a remark of deferring to give the world a true notion of the character and talents of Mr Addison, which makes it much to be regretted that he did not carry out an intention he seems

to have entertained of giving some literary memorial of
his illustrious friend.

Steele's insinuation that the translation of the first book
of the Iliad, which appeared under Tickell's name, was
the production of Addison, which was also a common
impression at the time, does not appear to be confirmed by a subsequent examination of the MS., which is
in the handwriting of the reputed translator, with inter-
lineations by Addison; nor, whatever the real facts of the
case may have been, was there any reason for doubting
Tickell's capability for the work, as in the art of versification, at least, he was quite equal to Addison.

We find from Steele's correspondence in the course of
this year—which is the only available source from which,
in the dearth of information respecting this period, any
additional details, however slight, are to be gathered—
that the unfortunate Fishpool scheme was still in suspense,
and a source of anxiety and cost to the projector.

LETTER CCCCVIII.   *To Mrs Eliz. Steele, Molly Steele.*
Feb. 11, 1721-2.

MY DEAR GIRLS,—Your brother is, just now, at ease, after great torment
of the gravel or stone.   I love you all so tenderly that my tears are ready
to flow when I tell you that I am, dearest creatures, your most affectionate
father and most humble servant,   RICH. STEELE.

LETTER CCCCIX.   *To Mrs Eliz. Steele.*
March 31, 1722.

MY DEAR CHILD,—I beg your pardon that I made Mrs Keck's servant
stay so long; it was occasioned by a crowd of people importunate to speak
with me on my coming to town.*   I send you such tickets † as I can by

---

* " He was just then elected into Parliament for Wendover."

† " Either for the theatre at Drury Lane, or for some concert in York Buildings.
In the latter business, Steele was principally concerned, by which he did not
better his circumstances."

our present rules; and am, with joy in your hopeful behaviour and toward spirit, madam, your most affectionate father, and most humble servant,   RICH. STEELE.

Give my most humble service to your good and honoured guardian.

LETTER CCCCX.   *To Mr Gilmour.*

May 24, 1722.

SIR,—I have yours of to-day, consisting of a declaration that you shall be forced to do what you otherwise would not, by reason of my paying you L.15 instead of L.30; and that L.30, you say, will still leave me in your debt L.80, by balance ending in April. I should seem insensible, and not to know the nature of my own actions, if I should not on this occasion acquaint you that I am become your creditor from a great opinion of your talents, and making an expense in support of them at all hazards; and that all the adversity that befell the Fishpool, happened from your having been persuaded to throw yourself into the hands of Mr Dale, by the minister of. your parish, who introduced you to me.

If you calmly consider, you will very well know that you have never' had any disappointments from me, but what have been abatements of what I was inclined to do for you out of freewill and respect to you, with very hazardous hopes of gain to myself; and those abatements occasioned by unforeseen distress in my health and fortune, on which occasions you have always sent me a declaration of your being ready to join with anybody else in mortification of me.

I have said all this as it is extorted from me by your reproaches; but I have at the same time, in spite of all particularity towards me, a great sense of your merit, and an ambition of producing it for the good of the world as well as ourselves. If your labours come to nothing, I am, by a condition imposed on me by myself, a considerable loser; and if they turn to advantage, I am sure I have proportionate pretence to gain.

I thank God, I am, from great torment, restored to present ease; and hope the next dressing will give authority to my physician to allow me the use of my legs: and nothing shall be wanting, within the rules of honour, justice, and discretion, to promote the present project.*—I am, sir, &c.,   RICH. STEELE.

LETTER CCCCXI.   *To Mr Alexander Scurlock.*

York Buildings, May 26, 1722.

DEAR COUSIN AND COUNSELLOR,—After I have condoled with you upon

---

* "The Fishpool went into Brunsden's Dock, Nov. 1, 1722."—R. S.

the death of poor Jonathan, I must acknowledge the receipt of yours with L.30 drawn on Mr Horn by Mr Philips, which, with L.30 sent me before, and the L.40 which Marmaduke Williams sent in your absence, complete L.100 which I desired of you.

Had you sent it me at once, it had been better to me than L.200 : but I must submit to the inconveniences which a certain easiness and irregularity in my own affairs subject me to. Thus I only complain of myself; and hope, by the blessing of Almighty God, to put my affairs, and keep them, so much within my income, as not to put my friends in any future pain or trouble for me.—I am, sir, your affectionate friend and most humble servant, RICH. STEELE.

CHAPTER XXI.

THE RETIRED VETERAN.

Steele commences two other Comedies, "The School of Action," and "The Gentleman"—Both left in a fragmentary state—Continued decline of his health, aggravated by the state of his affairs—Takes his departure from London—Takes up his residence at Bath—His resolution of making his future residence in the country—Death of his only remaining son, Eugene—Correspondence in 1723—To his daughter, to Mrs Caney—Residence at Hereford—Proposals for his daughter—Urgent application from the Managers for his presence in London—Not complied with—Subsequent litigation with them by his trustees—Colley Cibber's account of the affair—Erroneous surmise of Lord Macaulay—Correspondence in 1724—To his daughters, to Right Hon. R. Walpole, from Messrs Wilks, Booth, and Cibber, to Mr Morgan, from Mr Morgan—Retires to his seat in Wales—Pursued by the malignity of Swift—Letter to his daughter, 1725—Adverse decision of the law-suit with the Managers—Paralytic attack—Letter to his daughters, 1726—His kindness in the interests of others—Receives an unexpected compliment—Last letter to his daughter, 1728—His love of nature and appreciation of retirement—His sympathy with the sports of the rustics—The sacred volume his constant companion—His decease—Notice of his family—His personal and literary character.

WITH what broken health and fortune permitted to remain of that mental activity and industry of which Steele, with all his recklessness and love of enjoyment, must be admitted to have displayed a remarkable example in his earlier years, before his health gave way, he now set himself to follow up his recent triumph with a double task. He had actually undertaken two comedies at the same time ; and, whether actuated by that self-deception to which all are liable, but persons of his ardent temperament are peculiarly prone, he had given expression to hopes of an early result which he was little likely to realise, or, as is more probable, there were officious people who knew more of his affairs than he did himself, it was currently reported through the press that he would probably present the town with another comedy in the course of the ensuing winter.   This was " The School of Action," in which he had made some progress, and a second, founded on Terence, which he had commenced, but left in a more fragmentary state, was entitled, "The Gentleman." Whether, if he had concentrated his efforts on one task he would have accomplished more, is difficult to say, for, though the rule is a good one, it is not invariable, and a change is often a stimulant.   But, though it is vain to speculate on that subject, we may be permitted to regret, if he was sanguine enough to anticipate an early completion of his labours, after his previous experience, the disappointment to which he and we were destined.

Some contributions to the periodical paper called *Pasquin* are also attributed to Steele at this time.

Towards the close of the year, however, in consequence of the continuance of his failing health, aggravated, beyond a doubt by the state of his affairs, and distress at the gloomy prospects of his family, he took leave of London in a state of great depression, as appears from an affecting confession to his daughter, and proceeded to Bath for the benefit of the waters, but with the resolution, if not formed previous to his departure, at least not long after, of making his future residence in Wales.   In this resolution he was, no doubt, actuated by the double motive of health and economy.

Fully to appreciate the state of his affairs, not merely at this time but in the past, it must be borne in mind that, while by his heedless and culpable extravagance or generosity his income was ever forestalled, his wife's property had yielded him but trifling benefit. It was mortgaged, and his mother-in-law's life interest absorbed what remained, and after her death it went to the education of the children.

To the accumulated troubles of Steele at this time, arising from the state of his health and the embarrassment of his affairs, which mutually tended to aggravate one another, there was added a bitter and irreparable affliction which he suffered this year in the loss of his only remaining son, Eugene, a youth of great promise, who seemed to inherit his father's talents, vivacity, and amiability. He had only attained the age of ten or twelve years. Had he survived, he might have been a great comfort to his father; but, in addition to other complaints from which he suffered, he appears to have inherited something of a consumptive tendency, probably from his mother, which was fatally developed by imprudent exposure. By this afflicting stroke Steele saw himself bereft of the consoling prospect of perpetuating his name in his offspring. But the sad intelligence, which reached him at a distance, was probably lightened by having been anticipated.

The following is his correspondence for this year :—

LETTER CCCCXII.   *To Mrs Elizabeth Steele.*

May 24, 1723.

DEAR CHILD,—I send the franks for Mrs Bullock, to whom I desire you to write with great gratitude and respect, alway remembering the great obligation you have to her for so tender an education. I am, dear Betty, your most affectionate father and most humble servant,

R. STEELE.

LETTER CCCCXIII.   *To Mrs Elizabeth Steele.*

July 15, 1723.

MY DEAR CHILD,—I have received a letter from you, but without a date; which, my dear, was a great omission. I ought not to find faults in so kind and so affectionate an epistle; but exactness is an excellent quality which every one may be mistress of, and therefore I would not have you want it. I am much better than I was, and attribute my recovery to the prayers of my dear children. I have taken a great deal of pains to serve the world, and hope God will allow me some time to serve my own family. My good girl, employ yourself always in some good work, that you may be as good a woman as your mother. Pray remember me to dear little Molly; and know me for, madam, your affectionate father and humble servant,

RICH. STEELE.

LETTER CCCCXIV.   *To Mrs Elizabeth Steele.*

Bath, Oct. 1, 1723.

MY DEAR CHILD,—This confesses to my dear children, that I came to this place three weeks ago with a very heavy heart; but I hope I am now better, and desire Betty to write to me, and let me know what she hears from Mrs Bullock, and the like accounts, for my soul is wrapped up in your welfare; and I am, dear children, your most affectionate father and most humble servant,

RICH. STEELE.

Direct, " To Sir Richard Steele, Member of Parliament, at Bath."

LETTER CCCCXV.   *To Mrs Martha Caney.*

Bath, Nov. 2, 1723.

MADAM,—I had a letter from you to supply you with money on account of my lodgings at your house, which I am very sorry I was unable to do. But when I come to town, I shall make it my immediate care to discharge it; but, as I believe all the time I shall spend in the country will hereafter be at the Bath, or in Wales, I beg the favour of you to take this letter for a dismission of the lodgings at Fulham; and believe me to be, with great truth, madam, your most obedient humble servant,

RICH. STEELE.

LETTER CCCCXVI.   *To Mrs Elizabeth Steele.*

Nov. 20, 1723.

MY DEAR CHILD,—I acknowledge the receipt of your kind letters, and desire you to write to me once every week, which will be a great comfort to me, and, I hope, hasten my recovery and our meeting.—I am, dear child, your affectionate father and most humble servant,

RICH. STEELE.

Love to Molly.

LETTER CCCCXVII.   *To Mrs Elizabeth Steele.*

Nov. 22, 1723.

MY DEAR CHILD,—I have your letter, with the news of Eugene's death,* and your reflections thereupon. Do you and your sister stay at home, and do not go to the funeral. Lord grant me patience ! Pray write to me constantly.—Your affectionate father and obedient servant,

RICH. STEELE.

Why do you not mention Molly ?   Is she dead too ?

LETTER CCCCXVIII.   *To Mrs Elizabeth Steele.*

Bath, Dec. 2, 1723.

DEAR BETTY,—I have your letter of the 30th from Mrs Snow. I writ to Mrs Nazerean in great concern, not hearing from you, and desired her to chide you very severely, if you were in health, for omitting to write me in the distress you must needs think I was in when I heard nothing of you ; your mourning was no manner of excuse, for you might have found time to write to your father, whatever other business you had. I desire you would give my most humble service to Mrs Snow ; I know not how to behave myself under the obligation of your being such a trouble as you must needs

---

* Eugene Steele, named in honour of Prince Eugene, was born March 4, 1712. "He was," says Nichols, "some years under the care of Mr Solomon Lowe, of Blythe-house, Hammersmith, who gave him the character of a sprightly lad of fine parts. He was afterwards a hopeful scholar in that noble foundation where his father was educated, the Charter House. Not long after he was taken home to his father's house in York Buildings, being indulged (as his genius lay that way) in acting plays in the great room there, called the *Censorium*,—his constitution is said to have been hurt by frequent colds. He appears also to have been grievously tormented with the stone, and was cut for that terrible disorder by the celebrated Cheselden."

be at her house. Let me know as soon as Mrs Bullock comes to town. My service to Molly.—I am, dear Betty, your affectionate father and most humble servant,   RICH. STEELE.

LETTER CCCCXIX.   *To Mrs Elizabeth Steele.*
                                                 Bath, Dec. 14, 1723.

MY DEAR CHILD,—You must pardon me if I write you by a servant's hand, because I have a great deal of business to do to-night, and therefore cannot, under my present infirmity, do it in my own hand. I know nothing of the gentlewoman with whom you are left, but depend very much upon Mrs Bullock's conduct and judgment. You say the gentlewoman who is your governess is a very well-bred woman. If she proves so to me, I shall honour her as my sister, for the justice and kindness she shews you. Pray shew her this letter, and tell her so. You say she never was abroad in any dependent way before. Pray desire her to write to me, to let me know what terms she is upon, that I may proceed accordingly for her service. I am, my dear child, most tenderly affected with the kind and prudent expressions in your letter ; but cannot speak my mind to you till I see you, which I hope will be at the time the Parliament meets.—I am, dear Betty, your most affectionate father and most humble servant,
                                                 RICH. STEELE.

Give my love to your sister Molly, and service to Mr Snow and Mrs Snow.

LETTER CCCCXX.   *To Mrs Elizabeth Steele.*
                                                 Bath, Dec. 21, 1723.

MY DEAREST, DEAR CHILD,—I have yours of the 19th, for which I thank you. Am preparing to come to town. God grant a happy meeting between you and your most affectionate father, and most humble servant,
                                                 RICH. STEELE.

We have little trace of Steele's engagements in the following year (1724,) nor does it very clearly appear where he resided. But it is likely that he left Bath early in the spring, and it was probably at this time that he took up his quarters in the city of Hereford, and that he spent part of his time at Carmarthen, though he does not appear to have retired permanently to that place till the next year, as we find him at the former place in the spring of 1725. Whilst at Hereford, he lodged in the house of a mercer, who was his agent and receiver of the rents of his wife's estate.*

We find, from his correspondence, that Steele had at this time proposals for his eldest daughter, who, then scarcely sixteen, afterwards became the subject of matrimonial contention among numerous claimants, a duel having been fought about her by two of them at Bath. She was afterwards married to the Hon. John Trevor, and thus became connected with the Marlborough family, into which her husband's sister was then recently married.

In the autumn of this year, as will be seen in the correspondence, Steele received a very urgent letter from the managers of Drury Lane, requesting his immediate presence in town to concert measures in what they represent as a very critical state of the affairs of the theatre. But he appears to have been so hurt by their treatment of him, that their representations failed to draw him from his retirement. It is to be regretted that we have not got his reply to this letter. Though generally represented as prior to this period, it must have been subsequently that he made the assignment of his share in the theatre for the benefit of his creditors, and the trustees commenced a litigation with the managers, which was decided against him in 1726. The only account of this affair we have is that written by Colley Cibber, which on that account, and as it is written with his usual liveliness, is here given necessarily some-

---

* Nichols mentions a gratifying proof he received at this time of not being forgotten in his solitude, by having inscribed to him a small production entitled "Remarks upon Dacier," by his friend Dr Parnell; but, as he died in 1718, there must be some mistake in the matter, at least as to the date.

what condensed. But though he speaks with great good
feeling of Steele, the reader is requested to remember that
it is written by an interested party, and we have not Steele's
explanation of the facts, but we have in a former correspondence his very strongly expressed remonstrance to
the managers on what he regarded as their very illiberal
treatment of him, and even having been entrapped into
some concessions to their interest.

"In all the transactions of life," writes Mr Cibber, with much good feeling, "there cannot be a more painful circumstance than a dispute at law
with a man with whom we have long lived in agreeable unity. But when
Sir Richard, to get himself out of difficulties, was obliged to throw his
affairs into the hands of lawyers and trustees, that consideration then
could be of no weight: the friend, or the gentleman, had no more to do in
the matter. Thus, while Sir Richard no longer acted for himself, it may
be no wonder if a flaw was found in our conduct for the law to make work
with. About two or three years before the law suit commenced, upon Sir
Richard's totally absenting himself from all care and management of the
stage, which, by our articles, he was equally and jointly obliged with us
to attend, we were reduced to let him know that we could not go on at that
rate; but that, if he expected to make the business a sinecure, we had as
much reason to expect a consideration for our extraordinary care of it;
and that, during his absence, we therefore intended to charge ourselves at
a salary of L.1. 13s. 4d. every acting day (unless he could shew us cause to
the contrary) for our management. To which, in his composed manner,
he only answered, that, to be sure, we knew what was fitter to be done
than he did; that he had always taken a delight in making us easy, and
had no reason to doubt of our doing him justice. . . . He never once objected to, or complained of, this for near three years together. . . . The
cause came to a hearing before Sir Joseph Jekyll, Master of the Rolls,
in the year 1726. Though no man alive can write better of economy than
he, yet perhaps he is above the drudgery of practising it. Sir Richard then
was often in want of money; and, while we were in friendship with him,
we assisted his occasions. This compliance had so unfortunate an effect
that it only heightened his importunity of borrowing more. The more
we lent, the less he minded us, or showed any concern for our welfare.
Upon this we stopt our hands at once, and peremptorily refused to advance
another shilling, until, by the balance of our account, it became due to
him. This treatment (though we hope it is not in the least unjustifiable)

so ruffled his temper, that he was at once as short with us as we had been with him ; for from that time he never came near us. Nay, he not only continued to neglect what he ought to have done, but did what he ought not to have done. He made an assignment of his share without our consent, in manifest breach of our agreement. . . . But supposing his assigning his share may have done us no great injury, there is a particular reason to believe that his neglect did : his rank and figure in the world, while he gave us the assistance of them, were of extraordinary service to us. The issue was, that Sir Richard, not having made any objection to our charge for management for three years together, as our proceedings had all been transacted in open day, without any intention of fraud, we were allowed the sum in dispute above mentioned. Sir Richard not judging it advisable to apply to the Lord Chancellor to overturn the award, both parties paid their own costs, and thought it their mutual interest to let this be the last of their law suits."*

Lord Macaulay has ventured on a remark in reference to Steele, implying that his difficulties arose from gambling. This would be fully adequate to the solution of the difficulty certainly, and if Steele had been addicted to it he would have had to bear the reproach as he best might, in common with some remarkable men, such as Fox, who should have been above such a vice ; but, while he got the greatest credit for having made a crusade against the gamblers of his day, no contemporary, nor indeed any subsequent writer, but the eminent one above named, ever insinuated participation in that vice against him. The surmise therefore, however plausible, must be dismissed as unsupported by evidence or authority.

The correspondence for 1724, which follows, is somewhat more general :—

LETTER CCCCXXI.   *To Mrs Elizabeth Steele.*

Bath, Jan. 8, 1723–4.

DEAR BETTY,—This is to let you and your sister know I am in good

---

* Cibber's " Apology," chap. xvi.

health, and, dear creature, your affectionate father and most humble servant,   RICH. STEELE.

My service to Mrs Baker.

LETTER CCCCXXII.   *To Mrs Elizabeth Steele.*

April 5, 1724.

MY DEAR LITTLE GIRLS,—Pray send me word when Mrs Evans and you begin your journey, and let her know she shall be well received here by all us country people. God send us a happy meeting! Dear child, your affectionate father and humble servant,   RICH. STEELE.

Give my service to the good old man, and to his son, and his sons, and to his cousin Betty.

LETTER CCCCXXIII.   *To Mrs Elizabeth Steele.*

April 8, 1724.

DEAR BETTY,—I desire you to be carefully dressed to-day in your black, in order to receive a visitor in honour of your brother; let your sister be in her white; and be both as cheerfully suited as you can be. I shall call upon you soon after dinner, and am your friend upon all occasions.—Dear Betty, your obedient, faithful father,   RICH. STEELE.

LETTER CCCCXXIV.   *To Mrs Elizabeth Steele.*

June 25, 1724.

DEAR BETTY,—I was much troubled to find you were sent to my lodgings with your keys. I hope you will find everything right there. But be exact in all your affairs hereafter, and we shall meet with fewer disappointments than we have hitherto met with.—I am, your affectionate father,   RICH. STEELE.

LETTER CCCCXXV.   *To the Right Hon. Robert Walpole.*

Carmarthen, Aug. 10, 1724.

SIR,—It is reported here that Mr Clavering, now treasurer of St David's, is to be made Bishop of Llandaff.

In case that happens, I beg your favour to Mr David Scurlock to be steward of St David's. The Bishop of Salisbury and Dr Clarke will both give him their good character; and you will oblige the gentry of these parts, who know he is well allied here, as well as you will do what you have always done to your creature, and most obliged, most obedient, humble servant,   RICH. STEELE.

LETTER CCCCXXVI.   *Sir Richard Steele to Mr Morgan.**

Dec. 7, 1724.

SIR,—I had the other day the honour of a message from you by Mr Pritchard, with an account that you had the greatest respect and love for my daughter, and a request of my permission to make your address to her. I told Mr Pritchard that " he who was to have her must win her and wear her ; that she was a girl of good sense, and I should take that with her in whomsoever pretended to her ;" but, upon speaking of the same subject that evening, and mentioning your civility for her to her, she told me with a great deal of calmness and ease, that "she was very young, and very well contented to wait her time and choice under my care ;" and begged of me to let you know, that nothing could do her a greater offence than such an application. I told Mr Pritchard this the same evening ; but I cannot forbid it with more earnestness than I do now, and desire you would give my service to your father, to whom I am, as well as to you, sir, your most obedient, humble servant,   RICH. STEELE.

LETTER CCCCXXVII.   *From Mr Morgan.*

Dec. 9, 1724.

HONOURED SIR,—I came on purpose, on Friday evening, to wait on you, in order to return you thanks for all favours, but particularly the honour you were pleased to do me, in signifying your and pretty Mrs Steele's thoughts in relation to her unfortunate, though sincere, humble servant. But it seems my visit was unseasonable ; and, since that time, I have not been very well, so hope you will pardon me for not making my acknowledgments earlier. Mr Pritchard was very just in delivering me your messages ; but the last at once awed me into silence, otherwise I should not have been under the same roof without paying my respects to you ; but when I found my company was rather an offence than otherwise, I chose to withdraw. It is with the utmost concern that I observe the young lady is pleased to conceive a particular prejudice to me. However, notwithstanding all that, I must beg leave to assure you that I shall always have the utmost veneration for worthy Sir Richard Steele, and his fair, but cruel daughter, though with a disinterested view ; and I sincerely wish her all the happiness imaginable in her choice ; for, since the lady, as I apprehend, is pleased to command my silence, I must acquiesce under the severe sentence, and shall endeavour to avoid giving either of you any offence ; but, on the contrary,

---

* " From a paper in the handwriting of Lady Trevors, entitled, ' An exact copy of a letter my father wrote to Mr Edward Morgan, in answer to a message he sent him by Mr Pritchard, December the 6th, 1724.'"

if ever it lies in my way to be serviceable to you or yours, none shall be readier to obey your commands than, good sir, your most obliged and most obedient humble servant,   ED. MORGAN.

LETTER CCCCXXVIII. *From Messrs Wilks, Booth, and Cibber.*
                                                    London, Dec. 12, 1724.

SIR,—We have long wished for your coming to town, but are now obliged to desire you to make all possible speed to us. Our audiences decrease daily, and those low entertainments which you and we so heartily despise, draw the numbers, while we act only to the few who are blest with common sense. Though the operas are allowed to be much worse than they were formerly, yet they draw much better audiences; and some persons of distinction not to be named have encouraged a set of *French comedians* to come over by *subscription*, who are to act next Wednesday at the little theatre in the Haymarket. Thus, while there are three playhouses exhibiting nonsense of different kinds against us, it is impossible we should subsist much longer. Both the courts have forsaken us. All we can do is to make the best of a losing game, and part from the whole upon the best terms we can. No person living, but ourselves, is sensible of the low state we are reduced to, therefore we need not observe to you how very needful it is to keep the secret.

There are several persons of fortune that, we have reason to believe, would be glad to purchase our interests, and put it upon the foot of the opera, by fixing the direction into an *Academy*, which is, we think, the only way to support and perpetuate the English theatre. We have nothing more to add, but our hearty wishes for your health, and quick arrival among us, and in the meantime to beg your speedy answer.—We are, sir, your most obedient, humble servants,
                                        ROBERT WILKS, B. BOOTH, C. CIBBER.

P.S.—Our profits were ever more than double to what they have been this year, and we are very far from any hopes of their growing better. Our proposal of parting with our interests will still leave room for any of us to be adventurers upon this new scheme, in what proportion we please.

LETTER CCCCXXIX.   *From Mr Morgan.*
                                                    Dec. 19, 1724.

HONOURED SIR,—I am so much at a loss for a sufficient apology for my importunity on this occasion, that I submit myself entirely to your clemency, which, by all accounts, has hitherto been very extensive, but particularly so in favour of the distressed: which, since it is my misfortune to be one of that body at present, I hope to meet with your indulgence, if not compassion.

Self-preservation is what is natural to most; and with that view, I flatter myself, you will pardon me if I once more beg a favourable thought from you, and, if possible, from the young lady your daughter; for her most irresistible charms have, in my own defence, obliged me to be thus troublesome. Give me leave, then, dear sir, to tell you, that I find it impossible for me to avoid having the utmost love and respect for pretty Mrs Steele, though in pursuance to her severe decree, which I hope is not yet final, I have made it my study to act as agreeably thereto as possibly I could; for, rather than give her the least uneasiness, I would torture myself first. I do not doubt but my father's circumstances and mine have been rendered to you in a worse light than what, probably, upon a due inquiry, they may appear to be. I beg leave to assure you that my designs are grounded upon a foot of honour; and then, I hope, you will imagine those affairs must have come to light. However, it is a usual thing to meet with back-friends upon these occasions; but probably I may find them out at long run.

Were it possible the lady could conquer all objections to my person, I believe I should be able to convince you that my fortune is not despicable; yet I must own it is a trifle when in competition with so much personal merit, which to me out-balances fortune, any more than what may be absolutely necessary to render the affairs of this world as happy as may be; but were I master of ever so great a fortune, I should never think it so well bestowed as upon your daughter. I heartily ask pardon for trespassing so long upon your patience; so shall only beg that my most sincere humble service may be acceptable to the young lady, and that you would believe that I am, with the utmost respect, sir, your most obliged and most obedient, humble servant,   Ed. Morgan.

LETTER CCCCXXX.   *Sir Richard Steele to Mr Morgan.*

Dec. 20, 1724.

Sir,—I have the favour of yours of the 19th instant, about the same matter to which I thought I had fully answered before. Speaking of "back-friends" is unnecessary, for indeed nobody can have any power with me but what should be necessary for affairs of that kind concerning which I am talking; therefore nobody could possibly lay any exceptions concerning you or your family. But there was no dispute raised about that matter in the least; the young woman did not enter into any inquiry concerning your circumstances, neither does she yet. Therefore, I earnestly desire you will lay aside all thoughts of this kind: for the child is young and discreet, and utterly declares against admitting your courtship, which I

desire you would please to forbear, and you will very much oblige, sir, your
most obedient, humble servant,   RICH. STEELE.*

In the following year sometime, most probably, Steele
retired to Wales, with the intention there to fix his future
residence, and, with the consent of the mortgagees, took
up his abode at his seat of Langunnor, near Carmarthen.
Even there, the inveterate and detestable malignity of his
former friend, Swift, pursued him, representing the retirement which he sought for the sake of his broken health
and in the interest of his creditors—after having made over
to them an assignment of his property—as a refuge where
he,

> " From perils of a hundred jails,
>   Withdrew to starve and die in Wales."

Even if it had been true, it would not have been the less
cruel. But it was so far from being so, that, independent
of the perils being purely imaginary, there can be no doubt
that the claims of his creditors were fully satisfied, though
the arrangement, doubtless, left him very poor in the
interim. That this was so is clearly proved by the fact
that, after his decease, a considerable balance remained
to his daughters, though they failed to derive any benefit
from it by the conduct of a fraudulent agent. It must,
with regret, be acknowledged that Steele was not equally
wise in his generation with the Reverend Dr Swift, and it
was perhaps but natural that he who had gone such lengths
in doing the foul work of party, to earn the wages of mer-
cenary apostasy, should be prudent in guarding the trea-

* "From a paper in the handwriting of Lady Trevor, entitled, 'An exact copy
of an answer my father wrote to a letter of Mr Morgan's, December the 20th,
1724.'"

sure—small as it was in comparison with his aspirations—which he had scrupled at the use of no weapon to acquire. Steele's folly, resulting in his poverty, must have given him many a pang, doubtless, for the sake of those dear to him who were affected by it; but there was no sting in it. He had never wantonly injured a human being, and he had used his talents for the noblest purposes, and the benefit of his species—not in vilifying them. Nor—could he have inhabited the "hundred jails" at the same time—could they have made him such a hell as his malignant critic found in his own bosom in his latter years—goaded almost to madness by the effect on his fierce temper of the failure of his schemes of misdirected ambition and the hopeless ruin of the party to which, in an evil hour, he had transferred his allegiance, and lashed by the avenging furies which his cold-blooded selfishness to two of the most accomplished women of their time had nurtured there—women whom he had attracted by his talents, and whom he held year after year in a state of cruel suspense, and saw pining in wretchedness without realising the hopes he had inspired, while he monopolised their society, until at last both expired, weary of life, broken-hearted, and almost execrating him.

His correspondence grows gradually more scant, and this year there is but one slight missive to his youngest daughter.

LETTER CCCCXXXI.   *To Mrs Molly Steele.*

Feb. 6, 1724-25.

DEAR MOLLY,—My cousin Scurlock sends me word you are mighty uneasy for coming hither. My dear child, you stayed at your own request, and I am heartily glad that you think of coming to me, where you shall enjoy all the happiness that you can. I am glad also to hear my cousin thinks of coming with you when the coach comes to Hereford * in better time.

She shall have all the welcome this place will afford her, which you may tell her from your affectionate father,   RICH. STEELE.

The next year was marked by an important event affecting Steele, the adverse decision of the long-pending litigation with the managers, which has been already noticed somewhat in anticipation. It will have been noticed in the account given by Mr Cibber that he ascribed it to Steele's trustees and their lawyers, rather than himself, and this was still more distinctly stated in a part that, for the sake of brevity, was omitted. He states, among other circumstances not quoted, that two of the lawyers employed against them afterwards rose to be Lord Chancellors.

But events of a darker and sadder nature have been assigned to this period, though in other accounts made a year or two later. Whatever the precise time, however, the physical infirmity from which he had suffered for a considerable period, aided in its malignity by mental anxiety, which the capability of greater bodily exertion would no doubt have tended to dissipate, resulted in a paralytic attack, which ultimately impaired the vigour of his mental powers. All serious literary exertion after that afflicting event was, of course, out of the question, and, if it had not, would no doubt have been prohibited.

* "In 1725," ('23) says Mr Victor, "Sir Richard Steele left London. He retired to the city of Hereford, and was lodged and boarded there at the house of a mercer, who was his agent and receiver of the rents of an encumbered estate of L.600 a year, which Sir Richard obtained by his late wife: at his death it devolved to his two daughters."—Victor's "Dramatic Pieces, Poems, and Original Letters," p. 330, 1776.

Again his correspondence for the year is comprised in a single brief letter to his eldest daughter, complaining of her sending him a troublesome guest.

To Mrs Eliz. Steele.

March 3, 1725-26.

MY DEAREST CHILD,—You were indiscreet to send Sandy here yesterday night, for he is a gentleman I have some reason to know very well.

Give my most humble service to Mrs Scurlock and Mrs Bevans. There is no need of bidding you be civil to all you see kind to me.—I am, dear girl, your dutiful and compassionate father, RICH. STEELE.

The succeeding year was, if possible, still more scant in details, and the correspondence was *nil.* Mr Victor has, however, recorded some pleasing particulars of Steele at this time, from which it appears that, though he had unhappily survived the capability of promoting his own interests, his kindness in seeking to serve those of others had not forsaken him. "In the year 1727," he says, "when I was a *levee-hunter,* and making an interest with the first minister, that good old man, hearing of it, enclosed me an open letter to Sir Robert Walpole, that, I remember, began thus, ' *If the recommendation of the most obliged man can be of any service to the bearer:'* Sir Robert received it with his usual politeness." [*]

The monotonous serenity of Steele's solitude in that picturesque land which he had chosen as the scene of his closing career was occasionally pleasantly stirred with a little bland excitement, borne to him from the distant busy world in a breath of incense sweetly soothing, both as an evidence that he was not forgotten, and reviving

[*] Victor's " Original Letters, Dramatic Pieces, and Poems," vol. i. p. 330, 1776.

reminiscences of his days of triumph. One of these,—recalling to the literary veteran his days of active service, when his lucubrations were a luxury as indispensable to every breakfast-table, of any pretension, as the tea and toast; to the invalid, his days of buoyant health; and to the recluse, his days of social distinction,—reached him at this time. It was a mere trifle, an epistle dedicatory, and important only as it was suggestive of reflection, like the inscription of a triumphal column read by a veteran warrior, telling him of the field on which he had won his honours. It was prefixed to a treatise, published this year, by the Rev. William Asplin, of St Alban Hall, Oxford, who had been a correspondent of the *Tatler* or *Spectator*.

> " *To Sir Richard Steele.*
>
> " *March* 2, 1727–8.
>
> " In the brightest days of Britain, when Bickerstaff presided in the chair of wit, and o'er this happy land showered *manna* down, which suited every taste, I had the honour (though unworthy and unknown) to be accepted as an humble correspondent. And it gives me now a melancholy reflection, when I am once more inclined to visit the world in print, that the only person who introduced me to it is himself retired. To be an intruder upon solitude, I am conscious, is rudeness ; but, as the greatest souls have never been so much adored as when departed, suffer me, sir, to approach your recess (which ought to be sacred) with the reverence due to the genius of our isles, and to make this small oblation of gratitude to the immortal *manes* of the *Spectator*."

A brief note to his younger daughter closes the correspondence of Steele for the year and for ever.

LETTER CCCCXXXIII.   *To Mrs Mary Steele.*

July 22, 1728.

MY DEAR, DEAR MOLLY,—I write to you because Mr Duke is going to Bristol. I desire you would give my service to Dr Lane ; and remember, dear Molly, your ever loving and affectionate father,

RICH. STEELE.

We have little definite information of the manner in which Steele employed himself in his retirement, amid scenes so very different from the bustle and gaiety of the life to which he had been so long accustomed. But incompatible as the present might seem with enjoyment to one who had lived such a life as he had done, or one of his disposition, yet we find, scattered over his writings, numerous indications of his ardent love of nature and his appreciation of retirement. Speaking in one place of the encroachment of artificial habits, and the changes of modern hours, compared with those of former times, or even what might still be found in the country, he launches out in praise of the early, or what he calls the still hours of the day, in these terms:—" The mind in these early seasons of the day is so refreshed in all her faculties, and borne up with such new supplies of animal spirits, that she finds herself in a state of youth ; *above all, when the breath of flowers entertains her, the melody of birds, the dews that hang upon the plants, and all those other sweets of nature* that are so peculiar to the morning."* And he compares with this the loss of the " exquisite taste of life " by him " who does not come into the world till it is in all its noise and hurry." Now these sweets thus casually glanced at as peculiar to the morning are also peculiar to the country, and to one possessing the tastes and sympathies here indicated, retirement could not be uncongenial or synonymous with dulness. In another paper, speaking of that calm and elegant satisfaction, as he felicitously expresses it, "which is the true and proper delight of men of knowledge and virtue," he adds, " Such a frame of mind raises that sweet enthu-

* *Tatler*, No. 263.

siasm which warms the imagination at the sight of every work of nature, and turns all around you into picture and landscape." *

Indeed, it is incredible that he who had sketched the immortal portrait of Sir Roger de Coverley, that model country gentleman, and had so considerable a hand in the filling up, should have been without strong appreciation of the pursuits of rural life. He has there referred more pointedly to the charms of the country than any of his coadjutors in that celebrated series. In his second paper on Sir Roger's courtship of the perverse widow, he says:—
"To one used to live in a city, the charms of the country are so exquisite that the mind is lost in a certain transport which raises us above ordinary life, and is yet not strong enough to be inconsistent with tranquillity. This state of mind was I in, ravished with the murmur of waters, the whisper of breezes, the singing of birds ; and whether I looked up to the heavens, down on the earth, or turned on the prospects around me, still struck with new sense of pleasure."† This subject is alluded to merely that the closing years of so genial a spirit should not be associated with anything like banishment and gloom, as the malignity of Swift suggested.

But ere the curtain falls, one little trait, that has been recorded by an authority previously quoted, must be presented. "I was told," says Mr Victor, "he retained his cheerful sweetness of temper to the last; and would often be carried out of a summer's evening, where the country lads and lasses were assembled at their rural sports,—and, with his pencil, gave an order on his agent, the mercer,

* *Tatler*, No. 89.   † *Spectator*, No. 118.

for a new gown to the best dancer."* That is a characteristic picture, forming a fitting close of the life-story of
one so genial, who, like the Vicar of Wakefield, delighted
in the sight of happy human faces, and in contributing to
produce them.

With such associations, and with only one other fact,
that the sacred volume is stated to have been his constant
companion and the source of consolation in his more
serious hours, — it is pleasant to close the story of
Richard Steele; and it only remains to add, that he paid
the last debt at Carmarthen, September 1, 1729,† at the
early age of fifty-eight, and his remains were laid, in
accordance with his own desire, in the town chancel.

Of Steele's family, Richard had died in infancy, Eugene
in his boyhood in 1722, and Mary, his younger daughter,
at Bristol, of a lingering consumption, April 18, 1730.
Elizabeth, the elder, married the Hon. John Trevor,
one of the Welsh judges, afterwards Lord Trevor of
Bromham, May 31, 1732.‡ They had one daughter,
Diana, who, like Addison's, though beautiful, was of weak
mind.

It is needless to trace any elaborate character of Steele
after the foregoing details, in which it is sufficiently por-
trayed. But it may be proper to glance at the salient
points in the scattered materials. One obvious characteristic which influenced his destiny at every stage of
life, was his ardent and impetuous feelings, which, though
united with good judgment, sometimes got the mastery, and
had the effect of producing an exaggerated estimate of the

* "Original Letters, Dramatic Pieces," &c., p. 330.
† *Weekly Medley*, Sept. 13, 1729.   ‡ *Universal Spectator*, June 3, 1732.

immediate object of pursuit, and giving additional tenacity
to an aim once adopted. We see this exemplified in his
first rash plunge into life as a guardsman,* and his equally
precipitate and imprudent dash into politics. Of the in-
fluences which acted on his mind in inducing the former
step, beyond the general feeling in youths of spirit in
favour of a military life, and his great admiration of the
illustrious William, we know nothing, though we learn
from himself that the result of it was to lose him the
reversion of a considerable estate in Ireland. In the latter,
he feared for the interests of liberty, civil and religious,
and, like Uzzah, raising his hand to support the ark, which
appeared to him tottering, received from his opponents,
not indeed an equal punishment, but one terribly cruel
and unscrupulous, and from the friends of the cause scant
compensation for his sacrifices and his zeal.

With the exception of his besetting infirmity of extravagance and want of attention to economy, for which there
is little to be said, and his undue indulgence in convivial
pleasures, he was exemplary in all the relations of life.
His frank, engaging demeanour, the sweetness of his
temper, the warmth of his affections, his eminent good
nature, amiability, and generous qualities, made him
generally beloved ; whilst the additional attractions of his
wit and humour made him courted in society, with the
drawback, unfortunately, of leading to excesses at convivial
meetings, of which they were the chief charm. In extenua-

---

* He appears to have left Merton College, Oxford, where he held a scholarship,
in the year 1694, after a three years' residence, his name not being found among
the records after that date. We are indebted to the kindness of the Rev. J.
Griffiths, M.A., keeper of the archives, for this information.

tion of this error, however, it is but just that the habits of
those times should be borne in mind. He was an affectionate
and tender husband, almost to weakness, an indulgent and
fond parent, a warm friend, a delightful companion, a
firm and enlightened patriot, as displayed not merely in
the question of the sucession, but in his strenuous opposition to the nefarious South-Sea scheme and the pernicious
Peerage Bill, which would have converted the constitution
into an oligarchy. Though himself a member of the
Establishment, he was the firm advocate of toleration to
all others; and, though zealous to an extreme in the political views which he approved, he suffered reproach for
advocating clemency to the fallen. His religious impressions were strong, and formed the consolation of his closing
years; and in all his writings he was the warm friend of
virtue, which he drew in such charming colours as to
make universally attractive. He was a friend to all
the friendless, and in his general benevolence bounded
only by his limited means. But his desires and intentions
in all the affairs of life, were marred by his unfortunate
want of prudence, which left as great a disparity between
his aspirations and his acts almost as in the case of Ham-
let. His debts—which amounted to the comparatively
trifling sum, as it would be considered in mercantile transactions, of L.4000, and a considerable portion of which was
no doubt the result of the unprincipled conduct by which
for several years he was deprived of what he justly considered a certain income—were fully liquidated before his
death by the assignment he made of his property for the
benefit of his creditors, leaving a considerable balance
(about L.1400) to his credit.

Of his literary character a few observations may be added. Appearing at an era subsequent to a long succession of civil wars and party conflicts, and during the existence of a continental one of ten years' duration, when all literature almost had become extinct, he revived the memory of the past and made fresh additions to the common stock, by directing public attention to the existing productions of genius in the various departments of letters, and himself inaugurating one additional. He brought into notice, in particular, the surpassing merits of Shakespeare and Milton, neglected and almost unknown to a degree that appears now utterly incredible. In addition to these, there existed many high names in almost every department — Bacon and Boyle, Spenser, Ben Jonson, Dryden, Cowley, and many others. But letters seemed a thing apart from the interests of society and the living world. No one had yet arisen to reconcile them, unless indeed the dramatists who ministered to the popular recreation, and they and society in that age seemed mutually to have corrupted one another. Society was leavened with an unprecedented viciousness from the time of Charles II., and the dramatists pandered shamelessly to the popular taste. But, apart from these, no one had yet undertaken to write on topics and in a manner that would have an attraction for all, which, in the phrase of Bacon, would "come home to men's business and bosoms," and be read by those not professedly literary. To this task Steele set himself as the business of his life.

After having first tried his powers in the interesting little moral essay, entitled the "Christian Hero," he next set himself to reform the comic drama from the unpa-

ralleled licentiousness that had characterised the writings
of his predecessors in that department, and produced a
series of unexceptionable and admirable comedies, which
Mr Thackeray thought "such pleasant reading, and their
heroes such fine gentlemen."* He then, after some interval, began his celebrated series of periodical papers
commencing with the *Tatler*, which adopted a motto implying that its range extended over the whole field of life.
With a dramatic framework and the machinery of a club,
the whole was invested with a living and personal interest,
and wit, and humour, and reason were brought to bear on
the follies and vices of the age in a continuous battery.
Such pleasant raillery and ridicule gained a ready hearing,
and gave delight, when acrimonious, dry, didactic reasoning
would have utterly failed. With the delineation of character and manners, it combined literary, critical, and
ethical disquisitions, "to allure the reader," as it was expressed in the concluding paper, "with the variety of its
subjects, and to insinuate the weight of reason with the
agreeableness of wit."

* One of the causes contributing to this effect, in the opinion of Mr Thackeray,
was his warm but rational appreciation of the female character, by which he is
distinguished from all preceding writers, particularly among his contemporaries.
"All women especially are bound to be grateful to Steele, as he was the first of
our writers who really seemed to admire and respect them." After referring to
Congreve, to the women of Shakespeare, and to Swift, he adds, "Addison laughs
at women equally; but, with the politeness and gentleness of his nature, smiles at
them, and watches them, as if they were harmless, half-witted, amusing, pretty
creatures. . . . It was Steele who first began to pay a manly homage to their
goodness and understanding as well as to their tenderness and beauty. In his
comedies, his heroes do not rant and rave about the divine beauties of Gloriana
or Statira, as . . . in the chivalry romances and high-flown dramas just going
out of vogue; but Steele admires women's virtue, acknowledges their sense, and
adores their purity and beauty with an ardour that should win the good-will of
all women to their hearty and respectful champion."—*Lectures on Humourists.*

In the *Tatler*, with the exception of one or two short essays and some occasional hints, Addison, who was then officially engaged in Ireland, did not commence his contributions until after the appearance of eighty numbers, when the work was a decided success, and then came to partake, and possibly to heighten, the triumph of his friend. In the *Spectator* they worked simultaneously from the first, and almost alternately.*

We have the most unequivocal contemporary evidence of the eminent success of these exertions for the public good. In a tract published in 1711, and attributed to Gay, among other circumstances from being signed with his initials, after stating the great and general regret caused by the recent decease of Bickerstaff, the assumed name of the *Tatler*, the writer adds :—

" It is incredible to conceive the effect his writings have had on the town ; how many thousand follies they have either quite banished or given a very great check to ; how much countenance they have added to virtue and religion ; how many people they have rendered happy† by showing

---

* " Of all our periodical essayists," says Mr Hazlett, " the *Tatler* has always appeared to me the most accomplished and agreeable. For myself, I . . . think at least there is in the last work (the *Spectator*) a much greater proportion of commonplace matter. . . . On this account my pleasure in reading these two admirable books is not at all in proportion to their comparative reputation. The *Tatler* contains only half the number of volumes, and I will venture to say, at least an equal quantity of sterling wit and sense. The first sprightly runnings are there; it has more of the original spirit, more of the freshness and stamp of nature. The indications of character and strokes of humour are more true and frequent; the reflections that suggest themselves arise more from the occasion, and are less spun out into regular dissertations."—*Lectures on the Comic Writers.*

† " I owed this acknowledgment," says Mr Hazlett, after speaking of Steele, and the remark may be quoted in confirmation of the above, " to a writer who has often put me in good humour with myself and everything about me, when few things else could, and when the tomes of casuistry and ecclesiastical history, with which the little volumes of the *Tatler* were overwhelmed and surrounded, had tried their tranquillising effect upon me in vain."

them it was their own fault if they were not so ; and lastly, how entirely they have convinced our fops and young fellows of the value and advantages of learning. He has indeed rescued it out of the hands of pedants and fools, and discovered the true method of making it amiable and lovely to all mankind. In the dress he has given it, it is a most welcome guest at tea-tables and assemblies, and is relished and caressed by the merchants on the 'Change.

" Lastly, his writings have set all our wits and men of letters upon a new way of thinking, of which they had little or no notion before ; and though we cannot yet say that any of them have come up to the beauties of the original, I think we may venture to affirm that every one of them writes and thinks much more justly than they did some time since." *

And in an obituary essay on Steele, published in 1729, shortly after his decease, the writer thus emphatically speaks of the great public benefit conferred by his writings and those of his coadjutors :—

" To him (Sir Richard) we owe that invaluable work which he commenced in the *Tatler*, and, assisted by the immortal labours of his ingenious friend, Mr Addison, carried into numerous volumes. Here he began a work which at once refined our language and improved our morals. None ever attempted with more success to form the mind to virtue, or polish the manners of common life ; none ever touched the passions in that pleasing prevailing method, or so well inculcated the most useful and instructive lessons. I say none did ever thus happily perform so important a work as these illustrious colleagues, who, by adapting themselves to the pleasures, promoted the best virtues of human nature ; insinuated themselves by all the arts of fine persuasion ; employed the most delicate wit and humour in the cause of truth and good sense, nor gave offence to the most rigid devotees or loosest debauchees, but soon grew popular, though advocates of virtue.

" This was laying the axe to the root of vice and immorality. *All the pulpit discourses of a year scarce produced half the good which flowed from the* Spectator *of a day*. They who were tired or lulled to sleep by a long and laboured harangue, or terrified at the appearance of large and weighty volumes, could cheerfully attend to a single half-sheet, where they found the images of virtue so lively and amiable, where vice was so agreeably ridiculed, that it grew painful to no man to part with his beloved follies ;

---

* " The Present State of Wit," 1711.

nor was he easy till he had practised those qualities which charmed so much in speculation. Thus good-nature and good sense became habitual to their readers. Every morning they were instructed in some new principle of duty, which was endeared to them by the beauties of description, and thereby impressed upon their minds in the most indelible character.

"Such a work as this in a Roman age would have been more glorious than a public triumph ; statues would have been raised, and medals would have been struck in honour of the authors. Antiquity had so high a sense of gratitude for the communication of knowledge, that they worshipped their lawgivers, and deified the fathers of science. How, then, must they have acknowledged services like these, where every man grew wiser and better by the fine instruction."[*]

It has been said with much justice that nothing has contributed more to depreciate Steele, in comparison with his friend and coadjutor Addison, than his frequent negligence in reference to style. If the question that has been very needlessly raised respecting their relative merits had gone no further than the greater general equality and finish of style, the admirers of Steele would have been obliged to give up his cause as hopeless. Though matter is undoubtedly the primary aim in theory, yet practically it will be found an almost invariable rule that it is style which imparts to literary productions their permanence and popularity. But there are various qualities of style, even in its most limited sense, and the superiority in general finish and elegance being conceded to Addison, we think it is equally undeniable that there are others, and some of the very highest—such as simplicity—in which the advantage must be allowed to rest with Steele, and that not in a merely verbal sense, but as indicating a quality of mind. This carelessness of Steele in too many instances, his occasionally involved sentences, and neglect in the choice of

[*] "An Essay Sacred to the Memory of Sir Richard Steele," from the *British Journal or Censor*, Sept. 13, 1729.

his phraseology, are indeed much to be regretted, the more so as we see that they were defects not unavoidable; for, when he allowed himself proper leisure, and gave himself thoroughly up to his subject, he wrote with unexceptionable clearness and accuracy, and, at his best, with a force, a richness, and a fervour, we think, superior to Addison. His faults of negligence may probably be attributed to several causes. The very title of his paper, and the comparatively limited views with which he commenced until the importance of his labours became apparent, and the consciousness of his own powers developed, seem to have led him to the adoption of a most objectionable theory, that, as he stated it, of " writing in an air of common speech." Wordsworth commenced with the application of the same theory to poetry, in which it is still less admissible. Fortunately, however, Steele did not adhere strictly to his rule, and when he came to write in conjunction with Addison, many of their papers would not be easily distinguished, after all that has been said upon the subject, by a mere reference to style, nor their respective portions in those which were joint productions. The bustle and excitement in which he kept himself, and the want of the serenity and methodical habits of Addison, contributed to the same effect; and being the responsible writer, and obliged to make up any deficiency, the natural result .followed under the circumstances, that he frequently did it negligently. There is a tradition that he was often hunted up with difficulty with an urgent demand for " copy," and would write what was required in a back-room of the printing-office while the press waited.

Though not affecting the character of a professed critic,

or dealing generally in elaborate disquisition or analysis, Steele has afforded frequent examples of the justness and accuracy of his taste in literature and the fine arts, and the keenness of his relish of their beauties and merits, which he has pointed out with much acuteness and discrimination. In what concerned the drama he particularly interested himself, and gave a series of admirable strictures on the subject, which had the most beneficial effect upon both actors and audience, and tended materially to rectify the depraved taste of the times. Their obligations to him for this service were warmly acknowledged by the actors themselves. By one of the most striking examples on record of the capriciousness of public taste, Shakespeare, with all his surpassing merits, was supplanted by a number of inferior dramatists, now no longer heard of, with the exception of Dryden, who, though of the first order otherwise as a poet, was only second-rate as a dramatist. From an early period of his labours Steele took every opportunity of extolling his merits, as well as those of Milton,—the former of whom had not merely been superseded on the stage, but had sunk out of notice in the closet to a degree now scarcely conceivable; while the latter, from political circumstances in a great measure, and his connexion with a fallen cause, had made but little way with the public. In these casual notices and quotations, Steele was among the first to direct attention to his merits, long prior to Addison's more elaborate critique.

The admiration and appreciation of the higher order of poetry and the drama which he displayed, and endeavoured to diffuse, was also extended to the sister art of painting, which he sought in like manner to elevate from its depressed condition. He recommended the cultivation

of historical painting to our artists, and suggested a number
of subjects, with remarks displaying much acuteness and
knowledge of the subject.   Mr Hazlitt—and he was an
authority on such subjects—has characterised one of his
art papers, that on the cartoons of Raphael, as " the best
criticism in the *Spectator*, of which Mr Fuseli has availed
himself with great spirit in his lectures."

Whatever may have been the imaginative powers of
Steele, he seldom displayed an ambition to soar beyond
"the visible diurnal sphere."   He seemed to agree with
Pope in the sentiment—

> " The proper study of mankind is man ;"

and it was in calling into existence imaginary beings, with
whom he crowded his pages, and investing his creations
with the most varied characteristic attributes, combined
with a moral aim, that he chiefly displayed the fertility of
his invention.   But, though he seems not to have delighted
in an equal degree with Addison in *visions* and *allegories*,
he has notwithstanding given us several pieces of this description.   In No. 514 of the *Spectator*, we have a very
ingenious " Vision of Parnassus " from his pen.   Of the allegory of Arcadia, also, concluding the series of papers on
pastoral poetry in the *Guardian*, he is the only recognised
author.   In No. 141 of the *Guardian*, likewise, he has alle-
gorised the principal events of his life, and in No. 2 of the
Reader has given us another allegory having also a personal
reference.   The former of these, particularly, affords a
beautiful example, that if he generally left this species of
production to Addison, it was not for want of the capability to excel in it, but that he loved other things better.

Addison's great partiality in that way is the more remarkable, as even in poetry, where it is most suitably employed,
he had formerly objected to it, and had ventured to speak
of its use by one of the greatest masters, Spenser, in such
terms as these—

" The long-spun allegories fulsome grow." *

Of his power over the pathetic, his dramas, though
comedies, afford numerous felicitous examples, but the
" Conscious Lovers" in particular, to a degree that makes
it trench almost on the province of tragedy. It is also remarkably displayed in those wonderful little tales and narratives he has given us, particularly in the *Tatler*—including
the account of the couching of the young man born blind ;
of the shipwreck in connexion with the young Cornish
couple ; of the Lover's Dream with reference to Dover
Cliff, (which, though ascribed to Addison, modern critics
agree that, from the circumstances, it must have been related to him by Steele, but more than this, it bears the im-
press of his manner) ; of the burning of the lovers in a
crowded theatre ; of the young man who shot his intended
bride by mistake ; of the domestic scenes in the two papers
where Mr Bickerstaff renews his acquaintance with an
early friend ; and in the other papers, the touching tale of
" Inkle and Yarico," and the story of Alexander Selkirk,
which formed the groundwork of the romance which immor-
talised Defoe. These brief tales possess a charm of vivid-
ness, of simple beauty and pathos, that for a parallel we
should be at a loss where to look except in some of the Old
Testament domestic narratives. Well, indeed, might he say,

* " Verses on the Principal English Poets."

as he does in his concluding paper, "I must confess it has been a most exquisite pleasure to me to frame characters of domestic life." And certainly scarcely less exquisite is the pleasure he has afforded his readers in these sweet and touching and instructive pictures. Of the possession or appreciation of the pathetic, Addison's writings, with all their finish, scarcely afford the slightest indication. The possession of this quality, in conjunction with humour, must be admitted to form the most exquisite and delightful of mental combinations, and especially when we feel that we are not being imposed upon by a mere affected or whimsical sentimentalist. That is but an arid soil on which, however brightly the sun may shine, its effects are not mitigated by the dews and showers.

Of his humour and delineation of character, the latter of course including invention, his dramatic writings also afford many happy examples. But in addition to these, he had mingled so variously with men, and was so quick an observer—though, it is needless to say, not an ill-natured one—that when he started his periodical papers his mind was furnished as a gallery with such portraits, from which he drew at will. To particularise these generally would exceed all reasonable limits, but the leading *dramatis personæ* in his different series of papers, which were almost all struck out by his own hand, may be briefly referred to. The character of Bickerstaff, so humorously conceived and well-sustained, with his astrological and censorial pretensions and genial philosophy, forms a sort of pervading spirit throughout the *Tatler*, and affords scope for much pleasant raillery, satire, and mingled seriousness. His three nephews are made the vehicle of expressing some general views on education and the training of youth, whilst his half-sister, Jenny Distaff, is the representative of the sex, and her history, with the account of her marriage, and of her husband Tranquillus, forms an episode of some extent, and the ground of many pleasant and instructive pictures and precepts referring to the matrimonial state. Supplimentary to Mr Bickerstaff's knowledge of the occult sciences, he obtains the aid of a good genius or guardian spirit, whose aerial facilities are placed at his disposal in the discharge of his censorial functions. This familiar, under the title of Pacolet, is the medium of some useful raillery and satire ; but was not made of so much avail as was probably at first designed.

In addition to these, he exercised his invention and humour in sketching the characters of Mr Bickerstaff's club at the Trumpet—a knot of old smokers and story-tellers, whose recollections went back to the era of the civil wars, and who had a profound contempt for the degeneracy of modern times. Among these Mr Bickerstaff was reckoned as the chief wit, which did not lessen his satisfaction in their company, and was sometimes designated the philosopher, but not allowed much knowledge of the world. Another kindred sketch may serve to throw light on his feelings towards them. It is that of one of the class of easy friends, who, without any shining qualities, and exempt from any obtrusive faults, who never contradict us unless we should chance to speak ill of ourselves, make their way to our esteem rather by an air of complacency to whatever we say or do than any gross adulation. One such Mr Bickerstaff says he often smoked with, who made it a point to light and to be out at the same moment with himself.

" This," he adds, "is all the praise or assent he is capable
of, yet there are more hours in which I would rather be in
his company than in that of the brightest man I know."*
The old decayed courtier, too, whose portrait he has struck
out, was among the members of this dull, but good-natured
company. " The man," he says, " has but a bare subsist-
ence, just enough to pay his way with us at the Trumpet ;
but, by having spent the beginning of his life in the hearing
of great men and persons of power, he is always promising
to do good offices, and to introduce every man he converses
with into the world. He will desire one of ten times his
substance to let him see him sometimes, and hints that he
doesn't forget him. He answers to matters of no consequence with great circumspection ; but, however, maintains
a general civility in his words and actions, and an insolent
benevolence to all whom he has to do with. This he prac-
tises with a grave tone and air ; and though I am his senior
by twelve years, and richer by L.40 per annum, he had
yesterday the impudence to commend me to my face,
and tell me 'he should be always ready to encourage
me.'"†

After the sketches of the *Tatler* Club, the invention of
Steele was next displayed in that of the *Spectator*, including the immortal portrait of Sir Roger de Coverley. Addison, with his fine taste, at once recognised the beauty and
merit of the latter, and took the child of his friend to his
bosom. He adopted it, devoted himself to it with a jealous
care, and has probably left it more carefully provided for
than its more negligent parent might have done. Yet even

---

* *Tatler*, No. 208.   † *Ibid.*, No. 127.

in this one series, the credit of which is usually thought to
belong exclusively to Addison, and to which he brought all
his art, gave some of his most finished touches, and im-
parted such delicate and varied tints—the part that, perhaps, after all, gives most individuality and interest to
the whole—the sketch of the charming but perverse widow,
and her influence on the history of the good old knight—
was contributed by Steele.　His share altogether in that
series, in addition to the original creation, was seven papers,
or nearly a fourth part of the whole.　In addition to Sir
Roger himself, who was intended as the representative of
the country interest in its best form, with nothing shining,
but with a simplicity, benevolence, and good-nature characteristic of the English gentleman, we have the contrasted
portrait of Sir Andrew Freeport, a great merchant, with
his shrewd keen sense, the representative of the industrial
and moneyed interest ; the Templar ; Will Honeycomb,
the man of the world ; Will Wimble, the representative of
younger sons ; Captain Sentry, the nephew and heir of Sir
Roger ; and the divine—all the creatures of Steele's prolific
invention.　The distinguished coadjutors seem at first to
have regularly contributed alternately.　On a Thursday we
have the whole design opened up, with an account of the
Spectator himself, by Addison.　On the Friday, Steele follows, with an account of the club.　Then, after a considerable interval, Addison, on a Monday, introduces us to
Coverley Hall, and on the Tuesday Steele makes us acquainted with the Coverley household and its economy.
Addison gives us an account of the guests, and Steele follows by introducing us to the Coverley gallery of family
portraits, with Sir Roger himself as the guide.　Without

further pursuing the subject, or more than referring to the
subsequent sketches in the *Guardian*, we may add that,
while we delight to acknowledge the incomparable elegance
and finish of Addison, both in his writings generally and
in this unique series of literary paintings, we must equally
do justice to the peculiar excellence of Steele.   Though he
may be inferior to Addison in elegant dissertation or allegory, (in which, however, we have seen that he was well
able to bear his part,) yet, if we consider the immense
variety of masterly sketches of character with which he
has vivified and peopled the various series of these celebrated papers, it seems impossible to deny his superior
invention in that respect.   In what is peculiar and characteristic in these classic serials, as distinguished from
other collections of essays, the " teaching by examples,"
the dramatic portraiture of life and manners,—in the immense amount and variety of the offspring of his invention,
without exhaustion and without repetition, Steele stands
to this day unapproached either by contemporaries or successors.   Nor less unquestionable is the precedence he
takes in his control over our softer emotions.

Among the many lessons which his genial sagacity inculcated is, that the *nil admirari* is the shallowest of philosophy and most miserable of criticism.   In illustration of
this, we have known of one who showed the greatness of
his mind by speaking contemptuously of the Rhine, and of
another who, after some hesitation, acknowledged that
Niagara was " very pretty."   But the admirable works of
nature and of art, despite their critics, whether eminent or
obscure, will continue to shine on ; and among the latter
we do not fear for the fate of what has been bequeathed

us by the pen of Steele—like the luminary of day, giving
vitality, warmth, and brightness to everything it touches,
and extracting something good or agreeable from all,
whether trivial or great ; like it, when in the camera,
under the hand of the artist, it imprints with an instan-
taneous but unrivalled minuteness and fidelity of little
touches, its vivid pictures ; and like it, too, when passing
over the dial in the garden, it leaves its shining and suggestive but quiet moral, only indicated by the opposing
shadow which it throws.

APPENDIX.

SOME LETTERS OF STEELE WITHOUT DATE.

LETTER CCCCXXXIV.   *To Mrs Steele.*

I beg of you not to be impatient, though it be an hour before you see your obliged husband and humble servant,   RICH. STEELE.

LETTER CCCCXXXV.   *To Mrs Steele.*

My attendant, you mention, is dismissed till night. I am to meet the people I have to do with at such hours as will consist with going to Mr Boyle's.* Pray be advised and content. I must go to know what will become of us with relation to this office.†

LETTER CCCCXXXVI.   *To Mrs Steele.*

Half hour after nine.

DEAR PRUE,—I was coming home from the office, after having received some money, but am invited to supper to Mr Boyle's. God be thanked, all will do well ; and I rejoice that I had the spirit to refuse what has been lately offered me.

Dear Prue, do not send after me, for I shall be ridiculous. I send you word to put you out of frights.

---

* Then Secretary of State, and afterwards Lord Carleton. As Chancellor of the Exchequer, he had waited upon Addison at the instance of Lord Godolphin, with reference to his poem in celebration of Marlborough's victory at Blenheim.

† This was probably when he was seeking to succeed Addison as Under-Secretary, shortly before the publication of the *Tatler*.

LETTER CCCCXXXVII.   *To Mrs Steele.*

MY DEAR,—Upon my honour and salvation, I hide nothing. Your generous declaration towards me makes me melt into tears. Mr Boyle has desired me to dine with him, which at this time I must not deny. As soon as I have dined, I will come to you. Pray send not thither.

Dear Prue, talk thus, and govern yours,   RICH. STEELE.

Pray be careful of Lugger, &c.

Tell Mr Nutt * I shall call upon him wherever he is to be in the evening ; but do not enter into any discourse with him, for reasons I shall tell you.

LETTER CCCCXXXVIII.   *To Mrs Steele.*†

DEAR PRUE,—I shall not come home till five o'clock, at which time I have good news to tell you.

LETTER CCCCXXXIX.   *To Mrs Steele.*‡

DEAR PRUE,—Don't be displeased that I do not come home till eleven o'clock.—Yours ever,   RICH. STEELE.

LETTER CCCCXL.   *To Mrs Steele.*

Friday morning.

MY DEAR,—Cousin is much as she was, but rather weaker. Pray let the boy be immediately sent back with my linen, after you have told me, under your hand, that I am in your favour, and that you are well ; which can only make happy your obedient husband,   RICH. STEELE.

LETTER CCCCXLI.   *To Mrs Steele.*

DEAR PRUE,—Forgive me dining abroad, and let Will carry the papers to Buckley's immediately, and leave the other letters at Ashurst's.—Your fond, devoted,   RICH. STEELE.

LETTER CCCCXLII.   *To Mrs Steele.*

DEAR, DEAR PRUE,—Forgive me that I do not dine at home, having

---

* Printer of the *Tatler*.   † " In Berry Street."
‡ " At Mrs Sewell's, in King Street, Westminster."

very particular business to concert with a gentleman who is with me.—
I am, yours affectionately, constantly, tenderly, RICH. STEELE.

LETTER CCCCLXIII. *To Mrs Steele.*

St James's Coffeehouse.

DEAR PRUE,—Send me word how you do; I have not got the money
yet, but I am going to try elsewhere.—Yours, with the utmost affection,
RICH. STEELE.

LETTER CCCCXLIV. *To Mrs Steele.*

6 o'clock, Tuesday.

DEAR PRUE,—I wish our private affairs were as happy as the enclosed
will show you the public are. I am going to the Temple. After I have
been there a little while, I 'll to you.—Yours faithfully,
RICH. STEELE.

LETTER CCCCXLV. *To Mrs Steele.*

DEAR, DEAR PRUE,—Pray forgive me that I do not come to dinner.
Salkield goes out of town before three ; and I cannot conclude with him
if I miss this opportunity.—I am, your obliged husband,
RICH. STEELE.

LETTER CCCCXLVI. *To Mrs Steele.*

Indeed you are ill-natured in talking to me at this strange rate. The
place * is of your own choosing, before one I liked better. I will come
to you in the afternoon, and, if you are able, bring you to town.

It is wonderful, when you know what I had to do last night, that you
will talk so to me thus.—Yours ever, RICH. STEELE.

LETTER CCCCXLVII. *To Mrs Steele.*

PRUE,—It is unworthy your virtue and merit to be diffident. I'll
warrant you all will be well before to-morrow night. I will come home
then with cash, and everything else that can please.—Yours faithfully,
RICH. STEELE.

---

* Hampton Court.

LETTER CCCCXLVIII.   *To Mrs Steele.*

Buckley's, 8 o'clock.

DEAR PRUE,—I have yours, but cannot imagine what I omit that is kind. I suppose you would not have had me avoided the gentleman I named to-day ?

I am come hither, and not one word* ready for to-morrow.—In haste, yours,   RICH. STEELE.

LETTER CCCCXLIX.   *To Mrs Steele.*

Pray, Prue, look a little dressed, and be beautiful, or else everybody will be entertained but the entertainer ; but, if you please, you can outshine the whole company, and my costly lustre. Come in good humour.—Yours,   RICH. STEELE.

LETTER CCCCL.   *To Mrs Steele.*

Whether I deserve it or not, I humbly desire you will smile upon me when I come into your presence. I wait for your answer, who am, yours tenderly,   RICH. STEELE.

LETTER CCCCLI.   *To Mrs Steele.*

DEAR CREATURE,—I go away because you will have it so, but I have been guilty of nothing that ought to exclude me from the happiness of being yours.

You will take this for an argument how much I am, dear wife, yours,   RICH. STEELE.

LETTER CCCCLII.   *To Mrs Steele.* †

DEAR PRUE,—It is a strange thing, because you are handsome, you will not behave yourself with the obedience that people of worse features do— but I must be always giving you an account of every trifle and minute of my time.

I send you this to tell you I am waiting to be sent for when my Lord Wharton is stirring.   RICH. STEELE.

---

* Of the *Gazette.*
† " At Mrs Binn's, at a mathematical maker, Dean Street."

LETTER CCCCLIII.   *To Mrs Steele.*

4 o'clock.

DEAR PRUE,—Take this boy to sit behind you in the boat ; and put on your mask, and come to Somerset Stairs. From whence send him to call me from Nutt's, where your servant [waits] for your arrival to visit my *grand-daughter.** RICH. STEELE.

LETTER CCCCLIV.   *To Mrs Steele.*

DEAR PRUE,—Send word when you are ready and hoods on, and I'll come for you. RICH. STEELE.

LETTER CCCCLV.   *To Mrs Steele.*

Young Man's Coffeehouse.

DEAR PRUE,—I have not yet been at the Savoy,† but stay near the Devil Tavern till I see Will Elderton.

Do not be out of humour, for all will be easy in an hour or two.—Yours, RICH. STEELE.

LETTER CCCCLVI.   *To Mrs Steele.*

DEAR PRUE,—I desire you to dress yourself decently before you appear before me ; for I will [not] be so easily pleased as I have been, being now in a fair way of being a great man.—Yours ever, RICH. STEELE.

LETTER CCCCLVII.   *To Mrs Steele.*

DEAR PRUE,—I propose setting off in the morning at five o'clock to Windsor, at which hour the coach will be at our door. I stay at the office now, to despatch as much of the *Gazette* as I can to-night.—I am, your obliged husband, RICH. STEELE.

LETTER CCCCLVIII.   *To Mrs Steele.*

After eight.

DEAR PRUE,—I send this to acquaint thee that I shall come home about

---

* There is no explanation of this, unless Mrs Aynston was so called.
† " Where the *Gazette* was printed."

an hour hence, and desire, in the meantime, that the boy may rest, for he has been up ever since five.—Yours tenderly,   RICH. STEELE.

LETTER CCCCLIX.   *To Mrs Steele.*

It is now professedly point of party, and I am required to be here, because a great man advised it yesterday.   But the remainder of the money will be ready, by means of Martyn and Elderton, before two o'clock to-morrow.   In the meantime, I am contented, and desire you not to come hither till early to-morrow morning, between seven and eight, at which time I would have you be with me precisely.   I sent young Elderton to the nurse's, and the child is much better.—Yours, with great truth now, and with care hereafter,   RICH. STEELE.

LETTER CCCCLX.   *To Mrs Steele.**
                    Rummer Tavern, Covent Garden.

DEAR PRUE,—I am just going to Jeffrey's; have settled my matter with Mr Potter, who lends me the money.

I desire you would go to bed at home, and be of good cheer.—Yours ever,   RICH. STEELE.

Martyn never came near me.

LETTER CCCCLXI.   *To Mrs Steele.*

I have four tickets for the music to-night.   If you will send for Mrs Keck, we will go altogether, or, if you please, only you and your most obedient servant,   RICH. STEELE.

LETTER CCCCLXII.   *To Mrs Steele.*
                    Hampton Court.

DEAR PRUE,—I am going to Watford, and shall be at home to-morrow. The coach is passing, so can say no more.—Yours ever,

RICH. STEELE.

LETTER CCCCLXIII.   *To Mrs Steele.*

If you have not a coach of your own, come to me in a chair, and we will be together all day, which will be a great favour to yours most obediently,

RICH. STEELE.

---

* " Berry Street."

LETTER CCCCLXIV.   *To Mrs Steele.*

DEAR PRUE,—I will be at Desmaiseaux'; and if you will spend the evening with me, please to call on me at the corner of St James's Place, and I'll go with you. If you do not like this proposal, send word.—Your humble servant and obedient husband,   RICH. STEELE.

LETTER CCCCLXV.   *To Mrs Steele.*

DEAR WIFE,—It is an unspeakable trouble to me that I ever let fall a passionate word in return for any impatience you show about the provision I make for you. I am indeed. [It is indeed?]

I take all the pains imaginable, and love you better than tongue can express.—Yours faithfully,   RICH. STEELE.

LETTER CCCCLXVI.   *To Mrs Steele.*

DEAR PRUE,—It is impossible for me now to get a coach, and it is [a] very bleak and raw night. I must, therefore, stay here, or lose all my pains for want of despatching what I have been about. Except your uneasiness, I am perfectly well and pleased.—Ever yours,   RICH. STEELE.

LETTER CCCCLXVII.   *To Mrs Steele.*

MY DEAR,—The coachmen were so very dear that I have taken places in the stage-coach, where we are to be exactly half-an-hour after one. Pray give my duty to my mother, and excuse that I cannot come to receive her commands. Put money in your pocket. Give necessary orders for the house to be in readiness against our return.—Yours ever,   RICH. STEELE.

LETTER CCCCLXVIII.   *To Mrs Steele.*

DEAR PRUE,—I cannot answer yours to all points till I have received answers to two or three letters, but will write in the afternoon.

Be sure to keep Mrs Keck.—Yours,   RICH. STEELE.

LETTER CCCCLXIX.   *To Mrs Steele.*

DEAR PRUE,—If you and Mrs Edwards can make use of these tickets which were given me, I shall be glad; if not, send them back, and I will give them to other people, for I will not go myself to any public diversion, except you are of the assembly.—Yours ever,   RICH. STEELE.

LETTER CCCCLXX.   *To Mrs Steele.*

DEAR PRUE,—I have read yours concerning the Anniversary Sermon, and the impertinent ill-bred behaviour upon it, with indignation, and your mention of tears that it drew from you put me in a rage as great as ever I have been in. We will take care to be above the necessities of life, and that will support our minds to contemn such low spirits, and all their imaginations. I cannot but pity the way of life you are in, without one body to converse with whom you like. I do not know whether I have told you the news of Mrs Sartre's * marriage at Bristol to one Mr Combs, who is an agent of the army. He is a very handsome fellow, and she has, without much reserve, given herself wholly to him, without care of a settlement, even of her own, but in very loose words.

Had I been present when the young gentleman was so pert at table, I should, I believe, have spoiled his stomach. I cannot but fancy, when you and I come to talk, such vexations from such mean objects will vanish.— I am, dear Prue, with the strictest truth, your faithful and obsequious husband,   RICH. STEELE.

LETTER CCCCLXXI.   *To Mrs Steele.*

If you have that paper, keep it safe. It was offered me, but rejected. Nothing of yours is unsafe by me, and I contemn him.

---

* Addison's sister. Mr Sartre died in 1713. She survived till 1750. See notice of her by Swift, vol. i., p. 223.

INDEX.